Emma Stirling was bo.... her early childhood lived in India. With her husband and two young children, she went to live in what was then Southern Rhodesia and Nyasaland, where another two daughters were born. She has since returned to the United Kingdom and now lives in London. She started writing in 1974 and has had a number of romantic novels published under a pseudonym. She is also the author of *A Field of Bright Poppies* and *The Cockleshell Girl*. Besides writing full time, she is kept busy with her family and three grandchildren.

Clover Blossom

Emma Stirling

HEADLINE

First published in 1992
by HEADLINE BOOK PUBLISHING PLC

First published in paperback in 1993
by HEADLINE BOOK PUBLISHING PLC

10 9 8 7 6 5 4 3 2 1

ISBN 0 7472 3870 7

Printed and bound in Great Britain by
HarperCollins Manufacturing, Glasgow

HEADLINE BOOK PUBLISHING PLC
Headline House
79 Great Titchfield Street
London W1P 7FN

This book is dedicated
with love to my sister,
Helen Patricia

Prologue

Today the weather was changeable. Holidaymakers emerging from their hotels and boarding houses were instantly buffeted by the wind which tunnelled down the narrow streets like a draught down a chimney. It was a cold wind, smelling of the sea, but when the sun burst out from behind the racing clouds, the brightness was dazzling, full of glare. Overhead, gulls screamed and floated, their wings outspread against the sky.

It was the kind of day when the small end-of-pier theatre did excellent business. The beach was too windy for all but the very hardy, and families made their way hand in hand along the length of the wooden pier to take their seats in the exciting dimness of the theatre. Children fidgeted, and asked how long before it started. Sit still, a harassed mother told them, else they'll ask you to leave. They don't like troublesome children in their theatre.

The children sat on the edge of their chairs, wide-eyed, gazing at the drawn curtains, as though willing them to open. You had to get there early if you wanted a good seat and sometimes it would be a long wait. But when the curtains did eventually open, the waiting was worthwhile.

The Pierrot troupe that began the show was greeted with whistles and loud applause. They danced and sang and those of the children who had never seen the inside of a theatre until now slid further onto the edge of their seats, hands grasping tightly to the back of the seat in front of them and gaped.

It was like some magical fairy land discovered for the first time. When the Four Blossoms came on, the applause was deafening. The children were urged by their mothers to sit back and enjoy the show from a proper angle. Their eyes never once leaving the colourfully arrayed figures on the stage, they did as they were bid, hardly daring to blink in case they missed something.

A man and a boy, dressed in loud yellow and black checked suits, scattered sand from a small bag onto the boards and did a sort of shuffle dance, gracefully gliding across the stage. As they danced, the man told gags, silly gags that had the audience screaming with laughter. No matter how many times they had heard them they always earned a laugh. After that a pretty woman with long brown hair, holding a little girl by the hand, joined them. The woman was dressed alluringly in pale mauve chiffon with a long matching scarf that she trailed on the stage as she danced. The girl joined in and they ended by combining their voices in a song, accompanied by the man on the piano. There was more, too much for the awed children to take in: a man with a black face, only they could see where the black ended at his collar, singing 'Old Man River'; another man with ginger hair who told more gags and seemed to fall over his own feet; and, most magical of all, a troupe of acrobats who leaped and jumped as though they were made not of flesh and bone but of rubber.

The audience whistled and stamped their feet, unwilling to let even one of the performers go without an encore. They whistled loudest for the Blossom family and the curtains drew back time after time for them, while they bowed and waved. The children would never forget it. Especially the little girl. Clover Blossom, Mam said her name was. Dad nodded wisely. 'She's no bigger than tuppence worth o' mince but it's all there. Mark my words, that girl'll go far.'

Chapter One

Clover always thought that she and Eddie were two of the lucky ones. Every summer they lived in the most exciting place on earth. Joy bubbling up inside her, she would race with Eddie along the sea front from the boarding house where they stayed, hardly able to wait to get sand in her shoes, hair and pockets. Nearing the sea front, she would close her eyes, holding Eddie's hand tightly, the better to smell the fresh, tangy salt of the water, knowing when she opened them all she would see was the glittering, shining sea stretching away to the other side of the world. Eddie had corrected her on this, saying it only stretched as far as Ireland, but Clover preferred her own version.

Blackpool, further along the coast, had electric trams that tore along at an alarming speed. They ran all the way to the North Shore, where sandhills with long coarse grasses flanked the beach, the promenade narrowed and the sea walls sloped steeply down to the sand. One day, Bert promised, their act would be appearing in Blackpool. But for Clover this small, more homely seaside town was just right.

Bert, too, looked upon these summers as the most wonderful part of his life. Adele, with her soft, fine brown hair and quick intelligence, was a warm and caring mother to their children and a loving wife to him. The act he had so carefully put together was welcomed in every northern seaside town worthy of its name. But since the birth of Clover, Bert had decided that Newcombe was best for them. As his fortieth birthday approached, stability was becoming dearer to his heart.

Theatre digs were kept for them every summer. Beds were two shillings a night. But Ma Ruggles – landladies were always called Ma – made special weekly rates for members of the Summer Follies who boarded with her. Her guests bought their own food and she cooked it. Visitors new to the establishment would always give a quick glance to see what the previous lodgers had written: 'Comfortable!' 'Cooks as well as the wife.' 'A home from home.' There were no adverse comments written in Ruby Ruggles' guest book. No one would have dared. They certainly wouldn't have been welcomed back the following year.

Ma Ruggles kept a comfortable house, clean bedrooms with the bed linen changed regularly, a warm parlour where guests could gather to compare that evening's audience with the previous night's. The parlour was respectable with antimacassars, stuffed birds under glass domes, a bowl of wax fruit on a bobble-fringed table runner and a shining brass fire screen. Autographed photos of the more important artistes who stayed there took pride of place on the walls.

Summer months would find the Blossoms lugging in the huge wicker baskets that contained their livelihood – costumes of fine silks and gossamer chiffon and sparkling sequins. Clover told everyone she had been born in one of those trunks between shows. Not entirely true, but near enough.

The child had arrived so suddenly it had taken everyone by surprise. Eddie, born four years before, had taken hours; twenty-two hours to be precise. The Blossoms had been delighted with their son. The small boy had been introduced into the act as soon as he could

6

walk, at first being led on holding Adele's hand, then dressed in a miniature copy of his father's yellow and black checked suit, joining Bert in a slow shoe shuffle that charmed their audience.

Adele had not been prepared for the speedy arrival of her little daughter. Indeed, she barely made it from the stage and into the dressing room that the Blossoms shared with the Morvellis, an acrobatic and juggling act consisting of mother and father and their two sons, when the pains that had been niggling her all day became too much to bear and she knew it was more than the indigestion she had first thought.

The dark, good-looking sons were sent packing, told to lose themselves until summoned. Luckily, they had already performed that evening and Madam Morvelli, black eyes flashing and still in her spangles, rolled up her sleeves and assisted until the doctor arrived.

Bert borrowed the stage door keeper's bike and raced through the streets to the doctor's house. He returned with laboured breath and the doctor following in his wake.

Later, wrapping the tiny pink and white bundle in a clean towel, Madam Morvelli handed it gently to the still disbelieving Adele. 'There, little mother, your very own girlchild. She has eyes the colour of the Madonna's gown and the face of an angel. This one will go far, you take the word of an old woman who knows these things.'

During the rest of that summer season, Clover was packed like one of the stage costumes in a basket lined with the rich crimson velvet of a cloak Adele sometimes wore on stage and laid in the wings while her family performed.

Her first memories were of lights and music and people applauding and the chorus girls bending over her and clicking their tongues soothingly as they hurried past.

7

The entire cast doted on her. Like Eddie, she was recruited into her parents' act as soon as she could toddle. Accompanied by Bert on the piano and dressed in a calf-length gown of white muslin over a ruffled petticoat, she lisped out a simple song. Delighting the audience with her cleverness and knack of remembering the words, she was led by her proud father for encore after encore. It was evident to all that he adored her, and that Eddie was relegated to second best.

Bert used to call her his 'nut-brown maiden', swinging her high and singing in his pleasant tenor voice, 'Ho, ho, my nut-brown maiden, you're the maid for me . . .'

It didn't occur to either Clover or her brother that their lives were any different from other children's. Growing up in the theatre, arrangements were usually made for tutors to be brought in to give the music hall children lessons. During the winter months, which they spent in a small town called Moorfield, some thirty miles inland, they were able to go to proper school. Bright, intelligent children, the Blossoms learned fast and could read and write in a fine, firm hand when they were quite young.

Clover loved every minute of her life. But the time she liked best was when there was no matinée and she was free for the afternoon. She would escape along the pier, looking forward to being able to paddle, to feel the sand between her toes. As a very little girl it seemed to her that the pier was very, very long and her legs would never get her to the squeaky old turnstile that guarded the entrance from the promenade.

Hurrying over the grey planks she was fascinated by the water that swirled below, endlessly advancing, flinging itself against the weatherworn piles that supported the pier, retreating to start all over again. Sometimes, out at sea, beyond the lights that blazed atop of the small theatre, spelling out the words, Summer Follies, dark

8

clouds warned of an approaching storm. Bert always said bad weather was good for business, for then all the holidaymakers would seek shelter from the wet.

Bad weather might be good for business but Clover preferred the days when the sun shone and the beach was dotted with families. Children built sandcastles and ran to the edge of the sea to bring back buckets of water to fill the moat surrounding their castle while their bigger brothers played a makeshift game of cricket, using pieces of driftwood as wickets. When the water was warm enough, Clover would stand knee-deep, skirts held daringly high, and gravely inspect the small family groups all enjoying themselves on their summer holidays. Sometimes, according to her mood and always with a slight sense of disloyalty, she would try and picture her own family like that; plain, ordinary folk who lived in a house with a garden front and back, a father who went out to work every day and came back in time for supper in the evening, a mother who stayed at home and took care of the house and children.

Impossible to imagine her own handsome father and blithe spirit of a mother in such commonplace roles . . .

She loved the deckchair man with his ticket machine that went 'ting-ting' every time he gave out a ticket. Tuppence for two hours and you had a choice of staying on the beach or carrying the canvas contraption up to the pier. Even when the wind was fierce, a number of brave souls would try to find sheltered spots and relax as best they could in their deckchairs, trying to look as though they were enjoying themselves.

Some of the men were daring enough to remove their jackets, revealing braces and high white-collared shirts, the collars so stiffly starched that Clover wondered how they didn't cut into their necks. She much preferred the

cream silk open-necked shirts her father wore and the
smartly tailored blazer.

The women wore their cardigans tightly buttoned at
the throat and smiled a lot, thinking of what they could
buy the landlady to cook for their tea. A nice bit of
smoked haddock would go down well . . .

Along the beach would be great excitement where
children gathered to watch a Punch and Judy show.
Further out on the vast stretch of sand left wet by the
outgoing tide, small brown donkeys plodded patiently.
Their riders clutched timidly at the reins, turning
constantly to make sure the beaming parents were still
where they'd left them.

As she grew into her early teens, Clover would stay
so long on the beach that often Eddie was dispatched
to bring her home. She'd hear her name called and look
over her shoulder to where the boy – well, almost a
young man now, he was so tall and well built – was
hurrying across the sands towards her. 'Come on, Mum
doesn't like you to wander too far on your own.' His
gaze examined the bare pink feet and ankles and the
damp frills of the white petticoat. 'Tut, tut, just look
at you!'

'You don't have to worry about me, Eddie.' Clover
lifted her chin in a defiant gesture that had her brother
grinning. 'I'd never come to any harm here. It's like a
second home to me, this place.'

At eighteen, Eddie was the recipient of many an
admiring glance from passing girls. He was a strapping
lad, with dark wavy hair and dark eyes that warmed
when he smiled, as he was smiling now. His profession
was a source of amusement to other boys his age and
more than once he'd had to prove his worth with
his fists.

'Not that I'm in any hurry to get back,' he said. 'I've
just had another argument with Dad over the act. You

know I've been trying my hand at writing some of those syncopated tunes that are all the rage now? Well, I played them to Dad and he nearly hit the roof. Said he wasn't going to have any of that modern rubbish in the Blossoms' act.' Scowling, Eddie gazed out to sea. 'He lives in the past. He won't admit that the world has changed, and changed rapidly, since the war ended. Those songs, ragtime and jazz, are the kind of things young people want to hear. Not all that old claptrap.'

Clover felt sorry for her brother. There had been a right old shenanigans the other day when Eddie had declared the black and white Pierrot costumes worn by the entire cast in the opening number were 'old hat'. 'Nobody wants that sort of thing these days,' he'd told Bert glibly.

'Oh, so suddenly you're an authority on what the public wants and doesn't want, are you?' Bert's face darkened like thunder.

A few soothing words from Adele had Eddie saying he was sorry. The arguments were becoming almost a daily occurrence and Eddie knew they distressed his mother. Privately, Clover thought Eddie was right; the act was dated, but people seemed to like it and as long as they came and paid their money, the Four Blossoms would go on entertaining the summer crowds at the end of the pier.

Occasionally Clover met Miss Boyce, one of the theatre's wardrobe mistresses, on her walks. Incongruous in her neat, button-top boots, her unfashionably long skirts raised from the sand, the middle-aged lady would stride energetically along the beach. 'Come and join me, Clover,' she'd call, noting with approval the lovely flush the wind had brought to the girl's cheeks, the added sparkle to the blue eyes, the brown hair tossed into a mass of curls. Clover would run to her side and listen as the little spinster expounded on whatever subject

11

was exercising her mind that day. Very often it was the sad state of unemployment and the way the Government chose to ignore the plight of the ex-servicemen, hoping, she explained indignantly, the problem would go away. And she spoke of the suffragettes and their fight for votes for women. She opened Clover's eyes to all manner of things she would never have known otherwise.

One day, to Clover's surprise, Miss Boyce had spoken of her family, bringing up the subject quite casually as they walked across the sands. She told Clover of her own holidays in Blackpool when she was a child, visiting there with her parents and sister. 'She was a handful, our Ruth,' she said, smiling.

Feeling that a response was expected of her, Clover said, 'Where does she live now?' Somehow, she had always thought of Miss Boyce as being quite alone in the world.

Miss Boyce's mouth firmed and her eyes turned thoughtfully towards the sea. 'I wish I knew, dear. I haven't heard from Ruth in over twenty years.' After divulging that little bit of information she seemed not to want to discuss it further and Clover wondered at the underlying sadness in her voice when she spoke of her long lost sister.

Little Miss Boyce, as she was known to everyone in the cast of the Summer Follies, was the elder of the two wardrobe mistresses. As chief seamstress her job was to see that the costumes were kept clean and in good repair and replaced after every performance in their neat rows in the various dressing rooms. She confessed to Clover she despaired of ever teaching the chorus girls to hang up their garments. 'They seem to think that the floor, or the back of a chair, is the proper place for them,' she said.

The little seamstress was the kindest and most warm-hearted person Clover had ever known. She had been a loyal and true friend to Adele, acting as baby sitter in the days when Clover was taking her first hesitant steps, when she needed constant supervision. Miss Boyce had made herself so much a part of Adele's family that their problems were hers, the small dramas that erupted now and then part and parcel of her life.

She had watched Clover grow up from an engagingly spirited baby to the delightful young girl she was now, already showing all the signs of the beauty that one day would be hers. The little spinster was as proud of her as though she personally had had a hand in her parentage.

Today Miss Boyce had not been able to keep back the fact that tomorrow was her birthday. She had been smiling at something Clover had said and suddenly announced the fact, quickly adding that birthdays didn't mean anything to her any more, they only served to remind her that yet another year had flown by. 'But you must promise not to tell anyone,' she said. 'It will be our secret. Just between the two of us.' It embarrassed her when people smiled and looked at her, saying in an artificial way, 'Your birthday? Oh, many happy returns! Twenty-one again, are we?'

'You're not old,' protested Clover warmly.

'Old enough.'

Clover glanced at her consideringly. Difficult to guess her age, with her small, neat figure, the thick mass of brown hair, still without the slightest hint of grey, taken back into the tidy bun low on her neck and the gold-rimmed pince-nez that rested on her long, rather narrow nose.

'Sometimes I feel so much older than I am and whenever a birthday approaches I try to pretend that it isn't happening.'

'It will be our secret,' said Clover.

★ ★ ★

In spite of the fact of promising to keep it a secret, Clover couldn't help telling her mother. She had never kept secrets from her mother and she was sure Miss Boyce wouldn't mind. Adele looked at her, smiling, saying, 'So that's why she asked us to tea tomorrow afternoon! I'd forgotten her birthday is this month.' She shook her head. 'She's a case, isn't she? Keeping it quiet like that. But then, she has done ever since I've known her. Why, she can't be much more than in her forties and already she's talking and acting like an old woman.'

Gazing into the lively face now almost on a level with her own, for at fourteen Clover was quickly overtaking her, she said, 'We'll have to get her something special. Something she wouldn't buy for herself. Something exotic.'

Clover could not visualise the word 'exotic' in connection with Miss Boyce. The little spinster was too straightlaced for that. Not that she was absolutely sure what exotic meant. But if her mother said they were to search for something like that, then she supposed it must be all right.

'A silk scarf,' she suggested.

Adele nodded. 'One of those absurdly gauzy silk ones in peacock colours. She'd like that. She could tuck it into the neckline of those white blouses she wears.' Give the poor old soul a bit of colour, thought Adele, for Miss Boyce never appeared wearing anything but black and white with an occasional drab grey.

'Of course,' went on Adele, head on one side, 'we must be sure not to buy anything that would offend her.' That was Miss Boyce's favourite word. 'That offends my ears', she'd say about the loud music coming from the wind-up gramophone in the dressing room of the chorus girls, or 'That offends my eyes', observing the ever shortening length of their skirts, the dropped waistlines and the flattened chests. Flappers all, she said of them.

In her forthright way, Clover asked, 'Do you think a boy has ever been interested in her, Mum?'

'Little Joycie Boyce!' Adele laughed but not in an unkind way. 'Oh, I shouldn't think so for one minute. She always gives the impression that she thinks them a waste of time. She'd probably be a different person today if she'd met someone like your father.'

Clover tried to imagine the little spinster partnered with someone like the uninhibited Bert and couldn't.

The following day they decided to walk into the town's shopping centre and see what was on offer. Clover suggested the Chinese shop in the narrow turning off the High Street. She thought of the scarlet and gold lettering on the window and of the one particularly warm day when she had stopped outside the shop. The front door had been propped open to let the air circulate and she had smelled the heavy fragrance of sandalwood and rose petals coming from its dark interior, heard the thin musical notes of wind chimes moving in the breeze from the open door. All manner of fascinating things must be in that shop, just waiting to be discovered.

'Get your coat on then,' Adele said, reaching for her hat. She pulled the blue felt hat down over her hair, tucked in the ends that lay over her cheeks and, satisfied they were both dressed correctly, led Clover out onto the pier. After that morning's rehearsal they had not returned to the boarding house but stayed on at the theatre as there were things Adele had to attend to. As they let themselves out of the stage door, the wind caught them unawares, sending Adele's skirts ballooning, causing her to grab at the hem and giggle like a young girl.

'Oh, my goodness!' she gasped, 'this wind! Do you imagine there is a pier in the whole of England that isn't windy but always nice and calm?' Her grip tightened on Clover's hand. 'Come on, we'd better hurry. After we've bought the present we have to take tea with Miss Boyce and still be back in time for the first house. You know how your father hates it if we're late.'

Curtain up was at six thirty, by which time they had to have donned their costumes, the black and white Pierrot ones which Eddie had called old hat but which caused a stir in the audience when the curtains parted, applied their make-up and arranged their hair. There would barely be time to breathe.

The wind chased them all along the promenade and down the narrow turning where the Chinese shop was; it took all of Adele's patience and ingenuity to hold on to her hat and her daughter's hand at the same time. Heavily laden wagons, pulled by large shire horses, used this lane as a short cut to the busy High Street. The pavement, on one side only, was narrow and it was impossible for two people to walk abreast on it, one having to step into the road which was cobblestoned and slippery, a hazard in itself. Petitions had been made to the local council, asking for the heavy transport to be banned from using this route, but to no avail. Still they came, a constant danger and irritation to everyone.

The wind caught them afresh. The long, narrow street with its slight incline acted like a wind tunnel. Adele let go of Clover's hand and clutched again at her hat and then her skirts. With all the force of a North Sea gale, it whipped the long hair about Clover's face, across her eyes, temporarily blinding her. Behind her, Adele hurried to keep up, stepping off the pavement as she came abreast of her daughter. Her whole concern was with her skirts, holding them down across her knees. Too late she heard the sound of cart wheels behind her, the sharp clatter of a horse's shoes on the cobbles. She heard the warning shouted by the driver,

16

followed by a string of obscenities and then she was
falling . . .

Clover heard her mother's cry and turned to see the
blue felt hat with its perky little red feather at the side
vanish under the hooves of the frightened horse.

'I'll bake a cake,' Miss Boyce had promised. 'A special one.'

It was lovely to see how excited Clover had been at
the thought of a tea party, how her face had flushed
with delighted anticipation. Now, on the way from
the kitchen to the stairs leading to her own room,
Miss Boyce glanced into the parlour as she passed: a
couple of the other guests were huddled over the fire.
There weren't many days in this establishment, which
went under the rather pompous title of Guest House for
Ladies and Gentlemen (of restricted means), when a fire
wasn't needed.

She debated on whether to join them, thinking she
would be better able to watch for her visitors from
the large bay window overlooking the street. Then,
as Mrs Munday called out to her in the coy voice
she assumed whenever Colonel Atkinson was within
hearing distance, she decided against it. She hadn't
much patience with fools, and the Colonel, for all his
lofty rank and manner, was in her opinion a fool. She
had never been able to speak to him for more than
five minutes without wanting to box his ears. And Mrs
Munday, all dressed up and nowhere to go, in a silk
frock decades out of style, was no better. She simpered
at one of the Colonel's jokes and held thickly knuckled
hands out to the meagre flames, all the while making
fatuous remarks about the treacherous weather.

No, Miss Boyce decided, she would sit at her own
window upstairs and watch for her visitors from there.
Back in the room on the third floor, a room that was

17

tiny even for that house, Miss Boyce being judged by
the landlady to be one of her least important guests, she
gazed out of the window, parting the lace curtains with
a pale freckled hand. She had come to live here after
the death of her parents, a good few years ago now. She
had once or twice thought of changing her abode, but
her natural parsimony made her hesitate. She wasn't
exactly a pauper but the small legacy she existed on
wouldn't go far if she went to higher priced lodgings.
Leaning forward, nearer the window pane, the gold
pince-nez threatened to slip off the end of her narrow
nose. The cherry cake made specially, knowing how
much Clover liked glacé cherries, held pride of place
on its glass and silver stand on the table behind her.
Plates of sandwiches cut into dainty triangles with the
crusts removed, the way Miss Boyce had been taught in
her girlhood, surrounded it. The cake had one romantic
little touch that she hadn't been able to resist: a tiny,
solitary candle in its centre, waiting to be lit.

The landlady had given grudging permission to use
the kitchen that day and Miss Boyce was pleased that
the cake had risen so well. She was more used to facing
disasters with sunken centres, the fruit all huddled in a
heap at the bottom. This looked highly successful and
she imagined Clover asking for a second or even a third
slice and herself saying when Adele remonstrated, 'Oh,
please, do let her, Adele. Otherwise I shall have to eat
it all myself.'

Everything was ready: the pretty set of paper-thin
china that had belonged to her grandmother, the heavy
silver cake forks and knives set daintily to the side of
each plate. Now, all she needed to do when her guests
arrived was to pour boiling water on the tea leaves.

Letting the curtain drop, adjusting her glasses with
one finger, she picked up the piece of scarlet knitting
that lived in its tapestry-covered bag beside her chair

and made herself comfortable beside the fireplace. The gloves would be nice and warm and later she would begin on a scarf to match their brightness. Scarlet suited Clover, setting off the flushed cheeks, the springy dark hair that bounced on her shoulders when she walked. Handling the four thin steel needles had been a trial of patience at first but Miss Boyce had persevered and the results were pleasing.

The packet of cigarettes that she was never without lay on the table next to her. Selecting one, she leaned forward and lifted a long length of folded newspaper from the hearth, lit it in the fire and held it to the tip of her cigarette. Even now, after all these years, she still felt guilty whenever she lit a cigarette, her father's face appearing before her, stern and forbidding. She smiled and puffed gratefully, then settled herself in the old wing chair and began another row of knitting.

The tapping on her bedroom door brought another smile to her face and she quickly folded the knitting, putting it back into its bag. She called out, 'Come in, my dears. Tea is all ready. I expect you're ready for it, on such a windy day.'

The door was pushed open and her landlady stood in the opening, her strong yellow teeth gnawing at her lower lip. Miss Boyce frowned. 'What is it? It's draughty, you know, with that door open.' She paused, the landlady's whole demeanour shrieking that something was terribly wrong. Miss Boyce laid one hand across her mouth, the other going to the small silver locket that hung by a thin chain about her neck. 'What is it? What's happened?'

She heard the words 'hospital' and 'accident' and Adele's name, and before the woman could say anything further was already reaching for her hat and coat, buttoning it with trembling fingers.

Chapter Two

Bert Blossom would always remember the smell of that hospital. Its stink seemed to have settled into his clothes, even his skin. Never in all his thirty-nine years, except in a couple of instances in the trenches during the war, could he ever remember feeling so frightened.

The wait in the cold, echoing corridor seemed interminable. Uniformed nurses passed on silent feet, the soft rustle of their aprons the only sound of their passing.

Clover sat on the hard wooden chair, beside her father. Bert was ashen-faced, the back of one finger constantly brushing his small moustache with a nervous gesture. The silence was absolute, as though the sound of a voice might bring home to the small family the reason for their long wait. They had watched while Adele had been taken away, swing doors closing behind the trolley, hiding from their sight the marble-white face and cloud of silky brown hair that spilled over the pillow.

Clover was very frightened. It was all her fault. If she hadn't suggested the Chinese shop, if they had bought Miss Boyce's present from some other shop, then her mother wouldn't have stepped off the pavement, right in front of the horse and cart . . .

It seemed they had been sitting in that corridor for ages, eyes darting hopefully towards the entrance each time the doors swung open. This was some hideous nightmare from which she'd soon wake, Clover thought, with her mother smiling down at her, telling her everything was all right, that it had only been a bad dream.

Bert's hands were icy, his whole body tense with fear. He could still not believe the appalling thing that had happened. He felt the slight body of his daughter lean against him and absent-mindedly pulled her closer, desperately seeking the comfort he craved. The comfort that only the reassuring words of a doctor could give.

Eddie, white-faced and silent, sat on the other side of his father. He wanted so badly to hold Bert's hand but at the advanced age of eighteen considered himself too grown-up to show the emotions that were tearing him apart.

'How much longer, Daddy,' Clover's voice quivered with fatigue, 'before they let us see Mum?'

Her large eyes gazed at him pleadingly, and as though in answer to her plea one of the swing doors opened and a figure in a white coat appeared. The doctor was a tall man in his mid-forties. His face was grey and tired and his eyes as they gazed at the little group that waited for his news were dominated by the pain he witnessed every day of his working life.

Bert jumped to his feet, releasing his hold on Clover. His voice cracked as he said, 'How is she, doctor? When can we see her?'

It seemed to Dr Laing that no matter how many times he went through a scene like this it would never get any easier. He was just glad the man who faced him, hope written all over his face, had the support of his young daughter and son to help him through. Although, gazing down with compassion at the girl, the wind-swept hair and wide, terrified eyes, he saw that from now on the child would also need every grain of love her father could provide.

Bert noticed the barely perceptible hesitation and an icy hand seemed to clutch at his heart. Still the hope refused to die, even as the doctor said, quietly, 'Your wife is at peace now, Mr Blossom. We did all we could, but I'm afraid the head wound she sustained when she fell . . .'

He paused, not sure the man had understood the message he was trying to convey. Perhaps it was better to be like his colleagues, blurting out the words bluntly, precisely, so there would be no mistaking their meaning. Not try to wrap it up in flowery words and phrases.

It was Eddie who broke the silence. 'Are you saying that my mother is dead?' Spoken like that, it sounded so shocking as to be incomprehensible.

There was a swiftly indrawn breath from Bert, a narrowing of the eyes and for one awful moment Dr Laing thought he would strike the youth for actually daring to put the thought into words.

Conscious of a rising anger that threatened his taut control, Bert burst out bitterly, 'You mean my lovely Adele is gone? That you took her,' he made a gesture towards the swing doors with a trembling hand, 'wherever you took her and you let her die?'

'Mr Blossom, we did all we could. The brain damage was severe. I am very sorry.'

Bert's hands closed into fists at his sides. His face twisted and tears flooded down his cheeks. He turned his head and met the wide, still uncomprehending gaze of his daughter. He wondered how he was going to explain the thing that would bring her whole safe little world crashing down about her ears.

The arrival of Miss Boyce brought soothing words and comforting arms. But Clover was beyond listening to anyone. She had listened to the remarks made by her father and the doctor and they were only now sinking in. And suddenly she was off, running down the wide shining corridor without a thought in her mind but her mother. 'Mama!' The word she had not used for years was wrenched from her, in the silence bouncing from the dark green painted walls. Passers-by eyed her warily as she ran. 'Mama!'

She heard footsteps coming after her, arms came round her, caught her, held her. She fought to be free.

'Clover!'

It was Miss Boyce. And because she would never hurt Miss Boyce, just in time she held back the kick she had aimed at her ankles. With surprising strength Miss Boyce swung her round so that they stood face to face. Clover was already taller than the little spinster. She stared down into the eyes behind the pince-nez and cried, 'Don't you understand?' Her voice rose in a wail. 'My mother is hurt. I must go to her.'

'No, no, Clover. Listen.'

Clover tried to squirm away again and Miss Boyce took her by the shoulders and shook her gently. She'd known immediately she'd seen Bert's face, read the terrible news it contained. 'My dear, you *must* listen.' She glanced about her at the long sterile corridor, the carefully expressionless faces of the passing nurses. 'But not here. Come, let's get back to your father and Eddie.'

All of a sudden, Clover felt as weak and helpless as a kitten. Afraid that if she stayed here much longer she would either be violently sick or else lapse into an embarrassing show of hysterics, she allowed Miss Boyce to lead her back to where Eddie and Bert waited. Bert sat with his face buried in his hands, doubled over as though in agony. Eddie drew deep on a cigarette the sympathetic doctor had given him, his hands in his pockets as he stood a little way apart from his father.

It was nearly midnight when they got home. Miss Boyce had taken charge and they had travelled back to the boarding house in the comparative luxury of a taxi cab which one of the porters had called.

Bert was like a person on the point of death, his breathing laboured, a slight wheeze sounding each time he drew breath. Clover was bedded down, her face and hands washed, wearing a clean nightie. Eddie had gone to his own room, not wanting anyone to see the unmanly tears he could no longer conceal.

Miss Boyce had coped like the enterprising woman she was, although once or twice she had almost given way and tears poured down her cheeks.

Declaring she would stay for the rest of the night and make up a bed on the settee, she tried to persuade Bert to go to his own bed. Of all of them, he was the one who had taken it the most badly. Miss Boyce watched him, slumped in his chair beside the dead fire and her heart bled for him. He kept saying, over and over again, 'What was she doing in that street, anyway? It's so narrow. I've warned her a dozen times about using it.' He broke off, his face twisted with grief as Eddie came through the door.

The boy approached him and put his arm round Bert's shoulders, murmuring, 'Hush, Dad, hush.'

Bert glared into his son's face. 'And where were you, eh? Why weren't you with them, looking after your sister and mother?'

Eddie caught Miss Boyce's eye and drew back as she shook her head, warningly.

'Not now, Bert,' she said. 'No one's to blame.' She fumbled for a cigarette, striking the match so hard it broke in two. She reached for the burning end, not feeling the pain as the tiny flame licked her fingers. 'Don't talk about it tonight. Go back to your room, Eddie, and you, Bert, why don't you go to bed? I'll stay here on the couch, in case someone is needed.'

Not that there was anything she could do, she thought

miserably. Poor Adele, lying so still and cold in the side room of the hospital where they had allowed her family to see her, would never need anything ever again.

Bert rubbed his hand across his eyes. 'I can't do that, Boycie.' The old familiar nickname, given to the little woman years ago by Adele, caused a sob to rise in her throat as Bert went on, 'I wouldn't be able to sleep.'

She picked up the bundle of bedding given to her by Ma Ruggles and shifted it to the settee. Looking over her shoulder, she said, 'Why don't you have a drink? It might help calm you.'

Bert nodded, without looking up. Crossing to the old-fashioned sideboard, she poured a stiff brandy from the bottle Bert kept for special occasions and carried it over to him. Then, greatly daring, she poured one for herself. Although disliking the taste of strong drink, goodness knows this night – or rather this morning because by now it was well into a new day – she felt the need of something stronger than the cup of tea Ma Ruggles had pressed on her. Bert drained his glass and refilled it. By the time the third glassful had taken effect he was slumped even lower in his chair, his snores filling the room, joining the slow tick-tock of the wooden-cased clock on the mantelpiece.

Adele Blossom was laid to rest on a clear blue morning. Birds had only just begun to greet the day and the salt tang of the sea drifted in on the morning tide. Clover, her eyes dry now, was dressed in black from head to foot, as were Eddie and Bert and grim-faced Miss Boyce. The cast of the Summer Follies were present and many wept openly.

Eddie and Bert stood near, stony-faced, staring straight ahead. Clover knew her mother would be gazing down from heaven during the service and she didn't want to embarrass her by weeping like a baby.

26

She could almost hear Adele's voice: 'Nothing lasts for ever, my little love. Life is like a candle in the wind, so easily gone. Don't weep for me, but be happy . . .'

The vicar spoke words of comfort and made much of the glory of joining the beloved Maker in the hereafter. But Bert did not hear him. Deep in his heart he was reliving memories; memories of a young girl running to meet him, long skirts flying, eyes starry with happiness; her hesitant steps when he'd first introduced her to the excitement and glamour of the stage; the sea whispering far beneath their feet as they walked the boards of the old pier with other strolling couples, eyes for nobody but each other.

Adele, with her soft brown hair and laughter on her mouth . . .

He recalled the tender, cherished moments and wished with all his heart he could live them again.

Bert felt lost. A terrible feeling of emptiness washed over him. But today had to be faced, painful as it was. Somehow, he managed to hold back the bitter tears, to lift his chin high and let the memories block out all other feelings. That would be how he would have to live for the rest of his life, fuelled by the past, thinking only of the happy times.

Back in their rooms in the boarding house, he gazed at his young daughter, so like her mother it was heartbreaking, and struggled to find comforting words to say. Miss Boyce had vanished in her usual discreet manner, leaving the small family alone. Soon after that Eddie had murmured excuses and had also vanished. Bert had watched from the window and seen his son striding across the road, hands thrust deep in his trouser pockets, as though he would escape from his sorrow if he walked fast enough.

The words, when finally he spoke, came out brokenly.

'Oh, Clover, oh, my little darling! What are we going to do now, with your mother gone?'

And Clover had gone to sit on her father's knee, putting her arms about his neck, striving to reassure him, to make believe that everything would be all right. That God would look after them.

She held him close, unsure of how to handle this distraught man who was her father. She listened to his words of scorn, that God was too busy looking after all the rich folk to bother his head about the likes of them. He shook his head. 'No,' he said, 'in this world you take care of yourself, for if you don't, then no other bugger will.'

'Shhhh,' she crooned, 'please, Daddy, don't.'

'What a waste,' sobbed Bert. 'What a bloody, bloody waste.'

Chapter Three

Bert Blossom was brought up strictly. His father, a fiercely upright man with a fine, waxed moustache, had been a regular soldier, had given twenty-one years of his life to his King and country. Living in places as far apart as Aldershot and Zanzibar, Bert's mother had learned early to cope with married quarters. Once she told Bert that the dream that had sustained her through all those years was of a small cottage in the country, beside a bluebell wood and a garden where she could grow strawberries and roses. In none of the hot, dusty outposts of the Empire in which she had spent her married life had she been able to grow either. She'd tried and wept many a frustrated tear over the results. If it was not the weather it was the wildlife. Anything from ferocious black ants that carried every leaf and blade of grass to their nests deep in the red earth, to small animals that left neat pug marks over her carefully tended garden beds and nibbled at every green shoot in sight.

Although on retirement her husband would have preferred a small pub where he could lord it as a publican, the bluebell wood got its way and the family settled down when Bert was fourteen. His parents tried, in a despondent kind of way, to persuade him to follow some sensible, conventional line of work, such as joining his father's old regiment or becoming a bank clerk. But young Bert wanted none of those things. What he wanted was to get away from the stifling influence and petty-mindedness of the small village where they lived. To do what, Bert wasn't sure, but it didn't include either soldiering or office work.

He was a good-looking lad and had a way with the girls, on which he quickly capitalised, getting one young girl pregnant when he was eighteen. The enraged father, armed with an ancient rifle he used for hunting rabbits, demanded retribution. It would be marriage or he would blow the boy's head off. He could take his choice.

Neither option appealed to Bert. That night, when his parents were asleep, he slipped out of the house and left the village for good. The next morning his parents found a note from him, saying they weren't to worry and once he had made a success of his life he would come back to visit them.

He never did come back and the success he made of his life wasn't quite what he had planned when he'd sat in his tiny bedroom under the sloping eaves, dreaming of things to come.

After school, he had worked briefly for a local farmer (not the one whose daughter he had compromised), a Jack-of-all-trades doing whatever was required of him. When he was eighteen, for a short time he'd stood behind the bar of the Woodsman, an old and respectable pub on the village green. On quiet evenings, he would tinkle on the piano, sweet, sentimental songs that everyone knew and joined with him in the chorus. He discovered he enjoyed that. It gave him a sense of power, of fulfilment, especially when the customers at the bar stamped their feet for more.

Bert had a natural ear for music. Pleasant and affable, the customers liked him. So when he found himself over the hills and far away in a strange town, what better way of making his living than by playing and singing at the piano? The music hall offered employment opportunities which to the young and ambitious Bert were a Godsend.

From those humble beginnings he graduated to better things, practising hard and adding a few dancing steps to his repertoire. The impresario of the Pierrot show at the end of the pier found Bert's dark good looks and pleasant tenor voice to his liking and the lad was always sure of a summer job at the theatre. The black and white costumes were attractive. The male members of the cast wore black silk trousers and a top with a white ruffle about the neck and large black pom-poms down the front of the jacket. A black silk scarf tied dashingly about the forehead gave them a piratical look that the ladies adored. The female cast wore a short, frilly tutu with a neck ruffle and tall pointed hats with a white pom-pom perched on the top.

Many music hall acts went from year to year, performing the same act. Bert Blossom brought a new vivacity into his when in later years he introduced Adele.

It would remain in his memory as long as life itself, that first meeting with Adele, his words, 'If you keep your eyes closed you can pretend you're the Sleeping Beauty and I'm the Prince come to wake you up.'

Adele Vaughn came of a good family. Her life began on a tragic note: her father died seven months before she was born and her mother on giving her life. Her mother's two spinster aunts took her in, bringing her up as their own. It was not considered quite the proper thing for two unmarried elderly ladies to bring up a child but the Frost sisters looked down their aristocratic noses and ignored public comment.

Adele was always alluded to by her aunts as the 'posthumous' child and for years she thought she was afflicted by some terrible disease. She was seventeen when she met Bert Blossom, he just three years older. It was summer and Bert, dressed in blazer, white flannels and a straw boater with his wavy dark hair and narrow moustache, held the eye of every girl as he strolled along the pier.

Adele and her aunts were on holiday, staying at a very select hotel at the quiet end of the promenade. Normally, she told him later, Aunt Hazel and Aunt Bethany would never have let her out of their sight. But today, greatly daring, she had taken fate into her own hands and crept out without their knowledge.

Earlier, the two aunts had decided to see the show at the end of the pier. A once well-known ballerina was appearing there and Aunt Bethany rhapsodised over the last time she had seen her, when Bethany was a young girl, going with her Mama to the theatre in Manchester and watching mesmerised as the dancer weaved her magic spell from behind the footlights.

Holding the local newspaper at arm's length, Bethany said, 'It seems she will be performing excerpts from *Le Cygne* and *Papillon*.' Letting the newsprint drop into her lap, she added, 'We *must* go. We'll go to this afternoon's performance. I see there is a matinée.'

'Me, too?' asked Adele, hopefully.

'Of course, child. Aren't you also on holiday?' For all Aunt Bethany's forbidding manner, she was really very fond of her young niece. She didn't spoil her like Hazel did, but then Hazel, five years younger than herself, was still young and foolish in Bethany's estimation. She'd probably never be any different. But one had to make amends . . .

'Of course, child,' she repeated, 'it will do you good. A brisk walk along the promenade to the pier always works wonders, I find. It might just bring back the roses in those poor, pale cheeks. You've been so listless lately, Adele. I declare I'm quite worried about you.'

Adele knew what she meant. Not so much *listless*,

she thought, as *restless*. Restless for things she didn't understand. Lately she couldn't settle to anything, the embroidery she had once taken such pride in lay idle in her lap while she gazed out of the window onto the summer's day, the new novel she had so looked forward to reading abandoned on her bedside table.

Faint-heartedly, Aunt Hazel suggested, 'Would not the evening's performance be more exciting, sister? The lights on the pier and all along the front? The people out for their after-dinner stroll? It would be most stimulating.'

'And why should you find this sudden need for stimulation?' Aunt Bethany's gaze rested coldly on the younger woman. 'Isn't being here, in this beautiful hotel with all its comforts, with dear Adele and myself, stimulation enough?'

Hazel blushed crimson. 'Of course, dear sister. I meant no criticism.'

'Then it is settled,' Bethany said, with all the graciousness of the Queen bestowing a knighthood on some fortunate subject. 'We will attend the afternoon performance.'

It was a decision that was to change Adele's life. She often wondered what her future would have held had she not gone to that show at the end of the pier and laid eyes on Bert Blossom. Vastly different, she knew, from what it turned out. Marriage into a wealthy family, to a man of whom her aunts approved. What a bore!

The performance of the rather passé ballerina was greatly appreciated, although Adele had to stifle a nervous giggle when she heard the boards on the stage positively creak as the dancer executed one of her famous pirouettes and little puffs of dust rose from the stage about her pink satin ballet slippers.

But when a dark young man came on and, seated at the piano, sang in a broad Irish brogue, 'Peg, o' my

heart, I love you, don't let us part, I love you . . .' even
the little puffs of dust were forgiven.

She left the theatre in a dream, answering in mono-
syllables her aunts' questions as to whether she had
enjoyed the show. 'A bit of culture,' observed Aunt
Bethany complacently. 'You must agree, sister, we do
not see enough of it.'

After dinner, the aunts settled to their usual enter-
tainment of bridge, leaving Adele to her own devices.
There was a turbulence within her, seated by her
open bedroom window, listening to the sounds of
laughter and music coming from the Pavilion where
she understood there was dancing. Only the common
people went there, she had been told. Oh, how she
wished she was one of the common people! She had
always thought of boys as being strange and alarming
creatures. Thinking of them now, she felt her heart
fluttering with a trepidation she didn't understand.
Was she coming down with something? That would
really ruin her holiday.

Not that it had been much of a holiday so far. The
aunts thought they were acting in her best interests,
of course they did, but it wasn't much fun for a
seventeen-year-old young lady to be constantly squired
by two unmarried spinsters who seldom took their eyes
off you.

Adele could see men and women walking arm in arm,
heads bent as they whispered secrets. She sighed. What
sort of secrets would a young man whisper to a young
lady? Whatever they were, she decided, they would be
infinitely preferable to sitting here alone, dreaming
impossible dreams.

There was a soft knock. The bedroom door opened
and a girl came in. Dressed in the plain bibbed white
apron and mobcap of a maid, she carried a tray on which
was set a tall glass of warm milk and a small silver dish

of sugar cubes. She looked faintly surprised to see the occupant of the room sitting in semi-darkness. Placing the tray on top of the small table under the window she looked over her shoulder and said, 'Don't you want the light on, miss? It'll be pitch black in another few minutes.'

Adele grimaced. 'The way I feel at the moment, Molly, darkness suits my mood admirably.'

The two girls were much the same age and got on well together, for Adele showed none of the haughtiness displayed by her aunts towards those they considered the 'lower orders'.

Putting her head on one side, like a cheeky sparrow, Molly asked, 'What's up? 'As somethin' 'appened? Not bad noos from 'ome?'

Adele shook her head. 'No, Molly, but thank you for asking.'

Molly smiled. 'Just a blue mood, is it? Never mind, miss. It'll pass. Affects us all one way or the other some time, does life. A right bugger.'

Adele had been intrigued by Molly's accent. 'You're not from around here, are you?' she had commented one day when Molly was busy making the bed, smoothing the shiny satin counterpane over the blankets. 'Where are you from, Molly?'

'The Smoke,' was the laconic reply. Seeing the other girl's puzzled look, she added, 'London. South of the river. Brixton way.' Her hands continued smoothing the blue cover, palms flat, as though she took great delight in the cool feel of the satin.

'You're a long way from home! What made you come all the way up here?'

'Fell in love, didn't I.' Molly straightened, pressing her hands into the small of her back. 'Followed the bugger up 'ere – 'e was a seaman spending a few days in London while 'is ship was docked in Liverpool. Fell

35

in love and followed 'im north. I got work as a skivvy in a lodging 'ouse and then when 'is ship sailed I decided to better meself and come 'ere to the seaside. I ain't never seen the sea before this, 'cept the docks in Liverpool and you could 'ardly call that the seaside.'

'And your . . .?' Adele bit her lip, unsure of the term she should use. Boy friend? Sweetheart?

Molly said it for her. 'Me lover?' She grinned cheekily, bending towards the dressing table mirror, the better to examine an inflamed spot on her chin. 'Sailed orf into the blue, 'e did. Never 'eard another word from 'im. Just as well, for already I was gettin' fed up with the bugger. Swaggering as a dog with two tails, so 'e was, thinking I'd be waitin' for 'im when 'e came back.'

Adele laughed, envying Molly her freedom of choice; the way she chose to live, the words she chose to use. If either Aunt Bethany or Aunt Hazel ever heard her expressing herself so freely, she knew there would be pandemonium.

The blue mood took over again. And when Molly came nearer and placed a hand on her shoulder and said softly, 'Don't you want to talk about it, miss? Sometimes it 'elps,' it was as if a dam burst within Adele and all her pent-up emotions came flooding out. She began talking, the words spilling out in a torrent.

When the spate finally faltered and came to a halt, Molly picked up a sugar lump from the basin and popped it into her mouth, sucking it thoughtfully. Adele, half ashamed of her volubility, waited for her to say something. Bits of sugar lump went down the wrong way and Molly coughed and then looked at Adele and said, 'You poor little cow!' Adele's longing to be with people her own age, to laugh and walk in the moonwashed hours with a boy's arm about her waist, touched her compassionate heart.

Mind made up, she said, 'Well, instead of wishing, why don't you go? What's to stop you?'

Adele grimaced. 'My aunts would stop me. I'm not allowed out on my own after dark.'

Molly repeated herself. 'Poor little cow!' Thoughtfully she regarded the other girl. 'Well, you'll get nowhere by not takin' chances in this world, miss. Wouldn't you take one if it offered itself?'

'You mean go out there,' she nodded at the lighted promenade outside her bedroom window, 'without my aunts knowing?'

'And eat fish and chips out of a noospaper wi' lashings of salt and vinegar,' enthused Molly, getting into the spirit. 'Blimey, I wouldn't 'arf mind a bit of that meself, but I'm not finished 'ere until ten.'

Up at the crack of dawn, making fires and tea for the rest of the staff, bed was the nearest thing to heaven by ten o'clock.

But what the heck, Molly thought. A walk by the sea would do her good and the girl really looked in need of a breath of sea air herself with those large grey eyes gazing so pleadingly on a world that cared little for the happiness or otherwise of young girls, whatever their class.

Pale, too, she was, that delicately fine skin untouched by colour, a direct contrast to Molly with her coarse black hair and rosy cheeks. Adele's hair was as soft as the down on the breast of a robin, the colour of cinnamon sugar.

'It's only another 'arf 'our before I'm finished,' she told Adele. 'How about if I call for you then, we go for a walk, see what the big, wide world is up to?'

Adele's face was a study. Molly saw doubt welling up into her eyes and hastened to reassure her. 'Don't be nervous, miss. No 'arm'll come to you as long as I'm wi' you.'

Adele's mind raced, knowing she should reject the whole foolish idea, knowing full well she wouldn't. She drew a deep breath, her mind made up. 'All right, then. But only for a little while. And my aunts must never know.'

Molly's eyes danced with mischief. 'Me lips are sealed. I'll be trusting you as much as you're trusting me. It'll be, what do you call it? A *fait accompli*.' She looked smug at her use of the phrase, explaining, 'That was a favourite quotation of one of the guests 'ere. Used it all the time, so 'e did. Said I was a bright little madam when I asked 'im what it meant.' She smiled at Adele. 'It'll be our secret.'

Adele thought of her well-meaning but austere aunts, the fuss there would be if they found out what she was about to do. But some exhilarating sense of freedom filled her and she said, firmly, 'Ten o'clock, then. I'll be ready.'

When Molly came for her, one finger to her lips in a cautionary gesture, she was ready. Molly peered along the length of the corridor making sure it was all clear. ''S all right,' she breathed. 'Come on, Buttercup. I'd like to enjoy at least a couple of breaths of sea air before I'm caught.'

Adele shuddered and said with a plea in her voice, 'Oh, please, don't joke! I feel so nervous.' Never before had she disobeyed her aunts. For all they knew she was in her bed, sleeping the sleep of the pure of heart.

'You'll be all right,' Molly assured her.

The way clear, they managed to escape through the back door and down the brick path to the side entrance of the hotel without meeting anyone. The promenade was crowded. It was just as Adele had imagined it: the sound of voices and laughter, girls squealing as the wind tugged at their skirts, lifting the light summery material to show a pair of pale stockings and trim ankles.

They turned onto the pier, dropping a penny into the slot of the heavy old turnstile, pushing their way through as it went click-click-click. Molly bought a stick of bright pink rock from one of the many stalls selling all manner of things along the length of the long grey structure. She sucked it noisily as they walked. She offered it to Adele, but Adele shook her head.

She gazed down at the boards as they walked, seeing between the narrow spaces the reflected lights from the promenade glistening on the water – myriad colours: greens, blues, reds, white, a liquid rainbow moving with the surging waves. She had never seen anything like it or felt so free of restriction. Why should her aunts object, anyway? She wasn't doing any harm, although Molly was talking about 'Popping in to have a drink'. But there Adele knew she must draw the line. The only drink she had ever tasted was a light wine at special dinners, when the minister came to pay his respects, usually after the aunts had made a substantial donation to the organ fund or the church roof. Aunt Hazel maintained the wine was good for the blood and had had an argument with her sister when Aunt Bethany replied anybody could find an excuse for anything if they wanted it badly enough.

Deeply engrossed in the colour-washed sea, Adele didn't see the young man until they collided. She felt an arm go about her waist and heard a voice: 'Steady on. Best to look where you're going in this crowd.'

She looked up and recognised at once the face of the young man whose voice had held her so captivated earlier that afternoon. Unconsciously, she caught her breath and held it.

He smiled down into her eyes. Sensations that caused the coloured lights to swirl, the boards beneath her feet to tilt, had Adele momentarily closing her eyes. She felt herself actually clinging to him, to his sleeve, and, horror of horrors, his arm about her waist tightened.

She heard a voice, deep, melodious, whisper close to her ear, 'If you keep your eyes closed you can pretend you're the Sleeping Beauty and I'm the Prince come to wake you up.'

He told her, long afterwards, that her wide dreaming eyes and small, pale face had indeed made him feel like a prince come to wake her up from a long sleep. Tenderness had welled up inside him, an unaccustomed emotion that both surprised and excited him.

He heard her sigh. She would like nothing better than to keep her eyes closed, to savour this moment for ever. But if she kept her eyes closed she couldn't see the handsome face and the warm brown eyes gazing down into hers, the even white teeth that were revealed beneath the narrow moustache as he smiled. Or the straw boater perched on the back of his head, the dark hair curling forward over his forehead.

Dashing, she decided. Like someone out of those torrid romances she was so fond of reading and which she had to keep hidden from her aunts. Well, Aunt Bethany, anyway. Aunt Hazel would often borrow one from her when she'd finished it and she'd giggle like a schoolgirl over hiding places with Adele.

Adele had never been as close as this to a man before. Indeed, apart from her aunts' lawyer and the minister, her contact with members of the opposite sex had been extremely limited. She didn't in the least feel like the young girl who had walked these boards in the company of her aunts just a few short hours before. She imagined their horror if they were to see her now, right here in the middle of a thronging crowd, a brazen hussy, actually enjoying the feel of a man's arms about her waist as he whispered in her ear. She didn't even know his name. She should have taken note of it from the posters outside the theatre but she hadn't. Which made the feeling that she already knew him more uncanny than ever.

For his part, he thought her slightly fey and ethereal, but with an infectious sense of fun. 'A cut above you, old man,' he told himself as he listened to the low, well-modulated voice, noted the simple but expensive clothes, which only money and the best schools could have achieved.

By the time Molly reappeared from the nearby pub she hadn't been able to resist, he realised something else. He had to see this girl again.

Full of apologies, Molly fluttered her eyelashes at the handsome young man, looking from him to Adele. Taking in Adele's confusion, digging her in the ribs with a familiarity that normally she would never have dared, she leaned closer towards Adele and said, loud enough for Bert to hear, 'You're a sly one, I must say! Talk about still waters running deep and all that!'

The chimes of the town hall clock reminded her of the passing hours and she sighed. 'I suppose I'd better get you back, miss. Don't want the old Missis Frosts coming in to tuck you up and finding you not there, do we? The fat would be in the fire and no mistake.'

Adele couldn't help but agree, although there was little likelihood of either of her aunts entering her room at this hour, presuming her to be fast asleep. Even so, the thought was terrifying. When Bert asked, very daringly, if he could see her again, she hesitated.

'We haven't been formally introduced.'

'Oh, Lord love a duck!' said Molly, losing all patience. 'If that's all it takes, I'll do the bloody honours.' With a grand flourish, she announced, 'Miss Adele Vaughn, niece to Miss Bethany and Miss Hazel Frost. Although dragons are supposed to 'ave expired with St George these two, I assure you, my good man, are definitely of that species. So don't say you 'aven't bin warned. And,' turning her attention to an amused Bert, 'I know you, you're in

41

that show at the end of the pier. Bert Blossom, in't it?'

Bert admitted that he was indeed Bert Blossom and she went through the whole rigmarole again: a sweep of one arm, the names spoken in the kind of voice a butler might use for the season's crop of debutantes arriving at Buckingham Palace to meet the Queen.

With a fine disregard for the conventions, Adele continued to meet Bert in the afternoons while her aunts rested after their midday meal. With Molly as a willing accomplice, she would slip out of the side door of the hotel and into the narrow lane used by the tradesmen. Bert would be waiting at the far end, straw boater in hand, hair ruffled by the breeze; so good-looking that the breath would catch in her throat and she would pinch herself to prove that she wasn't dreaming.

Bert never forgot those afternoons, the summer sunshine on their faces, the sense of exhilarating freedom. It seemed the whole world had turned out in their best clothes, bent on enjoying the lovely weather. The deep blue of a cloudless sky; the brilliant greens of the lawns fronting the hotels; the flowerbeds along the promenade blooming in a profusion of vivid colour. Bert would tell her tales of his youth, of growing up in a hot country with all its alien smells and sounds. His memories were vivid of bright yellow and orange marigolds ringing a flagpole, the whole surrounded by chastely painted white-washed stones. The Union Jack snapping merrily against a deep azure sky while hawks swirled and floated on the hot winds above.

Adele drank it all in, each day captivated more intensely by this young man who was making such a difference to her life. She listened and sighed. 'You've been to all those places and I've never been further than Morecambe and Whitney Bay. And, of course, this place.' She made a small grimace. 'I feel a real dunce.'

Bert squeezed her arm. 'There's still time. We've got years ahead of us yet.' And she thrilled at his use of the word 'we'. Those meetings were of necessity short, for Bert had an early show to do and often an afternoon matinée. But they were made all the more sweet by their briefness. One afternoon, Adele, holding her skirts high to avoid the last of the night's rain that left the gutters swilling, was thrilled to see him seated high on the seat of a small pony trap. The reins were held loosely in his hand, his hat perched cheekily on the back of his head. His eyes watched eagerly for her appearance.

She ran the last few yards, hair and skirts flying. Bert, with one smooth, graceful movement swung himself to the ground and caught her in his arms. Holding her tightly against him he kissed her.

It was the first time they had kissed. She told him later that the whole universe stood still, the clouds paused in their windswept journey across the skies and bells rang in her ears. Coming from any other girl, this confession would have had Bert laughing coarsely. In his day he had kissed many a young girl, and some not so young. He was shaken now by the feelings that kiss aroused.

Such a chaste kiss, too. Adele's lips were warm and sweet and lay still beneath his. He did not want to frighten her away by becoming too aggressive and so was content to leave it that way, putting her from him after a moment and smiling down into her startled eyes. Waving one hand towards the cream-coloured pony and gaily painted red and white two-wheeled trap to which it was hitched, he said, deliberately casual, 'Like it? I thought we'd find a nice, quiet country lane out of town and just sit in the sun and talk.'

Adele's eyes shone. 'Oh, Bert, how wonderful! But can you afford it?'

'If I can't afford to take my girl riding for an hour then it's a poor show.'

Adele clapped her hands like an excited child and, disdaining the hand he extended, climbed unaided into the high seat.

The holiday was fast coming to an end and he knew that in another week she would be gone. He confessed that when the time came, he would find it hard to part, and shyly Adele nodded her agreement.

'Would you consider marrying someone like me?' he asked. A question that had been trembling on his lips for some days now. They had left the pony contentedly grazing on the green verges of the lane and now they strolled, hand in hand, Adele radiant in her gauzy white summer frock and white straw hat with its band of yellow daisies. At his words she felt her heart skip a beat. Then it began racing again with a speed that frightened her. For a moment she wanted to turn and run, not to have to face the question.

Gazing into his eyes, seeing the love and longing there, she knew there could be only one answer. 'I'd love to,' she said shyly and closed her eyes. She felt his mouth on her upturned lips. Opening her eyes she saw the triumph on his face.

'Good, let's break the news to your aunts, then.' His grin widened. 'How do you think they'll take it?' Adele couldn't repress a shudder. Without waiting for an answer, he went on, his voice teasing, 'We *could* run away together. Elope. I could borrow a ladder and climb up to your bedroom window and you could throw your case out and follow me down. It might be safer than facing your aunts.'

But they didn't. Adele had too much pride and love for her aunts for that. The following day she met him outside the hotel. This time choosing the front door, she led him by the hand into the private sitting room

Clover Blossom

used by her aunts. Together they faced the women
and proudly, head held high, for miraculously all her
first nervousness had gone and she felt she could face
anything, or anyone, she told her story with a plea for
understanding.

'You see, we love each other,' she said, her eyes
shining so joyously that Aunt Hazel felt tears start in
her own eyes. 'We want to get married.'

Bert would never rid himself of the memory of the
look of horror, quickly followed by one of hostility, that
flooded the elder sister's features. Hazel recovered first,
although her voice shook when she exclaimed, 'Don't
you think it would be manners to introduce us to the
young man before you talk of marrying him, my dear
Adele?'

It sounded so comical, Aunt Hazel looked so prim
and proper, Adele started to giggle. Aunt Bethany shot
her a glance of such icy rebuke that the giggle turned
into a hiccup and Adele took a deep breath, trying to
repress it.

Unceremoniously, Bert was sent packing with instructions never to try and see their niece again. To spare
Adele's feelings, he left quietly, although beneath the
calm exterior he was simmering with rage. The Miss
Frosts, he thought, had been aptly named. He'd never
met a pair of frostier old bitches in his life!

Clover had been fond of listening to her mother tell this
story. At this point she would let out a gusty sigh and
breathe, 'And what happened then? Did you run away
with him in the end?' She knew the answer, for this was
one of her favourite stories, the romance between her
mother and father. It had enlivened many a dreary day
when the rain slid down the windowpanes and it was
too wet to go out to the beach.

Adele had had a little money of her own and Bert had

a few pounds saved. They caught the train to Gretna Green and were married by the blacksmith in the time-honoured tradition over the anvil. It was all part of the magic, listening to her mother's reminiscences of that summer of long ago.

Adele would look down on the lively little face and smooth one hand across the glossy hair. 'If I hadn't, well, you and Eddie wouldn't be here now, would you?'

'Didn't you find it hard?'

'When you really love someone, Clover, you can face anything, go anywhere, live like a gypsy if you have to, as long as he's at your side.' She smiled, thinking of some of the digs they had used. Bert accepted whatever opportunities came his way, delighted to find his young wife had a natural gift for simple dance routines and a pleasant singing voice.

'And you never saw your aunts again?'

'No, love, I never saw them again.'

Clover felt she knew the two aunts intimately, although she had never met them and wasn't likely to. Not the way they felt about her father. She knew they lived in a big house with beautiful gardens in the country and had a carriage to take them everywhere. Aunt Hazel was her favourite. She imagined her as warm and motherly, if a little timid of her elder sister. Whereas Aunt Bethany would be sharp and full of rebukes. Clover was sure there would be a welcome from Aunt Hazel for a poor little niece without relatives and wished every year on her first Christmas pudding stir that one day they would all be together. Sometimes there was such a sad look on her mother's face whenever she spoke of her aunts. She didn't like her mother looking sad.

Bert had lost all touch with his own parents. In fact, he didn't even know if they were still alive. Listening to the others in the cast talk of visits at Christmas to aunts and cousins and uncles, Clover felt somehow cheated. Would she ever have an extended family of her own with whom she could stay and exchange family anecdotes and presents? She told herself there were plenty worse off than she was. People who had no family at all, not even homes. She'd seen pictures in the newspapers of slum dwellings where a mother sat in rags before a scanty fire, the baby on her knee covered in sores while another two or three young children stood about her, gazing solemnly into the camera. Bert had told her of people who slept in street doorways and begged for a living. If ever Clover saw a beggar, she would drop a penny – if she had one to spare, which wasn't often – into the grubby outstretched hand. Especially if it was a young girl. Her father was cross if he learned of her generosity, saying charity began at home and didn't she realise that the money she gave would only go towards purchasing a jug of gin? 'Beggars and gypsies,' Bert would lecture. 'You stay clear of 'em, my girl. A scurrilous lot. Pinch the fillings from your teeth if you gave 'em half a chance.'

Children might go without shoes, without cloth coats to keep them warm in the bitter Lancashire winter, but the people who made up the end-of-pier audience paid no heed to that. The Golden Age of Music Hall, the papers called it, and if one or two of the comics caused a blush to warm a lady's cheek, well, it was all good, clean fun. The King loved it and he would bring Queen Mary to enjoy it with him. Vesta Tilley, the darling of the halls, sang her famous song 'Piccadilly Johnnie', and the Queen was so distressed at the conception of a woman dressed as a man that she averted her eyes for the rest of Miss Tilley's performance.

Then somewhere in a little town in Europe a duke was assassinated and the world was swept into war.

The year Clover turned ten, Bert watched as men joined long queues outside recruiting offices. Acts in

the theatre suffered as men left. But the Four Blossoms
went on, gaining in popularity and strength as the
children were able to participate more in the act.

On one of their rare outings together without the children, Adele and Bert sat in the local cinema, enjoying
the slapstick comedy of Charlie Chaplin. Afterwards
the management showed a newsreel of goose-stepping
German soldiers and stretches of no-man's land marked
with barbed wire fences over which men struggled
bravely. The night sky was ablaze with gunfire, bursting
shells making it as bright as day. The straggly line of
men in British uniform advanced, fixed bayonets at
the ready.

Bert relived memories of his own childhood, of his
father in his khaki uniform, straight and fierce; he could
almost hear his voice saying, 'Come on, lad, no sitting
about while your country needs you.'

His arm tightened about his wife's shoulders. He bent
his head to Adele's, surprising himself by saying in a low
voice, 'You know, old girl, I think I'm going to have to
do something about this. I really don't think they stand
a chance without me.'

He would never know how Adele's heart sank at his
words. She gave a little laugh and said fondly, 'Bert
Blossom, my ever so modest husband!'

He kissed her cheek; mindful of the scandalised
glances of various middle-aged ladies sitting near them,
he grinned cheekily and kissed her again.

Responding, like thousands of others, to the Kitchener
poster with the pointing finger – 'Your Country Needs
You' – he was first in line at the recruiting office
barely a week later. Within days of joining up, Adele
and the children were saying goodbye to him on a
windswept station. All about them, women sobbed
into handkerchiefs. Adele was determined that Bert's
last view of her until his return would not be one of

a sorrowful, weeping face. She forced a smile, waving the handkerchief she would later use to dry her tears, instructing the children to wave, too. Clover was already in tears, seeing the train take her beloved father away.

Adele would never tell him how lonely she had found it, with him away. How austere the months had been during their winter sojourn in Moorfield. The meagre allowance she received from the army went nowhere and Bert had never been much of a one for saving. To help out, Eddie had borrowed a small, two-wheeled handcart and made a few shillings trundling it around the poorer parts of the district, selling the coke he had begged from the gas works. But it was a hard time.

Fleetingly, Adele had considered writing to her aunts. But their parting when she had left with Bert had been acrimonious and she did not think they would have changed; Aunt Bethany had threatened to go to the law if she continued with her wild scheme. But Adele had known it for the empty threat it was. Her aunts would never face the disgrace. She thought of them often, of their kindness and concern for her welfare. But she knew that if she had to make the choice again she would not have changed a thing.

Bert's army career didn't last long. Wounded almost immediately in France, he was invalided out of the army barely six months later. His shoulder wound never healed properly and he was declared unfit for further service. Adele welcomed him home with tears and kisses. Confused, he'd exclaimed, 'Go on, you daft woman! I'm safe and sound now, back home again. Why all the tears? You didn't cry when you saw me off but you're in floods of tears now!'

Adele sniffed. 'I know. I'm sorry, but it's just the thought of having you home again.'

Bert grinned. 'That bad, eh?'

'Bad?'

'Yes, having me home again.'

Adele punched him.

Their lives continued as though there had been no break. During the last of those grim war years, more people than ever wanted to be entertained. Work was always available for the Four Blossoms and it seemed to Bert that some benevolent deity had cast an approving eye over the small family and smiled. Until a pitiless fate decreed otherwise.

Chapter Four

Like a monster crouched for ever in some secret corner, the night of Adele's death towered up and spilled long shadows of misery across Bert's mind. Without Adele he felt rootless and he took to walking the streets, a morose and bitter man. Wrapped in his own despair, he was blind to his children's grief. Eddie took the brunt of his sharp temper. Young though Clover was, touching fifteen the summer of that year, her instincts told her that deep and lasting though her and her brother's sorrow was, her father's loss was different. Something quite beyond her understanding.

When Bert got tired of walking the streets, the cheerful sounds issuing from the Silver Mermaid on the prom beckoned and it was easier to join the cheerful company of fellow drinkers than to return to Ma Ruggles' boarding house and face the accusing frown of his son. Clover, bless her, was not one for blaming anyone. Clover would have a hot supper waiting for him and a smile and say, 'Eat it up quickly, now, before it gets cold.' Trying to be a wife. Trying to take the place of her mother.

Ma Ruggles told her, 'I've seen the sort of thing that's happening to your dad before.' She shook her head. 'With tragic results, love. Perhaps if I was to 'ave a talk with 'im . . . ?'

'Thank you for your concern, Mrs Ruggles,' an embarrassed flush stained Clover's cheeks, 'but it's only a temporary thing. We just have to have patience.'

Patience, Ma Ruggles thought, had nothing to do with it. You could have all the patience in the world but it wouldn't do a scrap of good for Bert Blossom. As she remarked to her next-door neighbour over a cosy cup of tea in one of her quieter moments, she could see there all the makings of a lazy good-for-nothing. 'Poor Adele must be turning in her grave the way he's carrying on.'

Miss Boyce put in a quiet twopenny worth, catching Clover alone one day at rehearsals. 'I'm deeply disturbed at what is happening to your father, dear. If there is anything, *anything* I can do, you will tell me, won't you?' She didn't say that, in her opinion, this was something Bert would have to overcome by his own inner strength. Which, since Adele died, seemed sadly lacking.

Clover squeezed the hand that held hers. 'Of course I will. Who else would I turn to but my dear Miss Boyce?'

Eddie made no secret of his exasperation with Bert's casual treatment of rehearsal times, his irritable comings and goings, and most of all the way the money Clover tried so hard to save for Ma Ruggles and other necessities slipped through Bert's fingers like sand on the shore. He resented bitterly Bert's carping attitude, the lip-curling scorn when again Eddie tried to suggest a new twist to the act or new music.

He and Clover had been trying out one of his compositions, an inventive and dazzling dance routine, their voices and steps cleverly harmonising while the Summer Follies' piano player did the honours. Some of the cast stopped to watch. A round of applause greeted their efforts and someone said, 'Why on earth don't you get Bert to introduce that into your act, Eddie?'

Eddie grimaced. 'Don't you think I haven't tried?

You know my father's opinion of this rubbish, as he calls it. He just won't see reason.'

'We'll talk to him,' murmured one of the chorus girls, 'get him in a good mood and persuade him to see the error of his ways.'

'You'll be lucky,' muttered Eddie morosely.

And of course Bert would have none of it. At rehearsals, Eddie would begin the introduction of a new song or dance routine and within minutes antagonism would spark between father and son. 'It'll be a long time before you start planning the act, boy,' Bert would say, tight-lipped, blustering. 'Don't you forget that I'm not an old man yet.' And, 'Watch those gags tonight, boy, and don't step on any of my laughs.'

'You kill your own laughs, Dad. You wait too long.'

'Are you telling me how to nurse a laugh?'

'No, but you can't keep on using that old-fashioned stuff. The audience want something new.'

'No, they don't. They want the good old "Why did the chicken cross the road" jokes that they've always laughed at. It's all part of our tradition.'

Eddie snorted. 'Tradition!' If it had been anyone but his father, Eddie would have told him what he could do with tradition. In his opinion the public wanted gay, lively songs and plenty of glamorous costumes, not the same old black and white stuff they had been looking at for years. All right, he knew the shows were as well attended as they had always been but then people on holiday would swallow anything. But that didn't mean the small end-of-pier theatres had to go on supplying inferior offerings.

Clover watched the men in her life hurt each other and tried not to come down too harshly on one side or the other. She loved them both and wished with all her sensitive being that things could be as they were when Adele was alive. But of course they never could be and

Bert and Eddie, like a couple of stubborn buffaloes, continued to lock horns.

With his eighteenth birthday come and gone, Eddie felt he had left his childhood behind and his thoughts were now concentrated on the battle to do what his instincts told was right. To lead the act of the Blossoms into a new era. Adele had known how to handle her two equally stubborn men, but Clover, listening to their angry voices, would shrivel up inside, hunching her neck into her shoulders and clenching her hands so tightly that her nails would dig into the palms of her hands. Eddie was aware of what these disagreements were doing to his young sister and tried to remain calm and not let his father's scathing rebukes get to him. But it wasn't easy and often he would forget and answer back, earning a sharp clip about the ear from an enraged Bert.

To all her entreaties, Eddie would reply, 'You're the one that Dad loves. He doesn't love me, never has. "This is my daughter, she's got a great future in the theatre, and this is my son who is getting too big for his boots and who would lounge about all day doing nothing if I let him."' He smiled, adding derisively, 'Everyone sees it but you, dear sister.'

'Oh, Eddie, you know that isn't true. Why don't you try and earn his affection, try to make things halfway pleasant between you? You can't win anybody's love by fighting with them all the time.' She looked up at him with appealing dark-fringed eyes. 'Why don't you give him a chance? Show him you really care?'

Eddie's lip curled. 'How am I supposed to do that, then?'

'Just tell him, show him by your actions. You'll see, it's the simplest thing in the world.'

One day at the beginning of September, when the season was nearly over and Adele had been in her grave for three months, Miss Boyce came upon Clover as she sat weeping in the stalls of the empty theatre. The cleaning women had gone and the building was silent. 'What are you doing here, Clover, all on your own?'

Clover hiccuped loudly, dried her eyes and gave Miss Boyce a wide smile to show she wasn't really crying. 'I wanted to say a sort of private goodbye to Mum,' she said. She glanced about her at the rows of tipped-up seats, the dust motes hanging heavily in the shafts of sunshine. 'She used to sit here during rehearsals and watch the other artistes perform. I feel she's still here, Boycie, that she will always be here.'

'I know, little love. I have that feeling, too.' Miss Boyce sounded on the verge of tears herself. 'And she will endure and that will be a comfort to us all.'

She thought wistfully of Adele's sweet expression, the cloud of soft brown hair. Clover was so like her mother in many ways that sometimes, as Miss Boyce watched her from the wings of the stage, performing her simple routine, she felt she was back in the days when the baby lay in the big wickerwork basket to one side of the stage and it was Adele in the spotlight singing her song.

Miss Boyce wished there was some way she could make life easier for Clover. She knew money must be tight for the family – Bert showed no signs of pulling himself together – and she had suggested that perhaps Adele's stage costumes could be disposed of. 'It seems such a shame,' she told Clover, 'for them to remain packed away when they should be out under the lights, being gazed upon by adoring young men.' She lowered her head, glancing across the top of her glasses at Clover. 'And they would fetch a good price . . .'

'You mean, sell them?' Clover said slowly. It seemed almost obscene, the idea of selling her mother's lovely things.

'You would get a good price for them.' Over the

years Miss Boyce had kept the garments fresh and clean and she had a pretty good idea as to their value. The materials were of the finest, silks and velvets, the sewing exquisite. She had done most of the sewing herself so she ought to know.

But Clover couldn't bring herself to ask for money for something that had been so close to her mother's heart. And so the costumes remained in their dark hiding place, like some faded ghost of poor, pretty Adele.

Miss Boyce patted Clover's hand. 'You'd better get back before Bert starts to wonder what's happened to you.' She squared her shoulders. 'And I'd better go and see to the costumes.'

A great deal of Miss Boyce's time as wardrobe mistress was spent ironing the many changes of costumes used in the show. Rows and rows of frills, with skirts so full they took an age to iron. As she bent over the fabric with one iron, a second would be heating on the gas ring. It was difficult to regulate the heating of the heavy flat irons and she constantly worried in case she burned a hole in the centre of some chorus girl's skirt or left a brown scorchmark on a muslin sleeve. In addition to the mental strain, these days it often made her back ache as well.

At least the winter months ahead would give her some respite, she reflected, although she was always sorry when the summer ended and the cast of the Summer Follies packed their belongings and moved on to their winter quarters. Some went to modest hotels, some to family homes where they got on everyone's nerves with their restless ways.

The Blossoms went to a small family-run hotel in Moorfield, near the Park, where they had been going for years. Newcombe's pier became a place of memories, deserted, with many stalls shuttered. The deckchair man handed out his last ticket. Only the man with the cockle stall who sold paper cups of the tasty shellfish stayed open. Lately, the Winter Gardens had taken to staying open all through the winter months and the pattern of things was changing, with many more holidaymakers coming for short breaks during the cold weather.

Miss Boyce stayed where she was. Years ago, when her life had changed so drastically, she had returned to this place and here she would stay. The memories Newcombe held were bitter-sweet and sometimes, walking the length of the promenade, she would pretend it was yesterday once more – the yesterday of the turn of the century . . .

Miss Boyce had not thanked her parents, much as she loved them, for their quaint sense of humour in their choice of name for her. They had thought Joyce sounded very dignified and ladylike. That 'Joyce Boyce' would subject her to all kinds of ridicule and name-calling at school never once entered their heads.

Their first child, Joyce's sister, was more suitably named Ruth. From birth, Ruth was a pretty little thing, with blue eyes and a mass of softly curling hair, while Joyce's hair seemed to have a life of its own. It was wavy rather than curly, often giving her the look, as their mother put it, of being dragged through a hedge backwards.

Joyce grew up a timid person, jumping when anyone of the opposite sex spoke to her, as different from her animated sister as chalk from cheese.

When she had just turned eighteen, Ruth eloped with a young man who had come to the house selling some new labour-saving invention for the kitchen. After that, the remaining daughter seldom escaped from the glare of the parental eye; Mrs Boyce had no intention of allowing the same thing to happen to the child who was born to take care of them in their old age.

Joyce was twenty-three when she'd gone on holiday to Newcombe that summer long ago with her parents. Unexpectedly she was allowed a measure of freedom one afternoon when her parents were persuaded to join some of the more elderly hotel guests in a game of bridge. Joyce slipped out of the front door of the hotel and down the garden path to the promenade, her heart thudding with excitement. Seldom was she allowed to do exactly as she wished.

She strode out, enjoying the blue of the sky; the sea today was calm and peaceful, gulls swooped and screamed, dived to devour the flotsam of a hundred picnics. On the sand below the promenade a young girl was being chased by two youths, her screams joining the cries of the gulls.

The brisk wind tugged Joyce's hair from the band that held it back from her face. Her ankle-length frock was of white cotton and its finely tucked bodice outlined her inadequate bosom and skinny legs. The colourful sign of a fortune-teller caught her eye and, after the briefest of hesitations, she went through its doorway, passing into a dark cavern-like place where a woman sat behind a small table which was covered by a black velvet cloth. She was a handsome woman, rosy-cheeked, with dark curly hair and large black eyes. A pair of golden earrings swung against her tanned neck. Gypsy Rose accepted Joyce's silver and told her she was about to meet a tall, dark, handsome stranger. Joyce smiled, thinking of her scandalised mother if she could see her now.

She spent ten minutes with the woman, listening to the sort of things the fortune-teller knew she wanted to hear. The magic still lingered as Joyce stepped out into the sunlight and continued her walk. The experience had brought a flush to her cheeks. Thinking of the long walk back to the hotel, she decided to sit for a while in one of the glass-sided shelters overlooking the beach.

Moments later a young man strolling past the shelter hesitated, caught by the sight of the girl with the flushed cheeks and untidy hair, and turned his steps to where she sat.

Joyce flinched timorously as he lowered himself beside her on the narrow bench. She experienced again that ridiculous thudding of her heart and unconsciously drew away as his shoulder brushed against hers. 'Sorry!' He had a nice smile and looked so friendly that Joyce relaxed. 'These shelters aren't very big, are they?'

Joyce thought of the gypsy woman's words: the tall, dark, handsome stranger! This man beside her could hardly be called tall, and he certainly wasn't handsome and his hair and moustache were mousy. Still, she consoled herself, even gypsy fortune-tellers couldn't be right all the time.

Too shy to answer, Joyce smiled back at the man. The shelter where they sat felt warm and isolated. They exchanged desultory comments about the weather and how crowded the beaches were this summer. 'We usually go to Morecambe Bay,' admitted Joyce, 'but this year we decided to come here.'

The young man looked at her appraisingly. 'We?'

'My parents and I.'

He nodded. 'It's very worthwhile though, isn't it? Although crowded, the beach is wonderful.'

Joyce nodded. 'Oh, yes, it's wonderful!'

He felt in his pocket and produced a packet of cigarettes. 'Do you have any objection to my smoking?'

She shook her head. 'Of course not. Do go ahead.'

'Aren't you going to join me?'

Joyce had never smoked. Had never even thought of smoking. She wondered what her father would say of a girl who smoked. Especially in public.

Seeing the challenge in his eyes, Joyce took one of the slender white tubes and placed it between her lips. Touching the end with a match, he grinned as the first puff had her coughing. Taking the cigarette from her fingers he broke it into small pieces and tossed it away and their joined laughter sent a flock of seagulls wheeling from the strip of beach below. 'It isn't everyone's cup of tea,' he admitted. 'A bad habit, though one that I can't break.'

Joyce looked at him shyly from the corner of her eye. 'Oh, I don't know. I rather like a man who smokes.'

'Remind me to smoke all the time when I'm with you then.' It was said so ingenuously that she couldn't take offence. Nor could she when a moment later she felt him drape his arm along the back of the bench, and one hand came to rest lightly on her shoulder. Suddenly faint-hearted, she hardly dared to breathe. The clamour of a group of gulls infringed on the moment. Gazing seawards, he said, 'Did you know that gulls are the reincarnation of dead sailors?' His arm stayed where it was. 'Listening to their cries, you could easily believe it, couldn't you?'

Joyce nodded, suddenly happy to agree with anything this young man said.

Later, when she said that her parents were expecting her back, that she'd told them she'd only be away a short time, he suggested they meet again at the same spot the following evening. She acquiesced rather than show herself up for the ignoramus she was, at the same time crossing her fingers behind her back in the childish gesture that wards off bad luck from telling a lie. She knew there was no way to avoid her parents' scrutiny in order to continue this holiday flirtation, sweet though it promised to be.

Although appalled at her own daring – she had promised to meet him and she didn't even know his name or he hers – she was even more shaken when a letter arrived at the hotel a few days later, addressed to her.

It began quite formally: 'My dear Miss Boyce, after our brief encounter I must confess I cannot get your sweet face from my mind. I saw you out walking the following day with people I took to be your parents and followed you back to your hotel. I hung around outside for a while, hoping you would come out again but you didn't. Then I saw one of the skivvies from the hotel running across to post a letter and waylaid her. When I described you she knew straight away who you were, revealing your name. Joyce! How it suits you! I slipped the girl half a crown and begged her to look up your address in the hotel register. I was there again the next night. As promised she came out and thrust a piece of paper into my hand. How I treasure that! For me it holds all the promise of the future. I fully understand why you couldn't meet me as arranged. Your parents, your father especially, seem very upright and proud people and have no doubt bright hopes for your future, which, I'm sure, does not include an unknown young newspaper correspondent who makes a pittance from his writing.'

The letter ended with a carefully formed signature: John Winters.

For long moments Joyce sat there, the letter face down in her lap, her heart thudding. Were her cheeks really as flushed as they felt? she wondered. If her mother asked her who the letter was from, what answer could she give? They would never allow her to write to a man to whom she had never been formally introduced. Especially after such a meeting, which she was sure they would view as a common 'pick-up'. Servants girls went in for meetings like that, not carefully brought up young ladies . . .

Her mother did not ask her; she never found out about it.

Back home after the holiday, Joyce replied to John's

letters and posted them in the red letter box outside the library on her weekly trips to change books. Oh, the agony of waiting for his reply, endeavouring to arrive in the hallway just as the post fell onto the mat before her father or the maid saw the letter.

Inevitably her father caught her one day with a letter from John in her hand. There was a terrible row. She thought all was lost as she watched her father read it and then pass it to her mother. Some little comment had her mother laughing. Very daringly she remarked to her husband that the young man seemed courteous enough and why shouldn't their daughter have a pen pal. It all seemed perfectly innocent to her.

Mr Boyce bucked at the term 'pen pal'. Whoever heard of such a thing! Really, young people nowadays . . .

Tired of being browbeaten by her bully of a husband, Mrs Boyce met his glare with fortitude. Caving in, he hummed and hawed and then declared tersely he supposed there was no harm in it. As long as the young man didn't make a nuisance of himself.

'We'll see each other again,' John wrote in his last letter. 'We'll find a way.'

Fate takes no heed of even the most worthy of people, and in 1899 Queen and country called its young men to arms. They sailed, untold thousands of them, into the blue horizon, to where Boer and Englishman for the second time in less than twenty years were fighting over a sun-baked country. In English towns, bands played 'Goodbye Dolly, I must leave you', soldiers in the new khaki serge uniforms marched, trying to look brave and responsible, while young girls threw flowers and called for them to come home safely.

Joyce's emotions fluctuated between happiness and despair. As the news filtered in from the Transvaal,

an energetic young war correspondent named Winston
Churchill sent despatches from the front line, which
gripped everyone who read them.

Just as realistically written, if not so well known, was
the news sent by John Winters. His letters to Joyce
brought the African country to life, the smells of the
dry red earth, the vivid blue skies and heat-hazy range
of mountains in the far distance.

'We sleep', he wrote, 'on the open veldt, with men
doing sentry duty on the kopjes. The nights are cold
and we have only blankets, sometimes just a greatcoat,
to cover us. I pass the miserable hours thinking of you,
wondering when I shall see you again. I will not in
this letter go into the dreadful details of scenes I have
witnessed or about the long marches in the burning sun,
the men falling in faints owing to the heat and hunger.
Or about the day the Boers came with a flag of truce,
asking permission to bury their dead. That sort of news
goes to my paper for I would not want to distress you
by telling of such things in detail.'

Joyce laid the letter down on her lap, lifting her head
to gaze out of the window at the cool, green garden
outside. What a different picture it presented to the
one John painted.

The letter continued: 'I received a batch of mail
from you and friends the other day and pray you
have received mine. The news from here, especially
the relief of Ladysmith, must have cheered you people
at home after the catalogue of such bitter disasters. For
my part, I believe the fighting to be nearly over, that
grown men will see sense and we will soon be on our
way home.'

In another letter he wrote, 'I watched this morning as
a young soldier came upon the body of a dead Boer who
was wearing a good pair of kid boots. Without the least
trace of squeamishness the soldier relieved the dead man

of them. He caught my eye as he laced them onto his own feet, saying in a broad Cockney accent, "Well, sir, 'e won't be wanting 'em again, will 'e?" He concluded the lacing and stood up, facing me with a cheeky grin. "And I can't find it in me 'eart to feel pity for a dead Dutchman." It brought home to me the depths to which ordinary men will stoop when fighting a war.' Joyce felt a quiver of distaste run through her at the description of the stolen boots. She reached into the deep pocket of her skirt and felt for the packet of cigarettes. Smoking them seemed to bring her closer to John. One day while shopping for her mother she had purchased a packet. After the initial spluttering when the smoke had caught at the back of her throat, she found them soothing to her nerves.

One letter that came contained a snapshot of John, already yellowing but clear. It was, he said in his letter, one that had been taken the summer they had met. At the moment it was all he could offer her. At the moment . . . But things would change and she must always keep that thought uppermost in her mind. The picture showed him with his hair in disorder from the wind, eyes squinting against a bright sun. It went into a locket she wore during the day under her blouse and at night next to her heart, concealed by the voluminous flannel nightgown she wore winter and summer. He haunted her dreams and she smiled, a small, secret little smile, and then gazed guiltily about her as though her thoughts might be emblazoned on her forehead for all to see.

And then, for months afterwards, there was no news. She was filled with a terrible anxiety, dismaying her parents with her lassitude. She puffed at her cigarettes, not caring whether her father caught her at it or not. She was smoking too many of the wretched things and had developed a cough as a result.

One day a brief paragraph on the front page of the morning paper drew her eye as a magnet attracts iron. In heavy black type it stated they were grieved to report that their newspaper's war correspondent, John Winters, had been killed during a skirmish with the Boers.

Joyce's hands came up to touch the chain about her neck, tracing the length of it until her fingers came in contact with the silver locket. It was as though an ice-cold wind had blown over her. In that instant her whole life crumbled and fell apart. Overnight the shy and lonely girl seemed to change into a brooding, testy woman, the picture of an ageing spinster, although she was still in her early twenties. What would become of her? she wondered bitterly. Was it really her fate to end up on her own, unloved and childless?

After her parents' deaths, some ten years later, her mother lingering just months after her father, her sole aim in life became the struggle to maintain the family home. She went without the things she needed in order to keep the house up to the standards her parents had required. But as time went on, it became increasingly difficult. She found that workmen became lackadaisical when dealing with a woman on her own and spent twice as long and twice the money on the job. She finally had to face the fact that it just wasn't practicable to remain in the house where she had been born and spent all her life. The small annuity left by her father was quite inadequate and she was forced to sell the house.

She faced a future of bleak loneliness, and felt lost. What is to become of me? was her constant worry. Where can I live, all alone in the world without the protection of a husband or father?

She decided that what she needed was a change. A change of scenery, somewhere she could begin anew. Why should it be only men who could rule their own destinies? She was a fully grown woman with all her wits about her; surely she should be capable of looking after herself? The memory of that seaside town where she had known such brief happiness came to mind and, surprising even herself by her impetuousness, she decided that there she would spend whatever future she had left.

The cheerless boarding house where she went was not entirely to her liking but it was all she could afford and was in sight of the sea which reminded her of her meeting with John. Over the years her imagination added detail and colour to the event until it became a much more romantic episode than that which had actually taken place.

The boarding house was a favourite with some of the more elderly members of the Summer Follies who considered themselves gentlefolk and scorned the type of digs the rest of the cast enjoyed. With time on her hands, Joyce found that her offers of mending and darning discharged neatly and economically were soon keeping her busy and earning her a few shillings to supplement her annuity.

When the position of wardrobe mistress at the show at the end of the pier became vacant, she was persuaded to apply for the job. The stage manager patronisingly explained the work that would be required of her. 'The last woman we employed left after only a season to get married,' he told her, clearly of the view that no woman could be trusted. 'Young people these days don't know when they're well off. Starting homes and families before they're out of childhood. So I have to ask, you understand, if it is your intention to get married?' Gazing at the thin, wan face he thought that most unlikely, and went on, 'If it is, then we shall have to seek elsewhere for a replacement for Miss Simms.'

'Heavens, no! I shall never marry.' She pressed her

fingertips against the locket. 'I intend to dedicate myself to whatever work I can get and will be happy with.'

'Champion, Miss Boyce. I can breathe again.' He pushed back his chair and stood up and Joyce felt like a midget beside the huge bulk of the man.

The proceeds from the sale of her parents' home she put in a bank, looking upon it as a bulwark against her old age. The decision to apply for the position at the theatre was something she never regretted. She was kept busy from morning till night and any of the chorus girls who had got herself in a 'fix' knew they could go to her for help and advice. Although the advice wasn't always acted upon, it always seemed to help. For the first time in her life, Joyce felt she was wanted. Not in the way her parents had wanted her, to fetch and carry, but in ways which she felt were beneficial. And, of course, there was always Clover.

Chapter Five

That first winter after Adele's death, when they were back in Moorfield, saw Bert more tormented and unsettled than ever. Every stick of furniture in the boarding house, the wide green stretches of the park, the benches on which they had rested during their long walks, all reminded him of his dead wife. He would spot a lone figure coming towards him along the street and for a heart-stopping moment think it was Adele. Not that he hadn't experienced this before. But in Newcombe it had somehow been more bearable. The landlady fussed over them, trying to anticipate their every need. Clover had finished her education at fourteen and so both she and Eddie were at a loss. Used to being kept busy, Clover wheedled her father into letting her accept a job serving behind the counter in a small general grocery store nearby, grateful for the ten shillings a week the grocer paid her. Eddie concentrated on his composing, using, with the landlady's permission, the upright piano in the sitting room.

Tapping her foot in time to the catchy music, the landlady said one day, 'You ought to try and get them published, Eddie. That sort of music's got very popular since the war. Too jazzy for me, mind, but the young people seem to like it. What's it called again?'

Eddie grinned. 'Ragtime.' He went into a rhythmic rendition of 'Everybody's Doing It' and the landlady shook her head in admiration.

'Well, I never!' she said then turned and went back to her kitchen chores.

Bert was in a fever of impatience to get back to the seaside. He missed the familiar surroundings of the Silver Mermaid and the company of his drinking cronies. In the past, sometimes he and Adele would go into a pub here on a Saturday night, choosing seats close to the fire, getting into conversation with the locals. It always surprised him how at ease Adele was in these surroundings, considering her gentle upbringing. She was a great favourite with the locals and many asked after her now, shocked when Bert told them what had happened.

'Shame, that young lass!' They shook their heads. 'Never know when it's going to happen, do you?'

At last it was time to return to Newcombe. Clover was happy to see Miss Boyce and the rest of the cast again. For a time everything went well. Then things between her father and Eddie became worse and more than ever Bert found solace in the company of the resident comic, Buster Bywater.

Buster was a middle-aged man who on stage made an affectation of wearing a shabby dressing gown and a white tropical topi. He told bad jokes and did conjuring tricks that always went wrong and was a great favourite with the public. He had a fondness for drink and young girls, the younger the better someone had once said in Clover's hearing. Affable on stage, away from the trappings of his act he was gloomy and petulant. He wore a toupee which sat on the top of his head, parted carefully to one side, a bright, gingery red. What remained of his own hair could be glimpsed underneath where it grew long and straggly on his neck. This always fascinated Clover and she found it almost impossible not to stare, never daring to catch Eddie's eye should he be near, knowing if she did they would both collapse in uncontrollable fits of mirth.

Usually a girl from the chorus would be Buster's companion for the summer. This year, however, Buster had surprised everyone by 'adopting' a girl who, he said, he had found one dark and stormy night. She was in a bad state and gladly accepted the food and shelter he offered. Although Ma Ruggles frowned on such goings on as she called them, it would have taken a tougher woman than she was to object either by word or deed to anything Buster Bywater did. Comedians were the *crème de la crème* of the music halls and Ma Ruggles was proud to include his name among her guests. Clover heard her confiding in her neighbour one morning as they swept the garden paths that she didn't trust that little madam Mr Bywater had chosen this year. A good, church-going woman herself, over the years Ma Ruggles had made many a judicious judgment about the people who stayed with her and this girl who called herself Imelda was in her opinion definitely suspect.

But Clover found her an agreeable companion. Starved for the company of girls her own age, she would watch for the comic to leave the house and then tap on the door of the room next to hers to have it opened by a smiling Imelda. Over those summer months she learned something of Imelda's history. But not by any means all of it.

At the beginning of that summer, a band of itinerant tinkers had come over from Ireland and among them had been Imelda. She hinted at being shunted from one 'aunt' to another; gruff old women who made use of her labour in various ways – minding the younger children, fetching water from the stream, keeping an eye open for the farmers as the tinkers illegally grazed their horses overnight in a field nearby.

Caught by a choleric farmer one evening, Imelda was dragged before the Newcombe police authorities and held overnight. The next day, cautioned and then released, she discovered that her 'family' had decamped, the site empty with only the remains of the fire and litter scattered everywhere to show they had ever been there.

Imelda searched for some clue, perhaps a sign scratched into a tree trunk indicating the direction they had gone. But there was nothing. Tired, hungry, for the local constables had omitted to feed her, Imelda wandered back into the town. A fine drizzle had started and she drew her plaid woollen shawl closer about her head and face.

The clock in a shop window said six thirty. It was that time of evening when the streets were almost deserted, the holidaymakers back in their hotels and lodging houses eating supper, the pleasure-seekers not yet out. As she stood staring with dull eyes at the face of the clock, the hunger pangs intensified and she clutched both hands across her stomach, bending from the waist.

She began to move forward, hugging the wall. The wind lifted the ends of her shawl and teased her long, unkempt hair, the rain increased and stung her cheeks. She crossed the road and plunged down a narrow side street. She walked as fast as she could, turning from one street into another, moving away from the centre of town, towards the promenade. Gradually the streets began to change and then she was passing grand buildings of red stone or grey granite; imposing hotels with large windows that overlooked the sea front. Once or twice she stumbled and almost fell. The globes of the gas lamps stretched into the darkness, and she progressed gradually from one yellow patch to the next.

The rain was now torrential, bouncing from the pavement in silver bullets. She pulled at her shawl and gazed about her in desperation. Noticing the glass-fronted shelters along the promenade, she hurried across to one, only to find it was already occupied by a young couple seated on the wooden bench, their arms entwined, heads close together. Like a small, dark shadow, she crept into the shelter and lowered herself onto the far end of the seat. Too engrossed in each other's company, the couple at first didn't notice the intruder. Then the youth raised his head and turned to look at her, his frown menacing.

The girl in his arms protested weakly, dragging his mouth back to hers, and Imelda saw her chance.

The girl's black leather handbag had fallen to the floor, unheeded. Imelda reached under the bench, the movement hidden by her long skirts, and then she was away, the purloined handbag thrust under the dark shawl. She felt no guilt. Her young life had been one of poverty and deprivation and she thought nothing of helping herself to another's possessions if they contained something she wanted. The question of right or wrong didn't come into it. Noble beliefs were for the wealthy and not for such as Imelda who had not even a last name with which to bless herself.

In her rough life there was no room for the soft or sensitive. She recalled how she'd once been handed three tiny newborn kittens and told to drown them as there were already too many cats in the camp and they couldn't afford to feed any more. To refuse that order would have meant a beating. Yet even now she felt a tremor run through her as she thought of how she'd filled the bucket from the stream and then, slowly and with great care, lowered the tiny bodies into the chill water. The pathetic creatures were but a few hours old, their eyes still tightly closed. They made weak mewing sounds as she pushed their heads under, closing her own eyes, holding them under the water until they ceased to struggle.

It was a traumatic experience for the young girl. But a steel thread of determination had been added to her character and in the life she was forced to lead this was no bad thing.

Safely away from the promenade, she paused before the steam-clouded window of the fish and chip shop. One hand fumbled in the silk lining of the stolen handbag. Her searching fingers encountered a comb, a folded handkerchief, the sharp corners of an envelope. No purse. With a curse that came straight from the camp fires of the tinkers, she flung the useless handbag from her. From the well-lit chippies, the warm yellow light and pungent smell of frying fish was overwhelming. Like a distressed animal, she wanted to throw back her head and howl her misery and hunger into the night.

Eventually, after suspicious glances from passers-by and hostile mutterings of 'Bloody gypsy' and 'Dirty Irish tinker', she found shelter in the doorway of an abandoned shop down an alleyway. Cold and shivering, she crouched, her knees drawn up to her chin, the damp skirt of her gown clasped tightly about them. The coldness wrapped her up, chill fingers snatching at her shivering body. By sitting quite still, trying not to move a muscle, it seemed not so cold. She whimpered in the darkness, her misery complete.

'Oh, sweet Jesus!' she implored, as the thought of being alone and hungry for the rest of the night filled her with despair.

It wasn't the name she had called upon but Buster Bywater who answered her prayer. She felt an arm slip under her shoulders, lifting her. A voice asked, 'Are you ill?'

Imelda licked her lips and tried to smile. Dizziness swept over her. 'I don't feel so good,' she admitted.

'Just let me shelter from the rain for a little while and I'll be on me way.'

The man gave a stifled exclamation as he gazed down into her face with its full sensual mouth and high cheekbones. Her black hair was loose and uncombed, tumbling down her back in a riot of tangled curls. The shawl had slipped and hung, wet and dripping, from her elbows.

Shrewdly taking in the overweight body and the flushed face, Imelda said softly, 'God 'ave mercy on us, but you must be Saint Christopher 'imself come to the salvation of the weary traveller!'

The comic habitually made the alley a short cut from the Silver Mermaid to his digs but never before had he been fortunate enough to stumble across such an enchanting tatterdemalion. And he had been called many things in his life, but never before a saint. He watched the raindrops beading her eyelashes, making her blink, and said gruffly, 'As you say, shelter is what you need.' Never knowing why he said it, he went on, 'Come back to my boarding house with me. It'll be safer than hanging around here.'

She tilted her head to one side. 'And then?'

Buster felt as though liquid fire coursed through his veins. After a slight pause, he answered, 'Let's worry about that once we've got you warm and dry.'

Back at the boarding house, he managed to get her up the stairs and into his rooms without the eagle eye of Ma Ruggles impeding their progress. He pushed the girl into the bathroom with orders to fill the tub with hot water and give herself a good scrubbing. And, taking stock of the situation, Imelda decided, prudently, that whatever happened later was infinitely better than walking the cold wet streets.

Imelda would have been shocked if anyone had labelled her as promiscuous. She had been raped by one of the tinkers when she was fifteen, not long after her grandmother died, and long ago had lost any feelings about the things men did to her body. On the whole, she despised men, using them for her own ends, taking what she could and playing one against the other without the slightest qualm. The tinkers at the camp had soon learned that only if they had something pretty to give her could they expect a reward. In fact, Imelda had stirred up so much ill feeling and jealousy among them that when the women had seen a chance to be rid of her, when she'd been caught by the farmer, they'd grasped it.

At first Eddie dismissed Imelda as an annoying, skinny child. After a while he revised his views. Meeting her on the stairs, brushing past her in the narrow hallway, had assured him she was every inch a woman and definitely not skinny. He recoiled from the thought of the lovely, dark-haired girl and her relationship with the irascible comic. In bed at night he would think of her and a sound between a groan and a sob would be wrung from him.

Meanwhile, his sister's friendship with Imelda grew.

'Don't you have any parents?' Clover asked her.

'No. I was brought up by my grandmother until one day she became ill. Calling out all day long, so she was, from her bed in the caravan. Taking her cups of tea, jam butties, when we had jam, when one of the women had bothered to gather the hedge fruits and make them into jam. If they hadn't, then a bit of bread and cheese and a pickle'd do her any day. Fair worn out, so I was. For two pins I'd have tipped the old faggot out of her bed and jumped into it meself.'

'Imelda!' Clover had to smile, not sure that she wanted to hear any more of Imelda's accounts of her grandmother.

'When we finally got a doctor, 'e said 'e'd never seen anyone as stubborn as that old woman.' She grimaced. 'We couldn't really afford a doctor but a few of the older men who had known 'er for years tipped out their pockets and sent someone to find one and bring 'im to the camp. The doctor said she needed proper treatment and so it was to 'ospital with her and she died.' They were sewing in Clover's bedroom and Imelda turned her attention to fastening off the button she was sewing on one of Buster's shirts.

Clover said, inadequately, 'I'm sorry, Imelda. It must have been terrible for you. How old were you then?'

'Sixteen years, all but a month.' She nodded. 'It was a nightmare, all right.'

Clover remembered her own nightmares, waking drenched with sweat, eyes wide, filled with the dark moving shadows of her dream: her mother's body lying still and huddled in the cobbled street, people milling around, nobody really sure of what to do.

She drew a deep breath and heard Imelda say in an unruffled voice, 'Since then I've 'ad to make my own way. You can't be choosy, you know, having to live like that.'

Unable to stop herself, Clover said, 'But why Mr Bywater? He's *old*!'

Defensively, Imelda murmured, 'He's bin kind and kindness is something I've not seen a lot of in my life.' She bit the thread of her sewing with small, even teeth, patted the shirt with a hand and went on, 'I've never known such a man for losing 'is shirt buttons.'

Eddie had come into the room while they were talking, ostensibly to enquire about supper, but really to feast his eyes on Imelda – which he did so shamelessly that Clover laughed and shooed him away. With that pensive look about him, Eddie exuded a charm under which many a young girl had fallen. Imelda, Clover thought, would be no different. She prayed they would be discreet.

Chapter Six

The sweetness of late summer lay on the air. Behind the seaside town in the narrow lanes dissecting the fields and woods, the smell of ripe blackberries, damp earth and grass combined in an elusive fragrance, hinting at the harvest thanksgiving to come.

Imelda had lingered far too long, searching for the herbs that her skill would brew into a soothing nightcap for Buster, ensuring an uninterrupted night's sleep for herself. She had come across the herbs quite by accident one day while taking a short cut through a small wood near where the gypsy camp had been located. She couldn't have said why she went there; perhaps unexpected nostalgia, perhaps just chance. All the same, she felt a sudden desire to see if the caravans had returned. It had been early summer when her people had deserted her. A few weeks' travelling might have brought them this way again. It had happened before.

Emerging from the cover of the trees she wondered what she would do if they were there. Would they receive her with affectionate cries of welcome or gaze on her with cold suspicion?

She didn't know whether it was gladness she felt or disappointment when she saw the field was empty. Deflated, she collapsed onto the log of a fallen tree. In a fit of pure pique she threw down the kerchief of red cotton in which she'd wrapped the herbs and began to pluck the full ripe blackberries from a nearby mass of brambles. Slim brown fingers darted out, squashing the ripe fruit in her vexation, thrusting them greedily into her mouth.

Imelda wasn't the only one to know of the short cut. Eddie could hardly believe his luck as he came closer and saw who was sitting on his favourite log. Purple juice stained her fingers and the front of her dress. It ran down her chin with one or two drops resting in the deliciously tender hollow at the base of her throat. Eddie would have given anything in the world to have been allowed to bend his head and lick the sticky sweet juice from the spot, to know he possessed the right to kiss the purple-stained mouth and whisper what a wild, fey little creature she was.

Instead he stopped a few paces away until, suddenly aware of another presence, she looked up. In a lofty voice she said, 'Well, what you looking at? 'Ave I grown two 'orns or somethin'?'

He actually blushed, then came closer, dropping onto the log next to her. 'I'm sure you would look perfectly delightful with two horns,' he said. 'Although you'd have to do your hair in a different style, wouldn't you?'

Grinning, he ducked as she lashed out at him with sticky hands. 'What makes you an authority on women's hair, anyway?' she demanded.

Eddie sat up again and his gaze inspected her face and then her hair solemnly. On her flushed cheeks, dark strands of silky hair lay like damp question marks, adhered to her skin by the blackberry juice.

She stuck out a narrow purple tongue at him. 'Well, cat got your tongue?'

He decided to change the subject. 'That stuff'll stain if you leave it on too long. There's a stream down there.' He indicated the narrow path that led through the trees. 'I'll wet my handkerchief and we'll try and freshen you up before anybody sees you. Can't have Buster seeing you like that, can we?' Though the name nearly choked him, still he managed a tight smile.

Moments later she sat quietly on the log while he wiped a wet handkerchief over her chin and cheeks, shyly rubbing at the spot above the opening of her blouse. The purple stains removed to his satisfaction – he got the impression that she couldn't have cared less whether or not she returned looking like an urchin after a rough and tumble picnic – he offered her his hand and helped her to her feet. With her arm linked in his, leaning against him slightly, they were almost out of the clearing when she remembered the herbs.

'The devil take it!' she breathed and lifting her skirts scampered back the way they had come. Moments later she reappeared, the red cotton kerchief in her hand. Seeing Eddie's frown, she explained, 'It's herbs I picked. To make a sedative for Buster. They'll 'elp make 'im sleep.'

His gaze sharpened as he digested the meaning of her remark.

'Maybe I shouldn't 'ave said that.' She looked at him, head tilted to one side. 'You'll not tell Buster I said that, will you?'

'What do you take me for?' he said angrily. She smiled and linked her arm in his again and they moved on.

The noise and clatter of the merry-go-round in the fairground they passed delighted Imelda. She loved the coloured lights, the delighted squeals of children as they whirled to the tune of 'Daisy, Daisy', the pricked-up ears and scarlet-painted nostrils of the traditional galloping horses with their golden saddles and reins. She remembered the fairs the tinkers haunted, herself mingling with the crowd, constantly on the look-out for a likely handbag held too carelessly or a pocket wide and gaping, easy to slip enquiring fingers into.

'Can't we go on it? It looks so . . .' She paused, searching for a word.

Eddie grinned and supplied, wryly, 'Stomach churning?'

She punched his arm. 'Don't be an old spoilsport. If you don't want to go on, then I'll go by meself.' She tossed her head and started for the box where the man was selling tickets. With a sigh, Eddie followed.

He paid for the tickets and lifted her, light as a feather, onto the carousel. She chose a wooden horse painted a bright, sun-burst yellow with scarlet trimmings. Eddie mounted the one behind her, a more sober chestnut. The music started and they began to move.

Sunlight yellow became her, he thought, watching like a concerned parent as she rose and fell before him, the motion becoming faster and faster as they whirled round. Imelda's dark hair streamed out behind her, the ribbon that held it becoming undone. Her small hands clung tightly to the brass pole ridged like a stick of barley sugar. There appeared to have been little sunlight in her life. How he longed to make up for that deficiency.

He made a silent vow, there and then, that he would make it all up to her. Somehow, sometime.

The carousel slowed and then stopped. He helped her down. Her hand tucked firmly under his arm, they strolled among the crowds. It was growing late. Soon they would have to retrace their steps back along the promenade, back to the theatre. Their day would be over. Small family groups, laden with tin buckets and wooden spades, the children fretful after too much sand and sun, were making their way home.

Lights were coming on now, each stall vying with its neighbour in brightness and colour. He threw coconuts, winning her a small doll with a silly little topknot of a curl in the middle of its forehead. The early evening dusk had settled. All about them was drowned in blue light, the air heavy with the smell of the sea and a mixture of candy floss and the paraffin used in the lamps. A man shouted, 'Hokey, pokey, penny a stick,' selling pink rock.

Imelda's excitement was boundless. Like a spoiled child, she wanted to see, and try, everything. Eddie was becoming uneasy, aware that time was moving on. He really should be getting back to the theatre.

He voiced his worries aloud and Imelda frowned. 'Just when I'm enjoying meself!' She looked to where gaily painted swingboats holding young couples, one at each end, pulling on ropes, rose and fell to accompanying laughter. Toffee-apple stalls were busy, the fortune-teller in her tent was doing a brisk trade. Imelda had never felt so free, away from the narrow, suspicious stare of Buster Bywater. Tossing her mane of wild black hair, ignoring Eddie's words, she began to make her way through the crowds. He heard her say over her shoulder, 'There's still plenty of time. I want to see everything before I go back.'

Eddie tried and failed to grab her arm as she pressed onward, attracted by the shouts of a large, very fat man in a checked suit. He stood on a small raised platform, thumbs hooked into the armholes of his waistcoat. Beside him was another man, dressed so immodestly that many a young lady averted her eyes as she passed with her escort. Dressed in long black tights and a black vest that showed a mass of thick greying hair, he stood with his hands on his hips, staring arrogantly into the slowly passing crowds. By his side was a painted noticeboard claiming that Charles Worth would take on any man who was willing to fight him.

'You see here a prize-fighter who could have been world champion had not cruel fate decided otherwise,' the fat man shouted in his hoarse voice. 'Of course, everything fair and above board, the Marquis of Queensberry rules apply here. Come on, lads, show your young lady how we separate the men from the boys.' He paused to gaze down at the small crowd that had gathered, faces turned expectantly upwards. The prize-fighter flexed his muscles, striking attitudes. Women in the crowd either blushed scarlet or breathed a long, barely audible, 'Ohhh!'

'He's a big lad, ain't he?' the promoter taunted. 'Not one any of you would choose to pick an argument with, I bet. Well, I'm telling you here and now, if any man here feels that he can stay on his feet for two rounds, just two rounds, gentlemen, he will win two golden guineas. Aye, two golden guineas for going two rounds with Charlie boy.'

He waited hopefully for an answer. No one seemed eager, although there was a lot of whispering. Imelda's fingers tightened on Eddie's arm. She made a charming little grimace. 'You're as big as him, Eddie. Bigger. And a lot younger. Two guineas, Eddie. Just think of it. Two whole guineas.'

With more reluctance than he felt, Eddie agreed. He won his two guineas amid lusty cheers of encouragement from the crowd. Bloody, but glowing with pride, he made his way back to where Imelda waited. She had pulled her light shawl over her head as he fought and now held one corner of it across her mouth, as though to stifle the small cries of distress the sight of his bloodied nose and cut cheekbone caused her.

'Christ-orl-bloody-mighty!' she breathed.

Like an Emperor offering his Empress the most precious of crown jewels, he held out his hand, in the palm of which lay the two golden guineas. 'For you,' he said, grinning from ear to ear.

Imelda held a finger to her mouth, made a soft kissing sound then laid it gently against his cut cheek. 'Poor baby,' she said, in a soft, crooning voice. 'Poor, poor baby.' But she took the money, slipping the heavy coins into the neckline of her blouse. Once back in Buster's apartment they would be added to the small hoard of coins and notes she already had hidden. Relieving Buster of his money had proved easy. After an evening spent with the 'boys', Buster would stagger home and collapse on his bed. Once asleep, nothing disturbed him. Certainly not the nimble fingers of Imelda going through his pockets. She would relieve him of all but a few shillings and some coppers, knowing full well that by the following morning he would not have the vaguest idea how much cash he was supposed to have on him.

All the noise and excitement had made her thirsty. Passing a public house, she stopped and grabbed Eddie by the arm, saying she fancied a drink. Eddie, not averse to the idea himself, followed her through the glass doors.

Half an hour later, like two naughty children late home from school they ran hand in hand to the nearest tram stop. Alighting at their stop, he pulled her into the shadows of a shop and kissed her gently on her parted lips. 'I'm real fond of you, Imelda,' he whispered. 'Even though I'll probably never understand you.'

'What's to understand?' She gazed at him under lowered lashes. 'Just as long as you remember who I am. You know what they say about silk purses and sow's ears? Well, that's me all over. I'll never change, Eddie, so don't expect me to.'

'I wouldn't want you to change. You're perfect.'

Back in the boarding house, she sat on the side of the bed and took stock of events. From an early age she had known that she was attractive to men, that she had the power to mould situations involving men to her own advantage. But sometimes it was more than that, a sixth sense that warned her in advance how it would be in her own best interests to proceed.

She stretched luxuriously, thinking of the tall, muscular young man whom she knew she could twist round her little finger. One hand went to her breast, against which the two heavy coins nestled. She smiled.

Bert Blossom stamped irritably up and down the cluttered dressing room. 'Who does he think he is, eh? You tell me that. God Almighty Himself, is that it?'

'Dad,' Clover forced a soothing note into her voice, 'Eddie'll be here. You know he's never let you down yet.'

'Aye, not yet, but the boy's getting mighty close to it. It would break his mother's heart if she could see him now.' Bert's handsome face went red with anger. He halted his frenzied pacing as the dressing room door opened and his son came in. Blood spattered his cheek and upper lip and Clover gave a gasp of dismay, one hand going to her mouth, while Bert's frown grew more fierce.

Bert watched Eddie cross to the small hand basin in the corner. 'So,' he began in a scathing voice, 'not content with all the other things you've done, you've been in a fight now! How do you propose to go on in that state?' He lifted his head, sniffing the air. '*And* you've been drinking.'

'Dad,' Eddie spoke wearily, 'it's only superficial, there's nothing wrong with me. Once I've washed my face I'll be fine. And I've only had one drink.'

'Oh, and that, I suppose, will sort out everything? Washing your face? You need more than that, my boy. A damn good hiding to start with and we'll go on from there.'

Fists raised, Bert advanced upon his son who stood erect, involuntarily raising his own fists in the classical prize-fighter's stance. Clover held her breath as they stood eye to eye. Then, with a muttered curse, Bert turned away. Over his shoulder, he growled, 'Look at your sister, she's never given me a moment's anguish, while you . . .' He made a gesture full of contempt. 'Any road, better not waste any more time. Go and get cleaned up. We'll talk later.'

The tension was still strong in the room and Clover applied the last of her stage make-up with fingers that shook, all the while keeping a wary eye and ear out for the slightest change in either of her menfolk. She felt that if for a moment she should relax they would be at each other's throats again. She had never seen her father so angry and Eddie's casual attitude wasn't helping.

She managed to have a word with her brother as they waited in the wings for their cue. 'What happened?' Her brow creased in worry. 'Was it a fight over some girl? You know what Dad thinks about that.'

He had no wish to bring Imelda into it so he grinned and said, 'I took on a pugilist at the fairground. I won two guineas.'

'Eddie!' Clover didn't know whether to be shocked or proud of him. She decided to be proud of him, although what Bert would say if he found out didn't bear thinking about.

As though reading her thoughts, Eddie whispered, 'Enjoyed it, too. The crowd cheered.'

There was no time to say more for the music changed and from the centre of the stage Bert glared across the wings at their tardy response.

A true professional, Clover put every thought from her mind but the immediate moment. She saw only the pale blur of faces behind the flickering stage lights, heard only the violins and piano, the regular beat of the drum.

At last the music faded and the curtain was lowered

to the accompaniment of clapping and some whistles. They waited for Bert to join them in the dressing room afterwards, Clover with misgivings, Eddie with a truculent frown. When time passed and Bert didn't put in an appearance, Clover said, on a note of relief, 'Maybe he's bumped into someone and they're talking.'

'Having a drink in Buster's dressing room more like,' retorted Eddie.

'You were going to tell me about the fight,' she reminded him. She seated herself in front of the large mirror and began to unfasten the silk rose from her hair. Their eyes met in the mirror. 'Didn't it occur to you that you might have been hurt, knocked out, even?'

'I never gave it a thought. Imelda was with me and when Imelda's with me I feel ten feet tall.' There, he'd admitted it, that he'd spent the afternoon with Imelda. He turned away.

'Did Imelda encourage you?' Clover asked. Although he was older than she was, the protective instinct she felt for her brother was strong.

He didn't answer her question.

'You're going to end up in trouble one day, Eddie, and I couldn't bear that.'

'Rubbish,' he scoffed with boyish bravado. 'Nothing's going to happen to me. Come on, little 'un, you're worse than an old woman, taking on your shoulders all the cares of the world.' His soft, confident voice soothed her and they were smiling when the door opened and Bert came into the room.

The drop of 'hard stuff' Buster Bywater had insisted on sharing with him had mellowed Bert considerably. Both Clover and her brother were surprised when he merely nodded a greeting and, still without a word, went behind the screen to change.

* * *

Imelda set herself deliberately to seek out Eddie's company. Hearing piano music one quiet afternoon, she stole down from her room to investigate.

Eddie sat at the old upright piano with its brass candlesticks, each holding a stub of candle, enabling the player to read the sheet music propped up on the stand. He looked up to see her in the doorway, her eyes fixed on him. He didn't stop playing but continued to let his hands glide gently over the piano keys, the sounds he made soft and restful to her ears. Like a silver stream of liquid music, she thought, surprised that she should feel this way. She wasn't one to listen to music as a rule. But this melodious stream of notes was something different.

She saw her feelings mirrored on his face and something moved inside her. It caused her to give him a wide, dimpled smile and she watched the colour flood his cheeks, saw the flames of hope light his eyes.

Inspired by her presence, Eddie played tunes of his own that set her foot tapping, her body swaying to the music. Her face glowed. 'Why, Eddie, you're real clever! Don't stop, go on.'

Lifting her skirts with her fingertips she executed a series of impromptu dance steps across the floor, swaying to the lively music. 'Has it a name?' she called, circling so fast her skirt flew out, showing a delectable pair of legs and ankles.

'Not yet. I've still to think one up.'

'You mean you wrote it yourself?'

'Yes. Like it?'

'I love it.'

'I've written quite a few. Like to hear some more?'

'Yes, yes, play some more.'

On her way through the hall, Ma Ruggles paused at the door and frowned. Never mind his father's ill humour, that young man would be facing the wrath of her most important guest if he didn't watch out. Buster

Bywater tolerated no interference in his affairs. And the way those two were carrying on – well, she didn't like to think what it might lead to.

She frowned again. That little arse-crawler, Imelda, was up to something and she hated to think what it might be.

The public house that Bert frequented, built at an advantageous spot close to the pier, was an attraction during the summer months and it didn't take much persuasion to entice Bert into its warm, smoky atmosphere. With its buzz of conversation, the bursts of laughter, the Silver Mermaid was infinitely more desirable than the windswept street on which he stood. It was early in the evening, he was not yet due at the theatre. Bert's conscience battled with the need for forgetfulness, the comfort that one drink, or several drinks, could bring.

Amidst boisterous laughter from his mates, Buster was in his element, doing the thing he liked best, entertaining a captive audience. His face was more florid than usual, his wig slipping slightly over one ear, his speech already slurred.

Thankful for the comforting bonhomie generated by the mass of bodies, Bert grinned and made for the bar. A couple only, he promised himself. Not enough to make him forget his lines or stumble in the dance routine he did with Eddie. Just enough to block from his mind the realisation that Adele would no longer join him in the old love songs for which the theatre crowd showed such affection.

'Bert!' His friends were calling, and he strode over, carrying his glass. The comic kept them entertained with a string of his risqué jokes and it seemed no time at all before he was laying a hand on Bert's shoulder and saying in a whisky-hoarse voice, 'It's late, man.

Look at the time! Your Clover'll be busting a gut and that Eddie'll give you a mouthful for being late.'

Bert sighed. 'Getting too big for his boots is that young man,' he said. 'Accused me the other day of spending too much time in bars and not enough practising the act.' Self-pity brought a tear to his eye, causing the other men around him to shake their heads and murmur soft words of sympathy. 'I know my dancing isn't what it used to be,' went on Bert, 'but nothing is with my Adele gone. She was my life, you know. My whole life.'

More murmurs of sympathy. 'Still an' all,' said Buster, tossing back the remaining drops of his drink, 'you still got the boy and young Clover. Now, there's a gal with talent. And such a good little homemaker. You're a lucky man, Bert Blossom, in more ways than one. Wish I 'ad someone half as thoughtful to take care of me in my old age.'

Sniggers from the listening men. 'Thought you 'ad, Buster!' said one, grinning from ear to ear. 'Don't that Imelda do that?'

Buster snorted. ''Er? Only good for one thing, she is, and I don't need to tell you wot that is, do I?'

There were more exchanged glances. 'Aye, but it's a change from just keeping your supper warm, like my old girl,' was the envious reply.

'More trouble than she's worth at times,' replied Buster. 'I've seen the way she looks at young Eddie, and she's felt the back of me 'and a couple of times for it, I can tell you. But don't make no difference. Might as well try and tame the wind as that girl.'

'Eddie?' Bert snorted with laughter. 'Now who's being daft. My Eddie knows better than to poach on other men's property.'

'We won't argue about that,' said Buster. 'Anyway, we'd better get you back to the theatre or his back *will*

91

be up. He's as big as you, remember, and strong wi' it, too. Likely to give you a scuffle if you looks at 'im the wrong way.'

They left the Silver Mermaid with their arms round each other's shoulders. The fresh air cleared Bert's head and he thought about his son, so tall and good-looking, of himself at Eddie's age. Childhood things left behind but still not quite a man. It was an uncomfortable age, as though you were wearing clothes that didn't quite fit and you longed to shed them.

Eddie, he had to admit, had been full of it lately, finding fault with everything Bert did, going on about improving the act, including jazzy songs, whatever they were! Bert's lip curled. Jazzy! What in the name of the devil was that? What was wrong with the old songs, the songs he and Adele had been singing for years? Songs about moonlit bays and harvest moons? Who wanted to listen to any other kind? Certainly not Bert Blossom.

Never once had he consulted his children on how the act should be run and he wasn't ready to start now. Clover was too young and immature to be considered and he wouldn't have dreamed of asking her opinion, anyway. What did a fifteen-year-old girl know? As for Eddie, hell could freeze over before he consulted him.

Bert arrived back at the theatre in a jocular mood. Buster and he parted in the corridor outside the dressing rooms and the comic gave him an unsteady salute before opening his own door and going inside. Bert knew there would be another bottle of the hard stuff hidden away in the dressing table drawer, acquired by Imelda from the off-licence along the promenade. Bert grinned. You couldn't help but admire the old codger! He could drink most men under the table and still appear on stage, albeit unsteady but carrying the act through to the very end.

Clover was already dressed. The frilly skirt and white cambric top with the heavily embroidered neckline and tiny puffed sleeves was supposed to represent an Hungarian peasant and looked, Bert supposed, suitably rustic in this north-west seaside town. Who would know the difference, anyway?

Bert lowered himself onto the chair before his section of the dressing table and stared at himself in the mirror. Then at the picture of himself in the silver frame. Aged about twenty, a slender strip of a lad, wearing white flannels and a blazer, looking as though he was about to burst into song – perhaps a number from one of the popular London shows that everyone was talking about. He felt tears come to his eyes. Catching the blue gaze of his daughter as she sat beside him at the mirror, he smiled and said briskly, 'Eddie not here yet, eh?'

'No, but I'm sure he won't be long, Daddy.' Clover lifted the heavy silver hairbrush that had belonged to Adele and fluffed out the fine curls that hung over her forehead. 'He'll be here in a minute.'

'Humph!' Bert ran one hand over his chin. 'He'd better be. I won't stand for the act going on late for anyone. Never have and never will. He knows that.'

Whenever Imelda was present, Eddie looked flushed and happy. The significance of the shared glances, the shy touch of hands, were impossible to ignore.

Today, Imelda wore a new ribbon, the colour of blue-bells, in her hair and looked breathtakingly beautiful. Watching her, Clover thought she must be aware that Buster would never countenance any kind of dallying with other men, and yet it did not stop her from making those subtle approaches to Eddie, an unspoken invitation in those dark, knowing eyes. An invitation that any young man with red blood in his veins would be tempted to accept.

Buster's foul temper was well known, especially after he had been drinking, and he hadn't been born yesterday. After a while, Clover began to notice the faint purple bruises that Imelda tried to hide. She began to wear long-sleeved linen blouses instead of the white cambric off-the-shoulder ones she had habitually worn, threaded with different coloured ribbons for each day of the week. The prim, high-necked blouses she now appeared in caused Clover many misgivings.

Imelda never showed any emotion and except for the bruises seemed to lead a perfectly normal life. But did she? What went on behind that closed door? Clover wondered. She did not think she wanted those questions answered. She had heard them quarrelling, Buster's voice raised in argument. Once, coming upon them at the end of a tirade, Clover saw him aim a glob of spit in the general direction of the fireplace and couldn't hide the shudder that went through her.

When she consulted Bert about it one day as he was having a late supper, he told her to mind her own business. 'Buster's developed a schoolboy crush forty years too late,' he grinned. 'Coupled with an extremely jealous nature. It's nothing to do with anyone else. If Imelda is prepared to settle for a life with a man like Buster, then that's her affair. He's a wealthy man, although he'd never admit it, and Imelda's well fed and can do more or less what she likes. It's not for us to interfere, lass.' He jabbed the air with his fork to emphasise his words. 'Imelda's no child. That one was never a child. She knows what's she's doing, don't you worry.'

But Clover did worry. And while she chafed over Buster's treatment of Imelda, Eddie was attempting a spot of self-analysis of his own. For the first time in his life he was in love. And miserable. Away from Imelda he felt stupid and couldn't concentrate, unable to accomplish the most simple of things.

That afternoon, strolling aimlessly on the promenade, hands thrust into his pockets, he would have walked right into her if she hadn't stepped aside. Coming to an abrupt halt, he stood with his back to the white-capped waves, gazing at her intently.

'You could do yourself a mischief,' she teased, 'not lookin' where you're goin'.'

He grimaced. 'Sorry. I was deep in thought.'

'Well, don't let it become a habit,' she murmured, leaning slender forearms on the top bar of the promenade railings. 'Too much thinking's bad for you, or haven't you heard?'

They stood so close, leaning against the railings, that he could smell that elusive fragrance of herbs from her silky hair. Her eyes followed a sailing ship far out at sea and he heard her whisper, 'God, I'd like to go wherever that boat is going.'

'We'll go together.' Startled at his heartfelt words, she gazed at him with a perplexed frown and he gave a low laugh and went on, 'Oh, not today, of course. But sometime.'

When she rose on tiptoe to kiss his cheek he blushed like a schoolboy. 'I think I'd like that.' She laughed. 'Just remember what I said about silk purses.'

'Don't change, Imelda. I never was very partial to silk purses. Useless things as far as I'm concerned. It's what I like about you. You're different from any other girl I've ever known.'

'I should hope so, too.' She smiled, a lazy, lascivious smile that made him want to pull her to him, to cover her lips with his own. 'I believe in being different,' she said. He drew a deep breath as she went on, teasingly, 'And you, Edward Blossom. What do you believe in?'

'Me. I believe in myself, in making something of myself.'

One finger twirled the top button of his shirt, her lips pursed. 'Good. I can see we have the same way of thinking.' Twirl, twirl went her finger. 'Did you mean what you said the other day about being real fond of me?'

From any other girl this would have sounded brazen. On Imelda's lips it sounded straightforward, without the slightest hint of coquetry.

'I would never say anything I didn't mean. Not to you, Imelda.'

The gleam of satisfaction in the dark eyes was quite lost on Eddie. 'Good.' She gazed at the westering sun sinking in a blaze of red and gold below the horizon. 'I'd better start back. Walk with me.'

It sounded like an order and he wasn't really ready to return to the boarding house yet, but because it was Imelda, Eddie followed meekly.

A short, stocky man drew back into the shadows of the narrow turning as they passed. They didn't see him; they saw no one, having eyes only for each other. But Buster Bywater saw them and his mouth tightened in an angry line as he watched her lift her arms to link them loosely about Eddie's neck as he dropped a kiss on her lips before they parted outside the boarding house. Then, with a punch of jubilation aimed into the air, Eddie stepped back and watched her go in. Buster waited five minutes before he went in himself.

Clover had been washing her hair. Emerging from the bathroom, she was in time to hear the raised voice coming from the hallway below. 'I won't stand for it, do you hear? You and that Mister Fancy-pants canoodling in public. Bloody little whore, that's all you are. Off with anything in trousers!'

A moment later, eyes black in a dead white face, hair in disarray, Imelda appeared on the stairs. Hard on her heels came Buster Bywater. He lashed out at her with the long thin cane he used in his act. Whistling through the air, it caught the fleeing girl across the shoulders and neck and Clover could hear the sharp intake of breath each time it landed. Without thinking, she stepped forward to the head of the stairs, waiting until the sobbing, trembling girl reached her. Without a word, Clover grabbed her by the shoulders and pushed her through the open door of the bathroom. She slammed the door shut and shot the bolt just as Buster reached the landing. She caught a glimpse of his choleric features, heard his angry shout: 'You stay out of this, Clover Blossom. It's naught to do wi' you. That brother of yourn's done enough mischief as it is. I'm going to teach that little bitch a lesson, so I am. One she'll not forget.'

Imelda screamed as the door shuddered under the force of Buster's shoulder. Curbing an impulse to scream as well, Clover shouted, 'Mr Bywater, get a hold of yourself! Imelda's not coming out of here until you do.'

There followed another assault on the bathroom door, one that had the two girls clutching each other, Imelda's sobs soaring to another scream.

'You hear me, you little cow? Let that gal out before I kick the bloody door down. Ma'll not like that and neither will your dad, faced with a hefty repair bill.'

Clover drew a deep, steadying breath. 'No, I won't.' Her voice was firm. It seemed to give Imelda courage. She leaned against the wooden panels, putting her mouth close to them.

'You're going to 'ave to give your word not to lay a finger on me before I set one foot outside this door, you old bastard,' she shouted. Her defiant words provoked a fresh explosion of rage. Then there was a sudden lull, as if Buster was getting his breath back. Clover, listening intently, could hear Ma Ruggles' voice from the landing outside, demanding to know what was going on. Clover laid a finger across her lips and the two girls stood silent, listening.

They couldn't make out the words, but whatever the landlady said, it had the power to send Buster to his room. Then the door handle rattled and Ma's voice came clearly. 'Clover, is that you in there wi' that girl? Better come out, there's good lassies. Mr Bywater's in a right old mood, I'm afraid he'll do hisself a misfortune if he doesn't calm down.'

Clover's mouth turned down at the corners. She looked at Imelda. 'Do you want to risk it?'

Imelda shrugged. ''Ave to sometime, don't I? Can't stay in 'ere for the rest of me life.'

Clover still looked doubtful. 'Will you be all right? You could always come to us for the night.' Pausing a moment, she went on, 'That remark made by Mr Bywater, about my brother, that he'd caused enough mischief. What did he mean?'

Imelda shrugged again, almost too casually. ''E's got a mind like a cesspit. Imagines just because I sometimes walk with Eddie, when we bump into each other on our walks, that we're up to no good.'

Clover sighed. 'I see. Well, if you're sure you want to go out?'

Imelda nodded and raising her arms began to tuck the thick strands of silken black hair back into a knot. With the resilience of the young, she patted Clover's hand, smiling. 'Don't worry, love. I can handle Buster.' She gave Clover a little push. 'Go and dry your hair else you'll catch your death of cold.' Assured, confident of her own attractions, Imelda was a different person from the frightened girl who only minutes before had cowered behind a bolted door.

Chapter Seven

Buster took to locking the door of his apartment behind him whenever he went out, leaving Imelda a virtual prisoner. The only time she was allowed to leave the room was when Buster was at home and he could wait for her to hurry back from wherever she went, or when she accompanied him. But these outings were becoming rarer and rarer.

She sat at the window, staring out at the busy street, and in her mind the icy cold anger began to turn to thoughts of sweet revenge. Memories of her grandmother's teachings stirred, the often quite illogical ramblings of an old woman who knew where in the forest the badgers came out at night and who could call a fox or a vixen to her side with a high, clear cry.

Her grandmother had been an amazing woman and her many talents included a fine knowledge of plants and herbs. She was acquainted with the cure for headaches and pains in the joints, carefully selecting suitable plants and drying them, small bundles hanging from the ceiling of her old caravan. Imelda would watch the old lady pound them into fine powder that later she would mix with camomile or some other herb tea.

Imelda remembered her becoming angry one day when she returned from the village with a brown paper bag containing half a dozen flypapers. The old lady tipped the little red rolls out onto the table and her lips tightened.

'They're for the flies,' Imelda explained unnecessarily. 'They've bin a blessed pest this year. You don't have to worry, Gran, I'll see to them.'

'Mucky things, those flypapers,' her grandmother grumbled. 'Dangerous, too. Arsenic-based poison, that's what's in 'em. Just you be careful how you handle them, my girl, and wash your hands well afterwards. Don't want you gettin' ill.'

Other voices. Other worlds. Recalling her grandmother's advice now, Imelda was filled with a sudden sense of purpose. Her fear of Buster's sudden violent outbursts, his habit of locking her away for hours on end, faded as plans formed in her mind, plans that would set her free from him forever. Often he teased her with the remark that the only way she would escape from him was if death took her first. He had made her very frightened, for she was highly superstitious and felt that with those words he had cast a spell on her.

Never slow to grasp an opportunity when it presented itself, Eddie's infatuation and mention of their going away together solved the frustrating problem of how she could escape – once she was free. Buster Bywater had to be dealt with first.

She heard the key grate in the lock. Buster had returned. He acknowledged her with a grunt and threw himself down into the large shabby armchair to one side of the fireplace. At once she was there, bringing his slippers, holding his booted feet in her lap, first one, then the other, kneeling before him on the hearthrug, untying the long black bootlaces.

Sitting back on her heels, she raised her head and smiled at him. She said the same things each night, asking the same questions in her clear, soft voice. She knew he had been having trouble with the woman who was his assistant and his mood depended on the way his act had been received. 'Did everything go all right? How was the new girl?'

Buster's bloodshot eyes devoured her body and she felt her cheeks growing hot. He reached out and ran a thick finger down one cheek. Fretfully she jerked her head away. In a disgruntled voice he answered her question. 'A bitch of an audience. A real bitch. They laughed in all the wrong places. And that girl was useless. Bloody useless. I've told 'er she's out on 'er ear at the end of the week. Too old. The audience wants someone with good tits and a firm little bum prancing around the stage as my assistant, not some slag old enough to be my mother.'

Imelda blinked. Exaggeration was a way of getting round most obstacles for Buster. The truth didn't overly bother him. Who was going to contradict him, anyway? Ma Ruggles was the only person Imelda had ever heard voice an argumentative comment over some outrageous claim he'd once made. And even she did it with an air of appeasement.

Imelda slipped the already warmed slippers onto his feet and made to stand up. Immediately he pulled her down onto his lap, grinning, pushing her skirts up with one rough hand. 'Buster!' She tried to wriggle away but he held her fast, the thick sausage-like fingers digging into her flesh.

'What's the hurry?' His free hand slid down her left leg, from thigh to ankle. The ankle was so slim his fingers closed about it easily. 'A bit skinny,' he said, 'but with pink tights and most of the men's eyes goggling at these little beauties,' he lowered his face into the neckline of her unbuttoned blouse, 'no one will notice.'

Imelda shuddered as he ground his mouth in the deep valley between her breasts. He hadn't shaved since last night and his bristly chin scratched the tender skin.

Reluctant to stir up one of his violent rages, she said, 'You mean you want me to go on as your assistant? Would I be able to do it?'

'Able to? Of course you'd be able to. All you've got to do is hand me my props and look pretty. Even you're not stupid enough to make a balls-up of that. Stupid, but not *that* stupid.'

Underneath the teasing words was the belligerence that she dreaded. Dreaded and resented, for she wasn't in the least stupid. Although uneducated, never having attended school, and she readily admitted that she could barely read or write, Imelda was as smart as any seventeen-year-old girl and a lot smarter than most.

She filed the insult away in her mind, to be avenged later, and thought of her grandmother who had taught her the hard way not to expect anything of any person except herself. And with those thoughts whirling around in her head, plus the knowledge that Eddie was already putty in her hands, she leaned towards the elderly man, resigned to acting her part.

The next day, in a hurry to get somewhere, Buster forgot to lock the door and Imelda slipped into Clover's room for a longed-for chat. But Clover was not there. Imelda hung around for a while but Clover did not return.

She was on the point of going back to her own room when the door leading from the landing opened and Eddie came in. Quickly he closed the door behind him. 'Imelda!'

'I came to talk to Clover but she doesn't seem to be in.'

'No, she had to do something for my father.' He looked at her, his gaze anxious. 'Are you all right? I haven't seen you for days.'

Her full lips curled. ''Course I'm all right. It'd take more than a man like Buster Bywater to get me down.'

Eddie came forward, took her hands, holding them lightly in his. 'I've been worried about you, not seeing you and all. I wondered if you were sickening for something.'

'Sick of seeing no one but Buster. That's why I wanted to talk to Clover. I always feel refreshed when I've 'ad a good gossip with Clover.'

'Yes, for her age, she's got a good head on her shoulders, has that little sister of mine.' The grip on her hands tightened. 'Did you mean what you said the other day, about wanting to go away?'

Imelda pursed her lips. 'Only when it suits me do I say the things I don't mean. And that will never be with you, Eddie Blossom. I like you too much.' She looked up at him. 'Why, have you decided on something?'

'Something, I'm not sure yet what it is. But when I am I'll expect you to be ready and waiting.'

'Oh, how I love a forceful man.' Standing on tiptoe, she kissed him full on the mouth, her lips warm and moist. 'Don't let it be too long.' Although she pretended she could handle Buster Bywater in any of his moods, in reality she didn't know how much more she could take of the disagreeable comic.

'If I had the means, I'd go right now, today,' said Eddie. 'But it's not going to be that easy. We'll have to wait for the right moment.' The right moment, too, to tell Clover of his intentions, and a pang, sharp as a knife, went through him at the thought.

The talk became so earnest that neither heard the sound of Buster's return.

He was waiting for her in the bedroom. 'Bloody little whore!' he shouted. His curled fist struck the top of the dresser with such force that Imelda jerked at the sound. 'Making sheep's eyes at that boy again, were you?' Every instinct warning her of what was to come, she pivoted on her heel and headed back to the door without a word. Her steps quickened as she heard him coming after her.

'God blast you, woman!' His angry voice thundered behind her. 'You're not going anywhere. You're staying right 'ere until I've taught you a sorely needed lesson.'

He caught up with her on the landing and grabbed hold of her hair, wrenching back so violently that a cry of pain was forced from her lips. Cruel fingers stabbed into her shoulder, digging into her flesh, and she stifled another cry. From behind, one arm came about her waist, the other hand covered her mouth and she was dragged back into the bedroom.

Once there he threw her from him so that she collided against the corner of the dresser and fell in a heap of skirts and wildly tangled hair onto the carpet. Slowly he stalked forward, his eyes, dark and evil, boring right through her. She crawled away. 'No, Buster, don't,' she pleaded.

His hands knotted into fists. 'You'll not be meeting your fancy man again behind my back,' he growled. 'Not again.'

She prayed that Buster's shouting would bring Eddie to the door, but he didn't appear and she could only suppose he'd left the room after she'd gone, even left the house.

The beatings Buster had given her before were nothing like the one he gave her now. Finally, reluctantly, he forced himself to stop. Breathing heavily, he stood staring at the girl lying curled up on the floor. 'Let that be a lesson to you,' he said, watching as she tried painfully to get up. 'I don't take the likes of you from the gutter and feed and clothe you for you to make eyes at another man.'

'I didn't . . .' she gasped, her hands pushing against the floor, trying to raise herself to a sitting position.

'We haven't ever . . .' She stared at him, her whole body burning with pain, hating him.

Ignoring her, he opened the door, then stood looking back over his shoulder. 'I'm meeting the lads. You just be sure you're still 'ere when I get back.'

Alone, she refused to give in to the tears that threatened, although every muscle, every joint, ached. She crawled to the bed, dragging herself up to it, thinking of Eddie and how different her life would be with him.

Eddie, who loved her . . .

A few days later Buster was taken ill with a sudden stomach complaint, but he refused to take to his bed. 'I'm all right,' he insisted. 'Whatever it is, it will pass in a day or two.' Lowering her eyes, Imelda agreed meekly that she supposed it would.

And a few days after that things finally came to a head between Eddie and Bert. Lately, Eddie had shown more restraint when Bert criticised and complained. In fact, the more Bert upbraided him, the quieter Eddie became. But that day, when there were just a few weeks to go before the end of the summer engagement, Clover heard again the raised voices and wished she could burrow her head deeper into the shabby old armchair where she was curled, reading a book.

She heard a door slam, then Eddie came into the room. His face was flushed with anger and slowly he paced the small room, his fists clenching and unclenching. Eventually he came to perch on the arm of her chair.

'Look, love, it's no use. I can't stay here any longer. I'm going away and I'm going to try and persuade Imelda to come with me.'

Clover said nothing. For a long moment she sat, letting his words sink in, feeling cold apprehension followed by swift anger spreading through her. Anger at the stupidity of two grown men.

Not waiting for her reply, he went on, 'I don't know why I've stayed this long. I'm young and fit and I must make a life of my own.' He stood up and again paced the room, too restless to stay still for long. 'And, before you start, Imelda's not influencing me in any way. With Imelda or without her, sooner or later I would have left the act. I'm going to find something I want to do, work hard at my composing, and when I've found what I want I'm going to work so damned hard at it that the whole world will hear of Edward Blossom. I have to be strong, Clover. I have to be independent, get away from Dad. There's music in my head that's struggling to escape. Dad doesn't want to listen and I know if I stay on, things will go on as they always have, the act never changing, Dad stuck in his old ways. I doubt he will ever change.'

'Oh, Eddie, don't do anything rash. How will you cope? Living God knows where, without a penny to your name?'

Gruffly, he answered, 'I'll manage. At least I'll be happy.'

'Are you sure? Will it make you happy knowing you'll be away from your family, hurting Dad so much? He'll know you did it to get away from him. Will that make you happy?'

He gave a small laugh, trying to coax a smile to her worried face. 'Oh, Clover, don't let's fight. What's happy, anyway? The pot guarded by the leprechauns at the end of the rainbow? Making a wish when you turn over the silver in your pocket at the first sign of the new moon? Happiness is something we have to strive for. I'll find it, not with the pot of leprechauns' gold but with Imelda beside me.'

Clover sighed. 'You haven't been happy with the act for a long time, have you? I remember even before Mum died . . .' She bit her lip. She knew he hadn't. All those arguments with Bert, the constant sniping, the blank refusal to alter the act even one little bit to bring it more up to date.

'Not happy,' Eddie admitted. 'But not exactly *un*-happy.'

'Do you love Imelda?'

He looked at her. 'Yes, I love Imelda. But my love for you, little sister, is different from anything I shall ever feel again. There is only one space in my heart for that and I shall carry it with me wherever I go. I'll take it out each night before I go to sleep and hope that the good Lord will notice it, lying there so pure and shining on my pillow.'

Clover felt a quick rush of tears start in her eyes. She stood up and crossed the small space between them, putting her arms about his waist. She leaned her head on his shoulder. She hadn't Eddie's poetic turn of phrase and all she could say was, 'I'm going to miss you.' She raised her head to look at him. 'You're going to make us all miserable, going away. You'll write to us, not forget we exist?'

'Of course I will. Whenever I have a minute to spare. I'll write such long screeds that you'll be fed up ploughing through them. I'll send them care of Miss Boyce. She'll see you get them safely, whether you're here or in Moorfield.'

The expression in his warm brown eyes was immeasurably sad and Clover's arms tightened about his waist. 'Imelda will take care of you,' she murmured. 'It seems she's been taking care of people all her life.'

Chapter Eight

Buster at last admitted he wasn't well and took to his bed. Imelda spent most of her time administering to his constant needs and demands. She would frequently be seen tramping upstairs from the kitchen with a mug of something nourishing. Those who had never had a good word for her commented on the loving attendance she bestowed on him.

To enquiries from friends as to his health, she would say, 'He has his digestive trouble again. He's been suffering with it on and off for some time now.' And she'd smile. 'But I'm sure it'll soon clear up and I'll tell 'im you asked.'

The attack that had brought Buster to his bed had been quite sudden and for the next few days he suffered cramps, vomiting and nausea which kept him in bed and unable to return to the stage. Despite his protests, an understudy had to go on in his place, earning jeers and catcalls from the audience who couldn't accept that artistes were as mortal as the next man.

'Haven't got money for a bloody doctor,' he exclaimed when Ma Ruggles suggested sending for one. 'Think I'm a bloody millionaire or something, do you?' Ma Ruggles avoided Imelda's eyes and left the room in high dudgeon.

Buster complained about everything and drove everyone mad with his constant thumping on the bedroom floor with his walking stick, demanding attention.

Imelda felt she was back in the tinkers' camp, nursing her old grandmother again.

Late September had brought with it an Indian summer and every time she opened the window, swarms of flies would come in. Made lazy with the heat, they droned about the room, settling on everything, driving Buster to near apoplexy. Reassuringly, Imelda said she would see to it and went out to buy more flypapers. The small circular rolls had to be unwound very carefully, avoiding the dark sticky stuff with which they were smeared. Once pinned to the ceiling, she left them there for days, sometimes as long as a whole week, until the desiccated bodies of dead flies completely covered the arsenic-based trap.

Buster's attacks came and went, sometimes so agonising that Imelda would sit in a chair by the side of his bed, holding his hand and murmuring soothing words. She felt no pity for him. He'd brought everything upon himself. At the beginning of their relationship he'd been abrupt with her, but kind, fussing over her as a father might over a favourite daughter. His gifts of chocolates and pretty blouses had pleased her. But it hadn't lasted, and his jealousy and beatings were intolerable. How could she feel pity for a man who treated her like a dog?

Nevertheless, she felt the time she had spent among these theatre people had not been wasted. Imelda firmly believed in learning from everything that came her way. A man like Eddie Blossom was a new experience for her.

Stirring herself, she peered into Buster's face. He'd fallen into a doze. Releasing her hand from his damp clasp, she went slowly down to the kitchen where Ma Ruggles stood guard over a huge pot of beef broth, simmering gently on the stove. The woman turned to look at her. 'How is he?'

Imelda shrugged, joining her at the stove. 'About the same. You know Buster, moans when he's ill, moans when he's not.'

Ma Ruggles frowned. She had never approved of the comic's relationship with this heathen girl. But then Buster had never been particularly choosy about the females he selected as summer companions. She often wondered what happened to them at the end of the summer and felt a certain satisfaction in the thought that this girl would go the way of all the others.

She reached for a thick mug and filled it full to the brim. 'Get that down 'im,' she said, handing Imelda the mug. 'Nothing like 'ome-made soup to put life into a body.'

Carrying the soup carefully upstairs, Imelda found Buster lying with his eyes open. 'I've brought you some nice beef tea.' She spoke softly, so as not to start the throbbing in his head that all week he claimed had been plaguing him. 'Come on, sit up now, don't spill it, it's hot.' She leaned across the bed, one arm slipping behind the back of the sick man. He made a grab at her waist, pulling her further onto the bed. She gave a squeal of pretended alarm. 'Careful! This stuff's hot. Wouldn't want you scalding yourself now, would we?' Tucking a linen napkin into his pyjama top, she added coaxingly, 'Now just you be a good boy and take this. Ma had it simmering all afternoon.' She began to spoon the rich-smelling broth into his mouth.

This was the side of Imelda that he liked. The soft, almost maternal side. For a moment he allowed himself the luxury of fleeting regret. He doubted he would find another girl who filled his needs so well. Pity she was such a little whore; he was painfully aware of the continued meetings between her and young Eddie. Despite the lesson he'd given her. If he'd been a few years younger, he'd have given Eddie a run for his money, for there was nothing Buster enjoyed more than competition, although he was a poor loser. It was easier to lash out with his fists at Imelda.

He smiled to himself and a trickle of beef tea ran down his chin. Lifting a corner of the white napkin, Imelda dabbed at it with absent-minded brusqueness. Her mouth, usually so full and sensual, was a tight line across her face. Her eyes, normally sparkling, were vacant and far away, as though concentrating on scenes inside her head. The speed with which she spooned the broth into his mouth increased and became so rapid that he had difficulty swallowing one spoonful before she was giving him the next. He spluttered. 'Hold on, will ya? You'll choke me to death at this rate.' He laughed and clutched both hands to his belly as a sharp pain shot through him.

Imelda looked at him questioningly. 'What is it?'

He shook his head against the pillow. 'That pain again. Like a flaming knife jabbing into me guts.'

'Well, have some more of this. You're probably hungry, that's what it is. You haven't eaten properly for days.'

The negative shake of his head became more pronounced. 'Don't want no more of that muck.' He wiped his mouth with his pyjama sleeve then snatched the cup and sent it crashing across the room, the contents spilling onto the carpet. 'I've 'ad enough of that to last me an eternity.'

Imelda made a prim puckering of her lips. 'It's your health,' she said pointedly, rising to her feet and crossing to retrieve the cup. Surprisingly, it was still in one piece. 'If you don't want to take care of yourself then you can't blame anyone else if you feel poorly.'

Poorly, he'd told Ma Ruggles when she'd used that same expression, was too bland a word for what he'd suffered for the past week. Imelda watched him, and wondered how much redder he could get in the face without exploding.

She left the room, leaving the door open, and crossed the landing to the bathroom, always a refuge from Buster's ungovernable rages. Through a crack in the bathroom door she could see through to Buster's bed, which faced the bedroom door. His bloodshot eyes seemed to be staring straight at her. Her small teeth caught at her bottom lip, biting hard. She stepped back a pace.

Eddie would be waiting for her. He'd told her days ago that at last he had made up his mind, his face so young and earnest it had touched her. Last night as they had passed on the stairs, he had pressed a folded note in her hand. 'I shall be waiting tomorrow evening in the fairgrounds by the old ticket office near the Ghost Train,' he'd written. 'If necessary, I shall wait all night. We must take our chances, Imelda, and we must take them now.'

She had spent the day in a fever of anticipation.

'What in God's name are you doing in there?' Buster shouted. 'Come and straighten these bedclothes. They're all over the place.'

Quickly, she recrossed the landing and went to him. She leaned over the bed, smoothing the rumpled sheets, and tried not to breathe in the stench of stale sweat that rose from the corpulent body.

She felt no disgust, concentrating her thoughts on Eddie, on his clean young body, his way of cosseting her, treating her like a lady. Worth all the tedious preparations of the sticky flypapers, constantly on edge in case someone came upon her as she scraped and gathered the evil mess. Not so long ago the newspapers had been full of accounts of a woman who had killed her husband by using the scrapings from flypapers. It had been a sensational case. The woman had been found guilty and hanged.

Imelda shivered. Compulsion drove her on; compulsion to cause him as much suffering as she could. If she could just ensure that Buster stayed ill long enough to enable her and Eddie to get away.

At last Buster fell into a deep sleep and she set about getting ready to leave him. The pretty blouses and the silk kimono were tied into a bundle. She looked about her, ever alert for the slightest change in the rhythm of Buster's measured snoring. Had she forgotten anything? Her eyes caught sight of his ginger toupee, abandoned on top of the dresser, looking like a scruffy cat. Her eyes glinted.

A few moments later she gave a sigh of satisfaction and sat back on her haunches as the ginger wig began to smoulder in the fireplace.

Soon, flames were licking at the material, and she reached for the poker, hooking the blazing wig on its end, watching as the flames consumed it. Buster had a great regard for his wig. It was easy to replace but this act of treason would hurt him more than anything else, she thought.

She jerked into awareness, hearing voices coming from one of the bedrooms as a door opened.

She stood up, unconsciously holding her breath. She heard footsteps descend the stairs and fade away. Still she waited, ears straining, every muscle tense. Finally satisfied that the way was clear, she picked up her bundle of possessions and carefully opened the bedroom door.

The shadowy landing was deserted. From the clink of crockery and the smell of boiling cabbage wafting up the stairwell, Imelda knew the guests would be seated at the table in the dining room, waiting for their dinner. Clutching her bundle, she fled down the stairs like a small dark shadow, avoiding the treads that creaked, eyes and ears alert for a sound or movement from the hall below. The voices from the dining room reassured her, for while Ma Ruggles' guests were eating, they wouldn't be about to wander into the hallway.

She experienced a brief sense of regret, thinking of Clover, of their friendship. Clover had been the only real confidante she had ever had. Would she ever forgive her for taking away her brother, leaving her and Bert to go on with their act alone? Other people's feelings had never bothered Imelda; she wondered why they should now.

A sudden tap-tapping of the cane Buster used to demand attention by banging on the floor beside his bed made her start, as though touched by a live electric wire.

She gasped, all her terror of the man returning to swamp her. She flew across the hall, her heart thudding painfully. She reached the front door. It resisted her desperately fumbling hands.

At last winning the battle with the door, she was out in the blessed darkness of the street, fleeing as though the Devil himself was after her. In her own superstitious mind he was, for it seemed to her that in her life with Buster Bywater, the comic had taken on all the characteristics of the hell on earth that would be hers if she was caught now.

After Eddie's confession to Clover about running away, nothing more had been said. Clover prayed fervently that it had been just a flight of fancy on Eddie's part and that a new day had made him see reason.

Bert's entrance on stage earlier that night had raised a few eyebrows. Looks were exchanged as he staggered across the stage, his dance steps clumsy and unco-ordinated. He fluffed the words of a song he'd been singing all that season, causing loud guffaws from the audience.

Eddie battled to conceal the mistakes while a confused Clover, unhappy and embarrassed, did her best to charm the disapproving crowd. In their dressing room afterwards Bert started an argument with Eddie that was still simmering when they sat down to supper. Bert immediately launched into a caustic inventory of the way Eddie had taken over the act. Without another word, Eddie pushed back his chair and made for the door.

Bert glared after him. 'Where do you think you're going? Sit down.'

'I'm not hungry.'

'I didn't say you had to eat. I said sit down.'

'I won't sit down with you when you've been drinking and are in this mood.'

Bert's chair crashed back. He followed Eddie to the doorway to shout, 'Don't you walk away when I'm talking to you, you young puppy. Come back here!'

Clover's lips tightened. 'Please don't, Daddy. Can't you see he's upset?'

'Well, I'm upset too. Or doesn't that count, me being upset? Only his feelings count, eh?'

Wordlessly, Clover shook her head, gazing pleadingly to where Eddie had been standing in the doorway. But he'd gone, the doorway was empty. Bert gave a low growl of disgust and returned to join her at the table. Clover blessed the fact, not for the first time, that they ate in their own room and not downstairs in the dining room where ears really would be flapping by now.

In the ramshackle hut which had once been used as a fairground ticket office, Eddie waited. Anger still churned inside him. Had he done right, walking out like that? No time to say goodbye to Clover. That was what hurt most, the thought that she would feel deserted. What if Imelda didn't come? He'd feel a fool, waiting here for God knows how long for someone who was sleeping quietly by Buster's side.

He shuddered and began to pace the dusty floor of the hut, rubbing his forehead, trying to silence his doubts.

The noise from the fairground almost drowned the soft tapping on the rickety door. When he stopped pacing to listen, it seemed to explode in his head. Jerking open the wooden structure, he gathered Imelda into his arms, his pulse racing.

'Buster didn't try to stop you?' he asked, gazing down into her eyes.

Her mouth quirked. Defiance sparked in her dark eyes. 'Didn't know I was coming, did 'e?' she answered. 'Would 'ave killed me if 'e'd known.'

Eddie attempted to gather his wits and his ebbing courage. 'Oh, Imelda, was it that bad?' His hands framed her face and there was a roughness in his breathing that excited her. The look in his eyes told her that he felt it, too.

Slowly he bent his head, still holding her face. His breath was warm against her skin. 'I love you, girl. I want to be with you always,' he whispered, his voice husky with desire.

His lips covered hers, igniting an immediate spark of pent-up longing in her. She arched towards him, her breasts flattening against the unyielding hardness of his chest. Beneath her outspread fingertips she could feel the muscles of his shoulders, the hair curling on the back of his neck. His mouth moved hungrily over hers and Imelda pressed closer, afire with an aching fever that made her skin burn to his touch.

This was not like the other times when men had kissed her. This was very different, disturbing in its intensity. She was trembling as Eddie's hands moved down her back. The roughness of his breathing increased, exciting her. She felt an odd mixture of relief and regret when at last he pulled away from her.

The sounds outside from the funfair, the tinny jangle of the merry-go-round, the shouts and laughter, the smell of the oil lamps, suddenly intruded and she whispered, 'I wish the world would go away, just for a little while.'

'It won't. We'll have to go away from it.' She looked so trusting, so eager, that he felt ten feet tall. Taking her face in his hands once more he kissed her gently. 'I'll never hurt you, Imelda. I'll take care of you always.' From now on he would be close to her, a happy, joyous prisoner made strong by their love. Their lives from now on would be a magic carpet of happiness, and he prayed their time together would go on and on and never end.

Still something urged him to add, on a tentative note, 'I don't know what we've let ourselves in for. Are you sure you wouldn't rather stay here? Buster would see you never went short of money.'

Imelda sniffed. 'You know what 'e can do with 'is money, don't you? He can wipe 'is fat old arse with it.'

Eddie gave a triumphant laugh and pulled her close again. 'My love, you have the most wonderful gift for expressing yourself!'

There was the clang of an engine, wheels rattling on a narrow track, shrill screaming, and the small hut shook to its foundations with the force of the Ghost Train as it hurtled from the dark tunnel just yards beyond the wooden walls. He smiled down at her.

'Better go,' he said. He eyed the bundle at her feet. 'Is that all you're taking?'

'All I've got,' she replied tersely. She slipped a small hand into the crook of his arm as he bent to lift the bundle to his shoulder. His own possessions were in a

battered old leather suitcase that had travelled with the
Blossoms for as long as he could remember. 'Where we
going?' she asked.

'We'll make for a large town, somewhere where
there'll be jobs. I'll take care of that.' He grinned.
'Maybe we'll get a ship to America. Would you like that?
The Morvellis, an act we knew years ago, have worked
there. They say it's an exciting place. Mrs Morvelli used
to write to my mother and keep in touch. She wrote that
all the opportunities in the world were there.'

Imelda squeezed his arm, her smile wide. 'Tell me
more about America. Where will we live?'

'New York.' It had come like a flash. 'New York is
the biggest town there. There'll be plenty of work for
me and before you know it we'll be rich and living
in one of those posh apartments in,' he shrugged,
nonchalantly, 'wherever the best apartments in New
York are. And we'll have a car. What would you say
to a smart yellow car with a leather hood that folds back
when the weather's fine and can be pulled over when
it rains?'

Imelda snuggled her head against his shoulder. 'I'd
say, yes, please,' she said softly. 'America sounds the
sort of place I've been looking for all my life.'

When the banging from Buster's stick had gone on
for longer than Ma Ruggles could countenance, the
landlady herself went upstairs to investigate. Buster
hung half out of bed, his hand still feebly grasping
the silver-topped cane, his face choleric. He gave her
a baleful glare, followed by a string of obscenities and
for the first time in her life Ruby Ruggles retreated
from the fury of a member of the male sex without
answering back.

A doctor was summoned. The first thing he asked
was the whereabouts of Mr Bywater's nurse. The term

seemed so much nicer than mistress or whatever they called them these days, he thought. Ma Ruggles replied that she didn't know. She'd given the girl a mug of beef broth for Mr Bywater earlier, and hadn't seen her since. She sometimes took her supper in the dining room with the other guests, but today she hadn't.

'Didn't you think that odd?' asked the doctor, looking at his watch. He was a tall, thin man with a perpetually worried expression emphasised by the pince-nez glasses on his nose.

Ma Ruggles bridled. 'No, I didn't. I assumed she was attending to Mr Bywater. It was only when that blessed banging went on for so long I thought it best to have a look-see.'

The doctor frowned. 'Banging?'

'Yes, with his walking stick. He bangs it on the floor to get attention. This time it fair drove me mad, going on and on like that.'

'He's been alone for some time, then? You say you have no idea where the young lady with him went to?'

Relishing her role, Ma Ruggles said, 'She probably went out to the chemists to get some more of those flypapers. We've 'ad to use a lot this year, the dratted things 'ave been so bad.'

Again a quick look at his watch. 'At this time of night, Mrs Ruggles? Surely the chemist would be closed now?'

Ma shrugged. 'Well, I don't know, do I? Maybe she got fed up nursing 'im and went off to meet a pal for a drink. No telling what she'd do next, even at the best of times. A right odd sort she was an' all.'

Buster Bywater was admitted to hospital and spent a couple of days feeling extremely uncomfortable and ill. Careful nursing pulled him through and he was discharged. The doctor warned him to cut down on his drinking and take things easy, not to return to work for the short period that remained of the season.

The Summer Follies being nearly at the end of their contract, it sounded reasonable enough. But Buster did not see it like that. The theatre was his life; how could he give up the excitement and adulation of his fans, not to mention disappointing them by his absence?

And he had every intention of being here when, and if, that dark-eyed gypsy bitch of a girl returned. Desert him after all he'd done for her, would she? He'd show her. He'd stay in Newcombe, forsaking the comforts of the hotel in Manchester where he'd spent the winters for more years than he cared to remember. And, by gum, he'd be ready for her if she did return.

Chapter Nine

After Adele's death, Bert had been asked why he didn't change the name of the act to the Three Blossoms. Usually an icy glare was the only answer he gave. Sometimes he would say, 'Why should we? That would be like denying poor Adele ever existed.' People understood. But when it became obvious that Eddie would not be returning, he was forced to rename it the Two Blossoms.

'I guess he's old enough to make his own mistakes, that brother of yours,' he said to Clover, his face tight with anger. 'But you and me are going on playing the act that made us what we are. The Blossoms. If he wants to quit, good luck to him. It's not going to make a scrap of difference to our act.'

Bert did his soft-shoe shuffle number, spreading a handful of sand over the stage and dancing to 'Swanee River', later accompanying Clover on the piano while she sang. They would end the act with a duet. Over the years, Bert's voice had taken on a deeper, rougher edge which blended well with Clover's clear, natural tones.

Somehow they went on, never missing a performance, although at times Bert seemed to be only going through the motions. He appeared to have lost all interest in whether the Blossoms remained on the bill or not, in spite of his earlier boasting to Clover. His visits to the Silver Mermaid became more frequent, more necessary to enable him to get through the day, and his work continued to suffer. Although Buster Bywater now spent less time in the public house, there were many other men who were only too willing to keep Bert company and buy him the occasional drink. Bert could not help feeling that in some way he'd been cheated. Life wasn't supposed to do that to a man, not when things had been going so well.

One Sunday afternoon the vicar paid them an unexpected visit. 'Ah, Mr Blossom,' he commiserated solemnly, 'it is all in the hands of the Lord. Remember, the Lord giveth and the Lord taketh away. It is not for us to question His judgment.'

'Aye,' Bert muttered, 'the Lord taketh away a hell of a lot when He feels like it.' He had already taken away his wife, the mainstay of his existence. Now He'd taken his son, although not in the same way. But it might as well have been, thought Bert. What would the Lord be demanding of him next? It didn't bear thinking about.

When the vicar had gone, and Bert couldn't understand why the man had come in the first place, for he was no churchgoer, not in that church, anyway, he poured himself a glass of whisky, disregarding Clover's frown of reproach. 'Got to keep my spirits up some way, love,' he said. 'To be a survivor you've got to keep going.'

And Clover did her best to do just that. But it was an uphill struggle and few girls her age would have been up to it. Bert was drinking heavily, using up the precious money, becoming increasingly unreliable. When she tried to prod his conscience with her anxieties, he would pat her on the head and say condescendingly, 'Oh, you leave things to me. It's not for you to worry your pretty little head about them.' And, teasingly, 'Why is my nut-brown maiden frowning today? Wondering if the ribbon we wear in our hair matches the colour of our frock, are we?'

Eddie's departure had wrought a change in Clover's

attitude to her father and the life they shared. Where at one time she would have smiled demurely and let his remark wash over her, now she had to hold back the sharpness of her tongue as she said, 'Wouldn't it be nice if that's all it was?' She shook her head. 'No, Daddy, it's more than that.' Chin lifted, she looked into the bleary eyes. 'Has Mr Ryder spoken to you yet?'

Bert flushed with anger. 'Yes, the great impresario did find time to have a word with me,' he blustered, 'but that's no concern of yours.'

Clover hesitated from saying that from the look on the producer's face after he'd watched their act, she thought it probably did concern her. Gregory Ryder owned the string of small theatres and enjoyed huge success in the various seaside towns. He had worked his way up from tea boy in a cheap music hall in a London suburb to the powerful man he was today. Fiercely ambitious, he used every trick he knew to reach the eminence he possessed today. His artistes considered themselves fortunate to be working for him and although he seldom interfered, he had all their records at his fingertips and demanded perfection.

A mop of thick, snow-white hair topped a pink face fleshy with good living. Although not as young as he used to be, he tried to keep himself fit and healthy and a good brisk walk along the promenade marked the beginning of each visit to the various seaside towns where his theatres were located. At all times his fingers were on the pulse of his rapidly expanding empire.

'We may not be playing to the Palladium,' he'd lecture to his assembled artistes, 'or performing before Their Majesties, the King and Queen, God bless 'em, but that doesn't mean to say we don't always give of our best. Business is business whether it's turns for a summer show or making metal washers.'

He had known Bert Blossom and Adele for years,

since before young Clover had been born. They had always worked for him. He'd been intrigued by the quiet, lady-like manners of Adele Blossom, and when years ago the little girl was introduced into their act, he knew he had a hit on his hands. To succeed in this business, artistes needed to have either a lot of luck or a distinctive style. The Blossoms made a welcome change from the usual run of jugglers and fire-eaters, of red-nosed comics with their secondhand, sometimes offensive jokes and the nautch dancers clad in diaphanous trousers and skimpy scarlet and gold boleros. The small family act was a favourite with the audience who looked forward each summer to hearing first Adele, then later Clover's sweet voice singing songs they loved. Brought a tear to the eye, did Clover's songs, interspersed as they were with half-serious, half-comic dance routines peformed by Bert and his son.

When Adele died they mourned her; now, with Eddie's departure, the act seemed to have died.

Mr Ryder had sat in his usual place in the auditorium a few evenings ago and watched Bert and Clover perform. First he'd been confused, then distressed when he realised the deceptively casual and then awesomely energetic steps that were Bert's trademark were missing. And it wasn't just Bert acting the fool, either.

He sat through performances on the next two evenings and things didn't get any better. Clover tried hard to make up for it, smiling more brilliantly than ever, joining in a simple dance routine with her father. But nothing could disguise the fact that the man was drunk.

Gregory Ryder sat staring at the stage, a sense of cold foreboding overtaking him. 'What's got into the man?' he wondered. 'Doesn't he realise he's fooling with his daughter's very future?'

Clover had such a promising voice and her air of fresh

innocence added immeasurably to the act. Dressed in a gown of apricot chiffon which seemed to float about her with every move, ending just above her knees, she stood in the centre of the stage, head high, hands folded in front of her and sang exquisitely.

Gruff with anger and disappointment, Ryder spoke to Clover, catching her on the way back to the dressing room. Bert had gone on ahead. 'When your dad's changed, love, tell him I want a word with him, will you?'

Bert was all blustering excuses when later Ryder approached him alone in his dressing room. 'It's only teething troubles while me and Clover try to get our act back together on our own,' Bert protested.

'Teething troubles my foot!' Gregory Ryder's eyes hardened. 'Bywater might be able to get away with it – after all, his entire act is based on falling about on stage – but I don't welcome it in my other performers. You've worked for me long enough, Bert, to know my rules about slackness. You're trouble, Bert Blossom, and Clover doesn't need that kind of trouble.'

Bert's face turned the deep red of a turkey cock; in fact, his whole demeanour was reminiscent of a turkey cock, down to the swaggering, strutting gait as he deliberately turned his back on the other man and walked to the door. His hand on the doorknob, he turned once to say, 'Do I take this as a warning, Mr Ryder? Or are you just being neighbourly?'

Ryder regarded him steadily. 'Take it any road you like, Bert. Just watch your step, that's all.' He drew deep on the cigar he was seldom seen without. 'You've got a gifted child on your hands. You should treasure her.'

'I'll bear it in mind,' answered Bert flippantly, and left the room.

His act the following evening was even worse. Ryder

watched from the wings with a frown of disapproval,
acutely conscious of the young girl beside him. That
wide, candid gaze would make most men squirm and
Ryder was no exception. A quick, bright girl, he
thought, it was a disgrace that her father should land
her in such a predicament. He recalled Adele and
immediately the sense of compassion was so strong he
almost tugged the new agreement he had been working
on from his pocket and presented it to Clover. It was a
contract that gave her uninterrupted work for the next
two years – in a proper theatre, where she would be
noticed, not just the end-of-the-pier spot they were
doing now. After two years it would be rewritten to
give her more advantageous terms, for then she would
be eighteen and a young woman.

She would never get another chance like this. That
drunken sot of a father was just a liability to her. She
might feel duty bound to stay with him, for there
was little doubt that her filial loyalties were strong,
but Ryder saw Bert only as a responsibility, one he
preferred not to have hanging about *his* neck. He'd be
a fool to allow any acts in his theatres to get so bad they
were booed off the stage, and that was precisely where
Bert Blossom's performance was heading.

Beside him in the wings a shamefaced Clover bit back
her tears.

'Don't take on, lass,' Ryder told her. 'It's not your
fault.'

On stage Bert was telling a joke, swaggering about
the stage, forgetting the sequence of the joke but
determined to divulge it to an audience that clearly
wasn't interested.

A few catcalls followed and Bert waved a clenched fist,
causing Ryder to say, tersely, 'I wasn't going to disclose
this to you, Clover, not yet, but I find I've no choice.'
Unable to meet the girl's wide-eyed stare, he went on,

'Your father'll have to shape up a lot better than he's doing if he wants to stay in my employment.'

He hated himself for the stricken look that shadowed the girl's face, but it had to be said.

Raising her chin, Clover said, 'My father has been with you for a long time, Mr Ryder. Since before I was born. You can't mean to toss him out, just like that, as though he was an old boot?' He cringed at the note of rebuke in her voice. 'I'm sure in a little while he will be fine. He's still shocked about Eddie, although he tries hard not to show it. And you know how badly he took my mother's death.'

He turned away, unable to bear the sight of tears gathering in her eyes. 'My dear, I would do anything in the world not to have to hurt you. But I really can't see myself continuing to turn a blind eye to the way he's carrying on. I hear stories about the lack of rehearsal, the times he's arrived late for the show, something completely out of character for your father, and I wonder how it's all going to end. Look at him now. He'll get more than catcalls if he carries on like this. The audience is getting restless.'

'I'll talk to him. He doesn't realise what he's doing.' It was an impassioned plea, but when Clover saw the look of pity combined with inflexibility Ryder gave her, she knew she was wasting her breath. 'You're not going to change your mind, are you? You won't give him another chance.'

Ryder thought again of the new contract, amending the wording in his mind. 'Clover, there's no other way of saying this except straight out. I don't want him. He's no earthly use to me as he is. And,' lifting a staying hand as she opened her mouth to protest, 'I don't hold a hope in hell that he's going to change.'

'But he will!' Clover rose like a bird to her father's defence. 'I know he will. I told you, he's upset about

Eddie and he still mourns Mum and sometimes he can't get through the next hour without a drink inside him.'

Ryder smiled mirthlessly. 'I commend your loyalty, my dear. And I pray that you never find that it's misplaced. I've seen men like your father before. Once they're on the bottle they reach for it again and again, whenever they encounter fresh troubles.'

Clover's face flamed and Ryder caught his breath, catching a vision of the lovely woman she would become in those flushed cheeks and snapping eyes.

'I would never have believed you to be such an intolerable man,' she said tightly. 'You've always been fair and above board with us, and my father has never once thought of working anywhere else but on your circuit.'

He shot her an inimical glance. He was not used to being told off by sixteen-year-old girls. 'I'm a businessman, Clover. Unfortunately, if I gave way to all the heartfelt pleas I hear from pretty young girls I wouldn't remain one for long. But,' turning the conversation away from the disgraced Bert Blossom, 'I do have a proposition to put to you. I can see no earthly reason why *you* should leave the show. The audience like you and soon you'll be able to take on a much more adventurous act, one with elegance and charm. In no time at all you could be top of the bill.' He eyed her keenly, pursing fleshy lips. 'Doesn't that appeal to you? Why don't you rejoin us next summer and see what happens?' He paused again, waiting for her reply.

She met his eyes squarely. 'And my father?'

Ryder spread his hands in a gesture of resignation. 'Your father doesn't come into it. I would only want you.'

'In that case, Mr Ryder, although I'm grateful for your offer, I'll have to say no.' It was said with a dignity far beyond her years. 'Now, if you'll excuse me, I must see to my father.'

Bert was stumbling off the stage followed by jeers and catcalls and one or two of the audience, who had come prepared, even threw eggs and rotten tomatoes. Gregory Ryder watched as she reached forward and helped pull Bert the last few steps. He said, raspingly, 'You must be dafter than I thought not to realise that he's using you as a prop.'

She gave him her brilliant smile. 'No doubt I can cope with it. Good night, Mr Ryder.'

He smiled. 'I know I'll regret it, but seeing that it's so close to the end of the season, tell your dad he can stay on until then. But I want no more nonsense like we've just seen, hear?'

Clover nodded, biting her lip.

In the dressing room, an anxious Miss Boyce waited, having witnessed the scene between Clover and Mr Ryder. 'It's all right, I'll see to him,' Clover told her gently. She waited until the decidedly shaken little woman left the room, closing the door firmly behind her, then turned to Bert.

He collapsed onto a chair and covering his face with his hands began to weep. 'I've done it now, haven't I, girl? I saw him talking to you at the side there, could tell by his face what it was all about. What are we to do, child, with your mother gone and now Eddie? Who'll look after us?'

It was an old cry. One that Clover heard in her sleep. Every instinct called on her to join him in a good, long weep, but she managed to steady her voice as she said, 'You know I'll always look after you, Daddy. Haven't I always said I would? We'll take care of each other. Everything will be all right, you'll see.'

'I know, my little love. We're lucky in that, we still have each other.'

She put her arms about the slumped shoulders, trying to comfort him. 'You're not to worry,' she whispered. She was used to saying that. It had become a habit. 'It'll be all right, Daddy.' She always said it, when she knew it was not all right at all. When she couldn't see far enough into the future to know if it would ever be all right.

Some of Ryder's warnings must have rubbed off on Bert; for the next few shows he seemed his old self, charming and affable, with hardly a fluffed line or a wrong step. Clover said a prayer of thanksgiving and did her best to avoid Gregory Ryder's judging eye.

A few days later, cheeks flushed with great excitement, Miss Boyce barged her way through the crowd of rushing artistes to the dressing room.

'See what *I've* got!' she announced in a voice bursting with joy. Waving a letter in her hand she approached to where Clover sat before the dressing table mirror.

'What is it?'

'It's a letter, silly.'

Clover gave a smothered cry and grabbed it from her, tearing open the envelope with fingers that trembled. It was just one single note of cheap paper and there were tears in her eyes when she looked up at Miss Boyce. 'It's from Eddie . . .'

Miss Boyce tut-tutted with impatience. 'I know that, you daft ha'porth. Didn't I recognise the handwriting? What does he say? Is he all right?'

'He says he's fine. Imelda's with him . . .' Miss Boyce gave an unladylike snort and tossed her head, deeply offended by the mere mention of the gypsy girl's name. Clover went on, 'They're staying at a place in Liverpool, with plans to get passage to America on a ship.' She turned the envelope over in her hand. Apart from the Liverpool postmark and the date, there was no indication of a return address. Eddie obviously didn't intend to be found.

'He says he will write and let us know definitely as soon as he can and we mustn't worry as he knows he and Imelda are going to be very happy together.'

'Oh, dear!' For a moment Miss Boyce seemed lost for words. Then she said, frowning, 'Sailing off like that could be extremely dangerous, couldn't it? All those rough winds and seas, especially with the winter approaching.'

Clover smiled, gazing into the little woman's anxious face. She knew Miss Boyce blamed Imelda for luring Eddie away. It was a feeling shared by many of the cast of the Summer Follies, especially since it had become known that she had deserted Buster Bywater when he was on the point of death. Heads nodded wisely, fingers tapped against a nose. It was well known Imelda had a knowledge of herbs, gathering them when she could. Who was to say she hadn't concocted something and fed it to Buster under the pretext of relieving his suffering? Who would know?

Loyal to her friend, Clover ignored the gossip. She had seen enough evidence of Buster's violent rages against Imelda but she refused to believe that even Imelda would sink to such wickedness. She kept remembering Imelda's words that day they had been talking: 'He's been kind, and kindness is something I've not seen a lot of in my life.'

Bert refused to become involved, rejecting all gossip as not being worthy of comment. When Clover handed him the letter, after the briefest of scrutinies he tossed it to one side.

'Right,' he growled. 'He'd do better to stay away if that's his attitude. I for one never want to clap eyes on him again. He'd just not better come crawling back thinking all is forgiven when he and that girl are starving and he finds work impossible to get. America!' If he was a man for spitting, Bert would have done that to show his disgust. 'And pigs might fly!'

Before the show the next night, Bert drank heavily. With a sinking heart, Clover watched him blunder his way through the act. As the jeering comments grew, he stopped to peer out over the audience. Holding one hand over his eyes to block the spotlight, he surveyed the crowded rows of seats, calling, 'Would you mind shouting a little louder, please? I didn't quite catch that last remark.'

'Get back to the bar,' yelled a man in a loud checked suit. 'Mebbe another couple of whiskies'll improve yer voice.'

The crowd erupted in laughter and Bert stepped right up to the edge of the stage. He gave a mocking bow and called, 'Gladly, sir. At least there I won't have to look at your ugly face.'

And Clover led her father off the stage amid jeers and catcalls.

Gregory Ryder informed Bert in no uncertain terms that his absence was preferable to his presence and as Clover refused to go on without him, they were left high and dry with a lot of time on their hands, most of which Bert spent in the Silver Mermaid. He also spent the precious bit of money Gregory Ryder had paid him in lieu of notice, money that would have seen them safely to the next job, if, as Bert constantly boasted, he ever felt in the right frame of mind to go after one.

Ryder had watched him walk to his dressing room after that last disastrous turn, not allowing himself to give way to the regret he was already beginning to feel. The show's welfare was more important than an artiste with too strong a liking for drink and a girl who was blind to the truth.

'Little tin-pot God,' said Bert virulently. 'Give 'em

a bit of power and they think they can jump all over you.'

Which wasn't entirely true. Ryder had always been very fair and had thought the world of Clover's mother. The impression the rest of the troupe got was that it would have taken very little encouragement from Adele for a different kind of relationship to spring up between them. But Adele, for all her sweet and unsophisticated ways, seemed to have the knack of handling the impresario without appearing brusque, keeping him at a distance but still being friends.

Ryder caught up with Clover before she entered the room after her father. 'Will you be all right?' Wanting to add that by 'you' he meant her and not her father. Bert Blossom's future wellbeing wasn't high on his list of priorities at that moment. He'd always liked Bert, but the man had let him down badly. One drunk in a show was enough. As he'd told Bert earlier, Buster Bywater could get away with it; the people who paid good money to see the show expected Buster to stagger around on stage and get his jokes muddled up. They didn't expect it from Bert Blossom.

To his question, Clover said, very quietly, 'You needn't worry about us, Mr Ryder. We'll be fine.'

Chapter Ten

The first thing they had to dispense with was their comfortable digs at Ma Ruggles' boarding house. Their savings were dwindling and the luxury of two bedrooms and their own sitting room was now out of the question. Ma Ruggles said she would be sorry to see them go even as her avaricious little eyes gleamed in anticipation of being able to charge the new lodgers a higher rent.

The day before they left, another letter arrived from Eddie, in which he said he and Imelda had booked their passage to America and he would let them know his new address as soon as they had settled in their new country. 'And don't worry,' he wrote, as though on a teasing note, 'I *will* marry the girl. Maybe one day you will be able to join us. Wouldn't that be grand?'

He made no reference to Bert, apart from a few brief words saying he hoped his father was well.

They found cheap lodgings in a boarding house in the back streets of the town, far from the prom with its noise and gaiety. Moodily, Bert eyed the dingy little room. There wasn't enough room to swing a cat; indeed, there was barely enough room for the black iron single bed and one bentwood chair that furnished it. Next door, an identical room would be Clover's.

'Don't look so worried, lass,' he said, trying to sound cheerful. 'And don't bother to unpack properly. I'll have us out of here in no time, you see if I don't.'

Smiling, Clover forced herself to believe him. Bouncing up and down on the bed that was to be hers, hearing its squeaks and feeling the springs piercing the thin mattress, she said, 'Of course we will, Daddy. I'll only unpack what we need and leave the rest in the cases.'

The saddest part was having to leave Miss Boyce and sell all of Adele's lovely costumes at last. Unknown to Clover and especially to Bert, who would have rejected out of hand any kind of help from that source, Gregory Ryder found a use for them in one of his theatres in Glasgow. The whole thing was arranged through Miss Boyce. Carefully altered, they would live again under the lights and be gazed upon, as Miss Boyce had so sentimentally put it, by adoring young men.

Clover found it difficult to come to terms with her new life. Used to being busy, she found the mediocrity of each day increasingly wearisome.

Although Bert's hopes remained high, there was still no sign of another job. Every night Clover would kneel beside her bed and ask God to guide her father's thoughts to finding more work. There were other, smaller, theatres in town, of the music hall type. They were very rough and once the Blossoms would have turned up their noses at any suggestion of working in them, but Clover was beginning to accept that they might well have to. They had to earn money from somewhere. All they had were two guineas she had managed to pry from her father, two shillings and a half-crown which she kept in the spare tea caddy on the mantelpiece.

Brushing her hair one night before going to bed, she had a sudden urge to talk to her father. The hairbrush still in her hand, she rose from the bed and crossed to the door in her bare feet. Her voluminous white flannel nightgown swirled about her legs and without knocking she pushed open her father's door. He was kneeling beside the bed, head bent, his hands clasped in prayer. Clover, scarlet with mortification, one hand going to her throat, murmured, 'Oh, I'm sorry. I didn't realise . . .'

Bert gave an embarrassed cough and, pressing both hands against the patchwork quilt, thrust himself to his feet. 'Just finishing,' he mumbled. Then, to Clover's surprise, he made the sign of the cross and her gaze fell on the mother-of-pearl rosary curled up on the pillow.

She had known her father was a Catholic, although he'd made many a joke about being a badly lapsed one, saying the Pope must surely have drummed him out of the Faith by now. She'd never once visualised him praying.

'You see, I'm not such a bad old bugger after all, eh?' he said, trying to cover both their embarrassment. 'I pray to your dear mother, asking her to intercede with the Virgin and all the saints on our behalf.'

Clover retreated to her own room, quite forgetting what she wanted to talk to him about.

It wasn't long before they fell behind with the rent. Clover began to dread bumping into the landlady. She would crack open the bedroom door and put an eye to the opening, watching and listening for the gimlet-eyed landlady before venturing out. If Mrs Marks knocked, Clover would stiffen into rigid immobility, holding her breath, praying that Mrs Marks wouldn't force open the door and march in.

In spite of her careful movements, the landlady caught her one morning with the words, 'I'd like a little word with your father. Tell him I want to speak to him, will you, dearie?'

Later she faced Bert. 'Daddy, the bills are mounting up horribly. And Mrs Marks wants a word with you.'

'Bugger Mrs Marks,' said Bert cheerfully. 'Sort out

the bills into dates and I'll decide which one to pay.' Lowering the newspaper he was reading, he gave her a fond smile. The gracious, generous, all-providing male dealing with a slightly precocious child. 'You mustn't worry so much about the bills,' he told her. 'My reputation is good. There are plenty of shopkeepers who are only too pleased to give me credit.'

'One or two have been pretty forthright lately,' she reminded him. 'There are a couple of final demands, and others, although polite, remind you how long they have been waiting for a settlement.'

'Tough luck on them,' replied Bert blithely. He rose, tossing the paper to one side, leaving the pages scattered on the floor. He bent to drop a kiss on the top of her head. 'Such a good little housekeeper. Don't let it worry you, love. We'll manage. We always have. They know they'll get paid eventually.'

Bert had the knack of avoiding landladies down to a fine art. Now, knowing he couldn't escape, for Mrs Marks laid siege to the hall, waiting to pounce as he passed, he would give her his most brilliant smile, white teeth flashing under his neat moustache. His eyes would crinkle at the corners in that endearing way he had and he would compliment her on her appearance. 'Why, I do believe you're looking younger every day,' he'd tell her with a broad wink.

Mrs Marks was a woman hardened to flattery from lodgers owing her money. But somehow with Bert Blossom it was different. She would simper like a schoolgirl, pleat the skirt of her wrap-around pinafore with nervous fingers and tell herself as he sauntered away that next time she would be firm and insist on something towards the rent arrears.

The days became cold and Clover took to going downstairs to the shabbily furnished sitting room, where the only coal fire in the house, apart from the kitchen range, threw out a dubious heat. Approaching tea time one afternoon, she sat listlessly in an overstuffed armchair beside the fire and watched the landlady's daughter, a gawky girl of twelve, squat before the fireplace holding out a glass butter dish to the flames. 'Mam couldn't spread it on the bread,' she explained to no one in particular. 'That scullery's as cold as an iceberg.'

In her free hand she held a discoloured, bone-handled knife with which she cut the butter into small pieces to facilitate the melting process. Between each slash, the ungainly girl put the blade of the knife to her mouth and licked off the melted butter.

Clover made a small *moue* of disgust. She felt she could not endure this place and its slovenly inhabitants a moment longer. These days a lot of her time was spent in trying to escape from her depressing surroundings.

She badly missed the companionship of the theatre, the bright lights and the gaiety. She missed Eddie and, in a strange way, Imelda who had become a real confidante. Apart from Eddie, Imelda had been the only one near her own age to whom she was close.

She wondered where Bert was. She hadn't seen him for hours. He could only have a few pennies in his pocket, and unless Buster Bywater was buying the drinks in the Silver Mermaid, Bert had nowhere to go. It was unusual for Buster still to be around, reflected Clover. Although the comic was fully recovered, he seemed loath to leave his comfortable rooms at Ma Ruggles and move on to his winter quarters.

Like a homing pigeon, Clover's steps took her to where she knew she would be welcomed. She felt the need of comforting and there was only one person to whom she could turn for that now. It was but a short walk to Miss Boyce's lodgings. She knew she would be at home. Miss Boyce was always at home. As she said herself, she wasn't one for gadding about.

'Clover!' There was joy in the little woman's greeting as she came down the stairs to meet her. 'How nice to see you.' She saw little enough of the girl these days, deliberately not visiting her and Bert for she knew how Clover detested the penury into which they had sunk.

Taking her hands, looking at her closely, she was suddenly concerned at Clover's wan and dispirited appearance. Anxiously, she said, 'Are you all right, dear? You look washed out.'

Clover forced a smile. 'I'm fine, Boycie. I just thought I'd drop in and say hello.'

Miss Boyce took her arm, urging her up the staircase. 'Come and have some tea. I bought some of those sultana scones you like this morning. We'll toast them and spoil ourselves. It's a long time since we did that.'

In her room she handed Clover the long-handled fork she used for toasting bread. 'Here, you toast. The fire's just right. I'll make the tea.'

Seeing Clover all right, she hurried out to the small room at the end of the landing that was used by the tenants as a scullery. A sink and small gas stove stood in one corner. Clover felt herself relaxing, soothed by the familiarity of toasting not only the scones but also herself before the cheerful fire.

Feeling refreshed by the tea and sympathy showered on her by Miss Boyce, Clover arrived back at the boarding house as dusk was setting in. She still had supper to buy and she cursed herself for not thinking of that before she set out. She should have taken the money with her and bought the food on her way home. Reaching up to the high mantelpiece, her fingers feeling for the tea caddy, she thought she could manage something nice without spending very much of the amount hidden there. As she lifted the gaudily coloured souvenir of Queen Victoria's Jubilee, she frowned. Prising open the lid, she stared down into an empty space. Her hands clutched the square tin so tightly that her knuckles whitened. Her feeling of contentment after the pleasant visit to Miss Boyce dissolved. She collapsed into the chair beside the fireplace, her head reeling.

Then with tightened lips she set out to find her father.

Her search led her back into town, but this time to the promenade, to the Silver Mermaid. Darkness was already creeping over the sea, and on the horizon a dark range of purple clouds gathered. The lights from the pier shone brightly through the evening mist. Outside the public house she asked an elderly man who had just pushed open the swing doors, about to enter, if he would be kind enough to see if her father was there. She described Bert and the man nodded, saying, 'Aye, lass, of course I will.'

Minutes later he came back with the information that no one inside matched the description she had given him. Clover thanked him and turned to walk away. She still couldn't believe that Bert would have stooped so low as to take the pitifully small amount of savings they still had. And yet she knew there could be no other explanation. They kept the door to their rooms locked, day and night. Each carried a key, for one of the first things Bert had done when they moved in was to get two keys made, an extra one for himself and one for Clover.

She stood looking about her. What now? Maybe Bert was already on his way home – although it would be early for him to return to the depressing surroundings of the boarding house. The lights of the pier beckoned, the few that the council saw fit to keep glowing all through the bleak northern winter. People still liked to stroll the grey boards and lean over the railings to watch the sea thundering below.

Suddenly, she heard her father's voice raised in song.

As she drew nearer, quickening her step, hardly able to believe her ears, she had to pinch herself to make sure she wasn't dreaming. It really was his voice! He didn't sound drunk or anything. In fact, couples standing around were listening with rapt attention. He was singing an old Italian love song, learned years ago from the Morvellis, and making a fairly presentable job of it, too, as he leaned with folded arms against the wooden railings of the pier.

Even so, Clover felt herself squirm with distress. Her lips firmed. She'd better get the silly old bugger home before he disgraced them by attracting the attention of the law. As she hurried towards the pier entrance, Bert finished his song and she saw him step back from the railing, throwing his arms wide to acknowledge the applause. Everyone listening clapped. A number cried encore. Clover could see couples giving him money, thrusting coins at him as he laughed and bobbed his head, accepting them benevolently.

By the time Clover had passed through the turnstile and reached him, he was already making for the pub situated so conveniently to one side. It was the same pub that Molly, the hotel maid, had vanished into all those years ago, leaving Adele and Bert to 'find' each other.

Clover grabbed his arm and literally dragged him back. 'Oh no you don't!' Her cheeks blazed, anger mixed with the embarrassment she still felt. 'You've had enough drink for one day by the look of you. You're coming home with me.'

Before he could open his mouth to protest, she went on, tightly, 'And I don't want any arguments, either. The shame of seeing you in a public place, making a spectacle of yourself, singing like that for money! Why, it's a wonder the constable wasn't down on you like a ton of bricks.' She stared him straight in the eye. 'It's called begging, Dad. You'll be standing on the corner selling bootlaces next.'

'Oh, Clover, darlin', you've a sharp tongue.' His eyes slid towards the swing doors of the small pub. 'Just one, my love, just to wet my whistle after all that singing. I'm as dry as the sands of the Sahara.'

'Not one,' said Clover firmly. 'Don't even think about it.'

Bert sighed. 'Oh, but you've grown hard with the years, daughter. When I think back to the sweet little girl you were . . .'

'Well, they can't shoot you for thinking,' said Clover grimly. 'Just keep it up, it'll do you no harm, thinking.'

Taken to task over the missing money, he produced a solitary coin which she suspected he hadn't had time to spend. With a longsuffering sigh, he handed it over, together with the coins he'd earned from his singing. 'Aye, a hard woman, Clover Blossom.'

The reason he gave for taking the money was so rambling that she put it out of her mind, resolutely turning her back on it but grimly cautioning herself that she must never let it happen again. As a hiding place, the old tea caddy was out.

Clover's mortification was complete when, returning from the bathroom one morning, the landlady confronted her on the narrow landing. It was too narrow to squeeze past, and with thudding heart Clover stood with her back pressed against the dark green door with the word Bathroom painted across it in big white letters. Silently she cursed herself for being such a ninny. But Mrs Marks was a formidable woman at the best of times.

'It's no good, you know,' she said in a harsh voice. 'It's a month now since I had any money from your father and I have a very presentable young gentleman eager to rent your rooms. If I thought your father would be able to pay, even in the next day or two, I'd gladly let you keep them. But as it is . . .' She shrugged, reading in Clover's eyes little hope of payment.

Clover found herself nodding, like one of those dolls you threw coconuts for in the fairground, the kind that jerk their heads up and down at the slightest movement and never seemed to stop. 'I'm sorry, Mrs Marks.' It sounded so banal, she tried again, in a firmer voice, 'I'm sure my father will settle everything once he gets round to it.' That didn't sound very good either.

'Aye, well, he'd better get round to it soon or you're both out on your ear, believe me. I've got a living to make, young lady, not like some who live the life of Riley while others wait for what's rightly theirs.'

The reference to Bert had Clover squaring her shoulders and looking the woman straight in the eye. 'My father always pays his debts, Mrs Marks.' He might be a bit slow about it, she thought wryly, but he paid them in the end. 'I will speak to him and I'm sure he will pay just as soon as he is able.'

'Aye, well . . .' Mrs Marks shook her head and walked away. She turned once to call back, 'And while we're at it, a hot bath is now one shilling instead of sixpence. With all the money I'm owed by some guests, my costs 'ave 'ad to go up.' Glowering, she moved on.

Bert was furious when Clover told him of the incident. 'She actually collared you on the landing, with all those ears flapping behind their doors, listening to every word?'

Clover's lips twisted. 'Yes, she did, and I think she means to tackle you in the morning.'

Clearly the charm he had practised on the landlady wasn't as effective as it once had been. In a quiet voice he told Clover to pack the few possessions they owned.

While she was busy doing that, he went out to find other lodgings. He took the tram, riding clear to the other side of town, knowing that if things didn't improve then the next move would have to be across country to another town.

Their old place in Moorfield was out of the question now. Cheap but decent lodgings would be difficult to come by. But he had friends in Moorfield, friends who had accepted drinks and favours from him in the past and would surely be willing to repay them now that his luck had changed. Maybe, after all, Moorfield was the place to go. Never once did he blame himself for their present adversity. If Adele hadn't died, if Eddie had still been part of the act – these were the thoughts uppermost in his mind.

He eventually found lodgings in a sleazy boarding house run by a down-at-heel woman who, although it was mid-afternoon, answered the door with rags still tied in her hair and wearing a food-stained dressing gown. There was a room the size of a broom cupboard for Clover with space only for a narrow wooden bed, while Bert was offered the use of the large front room. It smelled strongly of damp carpets and ancient soot. Glumly, Bert stared about him. But the terms were right and he thought Clover would be impressed by the pair of crimson velvet curtains that covered the bay window of the front room. The house had obviously seen better days.

Clover had heard of people doing 'moonlight flits'. It was a standing joke with comedians; Buster Bywater had a score of them based on that very subject. But never in her wildest imaginings did she think she would have to suffer the indignity of creeping down a dark staircase in the dead of night, pausing at every other step to hold her breath and listen. Snores came from behind closed bedroom doors. Bert held one finger to his lips, his eyes twinkling in the flickering shadows thrown by the gaslight left burning at the bottom of the stairs. Clover could have sworn he was enjoying himself.

She wasn't sorry to leave the boarding house, although she felt deeply ashamed that they were leaving owing money. Bert assured her he would return and pay every penny they owed Mrs Marks as soon as he could. And maybe, with the change of digs, would come a change in fortune.

Clover believed him. He was her father, wasn't he?

It didn't and they went through the procedure again a few weeks later, only this time the slattern of a landlady, being wise in the ways of impecunious lodgers, held on to their luggage, refusing to part with either of the battered suitcases until Bert produced the two weeks' rent he owed. This was disastrous for the two Blossoms. But Bert retaliated in his own way.

'Like it?' Grinning, he shook out the folds of crimson velvet curtain in front of Clover's startled eyes. She had noticed the brown paper parcel tied with string he had carried under one arm as they crept away. A cloud of dust rose from the folds of the curtains, making her sneeze. 'Not bad, eh?' he went on, complacently. 'I know you have a fancy for this colour. Plenty of stuff there to get your teeth into, my love. At least one new dress for you and, if you're clever enough, a jacket for me. We'd look a right treat, wouldn't we, dressed like that for our act?'

'What if she reports you to the police?' Clover still looked startled. 'Won't we get into trouble?

Bert scoffed. 'Won't know where we are, will she? I've tried the north end of town this time. Heard some nice things about the digs over there. Cheaper, too.'

The search for an opening went on, although Clover

suspected Bert didn't try too hard. Theatres in the town itself stayed open during the winter months, competing with the cinemas that were springing up all over. Only the end-of-pier shows closed their doors until the summer. Still, Bert thought, someone, somewhere, would want them. But it seemed his abrupt departure from the Summer Follies was well known in the town. He was classed as unreliable. No stage manager was willing to risk his show to such behaviour.

Bert had been out of work for three months. In the bitter December weather, with no money for beer or spirits any longer, he took to hanging around a small but busy café. A huge polished brass tea urn stood on the marble-topped counter, giving a warm glow to the room. The red and white starched curtains gave the place a homely look, making it popular with artistes who were 'resting'. Here they would sit, down at heel, with empty bellies, and order a cup of tea that would last them for hours. Deals were done at these tables, contracts examined. Well-known and not so well-known agents were seen amidst the fog of blue cigarette smoke. None, sadly, had anything to offer Bert.

With their frequent changes of address, it was difficult for any of their old friends to keep in touch. Miss Boyce discovered their latest address from Buster Bywater who had insisted on keeping track of them in case something came up that would suit them. Buster's fight was with Eddie, not his father, he told everyone. And if he waited long enough, maybe Imelda would come back . . .

Miss Boyce arrived on their doorstep one day when Clover's spirits were at their lowest ebb. Miserably she told the little spinster about the last landlady refusing to part with their luggage until the rent was paid in full.

Miss Boyce's cheeks flushed with indignation. 'But

she can't do that!' Then, after a pause, catching Clover's eye, 'Can she?'

Clover said she thought she could. 'Once we pay what is owing we will get our suitcases back but not before.'

When Miss Boyce asked whether Clover would consider it an interference if she offered to lend her father the money, Clover didn't know what to answer.

'You can't possibly go through a Lancashire winter without the thick underclothes and jerseys that that woman's holding on to,' Miss Boyce pointed out in her practical way.

'My mother would have gone without rather than borrow from anyone,' Clover said fretfully.

'Well, maybe, but really, I don't mind. I couldn't bear to think of you both cold and miserable, without your belongings.'

'But what about you? Won't you need it?'

'Don't be daft, child. I wouldn't be offering if I couldn't afford it.' She folded Clover's fingers round the notes. 'There, not another word.'

Clover took a deep breath, feeling her cheeks crimson with shame. 'If you're sure.'

'Of course I'm sure. Didn't I just say so? Pay that old biddy what you owe her and think no more of it.'

Clover smiled at her lovingly. She who could be sharp and cantankerous with other people had never been anything but kind and helpful to the Blossoms. Eddie had been fond of teasing her, saying she must promise never to marry until he was old enough to ask her himself, and the thin little face with its beaky nose would soften, and a hand reach out to tousle the boy's hair.

To make quite sure the landlady was paid, Clover suggested going herself. But Bert was adamant, insisting it was no job for a girl. 'She'll likely be insulting to you, love. I think you should let your old dad take care of this.'

'What if she accuses you of taking the curtains and makes trouble?' Clover asked. The woman could hardly have failed to notice their absence.

Bert shrugged, already on his way out. 'She's got no proof we took them. It could have been anybody in that house and by the look of some of 'em, they'd take the pennies from the begging bowl of a blind man.' He smiled. 'Don't you worry, soft words and a winning smile will have her eating out of my hand, and if that doesn't do the trick, an extra bob or two will keep her happy.'

Whatever wiles Bert employed, they worked. He returned with the suitcases and no more was heard from that particular landlady.

Miss Boyce brought over some Butterick patterns and with her help Clover laid the crimson velvet on the carpet of her bedroom and cut out a jacket for her father and a dress for herself, with a wide skirt – plenty of material so no need for skimping, said Miss Boyce. Later Miss Boyce gathered up the cut pieces and took them with her, against Clover's protestations, saying she would do the long seams on the machine she used in the theatre. The rest, however, Clover insisted on doing by hand.

It gave purpose to her days, stitching at that crimson velvet, watching the garments take shape before her eyes. The dress was in the style of her parents' youth, tight-waisted and flaring out over the knees. Bert said that it was much more elegant than the current fashion for ever shorter skirts and waists somewhere around the hips. 'Getting to look like a bunch of lads, so you are,' he grumbled. 'No shape at all.' On the front of the jacket she made for him she sewed black silk frogging, using a length of trimming Miss Boyce had given Adele long ago, along with lengths of cotton lace, ribbons in a multitude of colours, Broderie Anglaise. 'If they're any use to you,' she'd told Adele, 'please take them. They've been lying around for ages.'

As Clover sewed she thought of Eddie and wondered how he was getting on. And if Imelda, in that vast new country, was wearing short skirts and listening to jazz music. It had been some time since Eddie's last letter in which he'd told them about getting a passage aboard a liner sailing for New York. 'The cheapest fare possible,' he'd written. 'Practically steerage. I can only pray it will be a smooth crossing, for I fear we will have to spend most of our time out on the deck, the cabin being so small and cramped, shared by a number of us.'

Chapter Eleven

They had obtained passage on the *Empress of the Seas*, using almost the last of Imelda's hoard to pay for their tickets. The weeks in Liverpool, staying in lodgings, had depleted it and Eddie had had to be firm about the excursions suggested by Imelda. 'We can't afford it,' he'd say. Then, seeing the sulky pout come to her mouth, 'Once we're in New York we'll make up for it. I promise.'

He wondered if she was having second thoughts about sailing for she'd admitted that the short journey from Ireland when she'd first come over with the tinkers had had her stomach lurching something terrible.

In fact, even before they sailed, still in dock, the swell of the ship had her stomach doing all manner of strange things. Now they were actually on board, she wondered if she should have given more thought to this journey. Had she done the right thing? There was no question in her mind that leaving Buster Bywater was the right thing. She'd have done that sooner or later. But was her decision to travel to a strange land, to the other side of the world, with a man – well, a boy, really – wise? Misgivings plagued her. Feelings quite foreign to Imelda.

Eddie, now they were on board and the adventure underway, did not notice her moods and sullen silences. He was totally swept up in the excitement of the voyage, the sense of freedom away from the carping tongue of his father.

They settled into a routine of visits to the deck, brief visits in Imelda's case, for although she disliked the dark, stuffy cabin which they shared with an emigrant Irish family, she disliked even more the heaving deck with the green swell of the Atlantic Ocean so close and threatening everywhere she looked.

Keeping her balance while they strolled the deck was wellnigh impossible and she clung tensely to Eddie's arm, complaining bitterly. She longed to feel the firm earth under her feet again, not this nightmarish rolling motion of the ship; see buildings and people and traffic instead of the endless stretch of green water. The seasickness that had overtaken her on the first day out had been brief. One blessing, she supposed. Eddie enjoyed the fresh, salt-tasting air. With the natural grace and balance his dance steps had nurtured, the heaving deck under his feet was no problem.

They struck up an acquaintance with a good-natured, middle-aged American who introduced himself as Nick Farrel. Eddie wondered if the name should mean something to them, for he saw the look the man gave them as he said it. Nick Farrel was used to awe in a person's eyes when they heard his name. This young English couple seemed ignorant of his celebrity status. A refreshing change, he thought. Intrigued by the young couple, especially when he learned Eddie came from a showbusiness family, he talked of actors and other people connected with showbusiness, whom he seemed to know by their first names. 'Just you wait until you walk down Broadway,' he enthused. 'See for yourself all the lights and glitter. You're never goin' to believe it, nobody does at first. Make sure you don't miss Herald Square. It sure takes some gettin' used to.'

For Imelda, just visualising the scene dispelled some of the wretchedness of the tiny, claustrophobic cabin.

At last there was the excitement of seeing for the first

time the Statue of Liberty, holding aloft her torch of freedom. Eddie recited the words engraved at her feet: 'Give me your tired, your poor, your huddled masses, yearning to breathe free. The wretched refuse of your teeming shores. Send them, the homeless, tempest tossed, to me. I lift my lamp beside the golden shore.'

His arm about her shoulders, they stood at the rail of the ferry, marvelling at the sight. 'That's us, all right.' He smiled down at her. 'We're going to be happy, aren't we?' His voice held the warmth of a young man deeply in love.

'Of course, silly.'

'And now that we're here, I'll soon find my feet again. I'll give you a home fit for a queen. *Better* than a queen.'

Amidst the hustle and the bustle as they left the *Empress*, their new-found friend had found time to bid them goodbye and good luck. He felt in his waistcoat pocket and produced a small business card. 'Keep in touch. I'll be staying in this hotel if you ever want to contact me. I'll probably be there for quite some time.' Almost as an afterthought, he asked, 'Have you got someplace to stay?'

Eddie had to admit that they hadn't. Nick Farrel nodded and, taking a small notebook from his pocket, he scribbled a few lines on it and passed it to Eddie. 'Well, until you're settled, this will do as good as anywhere. It's cheap and the woman who runs it serves good grub – when she's in the mood, that is. Anyway, it'll suit you until something else turns up. Looking for digs in a place you don't know can be a daunting experience.'

New York was a hive of activity. Imelda had never seen, never imagined, there could be so many cars and people all in one place, all rushing madly about, the trolley cars crammed. She held tightly onto Eddie's arm, urging him to find Broadway and the famous Herald Square.

'First things first,' said Eddie. 'We've still got to find this address.' He glanced down at the piece of paper he held in his hand. 'We'll get ourselves settled and then we'll go out and explore.'

'And get something to eat,' begged Imelda. 'I'm starving.'

He gave her a fond look. 'When are you ever anything else?' he grinned. Imelda pouted and punched his arm.

The address to which they had been directed proved to be one of a row of crumbling terrace houses in a district that had obviously seen better days. Number 238 looked as though it might fall down at any moment and the glass panel in the front door was broken. Children of all ages and shades of skin played in the street, their voices competing against each other in order to see who could shout the loudest. Makeshift wooden stalls were parked in the gutters, selling all manner of things. As they approached the stone steps leading up to the front door, a couple of boys hurtled past, one deliberately barging into a fruit stall. Apples rolled onto the pavement and quick as lightning apples disappeared into trouser pockets and down the front of jerseys.

'Looks a lively enough place,' Eddie commented as he led the way up the steps to the front door. Imelda didn't answer.

The small garden was littered with refuse of every kind. There was a light in the front downstairs window and moments after Eddie knocked there was the sound of footsteps and the door opened a few inches. A woman's voice said, 'Yes, who is it?'

'We're looking for lodgings,' said Eddie. 'We were given this address by someone at the docks.'

There was the rattle of a chain and the door opened. 'You'd better come in,' she said and beckoned them to follow her along the dark corridor. The sounds of a baby crying and voices raised in argument filtered down from the upstairs regions. The woman opened a door at the far end of the hall and turned up the gaslight. 'It's all I've got at the moment. But for the money it's good value.'

Eddie looked about him. The room seemed reasonably clean with a thin carpet on the floor and a double bed against the far wall. The woman turned to face him. She was large and heavily built, running to seed and no longer young but still handsome in a bold, coarse sort of way. As she examined Eddie, a smile of interest lit her face.

'I'm Mrs Riley, Peg to me friends,' she said. 'What do you say about the room, then?' After the first astute look, she totally ignored Imelda. She smiled again at Eddie. There was an unmistakable invitation in that smile and Eddie felt his cheeks flush.

'My name is Edward Blossom and this is my fiancée, Miss Imelda . . .'

He hesitated, biting his lip, and smoothly Imelda murmured, 'Jones. Imelda Jones.'

'Well, that's nice,' the woman said. 'Although you not being married yet, I don't know if I should let you have a double room like this.'

'We plan to marry as soon as we can arrange it,' Imelda told her. 'In any case,' plumping herself down on the edge of the bed and smiling, 'I don't see why you should quibble as long as you get your rent.' Pointedly she gazed about her. 'It ain't exactly Buckingham Palace, is it?'

'All right,' said Eddie after a sleepless night of infants crying and the front door slamming well into the wee hours of the morning, 'so it isn't perfect, but we won't be here long enough to let it worry us. The first thing I've got to do is put out some feelers about the job situation.'

Imelda frowned. 'I thought you were going to take me to see the sights today.'

Eddie smiled. 'I suppose that would be more interesting. There'll always be jobs waiting for someone fit and young like me. Come on then, let's go and see the sights of New York.'

A weak winter sun shone, sparkling on the river, and while they still had money to spend the world for Imelda was full of energy and magic. They visited the Statue of Liberty by boat, climbing to a dizzy height up into the head, the wonderful panorama of the Hudson River spread at their feet. They walked in Central Park and strolled arm in arm along Broadway at night, gaping in amazement at the lights twinkling in the blue November dusk.

Eddie gave in to her pleas of going to a cinema to see a film advertised in blazing lights over the entrance: *The Heart of the Hills*. It was dark and warm inside and smelled of popcorn. They sat in the back row, Eddie's arm about her shoulders, and stole kisses. Tightly clasping his arm as they came out, Imelda said, 'You're much more 'andsome than that actor bloke. I bet you could act better'n 'im, too.'

'Imelda! That was John Gilbert!'

Imelda sniffed. 'So what if it was?' She gave his arm a squeeze. 'I still think you're better lookin'.'

With the resilience of the young, they settled into their new life quite smoothly. Imelda loved the free and easy life, making friends with their neighbours, answering questions about England as though she were an expert on the subject, making them laugh. They were a happy, extrovert crowd, a refreshing change from the class-ridden English who had made her feel as though she was still only a poor gypsy brat.

The days sped by until one morning they didn't have enough money to buy even a loaf of bread. It was time to face reality.

Time for Eddie to put to the test his assertion that there were jobs in plenty, just waiting to fall into his lap. In a town humming with the new, syncopated rhythms, his own compositions, a pile which he had brought with him, would sell like hot cakes. He would arrange a new act for himself, singing his own songs.

In this busy, bustling city, jobs as street sweepers, men who emptied garbage bins and those who washed up mountains of dirty crockery in the beetle-infested kitchens of pavement cafés, were easy to find. Eddie scorned them, resolutely persevering in searching for employment more to his talents. His feet burned from the miles of hard pavements he covered every day, from the stairs he climbed to the dusty offices with the names of the theatrical agents spelled out in gold on the frosted glass door.

'Blossoms?' The cigar-chewing agent regarded him from behind his cluttered desk. 'They're flowers, ain't they?' The sneer in the voice made Eddie want to squirm.

His voice calm, he explained, 'The Four Blossoms was the name of our act. A family act. My surname is Blossom.'

The man gave him a look of indifference mixed with scorn and reached for the telephone which never seemed to stop ringing. 'Sorry, kid, family acts ain't popular no more.'

'But it isn't a family act now – I sing and dance and play the piano. I've written some of my own songs. Look . . .' Ignoring the man's back, pointedly turned on him as he swung his chair round, Eddie reached into the holdall he carried, pulling out the sheafs of music. 'If you'll just listen to one, I'm sure you'll like it.'

The man waved him away, and continued to talk on the phone.

Car horns and the clankety-clank of trolley cars filled Eddie's waking hours. And there were people, always people, crowding the sidewalks, moving with great purpose. Gaunt faces and hungry eyes, all searching for a lost hope.

Tired and dispirited, he returned home, finding the beginning of each new day harder to face. Imelda, losing her temper one day, screamed at him, 'What do you think you are, anyway? Bloody royalty? The Right Royal Blossoms, eh? Can't do anything but singing and acting daft on the stage. Wouldn't dream of dirtying their 'ands with manual labour, would they? Oh, no, much too good for that!'

'Imelda!' Ashen-faced, Eddie rushed at her, grabbing her hands as they came up to rake his cheeks. 'Stop that. You don't know what you're saying.' He held her at arm's length and looked into her eyes and suddenly she was weeping, fat tears rolling down her cheeks, her mouth twisted in a little girl's petulance.

'Sweetheart!' He drew her to him. Clinging, she sobbed with all the passion of a spoiled child.

'I'm sorry. I can't help it. But I thought everything would be different, and it's not.' The reality Imelda had to face was the last thing she was prepared to accept: the certainty that she was pregnant.

Clover was also worrying about where the next meal would come from. When she questioned her father about work he became evasive, saying he'd got a couple of irons in the fire that looked promising. If she'd heard that once, she'd heard it a dozen times. The despondency that was her constant companion threatened to overwhelm her. Something had to be done.

The next time she was passing the newly opened Argyle Theatre, she stopped to gaze at the posters outside. They showed pictures of scantily clad girls and advertised a comic whose reputation she knew to be far worse than Buster's. You couldn't call this a family show, she thought. Not by a long chalk. Still, if it was what some people wanted, why not? The world had waved goodbye to the good-goody girls of pre-war days and the public was demanding all manner of things new.

Acting on an impulse, she pushed open the swing doors of the entrance and went into a cool, dark foyer. In for a penny, she thought. Squaring her shoulders she approached an elderly man who was busy sorting through books of tickets in a small glass enclosure. He looked up, suddenly aware of her, his eyes questioning. 'I'd like to see the manager,' she told him crisply. Her well-modulated voice and air of quiet dignity told him that this wasn't some tart off the street, out to make trouble, and he himself escorted her to the manager's office.

A dark young man looked up from the papers spread across the top of his desk. She met his gaze squarely, with no sign of nervousness. 'Damn!' he thought. 'What's that bugger Jack been up to now?' Jack Benson was the resident comic and girls appearing out of nowhere were becoming an aggravation he could do without. Still, this girl didn't seem to be one of those.

'The young lady wanted to see you, sir,' the elderly man said.

The manager leaned back in his chair, his thumbs hooked into the armholes of his waistcoat and nodded. 'All right, Michael. Thanks.' He waited for Clover to state her business. She did, haltingly, the words tripping themselves up, for suddenly all her calmness had left her and she was as nervous as a kitten.

He got up and, still not speaking, brought forward a chair from against the wall, placing it in front of his desk. He motioned for her to sit down. Clover did, arranging her skirts over her knees, conscious of the bold eyes that watched her. They brought a bright flush to her cheeks and she lowered her eyes, twisting her hands in her lap. At last he spoke. 'So you want me to give you a job, is that it?' He had a surprisingly pleasant voice, at variance with his looks which Clover thought rather rough and forbidding.

She nodded. 'My father and I have a singing and dancing act and he tells a few jokes.' She heard a groan and looked up sharply.

'I've got acts like that coming out of my ears,' he said matter-of-factly, not being rude. 'What's your father's name? Perhaps I know him. I haven't seen you before. I wouldn't have forgotten that face.'

Clover's chin tilted. 'My father is Bert Blossom and we were billed as the Four Blossoms. That is until my mother died two years ago and my brother left to go to America.'

Realising the manager was still studying her closely – dreadful man, he hadn't even introduced himself to her yet! – Clover pulled herself together and sat up straighter. He reached for a pencil and tapped it irritatingly on the desk top, his lips pursed.

'I know of your father,' he said. Pity, he thought. The girl's attractive in an unformed sort of way, with her pale, flawless skin and dark brown hair caught back from her face in a ponytail, the hair above her smooth forehead short and curly. The blue eyes that gazed at him were wide and questioning, like the eyes of a still learning child. Bert Blossom's reputation had spread ruthlessly and he had no intention of risking the very

promising show he had put together with so much effort
to a drunkard. Still, it was a damn shame, the girl looked
worthy enough, though hardly more than a child.

'And what do they call you?' he asked.

'I'm Clover Blossom.'

'The name suits you.' He startled Clover by swinging
round and completing a full circle in his swivel chair.

'A trick of mine when I'm faced with a question
I don't want to answer,' he grinned. 'It gives me a
moment's breathing space. Not that I need it in this
case, Miss Blossom. I'm sorry, but I have to tell you
I wouldn't touch you with a barge pole.'

Clover gasped at the crudeness of the man. Before
she could think up a sufficiently biting reply, he went
on, 'I hear your father is spending most of his time in
bars. That must be distressing for you. Everyone likes
a drink at the end of a hard day, but it can play the very
devil with a man's career if you give it half a chance.
Which, by the sound of it, your father has. Given it
half a chance, I mean.'

'My father meets agents and people, theatre people,
in bars and cafés. They spend a lot of time discussing
contracts over a drink.' It was the explanation Bert
had given her one day when she had asked the eternal
question about how seriously he was taking the problem
of finding work.

The young man looked at her and thought: My
God, here is all the composure of a woman combined
with the trusting nature of an eight-year-old! That
father of hers must be a right bastard to pull the
wool over her eyes like this. The pencil continued its
tap-tapping.

'How old are you?'

Clover hesitated, about to say eighteen, knew how
ridiculous that would be and spoke the truth. 'Sixteen.'

His lips twisted. 'A mere babe!' He sounded angry.

She blinked, unable to see any reason for his anger and not a little puzzled by it.

The young man watched the sunlight streaming through the window behind her, for it was one of those bright, sunny days that frequently occur on this north-west coast in winter. It struck unexpected golden lights in her hair. The blue eyes gazed steadily at him, accepting the fact that here was another blow to her self-esteem. It was an unenviable task, telling eager young girls, many of whom had run away from home, that they weren't suitable. 'Come back in a year or two,' he'd advise, seeing the eager light in their eyes fade, to be replaced by the dull look of rejection. 'Keep trying. If you're persistent enough and you've really got what it takes, you'll win in the end.'

He didn't need to give this homily to Clover. The girl was a professional, her background told him that much. She was quite likely talented, too.

She smiled suddenly. 'May I ask who sews for you?'

Startled by her question, he raised an eyebrow. 'Sews? You mean the stage outfits?' He shrugged. 'We have our own wardrobe mistress. Why?'

'I'll make a bargain with you.'

'What do you have to bargain with? Don't tell me you're a Paris-trained couturière as well as the mainstay of your father's act?'

She ignored the sarcasm. 'I can sew, make dresses and men's clothing, jackets and shirts.' She thought of Miss Boyce. 'I had an excellent teacher.'

All this in one little slip of a girl, he thought. Involuntarily, his eyes fell on the young breasts pushing at the material of her blouse.

'I can keep the dressing rooms clean, too, if you want.'

'Who is going to take care of your father while you're accomplishing all this?'

'I can. I'm strong.'

She looked anything but strong. Shaking his head, he grinned at her. 'I bet you could turn a house inside out and still come up smelling of lilacs.'

The office door opened and the elderly man poked his head in the opening. 'There's someone asking to see you, Mr Holt. That Mr Troon.'

'Hmmm.' Pushing his chair back, the young man stood up. Cocking an eyebrow at Clover he said, 'Don't think I haven't appreciated your offer, Miss Blossom, but as you can see, I'm busy.'

'Does that mean no?' Something inside Clover seemed to shrivel. After plucking up her courage, facing him so bravely, he was still turning her away like a valueless object. He was already at the door, holding it open, clearly in a hurry for her to be gone.

'I'm afraid so, my dear. Don't take it to heart.' His grin widened. 'I'll wager in another year or two men won't turn you down quite so casually.'

Feeling again the flush sweep up to the roots of her hair, Clover hurried out, drawing her skirts to one side as she passed him, as though the slightest contact with this insufferable creature would contaminate her.

The gesture wasn't lost on Harry Holt. Clover heard his amused chuckle as she crossed the foyer to the door.

Bert was furious when she told him what she'd done; she'd been unable to keep it from him when he asked what she'd been doing that morning.

'Do you want people to think I can't look after my own daughter?' he asked, his voice rising on an angry note. As usual, he'd been drinking. Sometimes it made him mellow and fatuous, at other times it was as if an entirely alien entity entered his body and took charge of his emotions.

She said, quietly, 'I was trying to help. You don't
know how bored I get, sitting in this flaming room all
day while you're out. I need to work, Daddy, need to
occupy myself. To get out and meet people.'

'And you'd meet them, would you, scrubbing floors
for some fat old producer and sewing until your eyes
gave out?'

'He wasn't old and he wasn't fat.' She thought of the
thin, hawk-like features of the young man behind the
desk, his barely concealed aggression, and added, 'But
you're right, of course. I just thought that if it would
bring in a bit of money—'

Bert caught her to him, holding her in a bear hug.
'I've told you before, you mustn't bother your pretty
little head about that. Doing menial work for someone
else! Ugh!' He pulled a comic face. 'Whatever would
your dear mother think? Bringing in money is my
department. Our luck must change sometime, good
fortune must look our way once in a while and smile
on us, and do you know, my love, I have a strong
suspicion that any day now it will.'

'Oh, Daddy,' Clover sighed, turning away from him.
She'd lost count of the number of times she'd heard him
say that. They were no nearer paying off their debts now
than they ever were. The money they owed Miss Boyce
nagged her conscience particularly. When would they
ever be solvent enough to repay her kindness? Worry
was like a sickness that settled within her, making her
lethargic and clumsy. The quicksilver mind that once
had been able to remember the words and music of
a new song or dance routine at the first playing was
now sluggish, unable to decide on a simple thing like
whether to buy a piece of skate for supper or mince for
a cottage pie.

Not long afterwards, Bert came home with the news
that he'd made up his mind. They would move to

Moorfield after all. He had friends in Moorfield, friends who would be only too willing to help him on his way.

Clover hated herself for the feeling of scepticism that overcame her at his confident words. Try as she might, she had no faith that the downward spiral they seemed to be trapped in would stop once they got to Moorfield.

And yet, what could she do but trust him, even with all the signs pointing in the opposite direction? Then, out of the blue, came an offer for Bert to help out at the Silver Mermaid. It seemed their regular helper had come down with a particularly nasty dose of 'flu and they needed someone in a hurry. It would only be until the man recovered, the barman explained, but the money might help. Bert accepted with alacrity. It proved to be for only two weeks. To Clover's relief she was able to pay back Miss Boyce and the rent on their present place and still have enough left over to purchase two single train tickets to Moorfield.

Maybe this time it really would be different, thought Bert. He would have to make it different if he was to keep Clover's affections. The damage this kind of life was doing to her was all too clear. If she went, life wouldn't be worth living.

Chapter Twelve

Bidding a silent farewell to the seaside town was almost a relief. A little of Bert's optimism had rubbed off on Clover, although there were tears in her eyes as she said goodbye to Miss Boyce.

Some of her hope left her when they arrived at the noisy, soot-stained station of Moorfield and Bert told her to sit on their battered suitcases in a corner of the platform and wait for him to return. 'I'm going to call on a house agent I know,' he explained. 'I'm sure he'll be able to fix us up with something.' He smiled and bent to tuck the woollen scarf more warmly about her neck. 'It won't be a palace, as the old song says, I can't afford a palace, but we'll make it as temporary as we know how, eh?'

Clover murmured that she understood. Before going he gave one last warning. 'Don't speak to anyone. If anyone tries to speak to you, ignore them. If they persist, call a porter. I shouldn't be long.'

Clover watched him walk away. He was away for so long that the more fatherly of the porters began to eye her with anxiety. 'You all right, love?' they called as they passed with their heavily loaded trolleys. Clover smiled and nodded, mindful of her father's words about not speaking to anyone.

At last she saw him coming towards her through the dusk. Bending to pick up the suitcases, he said, 'Sorry I've been so long, love. My mate wasn't in the office and I had to track him down.'

171

Catching a whiff of his breath, Clover had no trouble guessing where he'd found his mate.

Still, they were here at their destination, with, she presumed, an address to go to and hidden away on her person she still had some of the money Bert had earned at the Silver Mermaid.

Eventually they turned into a rubbish-littered street at the back of the town. Pausing outside a tiny house, with a narrow door and one small, paned window downstairs matched by another upstairs, Clover stared in dismay. It was identical to all the others that straggled down the hill where a murky-looking canal was guarded by a line of rusty railings. She heard Bert beside her say jovially, 'Nothing to write home about, I know, but it's a roof over our heads and my mate is letting us have it for peanuts.'

On entering the kitchen, smelling of soot and God knows what else, Clover had the thought that even peanuts would be asking too much.

The winter spent in that dilapidated house was one Clover would never forget. At Christmas they had a Christmas card from Miss Boyce, for Clover had written a short note, informing her of their new address, followed by a white lie that they were all right and settling down nicely.

The card stood open on the mantelpiece, next to the mahogany cased clock that had stood on various mantelpieces for as long as Clover could remember. The card with its picture of snow and scarlet berries and children skating on a pond of ice brought a brightness to that part of the room; the only brightness during that time of depression.

They spent most of their time indoors. Wrapped in blankets, they huddled over the cheerless fire. On the few occasions Bert could bring himself to venture into the icy weather to seek work, Clover would stand at the window, staring at the endless drip of the rain falling on the grim street and mean houses opposite.

She watched the boys with short trousers, their bare knees red with cold, the knuckles of their hands swollen with chilblains, as they tipped buckets of water on the sloping street. Overnight it would freeze and provide a grand slope on which to slide. She smiled as a young mother, just outside her front door, buttoned her little girl into a threadbare coat, lovingly tucking the child's long hair under a hand-knitted beret. The child stood quietly, accepting her mother's ministrations with composure, and then with a shrill 'Ta-ra' ran off to join her friends. One morning Clover had laughed when a cart, loaded high with potatoes, overturned just down the road, scattering its contents all over the cobbles. How the children swarmed over it, filling whatever they could find with potatoes, ignoring the driver's red-faced cursing.

It seemed things would never improve. Deep in her heart she knew Bert would never change. He would go on in the way he always had, evading his responsibilities whenever possible, a weathercock shunted by the wind.

'If we're very careful, we'll manage fine,' he said whenever she brought up the subject of seeking work herself.

'There's that general store where I worked last winter,' she said. 'I'm sure he'd take me back.'

But that was clear on the other side of town and would mean tram fares, there and back each day, taking quite a chunk out of the small wages he would pay her. 'Besides which,' Bert pointed out, 'you'd be leaving in the dark each morning and coming home in the dark.' He shook his head. 'No, my love, I don't think we've quite reached that stage yet. Something will turn up. You're not to worry. Let your old dad handle it.' He smiled reassuringly. 'After all, that's what I'm here for.'

But nobody was willing to employ an out-of-work stage artiste with bloodshot eyes and trembling hands.

Returning home one morning from a desultory walk, Clover's steps slowed as she came to a small corner shop. A group of women and children had gathered. They watched as a man in his shirtsleeves taped a notice to the window. It announced a half-price sale of dented tin goods: corned beef, condensed milk, baked beans.

Clover's fingers jingled the few pennies in her pocket. When the grocer went back into the shop and opened his doors for business, she was one of the first inside, jostling and pushing with the best of them. A tin of corned beef would make a good hash, topped with mashed potatoes, and the condensed milk in tea or cocoa would save on sugar.

Their only means of lighting was an ancient oil lamp. Leaving it as long as she could, eventually she would have to remove the glass and touch a match to the wick. The glass safely replaced, the small room was revealed in all its squalidness. The walls and ceiling, blackened by decades of coal fires and uncleaned chimneys, made it appear even smaller than it was, casting thick shadows in the corners. A heavy chest of drawers with a cracked mirror on the back faced the door, taking up one whole wall of the room, while directly in the middle of the kitchen a cheap deal table and two chairs filled what little space there was left.

Upstairs there were two tiny bedrooms, so cold it was agony to venture into them and Bert often slept on the tattered fireside rug before the grate, wrapped up in a blanket, ladling coal onto the fire before he slept.

The ordeal she found hardest to bear was the tiny red bites bequeathed on her by the various bugs that shared

the house with them. Waking one morning not long
after they had arrived, she had pulled back the blankets
and seen them in her bed, and when she removed her
nightgown and saw the weals where she had been bitten
and where she had scratched in her sleep, she had to
fight down the fit of hysteria that rose in her. Frantically
she began beating at the tiny creatures with her shoe,
then gathered the brown bodies together in a dustpan.
She carried them downstairs, shivering with revulsion
as she threw them on the fire.

When spring brought the tender green of new foliage
to the trees in Coronation Park and the daffodils lifted
their golden yellow trumpets to the sun, Clover hardly
noticed. She was still waiting for Bert to pull himself
together, to offer her new hope by coming home and
announcing he'd got a job. The friends of whom he'd
boasted, the ones who would do anything for him, had
not materialised. There had been no further addresses
from the 'mate' who worked in the estate office and
who had found them this place. Bert himself was silent
and withdrawn. All he wanted to do when he was at
home was crouch over the fire and wait silently for
the thin stews and chunks of bread that formed their
usual meal of the day. Yet through it all she remained
loyal and loving, ready to do battle with the world for
her father.

This evening Bert was late home from wherever he'd
spent the afternoon. Opening the front door, for the
evening was mild, she stood on the step, gazing forlornly
down the quiet street.

'Oh, Mum!' she cried inside herself. 'Oh, Mum!'
For a second, the image of her mother's face floated
in her mind, as though trying to comfort her. There
was a clatter of footsteps, breaking the illusion, and she
looked up hopefully.

But it wasn't Bert. It was the woman from next door,

a Mrs Kelly who had been friendly. 'Your da not home yet?' she enquired brightly. Her sharp eyes were full of speculation. The house next door had been empty for so long it had been considered derelict. Nobody could have been more surprised when the man and his daughter had come to see it and had moved in immediately. Mrs Kelly, like many others living near, had wondered about the history of the pair. They spoke with a good accent, the girl, anyway, not the broad vowels of the local people. There was much conjecture in the street for weeks after they moved in.

Clover shook her head at Mrs Kelly's question. 'No. I expect he met someone and they're talking.'

'Aye, well.' Mrs Kelly smiled knowingly. 'We all know what kind of talking men get up to when they get together. Especially if the meeting takes place in a pub.' She fitted the key into her lock, opening the door with a quick twist of her fingers. 'Your father would be late on the Day of Judgment, lass, but he will smile and the pearly gates will open and he'll be let in. It's a long time since I've seen such a good-looking man. And such charming manners! You must be very proud of him.'

Truthfully, Clover answered, 'Oh, I am, Mrs Kelly. There's none better than my dad.' She smiled and stepped back into the passageway, closing the door on what her neighbour no doubt hoped would have been a good gossip if she'd lingered on the doorstep. Mrs Kelly had that look about her, of wanting to know more about the father and daughter who had taken the house next door.

It was late when Bert finally arrived home. Clover flew at him as the key grated in the lock. 'Where on earth have you been? I've been worried sick.'

'I've been to Darnley.'

Darnley, she knew, was a largish place a few miles to the east. 'Whatever were you doing in Darnley?'

'I've got a job.'

Clover blinked, unable to believe her ears. Bert laughed. 'That's good news, lass, and when you hear good news you're supposed to smile.'

'Of course it is. Oh, Dad, how wonderful! What kind of a job?'

He came towards the fire, holding out his hands to the weak flames, and sat down in the hard chair. 'Now, just listen, love. It's only temporary. We'll be working as busy as ever in a couple of months, once the summer is here. The trouble is people are tired of seeing the same old faces all the time and want something new. That's what's been holding us back.'

Eddie had said the same thing, she couldn't help but think, but you didn't want to know. Stubbornly, she repeated, 'What kind of a job, Dad?'

'Paying the piano at the Darnley Arms.'

It wasn't quite what Clover was expecting, but she bent to kiss his brow before going to the old kitchen range and stirring the coals with the long iron poker. The warmth felt good and her spirits rose.

'Why, I think that's just fine,' she said, turning to smile at him.

He raised an eyebrow in an exaggerated gesture of surprise. 'You approve, then?'

'Of course I do.'

'Well, you've got to take the ups and downs in this business, especially these days. And as I said, it won't be for long, lass.'

The thought crossed her mind that with this job the temptation to drink would be that much greater. Lately, there hadn't been any money for drinking, which was the one thing in their new life for which she was grateful. Bert had suffered as much from that as from anything else.

She turned towards him, then stayed silent when she

saw his eyes bright with the prospect of working again. She hadn't the heart to put a damper on his pleasure by raising objections.

'What can I do to help?' she asked instead, crossing over to him.

He smiled at her, one hand lifting to smooth the hair from her cheek. 'You're a good girl, Clover. So understanding.' His little girl was growing up fast, he thought, losing that coltish girlhood he had loved. She was beginning to resemble Adele so much that at times it pained him to look at her, reminding him as it did of those early days of sun and laughter.

He suddenly gripped her hands in his, gazing at her so earnestly that for a moment she was frightened.

'What is it, Daddy? Is something wrong?'

'I'd better tell you straightaway that there's a catch in it. Now, don't say anything until I've explained, but I don't get paid for the job, just pocket the tips the customers give me.'

He didn't mention the fact that it would also enable him to get free drinks.

Clover looked thoughtful. 'That won't be much, will it? How will we manage?'

'Something, no matter how small, is better than the nothing we get now.' He gazed into her face, reading there the fading glow of hope, and was suddenly afraid. 'But together we'll manage, won't we? You won't ever let some man come into our lives and take you away from me?'

Her heart contracted with emotion and she hugged him tightly, feeling more inadequate than ever, trying to convey all the love she felt for this feckless man who was her father.

'Don't be silly. What man could take your place?' Responsibility for her poor, misguided father stretched clear into the future and for a moment the weight of it made her ache. She pushed it aside and knelt by his chair, her skirts spread out on the faded, threadbare carpet. 'I'll take care of you, Daddy. You know I will. As though you could ever believe anything else.' And she saw he was asleep, head sagging on his chest, a soft snoring coming from the parted lips.

Chapter Thirteen

The Darnley Arms was adjacent to the local music hall. It had an entrance leading directly from the music hall foyer and was a great favourite with the regular theatre-goers. During intervals the bar staff were kept busy and Bert soon became something of a celebrity.

Repelled by the thought of the long evenings spent alone in the miserable house, Clover begged to be allowed to go with him. 'I'll wait in the foyer of the theatre,' she said. 'There'll be seats there. I'll be all right.'

Bert looked doubtful.

'I'll be all right,' she said again, firmly. 'It will be better than staying here, all on my own, with nothing to do.' And, that way, she thought, I can keep an eye on you.

Bert was expected to perform only in the evenings. They fell into a pattern of the two of them taking the tram each day to Darnley. While Bert played the piano and sang all the old favourites, Clover waited on a shabby velvet seat by the far wall of the music hall lobby and tried to make herself as inconspicuous as possible. People came and went in a constant stream, the double doors leading to the auditorium swinging open to admit a drift of song or music. It was like lifeblood to Clover, that glimpse of a world she had been forced to relinquish.

One evening, not long after Bert had started in his

new job, the commissionaire of the theatre, an old soldier in a fancy uniform with gold epaulettes on his shoulders, invited her to stand at the back of the stalls. He felt sorry for the girl, sitting there so quietly each night, waiting for her father. 'Enjoy the show,' he told her, smiling. 'Better than waiting out here all on your tod.' He showed her to a spot in the shadows behind the last row of seats and gratefully Clover stood like a shadow in the warm darkness. At once, all the old familiar sensations were there – the tingling animation as the curtain rose on the lighted stage, the expectant murmur of a hushed audience as the music began. She hadn't realised she missed it so much.

The old commissionaire began to hold the seat nearest to the aisle in the back row for her whenever the theatre wasn't too full. One night a comedian who reminded her vividly of Buster Bywater took it into his head to indulge a noisy audience with jokes not usually in his repertoire. It was late, a second-house performance and no children in the crowd, and the customers roared with laughter as one blue joke after another flowed over the row of lights.

The commissionaire cocked an ear and then with flushed cheeks hurried Clover to the theatre foyer. 'Can't 'ave you listening to things like that,' he scolded. 'Whatever would your dad say?' He gazed at her, a worried frown on his forehead. 'Be all right, will you, lass? Your dad shouldn't be long.'

She smiled and assured the elderly man she would be fine. Left alone, she wandered over to the glass-fronted posters just inside the doorway leading to the bar. She pushed the door open the merest fraction, peering round its edge into the bar, and heard a voice call out, 'Come in, ducks! Don't dilly-dally in't door like that!'

On cue, Bert began playing the popular song, 'My old man said follow the van', and Clover felt herself being

urged into the crowded room veiled with blue cigarette
smoke and warm with the crush of bodies. Red-faced
men in shabby suits, bowler hats pushed to the backs
of their heads, stood about the long mahogany bar, their
images reflected in the fancy gilt mirror, glasses of beer
in their fists, all talking at the same time. The ladies with
them turned to look at Clover with speculative frowns;
then with a shrug, seeing no competition there, they
turned back to their glasses of port and lemon.

The landlady of the Darnley Arms, a large woman
with hair dyed an improbable shade of black, who went
by the name of Mrs Starkey although there was no
evidence of a Mr Starkey, watched the girl warily. She
wanted no truck with under-age clients.

Suddenly shy, Clover stood by the piano, turning the
pages of the sheet music Bert used, resolutely ignoring
the glasses of ale that stood on the top of the upright.
Then, urged on by a jocular crowd, Bert struck up the
chorus of a popular song, saying in a low voice, 'Come
on, lass, give us a song. They'll love it.'

Clover began in a hesitant voice, not really loud
enough to be heard over the voices and laughter. Then
someone called for silence and minutes later the entire
bar was chuckling as, gaining confidence, hands on
hips, cheekily she sang, 'I make 'im nice and comfy
then I toddles off to work, I do the best I can. For I'm
only doing what a woman should dooo – for 'e's only a
working man . . .'

The anthem of the poor, working woman earned a
shower of pennies which Clover quickly scooped up,
catching her father's delighted grin.

'More. More.'

Mrs Starkey didn't know whether to be pleased or out-
raged. Definitely under-age, she thought. Approaching
Bert at the piano, her only comment was, 'It's orlright
as long as there's no trouble. But lissen 'ear, young

woman,' turning to fix Clover with an admonishing eye, 'if the old Bill as much as pokes 'is nose in that door, you make yourself scarce. Understand?'

Clover drew a deep breath but before she could answer Bert laughed and said, yes, they understood. She needn't worry. Clover was a clever girl, she knew what was what.

'Orlright, then,' grunted the landlady and returned to her customers. By the look of her, she thought, the girl could do with a bit of sympathy, with that no-good charmer for a father.

The man who helped Mrs Starkey behind the bar stared at Clover. He had lank, greasy hair, already thinning on top although he was still young, and a full fleshy face. His small eyes watched her greedily. She didn't think she'd like to find herself alone in the same room with him. He sent a shiver down her spine. The moist brown eyes with their blatant message of desire disgusted her.

It seemed to Clover that the customers would never be satisfied. She gave them song after song, some funny, some sweet, smiling about her, eyes bright, and by the time Mrs Starkey had called 'Time' her handbag was heavy with the copper coins and even a few silver shillings.

When she was pressed to take a drink for herself by her enthusiastic audience, Bert had shaken his head and because he was uneasy about this new, attractive Clover who had emerged from the awkward, funny little girl who was no threat to anyone's peace of mind, he spoke more brusquely than he intended. 'My Clover does not drink. Never has and never will.'

They left the Darnley Arms with Bert promising he would bring her the next night.

They took the tram home and Clover opened the front door, mentally steeling herself for her nightly battle with

184

the cockroaches and other creatures. The chill, icy room seemed as barren as a wasteland after the bright sparkle and noise of the bar. She shouldn't, she told herself, begrudge her father his love of company. It was only when he was with people and had a few drinks inside him that he seemed to come alive. The thought crossed her mind that once the stage and an audience had had that stimulating effect on him, when Adele was alive, when her parents waited hand in hand in the wings for their cue, sure of themselves and their little family. Clover felt oddly detached from that earlier life, as though it had all happened to someone else.

Her father went to bed, admonishing her to be sure to get enough coal in the bucket to light the fire. She stood in the yard, taking deep breaths of the cold air. After the smoky atmosphere of the bar, it felt good. The stars looked down from a black sky and she sent a little prayer winging to her mother, hoping she approved of their latest venture.

'Wear that red velvet dress you made,' Bert suggested the following evening as they were getting ready. 'You look like a princess in that.'

'Some princess,' she smiled, lips curling. 'A dress made from a pair of old curtains!'

'The dress doesn't look old,' chided Bert, 'and even if it did, you'd still look like a princess. Besides which, it makes you look older. I wouldn't want some heavy-handed copper coming in and ordering you out because you're under-age.'

Bert's remark brought back Mrs Starkey's warning. She looked alarmed. 'You don't think that they would?'

'Try the dress on and see how it looks,' he advised. When she came back down into the kitchen, she held the full skirts out at her sides and twirled for Bert's inspection.

'Well, my goodness, look at you!' he said in a hushed voice.

'Will I do?'

'I should certainly say so. You're a sight for sore eyes, so you are.' With her hair coiled on top of her head and a narrow black velvet ribbon about her slender white throat, she did appear much older than her sixteen years. An observant eye, however, would have noticed the far from mature bosom and the rather wary look in the wide eyes.

For his part, Bert looked resplendent in his velvet jacket with the black silk frogging down the front, and that night he drew many an admiring glance from the lady customers.

Keeping herself and her father neat and presentable for their nightly appearances at the Darnley Arms was not easy. Washing clothes in tepid water without sufficient soap didn't produce very good results. The dirt that had accumulated in the small house over the years of neglect by previous tenants was a constant battle of scrubbing, and Clover's hands, small and well formed, were now red and swollen with chilblains. She tried to keep them out of sight when she performed at the bar

Washing her hair, too, was a problem. Unable to afford shampoo, she would save scraps of the hard green soap left over from the washtub, collecting them in a tin mug and then adding hot water from the kettle, stirring the bits with an old spoon until they were soft and could be worked into a lump. It did the trick, but the shine in her hair began to diminish when she found she couldn't use enough hot water for the final rinse. Not unless she wanted a bowl of icy water in which to wash herself before she went to bed.

Bert expected hot water for shaving and made a wry face when she tried to explain why she had to be frugal.

'The coal is nearly finished,' she'd tell him. 'I daren't heap too much on the fire to heat water or there won't be enough to cook supper.'

Again that wry face from Bert and she had the feeling he sometimes wished he was a hundred miles away, instead of standing arguing with this stubborn daughter of his. Undeterred, she pressed on. 'We can't have it both ways, Dad. Hot water or hot suppers. Take your choice.'

Lately, she had started to stand up to her father. Whereas at one time his nonchalant acceptance of their poverty had made her want to cover her face with her hands and burst into tears, now her anger would stir and she had to force herself to control it.

Things ought to have been better now that they had a little money coming in, although their earnings were erratic. When the mood of their audience was good, their takings would be worthwhile; on a wet, rainy evening, not so good. Either way, Clover saw little of it. Bert would take the money she had collected, sometimes not even bothering to count it, and it would disappear into his pocket, all but a few shillings which he handed to Clover, expecting her to run the household with it.

That evening, getting ready for their stint at the pub, Bert looked so tired that she felt a sudden wave of concern. The irritating little cough that he'd developed lately worried her, too. 'Are you all right?' she asked.

'Of course I am,' he said brusquely.

'Are you sure?' Anxiety made her frown. 'You don't look all right. You look washed out.'

Bert dismissed her fears with a gesture. 'I said I was, didn't I? Don't fuss, lass. You know I'm never ill.'

It was true. Clover could not remember him being ill once. But Bert was not the kind of man to admit it, even if he was. She lifted her old black coat from the nail on the back door and they set out for the tram stop. At least the fare for the tram was still forthcoming from her father's pocket.

The following day was Sunday, their day of rest, when they weren't expected to go to the Darnley Arms. Clover was in the kitchen, washing up after their midday meal when she heard Bert groan. She turned from the sink and saw him double over in his chair, his face contorted with pain. Quickly she crossed to him. 'Dad?'

'It's nothing, girl,' he wheezed. Raising his head he drew in a great lungful of air.

Clover's frown deepened as she looked at him. 'Can I get you something? A glass of water?'

'Water?' He tried to laugh and again clutched at his chest. 'Yes, perhaps that might be a good idea. And if you've got any of those Beechams Powders your mother used to take . . .'

While she ran upstairs to her room for the headache powders, he sat quietly massaging his chest. The white powder was tipped onto a spoon and mixed with a little milk, washed down by the water. Bert pulled a face at the bitter taste. Then within minutes he was telling her not to fuss, that he was perfectly all right. It was an attack of indigestion, that was all, brought on by over-indulgence in the grand, thick soup she'd been feeding him. This time it was her turn to laugh.

He spent the rest of the day sitting in his chair with the *News of the World*, reading the more innocuous bits aloud to Clover. He slept late the following morning and Clover begged him not to work that day.

'You're worse than your mother,' he scolded. 'I told you, I'm fine.' He grinned. 'Still, the thought of that smoky atmosphere and noise doesn't go down too well, I must confess.'

Surprised that he should even admit it she quickly said she would go over to the Darnley Arms with a note for Mrs Starkey, explaining why he couldn't come.

The pub hadn't yet opened when she arrived and the theatre next door was quiet and deserted. She went along a rubbish-lined back lane to where a wooden door opened onto a paved yard behind the pub. The large youth who helped in the bar was busy rolling beer barrels down a wide plank. He'd taken off his shirt, exposing a grubby, sweat-stained vest.

He stopped at sight of her, straightening and looking at her with speculative eyes. Clover felt herself shrinking inside at the sight of the fleshy, almost woman-like breasts outlined by the tight vest, the roll of fat about the hips and stomach. One hand scratching his shoulder, he stood grinning. 'Well, what you want, then?'

Clover explained about the message for Mrs Starkey. 'Give it to me, I'll see she gets it.' He held out a none too clean hand.

She hesitated. The proximity of the man frightened her but she wasn't going to let him see that. She shook her head, the dark hair flying about her face with the abrupt movement. 'No, I'd better give it to her myself. It's important.'

'Suit yerself.' He moved to the back door, pushing it open, still grinning, and indicated a long passage. 'After you.'

Against her better judgment, Clover preceded him down the dark passage. She paused when they reached the end where a door opened onto a large kitchen. She felt herself flinch as his big hands touched her back, pushing her before him. She glanced about her at the empty kitchen.

'Where's Mrs Starkey?'

He leered at her. 'Where she allus is, this time of the day. Prettying 'erself up in 'er room, getting ready for 'er customers.'

'Why did you bring me here, then?' Clover demanded,

the metal taste of fear in her mouth. Without waiting
for an answer, she tried to push past him to the door.

He blocked her way. 'Wanted to 'ave you alone for
a little, didn't I?' he said. 'What's the 'arm in that?
Watched you singing out there wi' the customers and
thought, she's a nice 'un, although she allus treats you
like you was a bit of dog dirt you'd trod on in the street.
Fancy a nice bit of skirt, I do, and they don't come any
sweeter than you, Miss Hoity-Toity.' Then he lunged
forward and grabbed her about the waist.

Long ago, between discussions on cabbages and kings
and the big, bad world, Eddie had taught her what to
do if she ever found herself in danger. Lifting one knee
sharply she aimed for his groin. He turned slightly and
caught the knee on his thigh.

'Bitch!' he grunted, and twisted her arms behind
her. He took both her wrists in his left hand and
bent over her. She clamped her lips tight and tried
to turn her face away, but his free hand held her chin.
His fetid breath filled her nostrils as his mouth came
down on hers.

He began fumbling with her clothing, trying to
unbutton her coat. Feverishly, she fought him, digging
her nails into his cheeks, into the backs of his hands,
drawing bright beads of blood.

She felt herself losing her balance; terrified of falling
with that huge, heavy body on top of her, with her
last ounce of strength she brought her knee up again,
catching him unawares. This time the blow connected.
He grunted and his hands left her body to clutch his
own, doubled up in agony.

Sobbing, she scrambled from the room and ran. Ran
back down the smelly dark passage, leaving the door
wide open behind her, out through the yard with its
litter of barrels, stumbling and tripping in her haste.
If he followed and caught her before she was out of

the quiet lane and back on the main road, she would be completely at his mercy.

She made it to the tram stop, gasping for breath and trembling as if with fever.

On the tram ride home, she sat with her head bowed, hunched in her seat, avoiding the curious looks of the conductor and other passengers.

By the time she reached her stop she'd managed to subdue the shaking somewhat. The long narrow street that sloped towards the canal was thankfully deserted. Children and adults alike would be indoors, having their tea. Lifting the latch on her own front door she stumbled in blindly, her hair in disarray, one sleeve of the old coat torn at the shoulder. Shuddering sobs broke out anew when Bert rose in alarm at the sight of her and took her in his arms. 'Hush, now, hush! It can't be that bad. Tell your old dad all about it.'

He spoke as he would have done when she was a little girl and had fallen and grazed her knee. Wildly, she thought, he doesn't understand! Hadn't a clue about things that men – fat, horrible, evil men – did to girls if they got them on their own. She wished with all her heart that Eddie was here. He'd sort that fat pig out, would Eddie. Hadn't he always said he'd break both arms of any man who tried to get fresh with her?

'Clover, what's wrong? For God's sake, what's happened?' demanded a bewildered Bert.

'That man,' she sobbed. 'That man who helps Mrs Starkey . . .'

'Benny Griggs?' Bert looked thunderstruck. 'He did this to you?'

Clover gulped. 'I ran and managed to get away. But he tore my clothes and his hands – his hands were everywhere . . .' She covered her mouth with her hands and made a rush to the back door and the tiny paved yard where the outside toilet was. Bert clearly heard her being sick in the bowl. He reached for his coat. Wiping her mouth with her handkerchief, Clover came back in time to see him open the front door. 'Where are you going?'

'Where do you think?' His voice was harsh, his face grim. 'You don't think I'm going to let him get away with this, do you? I may not be much of a provider, Clover, but I'm still your father and no man lays a finger on my daughter, not while I'm around to stop it.'

'Dad.' She bit her lip, her eyes pleading. 'Please don't. You've not been well . . .'

He still had that drawn look about him, and his lips had a faint bluish tinge. 'Please don't,' she repeated. 'I don't think he'll try it again.'

'He'll not get the chance,' growled Bert and left the house.

Clover waited, wishing she had something or somebody to distract her. When Bert didn't return after two hours she began imagining the worst, picturing her father lying senseless in some gutter, beaten to a pulp by the repulsive Benny.

Just as she made up her mind to investigate, slipping her coat about her shoulders, the latch on the front door clicked and Bert entered.

She eyed him intently, looking for bruises or signs of blood. She could see none, but there was a flush on his cheeks, taking away the ashen look. To her unspoken question, he said, 'Mrs Starkey was there when I arrived so I just up and told her what had happened with that turd listening in. He won't try it again, my girl, so you just put it out of your mind and forget it ever happened.'

Which, of course, was always Bert's way.

Sleep was a long time coming that night. Even though she washed as thoroughly as she could before slipping into her nightgown, she could still feel the hot pawing of his hands, his grunts as they battled. She tossed restlessly, awakening from a half sleep with a cry ringing in her ears. Late-night revellers in the street below joined in a chorus of 'Nellie Dean' as they staggered homewards from the corner pub. She lay on her back, clutching the blankets to her chin, eyes staring at the glow from the gas lamp below her window.

Had she cried out in her sleep? As she turned on her side to try and recapture the little sleep she'd had, the cry came again. More like a low groan, she thought. Flinging back the blankets, long slim legs flashing out of bed, she ran across the landing to her father's room. The door was ajar and she saw that the bed was empty, though rumpled. Restless, like her, unable to sleep, he must have gone downstairs to make himself a cup of tea.

As she crept down the narrow staircase it suddenly struck her how very quiet it was, only the tick of the old mantel clock breaking the silence.

Her father couldn't have fallen asleep in the chair, surely? she thought and grimaced, thinking how uncomfortable that would be. And by now the fire would be out. He'd be frozen.

Immediately she entered the downstairs room and saw his face, she knew Bert wasn't asleep. He lay crumpled in a heap on the hearth rug, the overturned chair across his legs. One hand still clung to the back of the chair where he must have tried to clutch it for support.

She gave a wail of anguish and ran to kneel by his side.

Chapter Fourteen

Clover's first thought was that she had to make her
father more comfortable. He was heavy, despite his
slimness, and it was a mammoth task for her to try
and lift him. But by alternately bullying and coaxing
she managed to get him into the chair where he sat
forward, his face tight with pain. Every few seconds
he gave a nerve-racking groan.

She fetched a blanket from the bedroom and wrapped
it about his shoulders. What to do? Oh, dear God, what
to do? He needed a doctor, that much was clear. But
could she safely leave him for the time it would take
to run down to where the doctor held his surgery, two
streets away? And at this time of night?

Her dilemma was solved by a knock on the front
door and Mrs Kelly's voice calling, 'Clover? That
you, lass? Is everything all right? I was up getting
a drink of water for young Freddy, 'e couldn't stop
coughing, poor little bugger, and 'e was keeping me
awake. I thought I 'eard a noise coming from your
kitchen . . .'

'Oh, Mrs Kelly!' Clover flew to open the front door,
gazing at the woman with an anguished face. She stood
in the doorway, an enormous plaid shawl wound about
her shoulders. At once her sharp eyes took in the
figure of the crouched man, his face chalk-white, shiny
with sweat.

'Eeee, lass!' She came further into the room. Clover

began to babble about getting the doctor, twisting her hands with worry. 'But I daren't leave him.'

Suddenly the competent Mrs Kelly was taking charge. 'Off you run and fetch the doctor, girl. I'll stay with your dad.'

Hurriedly, Clover slipped her coat about her shoulders, thrust her bare feet into shoes and then was running through the dark streets to where the local doctor had his consulting rooms. Old Dr Fraser had a good name in the community and she had no doubt from what she had heard about him that he wouldn't refuse to come. She'd worry about money later.

She was profuse in her apologies to the startled housekeeper who opened the door to her frenzied knocking. She had to see the doctor, she cried, her voice rising on a note of near hysteria. It was her father. She was sure he was dying . . .

The woman looked dismayed. 'The doctor's just been called out to a delivery,' she began in an almost indignant tone, then hesitated, taking in the girl's anguished expression. 'All right,' she muttered. 'I'll see what I can do.'

Clover was left standing on the doorstep while the door was closed in her face. She waited with an impatience that had her biting her nails in anxiety. Finally the door opened again and she was ushered into the warm hallway, comforting after the cold darkness outside. She heard a voice and looked up. A young man was descending the stairs, his gaze fixed intently on her face. He was good-looking in a tall, loose-jointed, particularly English kind of way. His hair was thick and fair and a bit untidy and he looked as though he ought to be wearing tweeds, striding across moorland with a Labrador at his heels instead of approaching her carrying the small black leather bag of a doctor. There was a certain clumsy charm in the way he came down the last of the stairs and towards her, his brown eyes examining her concerned, ashen face. They dropped to take in the long nightgown showing under the hastily donned coat, the slim white ankles in the unlaced shoes. 'I'm Adam Foley,' he said, 'Dr Fraser's partner.'

Listening to her description of her father's condition, the words tripping over each other in her haste, he said she was quite right to call him. He would get his coat and be with her in a minute. Clover heard the housekeeper behind her murmuring something about his other, earlier call and caught his reply that he'd be grateful if she'd wake Dr Fraser to attend to it.

'Please explain that I'm answering a call elsewhere and this one is an emergency.'

Hurrying by his side down the street, his raincoated figure towering above her, she had to break into a run every few yards in order to keep up with him.

Dr Foley insisted on getting Bert back up to his bed before examining him. Under the incredulous stare of the two females, he bent and lifted the sick man bodily, urging him up the stairs to the bedrooms. He turned once to call, 'Which room is it?' At Clover's answer, he added, 'One of you bring up a cup of tea, will you? He might enjoy it. I know I would.'

Mrs Kelly insisted on seeing to that, shooing Clover upstairs to be with her father. She found the young doctor giving Bert a thorough examination, after which he turned to her and said, 'Has he ever had a turn like this before?'

Clover remembered how her father had bent over double in agony in his chair on Sunday, laughing it off as indigestion. She told the doctor, who looked grim.

'I think it's his heart,' he said quietly. In his opinion, her father should be admitted to hospital.

Clover felt her own heart skip a beat. In a low voice,

she said, 'He can't, doctor. We – we haven't any money, not enough to pay hospital bills.'

'Don't worry about that.' His eyes were kind, smiling down at her. 'I'm sure we'll work something out.' Curiosity and concern competed within Adam Foley. The girl looked as though her self-control would snap at any moment. He felt it was important to keep talking as reassuringly as he could.

'Couldn't he stay here?' she pleaded. 'I'd take care of him.'

He sighed. 'Your father needs the kind of care you couldn't possibly give him, my dear. It's important that he has peace and quiet; coupled with good nursing. And no worries.' He smiled into the fear-filled eyes. 'I'll see to everything. I promise you.'

Clover lay huddled beneath the blankets until the cold grey light of dawn crept into the small bedroom. A dog, let out for its early morning run, began to bark, breaking the silence. In this street of mean houses there were no trees from which birds could sing their dawn chorus.

Peering into the mirror above the washstand after she'd washed her face, she saw circles of shadow, like bruises, beneath her eyes. She looked like an old woman instead of her sixteen years.

Dr Foley remarked on this when he suddenly and quite unexpectedly arrived just as she was having her breakfast. A cup of tea and a slice of bread and jam would have to suffice, she told herself, for her priority this morning was to get to the hospital and visit Bert. They had refused to let her stay last night, telling her to go home, that her father was in good hands. The young doctor had driven her home, dropping her off at the top of the street.

Now, standing bareheaded in the open doorway, he frowned down at her and said, 'Did you sleep at all, child? You look as though you've been up the entire night.'

'A little,' she hedged, not meeting his eyes.

'But not enough.' He eyed the slice of bread with its smear of jam, the cup of tea standing beside the plate.

Clover, suddenly conscious of her social obligations, said quickly, 'Would you like a cup of tea, doctor? I think there's enough in the pot.'

He was shaking his head. 'Thank you, but I've already breakfasted.' He smiled, lightening the situation. 'Try getting past my housekeeper without it!' He pulled a silver watch from his pocket and glanced down at it. 'I know it's early but I wanted to get to the infirmary before I begin my surgery. If you hurry you can ride along with me.'

As he spoke, Clover was reaching for her coat, one hand flying to her hair, checking that the tortoishell slide holding it back from her cheeks was secure. 'That's kind of you, doctor. As a matter of fact, I'm all ready.'

A feeling of relief enveloped her. To ride with the young doctor in his open car with the square windscreen high in front instead of the old rackety tram would be pure bliss. Dr Foley drove a dark green Austin, open at the sides with a canvas top that could be pulled over in bad weather. Today it was open and Clover relaxed on the leather seat with a feeling, if not of bliss, of something that came pretty close to it.

Moorfield Infirmary was situated on the outskirts of town, away from the smoking chimneys and other threats to a person's health. A grim, Victorian building, it stood back from the road, guarded by black iron railings. The hush inside was intimidating, the air wintry, the smell reminding Clover vividly of that shocking night they had waited to hear what the doctors had to say about her mother's injuries.

Bert was in a long ward of beds facing each other

across a highly polished floor. A nurse in a white folded headdress sat behind a small desk just inside the door. 'Samuel Amory Ward' was printed in black letters across one of the doors. Clover wondered who Samuel Amory was. The nurse smiled at Dr Foley but eyed Clover with suspicion, giving the impression that nothing and no one would get the better of her as far as her duty to her patients was concerned. Even though the morning was far from warm, some of the windows high above the beds were wide open, letting in the chill air.

The rows of sick men turned expectant faces towards the visitors as they walked between the beds. They came to one halfway down the room and Dr Foley stepped back to allow Clover near. She heard him murmur something about seeing her in a minute, then his quiet footsteps as he strode back down the ward.

For a long moment she failed to recognise the white-faced man who lay in the hospital bed. He looked smaller somehow, shrunken under the blankets. And oh, so much older! Still she smiled, taking the hand that lay outside the tightly tucked bedclothes. 'Hello, Daddy,' she said, trying to hide her shock.

He stared at her, for a moment speechless, his gaze resting on her face. Then: 'You took your time in coming,' he grunted.

Clover flushed. 'They wouldn't let me in last night. They said you had to have complete rest. Absolutely no visitors.'

'Not even my own daughter?' He'd got that pugnacious look about him, reminding her of his arguments with Eddie.

Not wanting to upset him, she said quietly, 'They know what they're doing, Dad. Anyway, the important thing is that I'm here now.' She leaned forward, squeezing his hand. 'How are you? Are you feeling better?'

'Sit down, sit down.' Peevishly he indicated the chair kept for visitors. The nurse who guarded the door left her desk and came to hover a few beds away. She kept a strict eye on her patients, constantly on the look-out for signs of discord.

Clover thought of Dr Foley, telling her quietly, 'He's going to have to change his lifestyle, Clover. The drink's not been doing him any good, not the quantities he's been taking.' Those thoughts uppermost in her mind, she spoke them aloud. 'You'll have to stop drinking, Daddy. The doctor told me—'

'Never mind what the doctor told you. I decide what I'm going to do, and if I want a drink then I'll have one.'

She stared at him with both pity and love. 'Oh, Dad!' she whispered, swallowing her tears, trying hard to understand this man whose self-pity and pig-headedness had all but ruined their lives. For several minutes there was silence while the nurse moved even closer, her eyes fixed with misgiving on her patient's face.

Clover's thoughts were on the past, of the mistakes and almost wilful self-destruction that had shadowed Bert since Adele's death. At last, as though sensing her concern, he said, 'That doctor told me how you'd run all the way to his surgery and practically dragged him along the street even though he was on his way out to another case.'

Clover smiled. 'I wondered afterwards what he must have thought of me, wild-eyed and looking like something the cat dragged in. I hope the poor mother held out long enough for the other doctor to get there. It was a woman in labour. I suppose I did wrong but he did tell the housekeeper to inform his partner . . .'

The nurse, who had arrived at the bed next to Bert's, busy on the pretext of tucking in already immaculate bedclothes, smiled and chimed in, 'Oh, those women are pretty tough, dearie. Most of the time they make do with the midwife or even the woman next door to help them out.'

Displeased at having the limelight directed from him onto some unknown mother, Bert said, 'Did my only daughter come here to discuss the advantages or otherwise of having a nurse or a neighbour to attend a birth or did she come to see me?' he demanded.

The nurse raised her eyebrows at his tone and retreated back to her desk.

With each visit, Bert seemed to improve. The nurses told Clover he was so much better it was a pleasure to have him in the ward. Clover smiled; Bert's favourite occupation was being fussed over by attentive women, she thought.

Despite that, he was still very pale, his cheeks sunken; he looked far from well. A few days after he'd been admitted, he told her on an afternoon visit, 'The doctor had a long talk with me this morning, lass.' His voice was subdued and a prickle of alarm ran down Clover's spine.

'Yes, Dad?' she murmured, taking hold of his hand on the bed cover. 'What did he say?'

'They want to send me to a sanatorium out in the country. They say my lungs aren't as good as they should be.'

'But I thought it was your heart. Dr Foley said it was your heart.'

'That, too. But they seem more worried about my lungs. The sanatorium's called Greenbay over Manchester way. I'll be off as soon as they can arrange it. It seems I'm in for a long rest, girl. No telling when I'll be home again.'

She could see how much the thought depressed him. Tightening his grasp on her hand, he said, 'How will you manage, Clover? They say I mustn't worry but how can I help it, knowing you'll be all on your own.'

'I'll be all right. And the time will fly by, just you wait and see. I'm a big girl now.'

He gave her a resigned smile. 'My brave little Clover Blossom! You wait till I get home, I'll make up for everything. The Blossoms will be on top of the bill again. This is just a temporary setback.'

She bent over to drop a kiss on his forehead, seeing signs of the other visitors rising from their chairs, denoting the end of visiting time.

'Of course it is, Daddy. I never felt otherwise. Just a temporary setback.'

The need for something to occupy her had her scrubbing the kitchen floor for the umpteenth time, for once lavish in her use of hot water. There was something marvellously therapeutic about scrubbing a floor, using up some of the nervous energy boiling inside her. With the money saved from the last few nights at the Darnley Arms, she was able to pick up some bargains in split bags of flour and sugar, a packet of margerine that was a turn away from being rancid and a few eggs that were going cheap because they were cracked.

Feeling warm and housewifely and proud of her ingenuity, she made a batch of scones and a gingerbread square. A parkin, Adele would have called it. The cakes would be a nice treat for her father. She would take them on her next visit. Covering them carefully with a piece of butter muslin, she placed them on the highest shelf in the stone-flagged pantry, safe, she hoped, from the tiny creatures with whom she shared the house – although they weren't as bad as when they'd first arrived. Cleanliness and lack of crumbs or food left overnight on a table were a great discouragement to them.

She never went back to the Darnley Arms. She wrote a letter to Mrs Starkey, informing her of her father's sudden attack, saying that no doubt when he was able he'd be in touch again – hoping against hope that that would never have to be. One of Mrs Kelly's brood from next door accepted the coin she offered and scurried off to deliver it. The message he brought back said how sorry Mrs Starkey was to hear her bad news and she hoped Mr Blossom would be better soon. Customers had never stopped asking when he and his lovely daughter were coming back and if they ever felt the need of earning a few shillings, well, they knew where to find her. She signed herself, 'With respects, Evangeline Starkey'. Clover had to smile. Someone less like an Evangeline she had never seen!

Although she tried to put on a brave face, her courage sometimes failed her. In the privacy of the dingy little front room, she would lay her head on the arm of the old settee and weep.

Dr Foley found her like that one morning, quietly sobbing as the fire in the grate slowly flickered and, despite her careful nursing, died away for the third time. The trouble was, the firewood stored in the small coal shed was damp, and in any case she didn't have enough newspaper to crumple beneath it to light it. Listlessly poking it, she remembered how expert Bert was at lighting fires and how every morning even before Mam set foot out of bed he would have one going nicely in the grate and a cup of tea waiting. She dried her tears and opened the door to his soft knock.

Adam Foley took the poker off her and stood it against the wall. Unable to bear the sight of her woeful face, he put his arms about her, feeling a rush of emotion he couldn't have begun to explain. Clover laid her head against the shoulder of his tweed jacket and continued to sob, innocently unaware of the feelings engendered in him.

'It won't light,' she sobbed. 'I can't get the blessed thing to light . . .'

He patted her back as he held her. 'Leave it,' he advised gently. 'I'll have a go at it in a minute. When you're feeling better. Then we'll have a nice cup of tea. All right?'

She gulped then nodded and he rocked her gently from side to side. His voice low and a little on the ragged side, he said, 'And after that I want to talk to you.'

At his words she stirred, lifting her face to look up at him. She nodded. 'Of course. You want to tell me something about my father?' His heart turned over as he gazed down into the large, luminous eyes, awash with tears. 'You want to tell me he's worse than you thought.'

'No. I want to talk about your future, little one.'

She smiled wanly at him, relieved at his words. 'Miss Boyce used to call me that.'

'Did she, now? A friend of yours, is she? This Miss Boyce?'

'The very best.'

He knelt before the black-leaded grate and coaxed the fire into life. 'That's just what I wanted to talk to you about,' he said as he sat back on his heels, wiping his hands on an old duster that lay beside the fireplace. 'Old friends and family.'

Clover shook her head. 'I haven't any family, only my father and a brother and he's in America.'

'And this Miss Boyce you mention? You said she was a friend.'

'She's an old lady, well, elderly anyway, at least

forty-five. I couldn't ask her for anything.' She looked at him closely, a frown marking her brow. 'Why are you asking me all this? Why are you interested?'

He rose and went to sit on the chair opposite; Bert's chair. Leaning forward across the bright glow of the flames, his hands between his knees, he said, 'You must realise, Clover, that you cannot stay here all by yourself. For one thing it isn't safe and for another what would you live on? I wouldn't want to see you go to work in the mills or domestic service, and from what I understand all that you've ever done is to appear with your family act on the stage in the summer months at the seaside.'

Clover pursed her lips, thinking of the Darnley Arms, trying to imagine what he would say if he knew about that short episode of their lives. Or the terrifying ordeal with Benny Griggs. Just thinking of it made the palms of her hands sweat.

Misreading her face, he went on quickly, 'Oh, don't think I don't approve of that kind of life. It was probably grand for you and your brother. But you had your family around you, your father there to protect you. It might be a long time before he can do that again, Clover. I'd like to know you were being looked after properly in the meantime.'

A dreadful thought came to her and from long ago she remembered her mother and a friend discussing a woman who had had to go into the workhouse. The friend said, 'She's got no one, poor soul,' and Adele said, 'How dreadful. It must be frightening,' and the friend said the poor were afraid to go into the workhouse. Everyone knew that once you entered those uncharitable portals, your life was not your own.

Her voice a whisper, Clover said, 'I couldn't go there. I'd rather try to manage on my own . . .'

His brows rose. 'Go where?'

'To the workhouse.'

He grimaced. 'Who said anything about the work-house? Really, Clover Blossom, what do you take me for? Some kind of monster? I'd take you in myself before I'd allow that.' His heart skipped a beat or two at the thought of this lovely young creature sharing his home and he looked away in case she read it in his face.

Her eyes studied him thoughtfully. 'You're very kind, Dr Foley. For such a busy man you've given me more than a fair share of your time.'

'A good doctor feels responsible for the welfare of his patients.' Thinking that sounded slightly pompous, he added, 'Part of a doctor's duty is to be concerned about the patients he tends.'

'But I'm not your patient,' she pointed out quietly.

'You could end up being my patient if I turned my back on your predicament and let you get on with it alone.'

'How long will my father have to stay in the sanatorium?' Clover asked.

'Probably for most of the summer. It wasn't just his heart, you know. His lungs . . .' Adam hesitated, loath to worry her further by telling her of the touch of tuberculosis the X-rays had revealed.

'We haven't any money, you know,' she said candidly. 'I don't know if we could afford—'

'There are certain beds they keep for . . .' He almost said charity cases but stopped himself in time. He didn't know how Clover would react to thinking of her father as a charity case. 'You needn't worry about that,' he told her firmly. 'Let's get back to you. Surely you have relatives on your father's or your mother's side?'

She thought again of Adele, of her recounting the fascinating story of her first meeting with Bert. 'There's my mother's aunts, two maiden ladies who brought her up after her own mother died. They would be really old now.' She looked at him, her gaze thoughtful. 'They would be my great-aunts, wouldn't they?' A flash of animation brightened the woeful look on her face as she thought of the two women whom her mother had adored but who had been so abruptly cut from her life. 'Aunt Bethany and Aunt Hazel,' she went on, 'and their last name was Frost.'

'And they lived – where?' prompted Adam.

She bit her lip. 'I'm not sure.' Where had her mother said she lived as a child? She could remember imagined scenes of a red brick house in its own pleasant gardens, Adele's descriptions of summer holidays taken by the seaside and her aunts' – well, at least Aunt Bethany's – severe rules of how a young lady should behave.

Watching her expressive face, he said coaxingly, 'Try to recall. They are very probably still alive and knowing your circumstances would, I'm sure, welcome you as warmly as they did your mother into their lives.'

He smiled at her reassuringly and she said, slowly, 'The town was Shackleton. Is there such a place? I remember her telling me now and the name stuck, it reminded me of the explorer, the one who tried to reach the South Pole.'

'Indeed there is such a place. In Yorkshire. Not too far from here. Are you sure? Shackleton?'

She frowned, thinking hard. 'I'm almost sure.'

'Of course, we could always ask your father. He'd know, wouldn't he? In any case, he'd have to give his permission.'

For a moment she looked uncertain. 'What if he

doesn't?' Would Bert have mellowed enough over the years to overlook past grievances?

Covering her hand with one of his, Adam Foley gave it a squeeze and said, 'Don't worry. I'll see to everything. We'll trace them somehow. I'm sure your father will agree, knowing it's for the best.'

Chapter Fifteen

Adam Foley came from an upper middle-class background. His father was the local well-liked doctor and the family lived in a semi-detached house on the outskirts of Canterbury. Adam's future was charted from an early age by his doting mother, although his father always impressed upon him that no man should be bound by his forebears.

Fortunately he had a leaning towards medicine, but his mother had been aghast when after qualifying he had expressed a desire to join a practice in one of the less salubrious towns of Lancashire. 'It's such a long way from home,' she moaned. 'We'd hardly ever see you.'

Helen, his elder sister, pulled a face. 'And they actually work down mines and in't mills up there,' she said, mimicking a broad northern accent.

His father listened but said nothing. He knew his son. Knew well the thread of obstinacy that ran though his character, knew that once Adam had made up his mind on something it would be near impossible to stop him. That he had chosen to follow in his father's footsteps was enough for the older man.

A loan from his father bought Adam a share of a practice in Moorfield where an elderly Scots doctor was considering retiring and returning to his native Edinburgh. Dr Fraser looked his visitor over with inquisitive scrutiny, asked a number of probing questions and decided he liked the open-faced young man.

'Start right away?' he asked. Dr Fraser didn't believe in wasting time. At his age time was precious and he prayed that however long he had left would be spent in his own land, doing the things he liked – once he'd seen this youngster settled in the practice and the ways of the people.

'Of course I can start right away,' Adam was telling him with a broad smile. 'The sooner the better is my motto.'

The ease with which Adam settled to the life of a doctor in a working-class district was still a matter of surprise to his parents. He was ambitious, not only for himself but also for the disadvantaged people who were his patients. He longed to better the lives made miserable by poverty and unemployment. At first the picture of uniform drabness and snotty, pale-faced children depressed him so much he wondered if he could really carry out what he had planned. He felt deep pity for the obviously worn out women and the scene as a whole made a deep, lasting impression on him. The lot of the poor was a hard one. It had always been so and it would continue to be so.

His commitment did not falter. Nothing was too much trouble. Long distances and rain-swept midnights meant nothing to him; if there was a call, he would go. And willingly. Indeed, Dr Fraser thought his young partner enjoyed the challenge. The dark green Austin helped considerably. The money had been well spent. Before that, Dr Fraser had attended his calls in a pony cart and although at first the car had startled a few of the more elderly residents of the street, they soon got used to it. And the patients, although at first wary of the new doctor and his 'posh' accent, soon learned to like and trust him.

Since their first meeting, Clover had been constantly on his mind; even when he was at his busiest, her face with those wide, troubled eyes rose up in his imagination to haunt him.

This had never happened to him before. Dr Fraser had warned him about becoming too involved with the patients and he had had to agree. But agreeing didn't solve his problem. Clover was still a young girl; as he understood, not yet seventeen. Her lack of artifice, her plucky battle against the poverty that surrounded her had him wanting to become very much involved.

He found himself increasingly eager to see her. Increasingly reluctant to part from her. Concerned about her welfare, he could see in the soft young face the image of the beautiful young woman she would one day become.

He was aware of her background, for she'd confided in him one day, telling him of the tragic death of Adele, of Eddie leaving, but not the reason for it or the way her father had sought refuge in drink. Neither did she tell him about the flights from one unpalatable boarding house to the next. Adam guessed much of the parts she left unsaid, and was aware, from her father's physical condition, that he had a drinking problem.

The determination that had led him to seek the kind of practice that would make him most happy, a determination his mother always referred to as 'Adam's pig-headedness', urged him on in his endeavour to trace the two elderly Frost sisters. Knowing the name of the town where they lived made the task not too difficult, for the two spinsters were well-known figures in the district. Enquiries at the local County Council were made. Within weeks two bewildered women were seated at their breakfast table in Shackleton, reading a letter from a doctor in Moorfield, explaining Clover's situation.

Hazel passed the letter back to her sister. 'Adele's child!' she said softly.

Bethany, reading her mind, answered sharply, 'That man's child, too, don't forget.' The old aversion for Bert rose in her, as strong as the day she had last set eyes on him.

'But a member of our family. We *must* help, sister. We simply cannot turn our backs on dear Adele's own little girl.'

Bethany did a quick calculation in her head. 'She would be – let's see – almost seventeen now, wouldn't she? Hardly a child. And I do believe young people these days can be extremely noisy, with their gramophone records and Charlestons. It would turn our life upside down, sister. Is that what you want?'

Hazel's mouth firmed into a stubborn line. 'She probably won't be like that at all. In any case, what if she is? It would do us good, a bit of gaiety and music in the house. Too long have we been stagnating here and I for one am sick of it.'

Bethany raised her eyebrows at her sister's rebellious tone but said nothing more.

Clover was alarmed at Bert's near fit of apoplexy, greatly exaggerated, when Adam, with Aunt Bethany's letter in his hand, sought permission for Clover to join them. But Adam spoke to him, making him see sense and he finally agreed that there was no other way.

'But mind,' he warned her, 'just as soon as I'm fit again you come back to join me. And you write and tell me if those two old bitches try to make your life a misery. Sick or not, I won't stand for that.' He pressed her hand. 'You don't know them, love. I do. I've seen them in action.'

'A lot of water has passed under the bridge since then, Dad. Who knows, they might have changed into the sort of lavender and lace little old ladies you read about.' Aunt Bethany's letter, although sympathetic, had a sort of stiff formality about it which didn't in the least sound like lavender and lace.

Bert grunted. 'More like arsenic and old lace,' was his laconic reply.

Two days later, Clover settled herself into a corner seat of the train and watched as Adam lifted her one suitcase onto the netting rack above her head. Everything she owned was in that suitcase. Her father's clothes and other possessions, including a thin silver cigarette case and a silver lighter, both with his initials engraved upon them would accompany Bert to Greenbay. The framed photograph of his wedding, standing with Adele beside a kilted blacksmith with a smithy in the background, and of Clover and Eddie as babies, together with the mantel clock, were removed by Adam and packed safely away with Dr Fraser's permission in his attic. The few blankets and bed linen they possessed had been clucked over by the elderly housekeeper before being washed and then aired thoroughly and stored on a back shelf in the roomy linen closet. The crimson velvet dress and jacket had been examined ambivalently, then folded neatly in a large trunk and also stored in the attic.

Now, Clover settled to enjoy the journey. She loved trains. Loved the smell of smoke that percolated into the compartment, the soothing hum of the wheels swiftly covering the miles. There were sepia-tinted photographs of country and seaside places framed behind thick glass above each seat, three on each side. Some she felt she should have recognised, so familiar were the views of long, narrow piers and formal flower gardens fronting the esplanade. One view, of Edinburgh Castle, had dark-suited men in top hats and walking sticks escorting ladies in long gowns with the hint of a bustle. All very pre-war. She wondered why the railway company didn't change them. They were so out of date.

She smiled at Adam who was seated opposite her. They had been fortunate in finding an empty carriage. Once settled he opened his newspaper and began to read aloud the latest reports of Benito Mussolini and his Black Shirts. 'Going to be trouble there,' he remarked and Clover smiled again, not in the least bit interested in some obscure little Italian dictator in Rome but very much interested in the countryside through which they were travelling.

It was all so beautiful; a thousand shades of green with a straight canal running alongside the tracks. Its surface reflected patches of blue sky and overhanging trees. She watched a gaily painted barge chug slowly by and wondered about the people who lived on it. Then wondered how her aunts would greet her, a girl turning up from nowhere, threatening to disrupt the peaceful tranquillity of their lives.

They had to change trains once. There would be a long wait for their connection and Clover plucked up courage to ask Adam to take her to the refreshment room. Tipping a porter to keep an eye on her suitcase, he took her arm and they entered the steamy atmosphere with its gleaming brasswork and long shining counter. A large silver tea urn hissed. Buns liberally sprinkled with sugar and slices of dark, very rich-looking fruit cake held pride of place on white plates with paper doilies.

They stayed there until the sound of their train echoed from down the line and Adam stood up and paid the woman at the counter. Again holding her arm, he led her out onto the platform. A branch line took them to Shackleton. The small town consisted of a narrow High Street fronted with small shops with old-fashioned display windows and low doorways. As the train steamed into the station, Clover could see where someone, probably the council, had made an effort to brighten the grey stonework of the buildings by hanging wire baskets resplendent with early spring flowers on the heavy iron lamp posts along the street. A hump-backed bridge spanned a fast-flowing river and a couple of children leaned over, dropping sticks into the water.

A definite improvement on Moorfield, Clover decided. Without waiting for the familiar grip on her arm, she jumped onto the platform. Adam reached for her suitcase. There were quick, light footsteps and an excited, almost girlish voice exclaimed, 'You've arrived! You're Clover! You *must* be Clover.'

Clover turned to find herself facing a woman a good head shorter than herself. She was dressed in a silk dress in shades of pale coffee and ivory. Elbow-length sleeves with three brown buttons sewn horizontally covered plump arms. The pretty face was unlined, the brown hair taken back in soft folds, waving over her cheeks and forehead. Bright blue eyes shone with a warmth that had Clover taking to her at once.

The woman held out a slim white hand. 'Hello,' she said, 'I'm your Aunt Hazel.' Glancing over her shoulder, a little timorously, she went on, 'My sister will be here in a moment. She is just making sure Frank parks the car correctly. He's getting so careless in his old age.'

Clover took her hand and shook it formally. 'I'm so pleased to meet you, Aunt Hazel.'

Hazel's smile faltered a little as Adam stepped down from the train. Lowering Clover's suitcase onto the wooden platform he politely raised his hat. Hazel blinked, obviously shaken at seeing a young man with her niece. 'And you are . . . ?'

Adam gave a little bow. 'Adam Foley, at your service, ma'am. For the moment, Clover's escort.'

'Oh, yes, of course. How silly of me.' Hazel gave a

nervous smile. 'It is very kind of you to accompany my
niece, Dr Foley. We—'

'Hazel!' Aunt Bethany's voice, high and imperious,
sounded behind them. She hurried along the platform
to where they stood. She was older than her sister by
some few years and although her manner was courteous,
Clover noticed how her sharp eyes flew from one face to
the other, lingering on her sister's flushed cheeks with
a hint of asperity.

Dressed in a dark brown ankle-length dress with a
slightly flared overskirt, years out of date, she looked
like something from a bygone age. Just like the sepia-
tinted photographs in the railway carriage. Adam stood
with his hat in his hands while introductions were made.
Clover was glad he was with her, for she would have been
completely out of her depth if she had been alone.

Although Adele had often spoken of her aunts, Clover
always got the impression she didn't reveal everything.
Now, seeing for herself the Miss Frosts, she could better
understand the turmoil caused in the young Adele's
breast by the arrival of the good-looking Thespian that
summer day on the pier.

They in turn saw a young girl with hair a couple of
shades darker than Adele's, eyes that were clear and
bright blue. There was a hesitancy about her that made
the soft-hearted Hazel want to take her to her bosom
and hug her tightly. Even the more prosaic Bethany
warmed to her.

Adam's eyes gleamed when he saw the elegant Rolls-
Royce Silver Ghost that waited for them in the car park.
Frank, the chauffeur, was an elderly man dressed in a
smart uniform of bottle green. He touched the shiny
peak of his cap and smiled warmly at the newcomers.
Adam was settled in the front seat of the car, next to
Frank, while Clover sat to one side of the two sisters on
the wide back seat.

Clover's first sight of the house brought a lump to her throat. This was the place where her mother grew up, where she'd spent her childhood. It was built of red brick, glowing in the sunshine, with trails of Virginia creeper partly covering one side. The drive ended in a semicircle before the front door, where Frank drew up with a flourish.

Clover's impression of the garden had been of green spaces with trees and flowerbeds, glowing with the yellows and reds and purples of spring bulbs.

Hazel alighted first, still nimble on her feet despite her age. 'Come in, come in,' she urged, ushering Clover towards the open front door. 'I'm sure you must be starving after your journey. Don't you find trains so dirty and depressing? I always feel as though I'm covered in soot after a journey in one of them.'

'While we were waiting for our connection we had something to eat,' explained Clover. 'But I wouldn't say no to a cup of tea.'

'Of course. And in the meantime, Sally will show you to your room.' Sally stood at the foot of the stairs, a girl in her twenties who looked friendly and smiled at Clover.

Although slightly thrown by the young doctor's unexpected appearance, the aunts insisted that he spend the night and journey back the following day. 'You must be tired,' they insisted.

'We've killed the fatted calf in honour of our niece's homecoming,' Hazel told him. 'You are very welcome to share it with us.'

He said he'd be delighted to stay.

The following morning, after a breakfast the like of which Clover had not seen for many a day, Adam walked with her for a long private moment in the garden. His gaze resting on the landscaped garden with its curving flowerbeds and smooth lawns, the bright green foliage of the trees, he said, 'Moorfield is going to seem pretty grim after all this.' He turned to face her, smiling, taking both her hands in his. 'You couldn't have picked a more perfect place to spend the summer if you'd been granted a wish from some kindly fairy godmother. And your aunts are excellent.'

'I know. Isn't it wonderful how they have welcomed me? I hope I won't let them down.' She grinned impishly at him. 'What sort of long, woeful tale did you spin them in your letters to make them so understanding?'

'They are ladies of the old school. When a member of the family needs help, they rally to the call.'

'They didn't have to. They don't even know me. And they hated my father . . .' She looked wistful for a moment, then brightened. 'And you didn't have to go to all this trouble for me, either. You and Dr Fraser must be busy with all the people I see queuing up for your surgery. I wonder why you did. Bother about me, I mean.'

'I told you. Part of a doctor's duty is to be concerned about the patients he tends.' It was said with a kind of raillery that had her punching his arm.

'And *I* told *you* I'm not one of your patients. Neither am I a child to be worried over. I can take care of myself.'

With the slanting early morning rays of the sun catching her hair, throwing unexpected coppery lights from it, he reached again for her hands, saying, softly, 'The way I'm feeling at the moment, I could think up all sorts of entirely different descriptions of you. But I'd better not.'

The imp of mischief was back in her eyes. 'Such as?'

'Clover!' It was Aunt Hazel, calling from the french doors behind them. 'If Dr Foley is to catch that train, he'd better hurry.' She stepped out onto the grass, walking over to where they stood.

Adam turned to smile at her. 'Just drinking in the beauties of your very pleasant garden, Miss Frost. Taking a breather, as you might say, before the return to the tall chimneys of Moorfield.'

'My sister remarked on a young man with your abilities working in a place like that,' said Hazel. 'There must be smart hospitals and clinics all over the country who would snap at the chance to have you on their staff.'

'Yes, well,' he said, 'it's a long story. One I won't bore you with just now. Maybe sometime in the future.'

Clover's face brightened. 'You'll come again?'

Aunt Hazel smiled and said, 'Yes, dear doctor, you must come again. Whenever you have time.'

'Got to keep an eye on this young lady here,' he grinned, looking at Clover. 'But yes, I'd like that. Whenever I have time, as you say. My partner is on the point of retiring so I shall be kept busy, organising a new partner.'

It was an effort for Clover not to clap her hands like a child in her eagerness. 'Oh, do please try!' she said. 'We will all look forward to your coming.'

'Don't forget, that's an open invitation, Dr Foley,' smiled Aunt Hazel. 'Now, Frank is waiting with the car. As I said before, if you want to catch that train, you had better hurry.'

As soon as they were back in the house after waving farewell, Clover excused herself and ran up to the room she had been given as her very own. 'It was dear Adele's room,' Hazel had told her with tears in her eyes. 'We've kept it exactly as it was when we started out on that last holiday together.'

'You must have expected her back, then?' Clover remarked softly.

'Not really. We hoped, of course, and prayed constantly, but we – or rather I – knew she would never return.' She felt in her skirt pocket for a tiny scrap of handkerchief, dabbing the corners of her eyes. 'Your mother wrote to us when Edward was born and then you. Bethany would not allow me to answer her letters and we never heard from her again. It was so sad, I would have liked to help but there was nothing I could do. Bethany has a very intractable nature, I'm afraid, and is used to being obeyed.'

Clover left it at that. She did not want to pry into their affairs, even though those affairs concerned her own mother. Some people, she knew, were made that way: inflexible, unyielding. Aunt Bethany appeared to be one of those people.

Gazing about the pretty bedroom, its soft pastel shades of apricot and pale green, the bedspread matching the ruffled curtains, the same delicate material draping the four-poster bed, she realised she should consider herself lucky that Bethany had relented enough to welcome the wayward Adele's daughter.

It had been lovely having Adam with them, if only for one night, and she smiled at the way the sisters had fussed over him, even Aunt Bethany, urging him to second helpings at dinner, pouring him a glassful of the twelve-year-old whisky they kept for the frequent visits of the vicar. He liked his tipple, they confessed with equanimity. Adam caught Clover's eye and pulled a comic face, making her giggle and turn her head away in case Aunt Bethany noticed.

Clover sighed, and hoped Adam would manage to pay them a visit soon.

Chapter Sixteen

Clover felt that she should be happy. The De Burney School for Young Ladies was run on genteel lines. The surroundings were pleasant and her new life with her aunts placid and secure. So very different to the old St Joseph's in Moorfield which she and Eddie would attend during their winter stay there. Where she would join the line waiting outside the stone archway with the word 'Girls' deeply engraved in the stonework overhead, while the straggle of noisy boys joined the 'Boys' queue.

The day after her arrival in Shackleton, Bethany had turned to her and without preamble brought up the subject of school. Clover had pointed out as politely as she could that she had finished school at fourteen. She looked from one face to the other. 'I really don't think . . .'

Hazel reached out and pressed her hand reassuringly. 'The De Burney School for Young Ladies is more of a finishing school, dear. It is very highly thought of. Pupils come from all over the country.'

'Because it sets such high standards,' broke in Bethany. 'Very high standards indeed. We thought that for the time you are with us, Clover, it would help accomplish some of the things poor, dear Adele was so cruelly deprived of passing on to you.'

They must think me a right little ruffian! Clover thought to herself. But as she had made the decision to be the perfect guest, agreeing with everything her aunts suggested, no matter how her own views differed, she smiled and replied goodnaturedly, 'I suppose it might be fun. Thank you.'

Aunt Bethany pursed her lips at the use of the word fun. 'School, in my opinion, is hardly "fun",' she murmured. 'The first thing we must do is pay a visit to Jessops in the High Street. For a school uniform,' she added, to Clover's enquiring look. 'Those things you are wearing and the ones you arrived in yesterday are hardly suitable.'

Hazel looked grieved. 'Oh, Bethany, dear, I thought how very nicely Clover was dressed. Of course, school uniforms are compulsory at De Burney's, I know, but . . .'

Bethany's cold eyes rested on her sister. 'Don't interfere, Hazel. I have my own opinions as to how a young lady should dress and Clover at the moment does not fit these at all.'

Clover glanced down ruefully at the cotton frock she had all but outgrown. A pale shade of blue, it had tiny white spots and a white piqué collar and small cuffs on the short puffed sleeves. Tight about the bust and too short, she knew it wasn't the height of fashion but she had washed and ironed it carefully and it had once been very pretty.

A few days later, outfitted in a pale grey pleated skirt of the finest wool and a long-sleeved white cotton blouse, pale stockings and black leather lace-up shoes, Clover was ready to face yet another episode of her life.

After breakfast the car was waiting for them on the driveway. The De Burney School was a pleasant drive through the countryside. The emerald green moors, their lushness broken by rocky outcrops of grey stone, stretched away into the distance. She felt her heart lift at the beauty of it all, promising herself that on the first opportunity that she got she would walk on these moors. Just looking at them reminded her of Heathcliffe and the dour house called Wuthering Heights. In her fertile imagination, she was already making up romances. But it wasn't the darkly forbidding visage of Emily Brontë's Heathcliffe she saw in her mind but that of Adam Foley.

She turned a startled face when Aunt Bethany beside her on the leather seat of the old Rolls said, 'Here we are.' There was a certain smugness in the glance she directed at the building before them.

Built of grey stone, in the Gothic style, the school was surrounded by lush lawns and rosebeds. Clover had never seen such elegance and space, except in a public park and that was usually litter-strewn, with children and dogs racing all over the place. The peace here was complete, the faint echo of girls' voices raised in song the only distraction. She supposed if she had to spend the next few months with her aunts, she could do a lot worse than spend them here.

Aunt Bethany smiled as Frank hurried round to open the car door. 'That will be the girls at their morning assembly. Your mother came here, you know. She had a lovely voice, so natural and pure . . .' Unexpected tears appeared in her eyes and Hazel pressed her arm lovingly.

'Don't upset yourself, sister,' she comforted. 'Adele was very happy here and we must remember that and not the unfortunate events that shaped her later life.'

Now, Aunt Bethany drove Clover to school every morning in the pony cart. The chestnut mare stepped out daintily over the rutted tracks of the country lane, rattling the very life out of a soul. 'Good for the liver,' Sally remarked cheekily when Clover had joked about this. 'Start you up for the day, that will.'

Sally was the youngest of the maids; a friendly creature who took the shy, sometimes bewildered Clover under her wing and tried to make her stay with the Frost sisters as painless as possible. Clover grieved for her father, confessing to the maid that she missed him terribly. Sally had placed a comforting arm about her shoulders and hugged her warmly. 'Never mind, ducks, p'raps it won't be for too long. They can't keep 'im in there for ever, can they?'

Arrived at the school, Clover would jump lightly to the ground and with one last wave at her aunt would cross the still damp lawn to where a group of girls hurried through the mahogany and glass-panelled door.

Then it was straight to the classrooms, no mucking about, whereas before, at St Joseph's, there would be giggles and secrets whispered behind raised hands and rough boys trying to pull your hair. Here was all sweetness and light. At least on the surface. Here the taunts were more insidious, spoken in well-modulated voices but still hurtful. Taunts like foundling and waif that had Clover glaring at her tormentors, eyes narrowed, longing to reach out and grab a handful of the offender's hair and tug at it until she squealed for mercy.

But that sort of behaviour was not encouraged in this establishment for the education of young ladies. Clover learned to enclose herself in a web of indifference where nothing could get to her. Calmly and serenely she went about her work and if her heart cried out for a real, shared friendship, someone to tell her secrets to, to collapse into fits of giggles with, she kept it to herself.

Sally, the maid, was her friend and ally, but Aunt Bethany discouraged any familiarity with the servants and Clover knew that Sally's family of widowed mother and two small sisters depended on the earnings she sent home every month. So any giggling had to be done where Aunt Bethany couldn't see or hear.

Clover made the best of it. If she wasn't really happy, she should be, she told herself, with all the care her aunts were bestowing on her. There was no word from Eddie, and Bert wasn't much of a one for putting pen to paper. Miss Boyce wrote frequently, keeping her up to date with theatre gossip. Adam wrote every so often and kept her in touch with her father's progress. Whenever one of his letters arrived, she would feel a quickening of her pulse, wanting to escape to a quiet place in the garden and read it without the enquiring eyes of her aunts on her face.

The aunts treated her very much as they must have treated her mother. Indeed, they often confused her with Adele. Hazel called her Adele more frequently than she called her Clover. The elderly ladies were, perhaps, even more strict with Clover, reminded constantly of the way Adele had absconded from them all those years ago. They acted as though Bert didn't exist, politely refusing when Clover asked if they would like to read one of the rare letters he did send. They had never forgiven him for luring away their beloved young niece to what, to them, was a wicked life upon the stage. Bethany left no doubt that in her opinion Bert was a licentious dissolute, preying on the emotions of a young, innocent girl who could see no further than the handsome face and charming smile.

One morning, happening upon her aunts discussing Bert, Clover felt resentment stir in her and said as calmly as she could, 'If you'd known my father, you wouldn't talk like that. He adored my mother and she him. When she died it was as if the whole world came to a standstill. There was no fun left in life. Daddy became quiet and gloomy and I know sometimes it took all his courage and willpower to go on doing the act without her.'

Hazel clicked her tongue in sympathy. 'Oh, my dear, I'm sure my sister did not mean to criticise your father. I'm sure his love for your mother was deep and sincere. But Adele was so young, had led such a sheltered life that we suspected that any young, good-looking man with charm would have found it comparatively easy to sweep her off her feet.'

Gazing at the fixed expressions, Clover reminded herself once again of her covenant with herself, that she would be the perfect guest. She bit her lip on the hot reply that hovered on the tip of her tongue.

Her aunts were sweet and meant well, but after the freedom she had enjoyed while growing up in the theatre, the restrictions they imposed upon her began to irk. They had no idea of the torments she went through at school, for when Aunt Bethany went to fetch her in the afternoon she put on a bright smile and to her aunt's questions about her day answered, 'Fine, absolutely fine, Aunt Bethany.'

After a while a few of the girls at De Burney's began to accept her, and Clover found her life changing once again. Occasionally she was invited out to tea, and her seventeenth birthday was celebrated with a sedate party for her new-found friends. Aunt Hazel was all a twitter. Supervising Sally's laying of the table in the conservatory, she told Clover, 'I'm so excited, it's been years since we entertained anyone to tea. When Adele was still with us she had friends all the time calling, talking like a flock of birds, chattering away nineteen to the dozen. Oh, it was such fun in those days.'

The summer was now well into its span and still Bert languished in the sanatorium at Greenbay, but although her aunts maintained a tight rein on her movements, Clover began to enjoy the luxury of not having to do her bit to earn the family living. She felt that for the first time in her life her waking hours weren't taken up by practising new songs or the steps of a new dance or, latterly, worrying about Bert and his drinking and how much money she could spend on food. It was heaven to be able to sit in her pretty bedroom, curled up on the window seat, reading to her heart's content, no longer fearful of indignant landladies bursting in on her. Aunt Hazel had delighted her by producing an old gramophone, a square boxy contraption that stood on a small table next to the dresser. The gramophone boasted a circular-type horn from which the music issued, in the best tradition of the pictures she'd seen with a black and white dog listening attentively to the sound.

Clover was allowed to accompany Sally to the village where a shop sold gramophone records – heavy black discs with the picture of the dog and the horn on their labels. Urged on by Sally, she purchased a number of records which she knew would raise her aunts' blood pressure a notch or two if they heard them. Sally giggled and as though reading her mind exclaimed, 'Aye, they will and all!' She picked up one, examining it with narrowed eyes: a recording of a popular male singer who was famous for his sentimental ballads. 'This should be good. I might get one meself if I can afford it next pay day.'

Clover immediately opened her purse. 'Let me . . .'

Sally held up a restraining hand, firmly shaking her head. 'No, I wouldn't 'ear of it, Miss Clover. If I'm meant to 'ave it, the good Lord will see that I've enough to pay for it. If not, then it means I'm not supposed to.'

Clover smiled. 'Does that apply to all you buy?'

'Yes, it does. 'Ow else are people like me goin' to stay out of debt!'

Clover had to admire her policy. Her father could do worse than follow such a course.

As soon as she got home she ran upstairs, Sally

making an excuse to follow her, mumbling something about seeing if fresh towels had been placed in the bathroom. Almost reverently Clover wound up the handle of the old machine, placed the arm with its fine silver needle on the outer groove and the two girls stood back, waiting to hear the first bars of the romantic song.

Clover tried a few steps of the new Bunny Hug, a dance that was sweeping London, so she had heard, stopping every so often to wind the machine when it threatened to grind to a halt.

'Yes, sir, that's my baby. No, sir, don't mean maybe . . .' The music filled the room. Heels kicking, hands flapping, she delighted in the syncopated rhythm of the number, trying to persuade Sally to join her. At first she hung back, shaking her head, saying, 'Oh, Miss Clover, I couldn't. My family don't believe in dancing. Not that sort of dancing.'

'What other sort is there?' cried Clover, enjoying herself immensely.

Sally giggled. 'My mam would say that kind of dancing was invented by the Devil hisself.'

Clover pulled a wry face. Her aunts would probably take the same view, she thought.

'Is that the kind of dancing you do on stage, miss?' Sally couldn't help asking, watching the kicking heels, the flapping hands.

Clover stopped to wind the machine. 'No, not this sort. My father is fairly old-fashioned about the act we do. My brother was always wanting to change it, bring in new songs and dances, but my dad wouldn't hear of it.' She wrinkled her nose, turning over the record to its other side.

'What happened to your brother, miss? I thought you 'ad no one but your dad.'

'He went off to America. For a while we heard from

him and then the letters suddenly stopped. I don't know what or how he's doing now. But, being Eddie, he's probably setting Broadway on its heels and too busy to write home.'

Sally shook her head in bewilderment. What a life this young girl must have experienced! And what a family! Light years away from her own hard-working mother and shy sisters.

The music had set her pulses leaping, her toes twitching and it didn't take much more persuasion from Clover for her to join in a slow waltz. The music of the new record was softer, closer to Sally's tastes, and the two girls were enjoying themselves enormously when the door suddenly opened and the startled face of Aunt Bethany appeared. Sally was sent packing back to the kitchen, while Clover was given a lecture on the unseemliness of becoming too friendly with the servants. Amazingly, Aunt Bethany didn't take it any further, just gave Clover a pitying look and closed the door quietly behind her, after announcing that tea was ready.

After that, the only times Clover saw Sally were when she was working, making up the fire in the sitting room – Bethany was always cold, feeling the chill on the warmest day – or bringing in the tea tray at four o'clock.

Clover felt more hedged in than ever. The De Burney School for Young Ladies was on holiday and so she found time hanging more heavily than ever on her hands. She missed the discussions on life that she'd enjoyed with Sally, the way the girl laughed off the hardships of her own life. Once when Clover mentioned Bert's drinking and how much it had worried her, Sally grinned and said benevolently, 'Well, 'e's a man, ain't 'e? They're all the same. Me old dad was like that. The times me mam found 'im in the gutter when 'e didn't come 'ome from the pub I've lost count of, I can tell you. Maybe, when 'e comes out of that place 'e's in, 'e'll be different. Maybe the fright'll 'ave cured 'im.'

Clover pulled a face. And pigs might fly, she thought.

There was no chance now of any more of those comforting little gossips. The weather was gorgeous and she longed to be able to run wild across the moors. She would sit at her open bedroom window, imagining the scene: herself, hair streaming behind her in chaotic disorder, running to meet someone who would catch her in his arms, lifting her high in an ecstatic embrace.

When she received a letter from Adam informing her that he would be up that way on business and would like to pay his respects to her aunts, her joy knew no bounds. Aunt Bethany read the letter Clover had dutifully passed to her. She said, 'I suppose there can be no harm in it.'

Hesitatingly, Hazel said, 'I did say he would be most welcome, sister, when last he was here. He seemed such a pleasant young man, a real gentleman, and I'm sure Clover would like to ask him questions about her father.'

Bethany looked at her with reproach but said nothing. Models of propriety, there was a lengthy discussion between the ladies as to the seemliness of a young, unaccompanied man staying overnight again in a spinster ladies' house. Clover listened and thought: Dear God in heaven, I hope if I never marry I don't get like that! The sisters finally agreed that there could be no harm in it. And, pointed out Hazel, goodness knows they had enough empty bedrooms . . .

Heavy gusts of rain driven by a strong wind arrived before Adam did. When Frank picked him up from the station, the gusts had reached hurricane force. As he hurried to open the passenger door for Adam it was almost torn off its hinges by the force of the wind. Clover watched as Adam struggled across the gravel to the front door, one hand held tight to his hat, the other clutching his small overnight case. The aunts clucked over him, bidding him go straight to his room to change. 'You're soaking wet,' exclaimed Hazel.

Adam grinned. 'Yes, the wind was so fierce that it blew the rain right across the station platform. The train happened to be early and so I had about ten minutes to wait. Not to worry,' he added disarmingly, 'I'll soon dry out.'

'Sally's put a fire in your room,' said Bethany, 'so it should be nice and warm.' She clicked her tongue. 'There really is no accounting for the weather, is there? And after such a perfect summer.' She turned to beckon to the hovering Sally to bring the doctor's case, and herself led him upstairs.

Clover watched from the hall. She didn't dare believe that he'd come all this way just to see her, even though on his last visit he had assured her he would. He'd mentioned business in his letter. Combining the two would be his target, she thought. She was silly to read anything more in his actions.

Alone with him for a moment after dinner while her aunts were fussing with Sally over a window left open to the storm, Clover tried to sound nonchalant when she asked him, 'Are you here on business for Dr Fraser?'

Her heart almost stopped beating and then gave a kind of somersault at the look he gave her. Naive as she was, there was no mistaking the tenderness in those dark eyes. Or the warmth in his voice when he said, 'It seemed a good excuse.' Their eyes met and held.

She wondered if she would ever be able to breathe normally again, her chest felt so tight. How humiliating if she fainted, right there in front of him, collapsing in a heap on her aunts' beautiful hearthrug.

Terrified that she would blurt out something stupid,

she kept silent. He said slowly, 'Dr Fraser bawled me
out for my lack of concentration and suggested I take a
few days off. A change of scenery is what I needed, he
said.' Still holding her gaze, he went on, 'I could have
told him it wasn't just a change of scenery I needed.
My greatest need was to see you, Clover.'

Her heart did another turn. 'To tell me the latest news
of my father?'

He laughed. 'Well, that, too. He's doing very well,
the nurses are all madly in love with him and he's taken
to striding about the sanatorium grounds as though he's
in training for the marathon.'

'So it shouldn't be too long before he's able to
come back?'

He didn't answer her question but said instead,
'Aren't you happy here? Your aunts seem only too
willing to have you stay for as long as you want.'

'Who wouldn't be happy in this lovely house, my
every need catered for? Of course I'm happy. And I
told you in my letters about the finishing school my
aunts are sending me to.'

He nodded.

'Even that's been edifying,' she said. 'I've made
friends with a few of the girls and been invited to
tea parties. All,' she grimaced, 'supervised by Frank's
stern eye.'

'But you'd still rather be with your father?'

The return of her aunts put paid to any further
discussion of this subject.

Seated at the breakfast table the next morning, Aunt
Hazel, who was always the first one down, said with a
girlish laugh, 'I think you may have an admirer.'

Clover made no reply, although her cheeks flamed,
telling their own story. Sally had just placed a silver rack
of hot toast before them and returned to the kitchen
for the bacon and eggs. A shaft of sunlight pierced the

watery blue sky and yesterday's storm seemed just a memory.

Reaching for a slice of toast, Hazel spread it with butter and then remarked casually, 'What do you propose to do today, dear?'

'I don't know. Did you want me to help you with something?' Secretly, she hoped she didn't, for more than anything she wanted to be alone with Adam.

Bethany arrived just in time to hear her last remark. Seating herself opposite her sister, she said briskly, 'Nonsense! You must get Frank to take you and Dr Foley out in the car. A drive out onto the moors. It would do you good.' She poured herself coffee from the tall silver pot. 'No, perhaps not. After all that rain the roads will be impossible, and anyway, today is Frank's day off.'

Clover wished they would let her and Adam decide themselves what they were to do. As long as she was with Adam she didn't mind what they did. And, let's face it, she thought, what choice was there in Shackleton, anyway?

'Sister,' Hazel broke in enthusiastically, 'didn't you say just last evening that the books were due back at the library? Perhaps Clover and Dr Foley would be good enough to return them for us? They could take the pony cart . . .'

'I hardly think Dr Foley has come all this way just to return books for two old women to a library.' Aunt Bethany's voice held a reprimand. Hazel, breathing through her nose, stirred her cup of coffee so forcibly that it spilt into the saucer.

Hastily, Clover said, 'I don't mind, Aunt Bethany. You know I love browsing around the library. It's not a chore, believe me.' Her look included Hazel. 'And if there's any other shopping that needs doing, I'll be glad to do that as well.' The presence of other people might stop her from making a fool of herself in front of Adam, she thought.

A shadow darkened the glass doors leading from the garden and Adam appeared. He was dressed in a Harris tweed jacket and grey flannels. Freshly shaved, his skin glowed in the chill morning air.

'I hope you don't mind but I woke early and couldn't resist taking a stroll round your beautiful garden. I tried not to get too muddy, keeping to the paths.'

'Good, then you must have worked up an appetite.' Hazel smiled at him archly.

'Starving,' he admitted. 'And I didn't mean to eavesdrop but I couldn't help overhearing your discussion about the library and shopping. To me it sounds an excellent idea.'

Without thinking, echoing Bethany's words, Clover said, 'But there must be other things you'd rather do?'

'I can't think of a single one,' he replied chivalrously and Clover was aware of the look exchanged between the two aunts.

It was decided that the weather was too unreliable for the pony cart; instead, Adam could drive the car himself. He was delighted. Since he'd first laid eyes on it, he'd been dying to drive the wonderful Rolls-Royce Silver Ghost. But after breakfast, a short, sharp rain shower put a halt to their plans. It was early afternoon before they set out.

Sitting beside him on the leather seat, Clover let herself sink into a dream in which she and Adam were lovers, surprising herself by her lascivious thoughts. But how could she help it, Adam so close beside her, his hands firm upon the wheel, his profile calm and so handsome as he studied the narrow road over which they drove. The wind whispered its messages in the silence.

White clouds raced restlessly overhead, chasing their own shadows over the stretch of moorland.

Being Saturday afternoon, the small town of Shackleton was busy. Wooden market stalls lined the square outside the town hall; voices bellowed their wares, all competing to outdo their neighbour. Everything that the farmer's wife and family could want was offered on those stalls. For the more affluent, the shops did a busy trade, people queuing at the baker's who made homemade bread and pastries.

It was after three when they emerged from the public library, its narrow doorway in the ancient grey stone building so low that Adam had to stoop. He took her arm and guided her through the maze of busy shoppers. 'Well, come on,' he said teasingly. 'Show me the sights of Shackleton.'

'That shouldn't take long,' smiled Clover. 'About two minutes if we take our time.'

They walked across the bridge she had seen from the train. He broke twigs from a riverside shrub and watched them as they sailed past on the peat-coloured water. Standing at her side, leaning against the stonework of the grey hump-backed bridge, he studied her bright, animated face. Although from the start he'd been attracted to her, he'd thought of her more as a child, needing help. This visit, after the few months they had been apart, had brought him up against the fact that she was growing up into a woman. And a damned attractive one at that.

Another sudden shower of rain had them running to seek shelter. The most likely place was the tea room across from the market square. It was cosy in an old-fashioned kind of way, with watercolours of local scenes on the white walls and small pottery vases filled with wild flowers on each table. Covered in crisply starched linen cloths, the tables were set for afternoon tea.

Adam hung his fedora hat on the hatstand in the corner and looked about him. 'Nice!' was his comment. They were lucky to get a table in the bay window. Busy housewives wandered in, gazing about them to see if there was anyone they knew whom they could join for a good gossip. Glancing out of the window, Clover saw a rainbow arching over the town. 'Quick, make a wish,' she said, drawing aside the net curtain so that he could see as well.

'Do people really wish on rainbows?' he asked.

'I always do. Quick, what would you like most in the whole world?'

'If I told you then it wouldn't come true,' he smiled.

'That's for stirring the Christmas pudding and pulling the wishbone,' she reminded him soberly.

'It's not only for those things, it's a time-honoured rule. If you reveal your wish, then it won't come true.'

'Time-honoured rules are meant to be broken.'

Her flippant answer surprised him and he said, 'You're tempting the fates. Don't you realise that?'

'The fates haven't been very good to me lately,' she said and gazed down at her teacup.

He reached over the table and covered her hand with his, feeling its soft warmth. 'Things will get better, I promise.'

Blushing, she looked again at the rainbow. 'It's almost gone. Better hurry.'

'I might as well wish for the moon. I'm as likely to get that as what I really want.'

His eyes bored into hers and she looked away, afraid to read what was expressed there. Afraid and yet longing . . . 'Oh, do hurry. It's fading fast,' she entreated.

'If it means that much to you.' His hand moved on hers, caressing the fingers, his thumb gently rubbing the knuckles. 'I wish that sometime in the future you will come back to Moorfield.'

She blushed again.

His hand continued to caress hers. 'Clover, my new partner arrives soon and I'll be too busy to get away. So it might be some time before I can see you again.'

A waitress with the rosy cheeks of a country girl took their order. Clover waited until she had gone before saying, 'I understand. I wouldn't expect you to.'

'But this isn't goodbye. I shall write and keep you in touch with how things are going. And maybe later, when your father's fully recovered and working again, maybe you'll consider coming back to help me in my work?' He paused. Another year and he could bring his feelings out into the open. At seventeen, a girl like Clover was too immature to know what she wanted, certainly far too young to consider marriage.

When she didn't answer, he said, 'Surely you're not thinking of going back to the precarious life of the stage after all you've already been through?'

'Of course.' Clover looked surprised that he should even have doubts on this issue. 'And thank you for your offer of a job, but my place is with my father.'

The waitress came back, carrying a tray on which rested a small brown pottery teapot, milk and sugar and the toasted teacakes they had ordered.

On the drive back they were silent, wrapped up in their own thoughts. Never had a weekend passed so quickly. It seemed no time at all before he was bidding them goodbye. He explained he had business in York to carry out for Dr Fraser, a detour that would take time.

Standing by the car, Frank holding the passenger door open, Adam brushed a closed fist gently across her chin. 'And just think on what I said about that rainbow,' he murmured. The sisters watched. It was quite obvious that the young couple were attracted to each other. Although it had nothing to do with her, Bethany thought the doctor would make a perfect match. But what was to happen when Bert returned?

Chapter Seventeen

Bert arrived on a bright October day when the garden was ablaze with late blooming roses and chrysanthemums.

The Miss Frosts stood in stunned silence at the open front door. Sally faded into the shadows at the back of the hall, her listening compulsive. She felt in her bones that something dreadful was about to happen.

Bethany, whose every instinct was to send him packing, looked down the length of her aristocratic nose and said icily, 'Why have you come?' Hazel, standing beside her, stared wide-eyed and anxious.

Bert Blossom gave her one of his broadest smiles. 'Why else but to take my daughter home with me, where she belongs.'

Bethany's gaze grew even more icy. 'Home? And where, pray, do you call home these days? Clover has been attending finishing school this past summer and is very happy. Her reports are excellent and she has made new friends, nice girls, with good backgrounds. Not like the ones with whom—'

'Oh, sister!' Hazel's voice broke on a sob. 'What is he saying? Does he mean to take Clover from us?'

'You've had my daughter for the past five months,' said Bert. 'Now I'm up and about, she's returning to where she belongs, under my protection.'

Bethany snorted. 'Really, I've never heard anything so ridiculous.'

There were light footsteps on the stairs behind them. Clover had heard the voices, recognised her father's. Jumping down the last three steps, her voice rising in welcome, she cried, 'Daddy! Daddy! Is it really you? Are you better? Have they allowed you home from the sanatorium?' She ran across the hall and threw herself into his arms.

Bert laughed, clasping her to him while her aunts looked on with horrified expressions. 'One question at a time, young lady,' he said. 'And it's yes to all of them.' He stood back, holding her at arm's length. 'Well, just look at you! All grown up and as pretty as a picture. The country air has certainly done you a power of good.'

'Oh, Daddy, I'm so glad to see you.' Clover felt so happy she could hardly express herself. He looked fit and rested, and with all the old charm back, as well as the arrogance that was part of his nature; the arrogance that expected everyone to fall in with his wishes without argument.

Ignoring the sisters, tucking her hand under his arm, he turned towards the garden. 'I'm better and I'm home for good. Come on, let's walk. It's so good to feel really free again, away from all those petty restrictions that place imposed on us.'

Acutely aware of her aunts' anguished stares as they walked away from the house, Clover felt as though a spell had been cast over her and that she could no more deny this man anything than fly to the moon. She had so looked forward to him coming back to get her, making up scenarios in her mind as to how it would happen. Now, although she was ecstatic to see him, to know he was better, a sense of injustice to her aunts battled with the joy of seeing him.

She hugged his arm closer to her body and said, 'Tell me all about it. Did the doctors say you were quite cured?'

'Never mind what the doctors said. Tell me what *you've* been doing this summer. What's this school the old trout mentioned?'

As they walked, Clover described the life she had been leading while Bert was away, mentioning Adam Foley's visit just briefly. Not making too much of it. 'That was kind of him,' murmured Bert thoughtfully. 'I remember all the trouble he went to to get me admitted to Greenbay. There was a waiting list, you know, so I was lucky to be admitted as soon as I was.' He nodded. 'Yes, very kind of him. It seems you had a better summer than your poor old dad could 'ave given you.'

She squeezed his arm. 'Oh, Daddy, don't say that. I missed you. You weren't all that great a letter-writer, either, you know. For all the pretty clothes and good food the aunts provided, I would rather have been with you in our old life.'

Something in the gentleness of her voice reminded him so strongly of Adele that sudden tears came to his eyes. 'Well, you shall be from now on, my little love. Let me tell you about the plans I've made for us . . .'

They sat on the low stone wall surrounding the goldfish pond and he spoke at length of his schemes, painting such a glowing picture that Clover wondered that she could ever doubt him, feeling a traitor that she did. She noticed that he stayed carefully away from the subject of Eddie. When she had first arrived at Shackleton, she had written and given her brother their new addresses. Now, tentatively, she said, 'Have you heard anything from Eddie lately?'

He shook his head, his mouth firming into a straight line. 'No, not a dickybird. Have you?'

It was her turn to shake her head.

'Well,' he went on, 'if that's how he wants it to be, that's how it will be. We'll concentrate on ourselves, my maiden. The Two Blossoms, eh? We'll make a go of it together, as we've always done.' He rose to his feet. 'Come on, let's go and acquaint the old dears of your decision.'

How could she harbour doubts when her father sounded so sure, so confident in the future he'd planned for them?

The two elderly women waited in the conservatory with its array of colourful plants in tubs and cushioned wicker chairs. When told of Bert's new plans, they looked stricken, seeing all their hopes for Clover falling apart. The soft-hearted Hazel clutched at the arm of her chair, placing the other hand across her heart. 'Oh, Clover!' There was a world of grief in that small utterance.

Aunt Bethany seemed too angry for words, glaring at Bert as though he were the devil incarnate. Then she controlled herself enough to announce, in a steady voice, 'You know, Clover, over this last summer we've become very fond of you. Are you quite sure this is what you want? A return to your old life? We don't want to see you making the same mistakes your poor mother made.' She felt such hatred for the man before her, could hardly bear to be in the same room as him, she didn't even try to hide it.

Hot words sprang to Bert's lips, words in defence of his wife. 'Adele did not make a mess of her life,' he objected harshly. 'On the contrary, she was very happy.'

Bethany sighed, reliving in her mind the whole acrimonious scene all over again. 'Really,' she began. 'You can't expect us to believe that—'

'Why don't we get Sally to make us a nice cup of tea?' Hazel broke in hastily, seeing the glint in her sister's eye. 'Then we can talk about it coolly. You know how dear Papa always used to say that discussion always helped.'

Since Cook was away, visiting a sick relative, Aunt Bethany suggested that Clover go with Sally to the kitchen to help with the tea tray.

In the kitchen, Sally busied herself with filling the kettle and placing it on the stove while Clover put out the teacups and saucers. There was an unnatural silence between the two girls, Sally loath to pry where she wasn't wanted, Clover too absorbed in her own disquietude to discuss this new event.

Sally jerked her head towards the round tin that held Cook's latest culinary offering. 'There's some fruit cake there, miss. 'Ow about putting some out on a plate? Your dad might fancy a bit.'

Clover did as she was bid, trying not to think too much about what might be happening in the room where Bert and her aunts waited. Curiosity got the better of Sally. She turned from the stove, the freshly made pot of tea in her hands. 'He seems a nice man, your dad. Very good-looking.'

Clover nodded, not wishing to get into a discussion while her thoughts were still in such a turmoil. Getting the message, Sally left it at that.

When they returned to the conservatory, Clover's eyes flew to where Bert stood, his back to the room, hands clasped loosely behind him, gazing beyond the long french windows at the garden. The air was electric, old hatreds bubbling below the surface.

'Put the tray down here, Sally.' Hearing Bethany's voice, he turned.

A faint feeling of resentment stirred in Clover. She'd guessed why Aunt Bethany had asked her to go and help Sally – to get her out of the room so the grown-ups could talk. They could shape her life without her raising objections to anything they said. But her father had come all this way to get her. What kind of a daughter would she be if she abandoned him now?

Besides, he'd been ill. He'd need her more than ever now.

Aunt Hazel poured the tea into delicate china cups, passing them to Sally to hand round. There followed small tea plates on which a slice of Cook's rich fruit cake rested. No one spoke.

Whatever had been said in Clover's absence obviously hadn't been met with approval by her aunts. From the surly look on his face, it was also obvious that Bert had refused to be swayed by any suggestions the two sisters had put forward.

At last Aunt Bethany spoke. 'Very well,' she said tightly, as though there had been no pause in the discussions, 'if that is your attitude then there is nothing more we can do about it. I do think, however, that you could have had the generosity to allow your daughter more time to make up her own mind. How can a girl of her tender years be expected to decide so hastily on something that will fashion her whole future?'

Clover put her hands to her hot cheeks, her eyes pleading for understanding. 'I'm sorry, Aunt Bethany, Aunt Hazel . . . I'm so sorry if I seem ungrateful. And after all you've done . . . But he's my father. He has only me. My place is with him.'

'My daughter, like her dear mother, has a mind of her own, as you see,' said Bert calmly. He turned to Clover. 'Go on, girl, get your things. I can't stand much more of this company.'

She heard Hazel's quietly repressed sobbing, Bethany's low mutter of condemnation, and knew she would never be welcomed into this house again. It was history repeating itself.

With one last look towards Sally, her shoulders sagging, Clover turned towards the door. Bert followed, his face completely devoid of expression.

Sally followed them into the hall. She hissed between her teeth, 'Come on, I'll 'elp you pack, miss.'

Clover ran up the stairs to her bedroom, wishing she was dreaming and would wake any minute, relief flooding her to find it was all a dream. On the porch, Bert waited, his lips pursed in a soundless whistle, his hands thrust negligently in his pockets, hat perched on the back of his head.

The two sisters remained in the sunny conservatory. Hazel had made an effort to follow Clover but had been halted by Bethany's sharp, 'No, sister, let them go.' Bethany wanted nothing more to do with the whole wretched affair. Hazel, as usual, was expected to follow her example.

Soon Clover came back down the stairs, carrying the same battered suitcase she had brought with her from Moorfield. She had decided to leave behind the pretty undergarments and frocks her aunts had persuaded her to purchase during the summer. The feeling was strong in her that she really had no right to them now. There was no sign of her aunts when she joined Bert at the front door. He turned to look at her. 'Come on, then, we're leaving.'

Leaving! Suddenly the word conjured up a dreary image of a dark night; of herself and her father creeping down a staircase, carrying their few possessions; of the white blur of a face peering out at them from a partly opened door, a voice saying, grudgingly, 'You'd better come in, then.' A never ending procession of dingy bedsits. It was like a partly remembered nightmare.

She realised Bert was talking, something about a train they must catch and suddenly she was turning, running back into the house, to the conservatory and her grim-faced aunts.

She hadn't realised how much it would grieve her to leave them. Hazel gave a little cry and ran towards

Clover, flinging her arms about her neck. 'Oh, thank God, you've changed your mind!'

Aunt Bethany said bitterly, 'I knew that man wouldn't have the guts to carry out an act of such treachery. Why, it's tantamount to kidnapping!'

Helplessly, Clover shook her head. 'I'm sorry, you'll never know how sorry I am, but I haven't changed my mind. I can't refuse to go with him. He needs me. He'll always need me. Please try to understand.'

'Why don't you stay a day or two longer, Clover? What are we going to do without you?' Hazel showed signs of hysteria.

From the open doorway behind them, Bert said flippantly, 'Worse things happen at sea! Come on, lass. I'm waiting,' and somehow it was all too much to bear. To her dismay, Clover began to cry; great sobs shaking her body. She covered her face with her hands, pressing her fingertips to her eyelids, willing the tears to stop. Crying could only make things worse.

And then Bert was putting his arms about her, cradling her, whispering to her not to be such a silly girl. Tightly clenched within her own grief, Clover stood rigid and unresponsive, hating herself for her show of emotion, her father for being the cause of it.

Finally he persuaded her to make a move. His arm still about her, Bert guided her to the front door and out onto the driveway. The gravel crunched under her feet, reminding her of the way the lovely Silver Ghost sounded whenever they started out on a drive. Sally ran after them on their long walk down the drive. There were tears in her eyes and she hugged Clover to her, begging her to take care of herself. The look she directed at Bert wasn't quite so benevolent.

From somewhere, Bert had obtained the hire of a small two-wheeled cart, pulled by a tired-looking horse. He had left it tethered just inside the main gates of the house and it was clear the horse had been enjoying a pleasant doze in the sun.

'Whoops-a-daisy!' he grinned and gave Clover a lift up, pushing from behind. Seated beside her on the wooden seat, he flicked the horse lightly with the tip of the whip. It broke into a trot. Turning for one last look, Clover saw the elegant house where she had spent the summer, sometimes happy, sometimes in misery, shrouded behind its trees. She wondered if she would ever see either of its two elderly occupants again.

'That Dr Foley was interested in what my plans were,' Bert said as they made their way to Shackleton station. He had already been back to Moorfield and collected his few belongings.

'And did you tell him?' Her heart did a quick skip and a jump as she spoke.

He gave her a keen look. 'Didn't see what it had to do with him. I was about to tell him when I thought better of it.'

Clover sighed. 'Oh, Daddy! Dr Foley's been so kind when he didn't have to be. He's just concerned for my – our, welfare, that's all.'

Bert noticed the hasty correction from the 'my' to 'our'. He grinned. 'Taken a fancy to you, has he? I'm not surprised. This summer you've grown up. Who'd have thought that living with those two old sourpusses would have made you flourish like that? You're going to be as bonny as your mother, bless her soul.'

'Course he hasn't taken a fancy to me.' He noted the touch of asperity in her voice and it amused him. 'What a thing to say! I'm sure Dr Foley has better things to do with his time than worry about our future plans.'

'Yes, well . . .' He fixed his gaze on the road ahead. They were approaching the town and the road was becoming busy. The horse trotted along briskly, sensing it was nearing home. 'I told him I'd heard of an opening at a place in Newcombe. A bloke I know said if I presented myself for work within the next few days I might strike lucky.'

'And how are we going to get there? What do we use for money?'

The question didn't faze him in the slightest. 'We'll get the afternoon train. The same bloke I spoke to lent me a few quid.'

The words were suddenly like a heavy weight, a link in a chain that was there to imprison her. Seeing the way her mouth tightened, he added quickly, 'As soon as I get my first pay I'll let him have it back. He's an old pal, he knows I'm good for it.'

There was a long silence while the trees and hedges alongside the road passed in a blur of colour, already changing to their autumn shades.

Glancing at her sideways, he repeated, 'You've grown up, haven't you?'

'I'm seventeen. The aunts gave me a birthday party and some of the girls from the school came. It was very nice.' A birthday card had arrived from him a week late and she had smiled and passed it to her aunts, saying, 'Daddy never could remember dates.'

Bert said, 'It's somehow hurtful, you not being a little girl any longer.'

'Daddy, I haven't been a little girl for a long time.'

'I've led you a pretty hectic dance, haven't I? Oh, Clover, if only everything could have stayed as it was when your dear mother was alive. But I have that old feeling in my bones that this time we'll be lucky. The Two Blossoms will be back again, as good as ever.'

In Shackleton, Bethany Frost gave instructions to the servants that everything Bert had touched was to be destroyed.

Wide-eyed, trembling, as though the very cup and saucer she carried before her on the tray would suddenly come to life and attack her, Sally hurried through to the kitchen. Watched disbelievingly by Cook, who had just returned and was peeved to have missed all the excitement, Sally dropped the cup and saucer into the sink. Cook winced as the delicate china smashed into small pieces.

The damask napkin on which Bert had dabbed his mouth was burned and the silver teaspoon tossed into the dustbin, later to be retrieved by Sally and sold for sixpence to the secondhand stall in the market. The chair on which Bert had briefly rested was, like all the other furniture in the house, an expensive item, one of a set that Bethany had had covered specially to her taste and so would be difficult to replace. Hazel begged her not to have it destroyed. It was carried by two of the servants into the paved back yard behind the kitchen quarters and scrubbed with hot water and disinfectant. Then it was left in the sun to dry. It was never the same again. The brightly coloured cushioned back and seat dried mottled, a permanent reminder to the sisters of that hated member of the male sex who not once, but twice, had disrupted the happy tenor of their lives.

The first person Clover contacted when they arrived in Newcombe was Miss Boyce. She was delighted to welcome Clover back. She had not seen her for almost a year. Eleven months, anyway. Eleven months in the life of Miss Boyce was a long time. And in that time Clover had grown into a young woman, a certain assurance and polish giving her a maturity that hadn't been there before.

'I bet your aunts were sorry to see you go,' she said. 'They will miss you.'

Tears threatened in Clover's eyes. 'And I shall miss

them. I'll try and keep in touch – if they will answer my letters.' Which wasn't at all probable after the way Bert had literally dragged her away from them.

Miss Boyce sighed. She recalled the fiasco of Bert's last performance with the Summer Follies, the boos and catcalls, and her heart went out to the girl who would never see her father for what he was, a feckless, irresponsible man who was his own worst enemy. She was delighted to have Clover back, but in her opinion Bert would have been better leaving her with her aunts.

Looking at Clover, she said, 'I saw Mr Ryder the other week, he was asking about you. Said to give you his regards next time I saw you.' She paused for a moment, then went on, 'And you know he said if you ever needed help . . .'

Clover's chin firmed. 'After what he did to my father? I wouldn't set foot in any of his theatres again, not if I was down to my last crust of bread.'

Miss Boyce shook her head. Stubborn to the point of obstinacy was Clover. Keeping up the pretence that Bert remained his old vital, decisive self, listening to his schemes and agreeing with everything he said.

His latest scheme proved to be another that floundered. There wasn't an opening for Bert and by the time they had found lodgings they could afford, Bert's money had all but run out. He had been careful to avoid the various boarding houses where they had stayed in the past. It was only too apparent that the gossip surrounding him was still fresh in the minds of both landladies and theatre managers.

Clover could quite easily have fallen into a slough of despair. After the summer spent in that lovely house with her aunts, her own pretty bedroom and the civilised surroundings of the De Burney school, she had little appetite for returning to the life of poverty she had shared with Bert. She decided it was time to take matters into her own hands. They couldn't go on living indefinitely off loans they had little hope of repaying, scrabbling from hand to mouth like this. Suddenly, words echoed in Clover's mind, a man's voice saying, 'I'll wager in another year or two men won't turn you down quite so casually.'

She thought of the hawk-like face, the dark good looks and made up her mind.

Chapter Eighteen

Although Imelda wasn't religious, had never been inside a church in her life except briefly at her grandmother's funeral service, the idea of a church wedding with all the trimmings had appealed to her. She pictured herself in white satin, a long, flowing train gliding across a crimson carpet after her, the coronet of orange blossom on her hair holding a delicately gauzy veil.

What she got was a hurried, almost furtive little formality in a dingy, ill-lit room in the local registry office. A middle-aged couple passing the steps of the building were unceremoniously summoned from the pavement as witnesses. The man clicked his false teeth throughout the proceedings, and the woman, even in that chill atmosphere, emitted a heavy body odour. The man who performed the ceremony gabbled the words at such a pace Imelda could hardly understand what he was saying. Only the pressure of Eddie's hand in hers made her aware of the fact that at one point she was supposed to answer, 'I do.'

She almost didn't, sudden doubts taking hold of her. She'd never really wanted to *belong* to anybody. She had once listened to Clover read aloud from a book of poetry about free spirits and independence, and although at the time she didn't fully comprehend the meaning of the words, she thought she did now.

A free spirit – to be that, surely, was everything a body could wish for. Over the years, a series of people had *owned* her: first her grandmother, then a succession of old biddies at the tinker camp, then Buster Bywater. She was sick of being owned. Although she loved Eddie – well, she was fond of him, at any rate, and she supposed that must be a kind of love – she had no desire to spend her life tied to one man.

The words of the marriage service echoed in the chill air of the depressing little room where not even a vase of flowers brightened the gloom. 'And forsaking all others, hold thee only unto him for as long as ye both shall live . . .'

A shiver went through her as she heard the words. They sounded so final, so cold-blooded. As long as ye both shall live! She really ought to have given herself more time. But as soon as her pregnancy was confirmed, Eddie had insisted they get married.

No day to remember this, all tied up in white ribbon and tucked away to remember when she felt blue, Imelda reflected despondently.

Afterwards Eddie, greatly daring, for as usual they were almost broke, hailed a horse and buggy to drive them around Central Park. They sat on the black leather seat, the driver flicking his long whip in showy fashion, caressing the rear of the glossy chestnut mare. He had tucked a plaid rug about their knees in recognition of the February weather. Eddie held her tightly, his eyes bright with love.

'Isn't this great,' he murmured into her ear. 'We'll bring our son here. The time will go so quickly we'll be doing it before you can say Jack Robinson.' His arm tightened. 'With maybe a little sister or two, eh?'

Imelda grunted, watching the New Yorkers who thronged the pathways, the children playing ball games on the grass. 'I don't know how we're going to keep the one we're having,' she said, 'never mind another two.'

'Our luck will change soon,' he told her. 'It's got

to.' He refused to be disheartened on his wedding day.

At the end of the ride he tossed a coin up to the driver. 'Here,' he said, smiling widely, 'buy yourself a new horse.'

The driver wished them luck, touched his hat, folded the plaid rug on the seat and drove away. Arm in arm they walked home to the dingy apartment and its noisy neighbours.

As the summer progressed, Imelda became clumsy and the slightest exertion made her breathless. The heat made her ankles swell, none of her clothes fitted her any more and there was no money to go out and treat herself to new ones. And her morning sickness seemed to last for most of the day. Thoroughly miserable, she took to lounging about the room at Mrs Riley's, which, although only meant to be temporary, was still their home. The streets that had once seemed so friendly and cheerful seemed to be filled with unhappy, poverty-stricken people. The neighbours with whom she had been on such friendly terms didn't seem so amiable any more.

She had come all this way, hoping for a better life, and had ended up with one as bad, if not worse. She stood at the window and watched the women in the back street in their ragged black shawls. The children were grubby, running hither and thither, pinching apples from a cart or trying to scrounge a dime from some likely looking passer-by.

At the end of the road, a water hydrant had been vandalised. The shrieks were loudest where a group of children, fully clothed, jumped in and out of the fall of gushing water, enjoying to the full the brief moments of emancipation before being moved on by some inter- fering cop. Imelda gazed at them dispassionately. She had no thought or aspirations for the child she carried. It was a burden to be endured, something she'd rather not think about. Her mouth took on a bitter twist and Eddie eyed the skirts fastened with a huge safety pin, or, more commonly, not fastened at all but left gaping, and blamed himself for all that had happened. He thought of his brave words to Clover: 'I'm going to work so hard at the thing I like best that the whole world will hear about Edward Blossom.'

However, the thing that he liked best was not for New York. No one was interested in a song and dance man, especially a limey, good-looking and brawny as he was, of whom nobody had ever heard. He met it everywhere he went. They had enough out-of-work piano players of their own without employing foreigners. He would have to face it sometime. In September the baby would be born and he would like to be out of Mrs Riley's and in something more comfortable before that. This was no place to bring up his child.

With a fierce determination, he decided he would accept whatever employment came his way. Already he had taken part-time jobs that were far beneath him; jobs that only lasted for a day or two. He would do almost anything rather than face one of Imelda's outbursts, he thought.

Reading an advertisement in the newspaper one morning for kitchen hands at the Ascot Hotel, the name rang a bell. Frantically he dug through the few possessions they had acquired, pulling out drawers, causing Imelda to glare accusingly when the contents of one spilled on the floor. Watching him, one hand pressed against her back, she said in a peevish voice, 'Maybe it would help if you told me what you were looking for?'

Eddie turned a despairing face towards her. 'That card Mr Farrel gave us. The one with his name and address on it. I'm sure it was the Ascot Hotel but I could be wrong.'

Reaching up to the mantelpiece, Imelda pulled out the small square card from behind the clock. 'You mean this?' She waved it in front of him, teasingly, transferring it quickly behind her back when he tried to snatch it.

'Imelda!'

She wrinkled her nose at him. 'All you've got to do is take it,' she murmured provokingly. 'A big, strong man like you against poor little ol' me!'

These quicksilver moods of hers never failed to arouse him. The moment he touched her, holding her by her shoulders, she seemed as always the most wonderful being in the whole wide world. Seeing the change come over his face, she moved closer and reached up to put an arm about his neck, her face pressed against his shoulder, and for long, long moments the elusive visiting card was forgotten. She was, he told himself, that treasured thing that other men talked about with envy: wife, mistress, soon to be mother. Hadn't he read somewhere of the theory that a person could only expect a certain measured amount of happiness in their lifetime and no more? There must be exceptions, though. God couldn't be so cruel as to snatch this wonderful happiness away before they had enjoyed it to the full.

His hands framed her face as he kissed her. Lifting her own hands to take his, she began to pull him towards the bedroom. 'Not now, Imelda,' he said. 'I've got to find this address.'

She looked sulky. 'Can't it wait?'

He shook his head. 'No, I'm afraid it can't, my sweet. There's jobs going in this hotel,' tapping the visiting card with one finger, 'and I thought while I was there I'd call and pay my respects to Mr Farrel, if he's still there. I won't be long.'

It was raining, wet and miserable with a cold wind blowing, as he set off to walk the crowded pavements in search of Nick Farrel and a job that not so long ago he would have scorned. In March, it had been like midsummer. Now, at the beginning of June, the rain poured from a leaden sky. He had never imagined New York in the rain, but always a place where the sun shone and people, if they put their backs into it, became rich overnight.

Reaching the hotel, he found that a queue had already formed. He joined the end and in an agony of impatience waited for it to move. It was at times like this that he realised fully just what he was up against. Finally the door at the head of the queue swung open and men began to filter through. Another long wait during which time the relentless rain crept under his collar, chilling him to the bone, dripping from the soggy brim of his hat, once set so jauntily. Then someone shouted from the end of the queue, 'The positions are filled, you guys, so there's no use you waiting any longer. Thanks for coming.'

There was a chorus of groans and muttered oaths and the dispirited men began to steal away, hands thrust deep into their pockets. Eddie went round to the front entrance, slightly uncomfortable to be on the receiving end of the uniformed commissionaire's suspicious stare.

Nevertheless, he opened the glass door for him and Eddie crossed the thickly carpeted lobby. The woman behind the desk gave him the same treatment as had the doorman. 'Can I help you?' she asked frostily. Although the words were polite, her tone said she didn't think there was much likelihood of that. She eyed the drowned rat of a young man with aversion.

'I certainly hope so.' Eddie gave her his best smile, watching her thaw a little under its charm. 'I'm looking for a Mr Farrel. Nick Farrel. I believe he always stays here when he's in town.'

'Mr Farrel certainly does stay here. He has a regular booking. But he left yesterday for California.'

He shouldn't have felt such deep disappointment, he thought. After all, it had been some months and Mr Farrel obviously was a busy man with other places to go to. Stubbornly he'd tried to make it on his own, without outside help. Now it was too late . . .

Back out on the street, he shivered and pulled the brim of the trilby hat down over his eyes, his shoulders hunched beneath the shabby raincoat. The bar on the corner beckoned like a beacon to a shipwrecked man. Imelda would have a go at him when he got home, but he felt the need so strongly he couldn't resist it. Not the need for the drink itself but for the sense of confidence, if only temporarily, it would give him. And the company of other men. He would have one beer and then go.

The beer turned out to be two and then three. A middle-aged man to whom he got talking and who that afternoon had turned up lucky on the horses insisted on buying the rounds. 'Might as well enjoy it while you can,' his new friend remarked as yet another glass was pushed into his hand. 'Once they declare prohibition, and there's talk that that could happen any day now, we're all goin' to have to join the temperance movement.'

A chorus of 'That'll be the day!' answered him from others at the bar.

At Eddie's puzzled look, the man – who had introduced himself as Stewart, 'Call me Stu, everybody does,' – explained. 'The manufacture, sale and transportation of all alcoholic liquor is to be prohibited. The big boys in Washington, in their infinite wisdom, imagine they know what's good for us, more than we do ourselves.'

'That's going to be tough,' remarked Eddie.

The man nodded. 'It sure is. So let's enjoy it while we may.' He beckoned the bartender for a refill. 'Lookin' for work, are you?' he asked Eddie.

Eddie nodded. 'Yes and it's bloody difficult, believe me.'

'What do you do?'

Eddie gave him a brief resumé of his background, adding that he was, in fact, ready to do anything for a living. Stu took a long pull of his beer, gazing thoughtfully at the young man over the froth-rimmed top. 'If you're interested, there's a job going in the men's room of the gymnasium of a pal of mine. Maxi Fields is his name. Well known in boxing circles.'

'Boxing circles?'

'Yeah, like in prize-fighting.'

Eddie nodded and Stu went on, 'It's not everyone's idea of heaven, working in a men's room. But it could be a step to something better and I know Maxi pays well for regular workers.'

Eddie did not care. Resigned to anything, even cleaning up after other people, he drained his glass and got up from the bar stool. 'Thanks, you're a pal.'

'It's not far from here, just in the next street,' said Stu. 'Say Stu sent you.'

Eddie smiled. 'I'll do that. And thanks again.'

Imelda was asleep on their bed when he got home. There was nothing prepared for a midday meal and so he set about making it himself. Later, feeling better, he walked round to the Maxi Fields Gymnasium. Someone called for Maxi, shouting there was a guy here to see him. Maxi looked him over, asked him a few questions, not showing any surprise at his background or English accent, and pushed a long-handled mop into his hand. 'Start now, can you?' was the only comment he made. Eddie nodded. 'Right. You keep the floor clean, make sure there's always a fresh supply of clean towels and don't let anyone drink on the premises. Or start any trouble. Our fighting takes place in the ring and nowhere else.'

He eyed the width of Eddie's shoulders, the muscular look about the boy and grunted, 'You surely look as though you could handle it.'

Maxi had all the characteristics of a boxer himself although Eddie later learned he'd never gone professional, preferring to train enthusiastic young men for the sport.

Eddie assured him he could handle it fine, proving his point one day when a couple of drunks barged into the gymnasium, intent on mayhem. Supporting themselves with an arm about each other's shoulders, they began singing and then making offensive remarks to everyone who was present. Eddie, quietly reading the paper in one corner, finally objected and threw them out.

Although Maxi Fields was impressed by the calm way he handled it, he said nothing. A few days later when one of the trainee fighters failed to turn up, he asked Eddie if he'd care to make a few extra bucks by taking his place. Eddie grinned. 'After the disinfectant smell of the men's room,' he said, wryly, 'I reckon I'd consider anything. But it's only fair to tell you that the only boxing I've done was at a fairground.'

Maxi gave one of his grunts. 'And?'

'I won,' grinned Eddie smugly.

Maxi laughed and thumped him on the shoulder. 'You'll do.'

A new cleaner was found for the men's room and Eddie's life took another turn. He trained hard and Maxi seemed pleased with him, although Imelda grew more fractious by the day, complaining constantly of the pain in her back, the way they never had enough money to buy the foods she craved; most of all of being left alone in the evening when Eddie was working in the gymnasium.

Eddie was patience itself with her moods. 'If we want to get out of this place, love,' he said, glancing round at the sombre room with its cheap furniture, 'then we've just got to grin and bear it. It won't be long, I promise. Maxi is putting me up for as many fights as he feels I can take. The money should start to roll in, for with the kind of opponent he's matching me against, I just know I'll win them all.'

Imelda refused to be appeased. Sulkily, she said, 'You sound just like your father. He was always one for the high-flying ideas that never came to anything. I thought you were different.'

Eddie didn't like being compared to his father. His cheeks flushed and he said, 'That isn't fair. You know I do my best. I've tried just about every agent in town, and there's not an opening anywhere. Do you think I'd have considered working in a men's toilet if I could have found anything else?'

Imelda turned away from him. 'I don't like you fighting. It keeps you out too late. I don't like that. I get lonely on my own. Besides,' she turned to face him, 'what if anything happened when you were away? What if the baby started? I'd be all on my own.'

'There's always Mrs Riley you could call. She would know what to do.'

'Mrs Riley?' Imelda's lips twisted with scorn. 'She's the last person I'd ask for help.' She had never forgotten how the landlady treated her when they had first arrived, before they were married. The sour looks she'd given her while blarneying Eddie.

Eddie frowned. 'Still, I'd feel better if I knew someone was keeping an eye on you when I'm out. I'll have a word with her.'

'I don't want you to 'ave a word with 'er.' Imelda's

voice rose. 'If you're not 'ere, I'll 'ave to manage on me own, won't I? I've seen many a gypsy baby born, helped in quite a few of 'em. Me grandmother always treated it as a natural thing.'

Eddie grinned. 'That's not what you were saying a moment ago. You really are the most contrary person I know.'

She placed both hands on either side of her swelling stomach and turned to gaze out of the window. 'You'll always 'ave the last say, won't you? What I say doesn't count.'

'Of course it counts.' He came and stood behind her, his arms about her bulging waist, his lips resting on her hair. 'You know I love you more than life itself. I want our baby to have the best start in life there is and if the only way I can do that is by prize-fighting, then that's what I'll do.'

She didn't answer and he sighed and turned away. He hadn't given any thought to the arrival of the baby, only to its welfare after it was born. On his way out that evening, he had a quiet word with Mrs Riley and was assured she would keep an eye out. 'She's not due until September,' he explained, 'but just in case anything happens before . . .'

Mrs Riley nodded. 'I understand, love. It's your first and you always worry more about your first. Just wait until you've 'ad 'alf a dozen, like me! The doctor told me last time I could do it standin' on me 'ead.'

'Well, Mrs Riley, that really would be something to see,' grinned Eddie.

He won his bout that night with a knock-out in the first round and acknowledged the cheers of the small crowd of regulars with clasped gloved hands and a wide grin. He wondered what Clover would say if she saw him now. Would she be proud of him or disappointed that he hadn't continued to pursue his career on the stage?

The thought reminded him that he owed her a letter. He wrote care of Miss Boyce and she forwarded Clover's letters on. Clover's excuse had been that she wasn't sure of where they would be staying and it would be safer sending them to Miss Boyce.

In spite of Imelda's moaning about his new job, she savoured the extra money he made and a month later they were able at last to move to a new home. Situated in a more wholesome neighbourhood, it consisted of two rooms and a kitchen on the second floor of an avenue lined with trees.

Peg Riley was sorry to see them go. Not sorry about Imelda, to whom she'd never taken, but sorry that she would no longer see Eddie's cheerful face as he passed her in the hall.

They were able to afford enough pieces of secondhand furniture to make it comfortable and for a time Imelda was content. Eddie still had to leave her in the evenings but Imelda made the acquaintance of two sisters who lived in the apartment above and a friendship quickly formed. Dot and Julie Amadeo were waitresses in one of the smart restaurants uptown. They worked irregular hours and one of the sisters was always at home. Flappers both, with skirts up to their knees and lipsticked mouths, they treated Imelda like a little sister. Dot was there when Imelda's first pains started and it was Dot who called a doctor.

An excited Maxi, who had just taken the telephone call informing him of the birth, met Eddie on the way to his dressing room after another successful fight. 'It's a boy!' the old man shouted, unable to control himself. 'A boy! What do ya know, a boy!' He sounded so much like the proud dad, Eddie had to smile.

At home he found an exhausted Imelda, tended by Dot. He bent over the bed, taking one of the limp hands in his. 'Why didn't you call me before?' he said.

'There wasn't time, Mr Blossom,' answered Dot. 'Her waters broke and then it was all stops out and action stations. The doctor himself barely made it in time.'

Eddie turned to look at the pink and white bundle lying in the wicker cot draped with white muslin that stood beside the bed. 'He's beautiful,' he said. 'Just like his mother.'

Dot giggled. 'His dad's not so bad, either.'

Imelda said weakly, 'Here I am, just got over child-birth and already me 'usband's flirting with the woman upstairs.'

'Correction. *I'm* flirting with *him*,' laughed Dot.

'Can I pick him up?' asked Eddie, longing to hold the tiny body in his arms.

Dot bent over the cot. 'I don't see why not. You are his father.'

Carefully, as if he was lifting the most precious glassware, Eddie gathered the baby to him and cradled him to his chest. Dot beamed and turned to smile at Imelda. She was thankful that Eddie was too occupied with the baby to see what she saw: the look of complete indifference on Imelda's face.

They christened their son James Albert, known as Jamie. And Eddie continued to win his fights. Money was no problem now. Imelda could buy almost anything she wanted. She had her new friends and the baby and with money in her pocket she could begin to live as she'd always wanted to. That, it seemed, wasn't enough for Imelda. No matter what he did, it was always wrong. There was no pleasing her these days.

He mentioned his feelings one day to Maxi Fields. 'It's the after-baby blues,' said Maxi, as though an authority on the subject. 'Lots of women go through it.' As Maxi had never married, or, as far as he knew, had any children, Eddie wondered how he could presume to know so much.

'And how long do you reckon that's going to last?' he asked grumpily.

Maxi gave one of his shrugs. 'As long as it takes, kid. As long as it takes. Who knows with women.' He raised his eyes to heaven as though in supplication.

They were in Eddie's dressing room, Eddie sitting hunched on the rubbing table, his hands dangling listlessly between his knees. Maxi reached out and clasped Eddie's shoulder with a big hand. 'Hey, come on, you've just had another win. You should be on top of the world. Imelda'll get over it. She's got the boy and you, what else could she want?'

How can I tell this kindly old man who has only my best interests at heart, thought Eddie, about Imelda and me? Since young Jamie's birth she had become a stranger. Seldom was he able to get close to her. She could freeze him with one look. The laughter and passion of those early days returned only briefly, fluctuating with her unaccountable swings of mood. Although he had never pretended to understand her, and probably never would, in bed they had been as one. In bed Imelda was warm and sensual, eager to please and be pleased. Now it seemed that just as things were going well, her body soft and yielding beside his in the big feather bed, young Jamie would open his eyes and his mouth at the same time and demand instant attention.

There was no way they could ignore him or leave him to cry himself back to sleep. There was nothing for it but for Imelda to get up and feed him. She had decided to breast feed him after a disastrous start with a bottle and patent baby food. Jamie had refused to take it, turning his head to one side and bringing it all back if Imelda insisted. Eddie had watched her force the rubber teat into the baby's mouth and hold it there until he was compelled to swallow. Finally a sullen Imelda would climb back into bed and turn her face from Eddie as though it had all been his fault.

And yet, for all her contrariness, he still loved her, forgiving her over and over again, even if at times he felt like taking her up and shaking her like a rag doll. She had given him Jamie and nothing in this whole, wide world could take the place of that fascinating little bundle.

As the months went by, it saddened him to realise that she didn't feel the same way about their son. He suspected Jamie bored her. What was more than a little worrying was the fact that she made no attempt to hide it. It was difficult to recall the Imelda of the old days in that seaside town in the north of England. She was always carping now, for ever finding fault.

'You're free to go out and see other people. It's me that has to stay in this place and look after him,' she said accusingly.

He laughed, trying to jolly her out of her sour mood. 'A happy prisoner?'

'No one in prison is happy. *He's* doing his best to create a prison for us both,' jabbing a thumb at Jamie. He sat in his cot, staring wide-eyed at his parents.

Eddie put his arms about her and tried to draw her close, ignoring her sharp resistance. 'So you're saying now this place is a prison? I thought you liked it. You said it was a hundred times better than Mrs Riley's.'

'If you only knew how alone I feel, Eddie, how afraid that we'll never be any different but always with a baby screaming, constantly at each other's throats.'

He let her go with a sigh, turning to reach for his packet of cigarettes and she went on, 'You haven't changed towards me, have you, Eddie? You would never do that?'

'You know my feelings towards you can never change.'

He lit the cigarette, drawing the smoke deep into his lungs. He shouldn't smoke; he knew Maxi Fields was dead against smoking. But sometimes, if he didn't have his hands occupied with something else, even holding a cigarette, he thought he might . . .

He shook his head as the thoughts raced about inside his brain. No, he could never hurt Imelda. Not Imelda . . .

Better that he made an excuse to go out rather than feel her resentment growing. Going out was his only defence, for he couldn't stand the accusation in her eyes. Or the petulant droop to her mouth.

She had begun to leave Jamie as soon as he got home from the gym, running upstairs to visit Dot and Julie Amadeo.

'I'll go mad if I don't hear another human voice instead of the yelling of that baby,' she would say. 'He's been at it all day.' She'd put her hands to her temples, pressing her palms against them as though trying to exorcise something she hated.

Often, when he came home, the child hadn't been bathed. Eddie would fill the tin bath with warm water, placing it on a spread towel in front of the fire. Jamie adored his bath and the kitchen floor would be awash after one of their sessions. After washing him, Eddie would lay him down carefully on a towel and begin drying him, not forgetting the area between fingers and toes. As he dried, he sang softly, one of those sweet old songs beloved by Adele. When Jamie was dried to his satisfaction, he powdered him, making a game of it, making the little boy chuckle. After which he slipped the nightgown over the baby's head and tenderly guided the fat little fingers spread like tiny starfish through the sleeves. Lastly he would reach for the triangular folded nappie warming by the fire and worm it under Jamie's bottom, securing it with a large safety pin.

After tidying up, Eddie would wash the dishes that cluttered the sink, some of which he knew had been there since breakfast. Then he'd sit with the baby on his knee, staring into the orange flames of the fire, waiting for Imelda. When the child became restless, he told him, 'Just a little while now and Mummy will be home and then you can have your supper and get to bed.'

She'd come in, taking her time, and fumble at the buttons on her blouse. Then sitting back on the low chair, the baby across her knee, she would relate all the latest gossip of the sisters Amadeo. Totally ignoring the infant, except to move him from one breast to the other, her face would be full of animation as she described the places, dance halls and fancy restaurants to which the girls had been taken by their boy friends. The jazz clubs with their ever present threat of a raid by the police fascinated her the most.

Eddie sat and smiled at the picture she presented, the gossip flowing unheeded over his head. 'You look like that painting of the Madonna with Child,' he told her.

She sniffed. She'd far rather look like Clara Bow, she thought, that movie star with the bee-stung lips. The extremes of her nature were still a surprise to him. She was a child at heart; impulsive, demanding, fretful, emotional. But it was all part of being Imelda.

His biggest worry, about which he had been brooding for some time now, was her prolific spending. She did not seem to be able to hold on to cash; if she had any, she spent it. He knew she had already spent the money he had earned from his last fight. For all Maxi Fields' enthusiasm, Eddie could see no future in fighting in the ring. Not unless he became big time and he knew perfectly well he wasn't good enough for that. He'd thought that all he had to do was present himself to the big city and they would all roll over and applaud. So much for his dreams . . .

Chapter Nineteen

At the Argyle Theatre, the man who guarded the door hadn't changed. Clover explained she wanted to see Mr Holt.

Sorrowfully, he shook his head. 'I'm sorry, dear, but Mr Holt's moved to Blackpool. Bettering 'imself.' He looked doubtful. 'I don't think you'd fit in 'ere at all, lass.'

A steely glint came into Clover's eye. 'Why not?'

The doorkeeper thought of the bawdy acts they were currently showing on matinées and in the evening. 'Well, you see, miss, the type of acts we 'ave now are changed. They're more – well, nearer the knuckle, like. You wouldn't do at all.'

Clover smiled again. 'Why don't we let your boss decide that?'

As she spoke there were footsteps behind her and a voice shouted, 'Bill! You out there?'

Turning, Clover watched as a middle-aged man approached the desk where the doorman sat. He was a beefy-looking man with thinning hair brushed sideways to hide his bald patch. His eyes, narrowing into slits, examined her rapaciously. 'Well, well, what have we here?'

He came closer and Clover, burying any sudden qualms she might have, smiled her warmest and said, pleasantly, 'Good morning. I was just explaining to your doorman that I would like an appointment to see the stage manager. I came once before and saw a Mr Holt. There wasn't an opening then but he told me to call in when I was interested.'

'Hmmm. Harry's no longer with us. Aiming higher these days is old Harry.' She spoke with a good accent, he meditated. Too ladylike for this show. Then he thought of her in one of those skimpy costumes the chorus girls were required to wear. She'd be a sensation. His eyes dropped to her legs, slim and shapely in the one pair of silk stockings she'd dared to take from her aunts. But something simple to start with, he decided.

'You're after a job, is that it?' he enquired.

'Yes.'

He nodded. 'The only vacancy I have just now is for a girl to carry on the name boards at the beginning of each act. And maybe stand in for any of the girls who fall ill. Think you could do that?'

'I think I could manage.'

'Good.' Thoughtfully, he considered the trim figure. Pushing his luck, he added, 'And to go into the auditorium in the interval and sell chocolates and cigarettes.'

Clover's smile beamed out. 'If you're offering, then I'm accepting. But don't you want to know anything about me? My experience, even my name?'

'I've seen you and your name's immaterial. You won't be getting billing.'

'Even so, it's Clover. Clover Blossom.' She spoke it with pride and he grinned and held out his hand.

'Nice to meet you, Clover Blossom. I've heard of your father, but you'll find I'm not a man to bear grudges. Start tomorrow, be here by ten. We'll get you fixed up with costumes and the girls can show you what to do.' Just before he vanished back into his office, he called back over his shoulder, 'And I'm Bobby Roxburgh.'

It was the first time she had stood up to Bert. 'No,'

he said, his tone emphatic, 'I won't have you debasing yourself by walking onto a stage to be ogled at by a crowd of men who—'

'It's a job,' she said firmly, 'and as you're fond of saying, Dad, every little helps when you've got nothing. Don't make a scene. Please! Maybe in a little while you'll find something suitable and things will really begin to look up.'

Miss Boyce, too, seemed far from happy when Clover told her about the job. 'I've heard about that place, Clover. It's very popular, by all accounts. But it caters to the rougher type of audience, I hear. Not exactly . . .' She broke off, looking distressed.

Clover smiled. 'Not exactly Summer Follies with a baritone singing "Old Man River" and Mum and me in our Pierrot costumes. Isn't that what you were going to say, Boycie?'

'You're being facetious now,' Miss Boyce objected.

'No, I'm not. I'm being realistic.'

In every way, the Argyle Theatre was different from the old end-of-the-pier theatre. To start with, it was much more ornate. There was a lot of gilt, with crimson velvet boxes and gold-coloured curtains that draped each side of the stage, held back by thick golden ropes. The backdrop was a painted canvas view of the fairground – the merry-go-round and refreshment tents, the Big Dipper towering over all.

The audience, too, as Miss Boyce had warned, was rougher; men on holiday, looking for a good time and, with money saved all year long, making sure they got one. At first, Clover felt shy and she could see Mr Roxburgh eyeing her with doubt, obviously wondering if he'd been wrong in his judgment. The costume they gave her to wear would have had her aunts (and Miss Boyce) reaching for the smelling salts. A short tutu made entirely of black satin, it had black net petticoats frothing above her knees and a large red silk rose sewn across the bosom. A frivolous thing that made her look older than her seventeen years. Long black silk stockings worn with high-heeled black patent-leather shoes completed the picture the stage manager had desired to create. The year was 1921. The year of the flappers. Women showed their legs and were proud of them. She was shown how to walk on before each act, smiling over the top of the boards she carried as the audience erupted in whistles and a few cheers. The boards gave the name of each act that followed and Clover was instructed to walk the width of the stage, fit the board onto an easel, then wink at the now noisy audience and walk off.

'Swing those hips,' Mr Roxburgh directed. 'And smile. Forget there's a depression. Give 'em their money's worth.'

The audience loved it. Soon her bashfulness ceased to bother her and as she made friends with the other artistes, she began to look forward to each new day. The fire-eaters, the jugglers, the girls who danced in the chorus line high-kicking their way across the stage and back, all became her friends. Some of the older artistes had heard of Bert and Adele and kept a fatherly eye on her.

The sale of cigarettes and cigars shot up. Men who had never been known to purchase chocolates bought boxes to give their lady friends. Clover learned to ignore the ribald comments that followed her progress, learning from the other girls that the best way of dealing with what they called the 'busy hand brigade' was a smart reply and a smooth step backwards out of their reach.

Bert was her chief worry though she tried not to let him see it. To her relief he told her one evening that the vacancy he'd first applied for at the Winter Gardens had again become vacant and they had offered it to him. 'As pianist,' he explained to a delighted Clover. 'Playing in the evening and at tea dances during the afternoon. It's not what I'm used to, but then neither of us is doing what we're used to, are we? Still, we're survivors, lass, and we'll survive this.'

A small niggle of doubt touched Clover. 'What happened to the other man they took?' she asked. 'He'd only been there a short time.'

Bert shrugged. 'Who knows? Or cares. The job's mine now, and they should know they won't get a better bloke than Bert Blossom to work for them.' He grinned smugly. 'I told you this time we'd be lucky. At least it's a step up from the last one.'

Clover thought of the Darnley Arms and the intimidating Benny Griggs and had to agree that indeed it was.

She worked long hours at the Argyle but still she found time to write to her aunts, a long chatty letter telling them where they were and what they were doing, without going into too many details. She said she missed them and sent her love to them both and to Sally and Cook. Also any of the girls who had befriended her from the school. Already that summer was like a dream, something experienced in another life.

There was no reply to her letter. After a month, thinking perhaps they hadn't received it, she wrote again. Weeks passed and there was still no reply. Bert, guessing her feelings, said, 'Don't let it worry you, love. If they don't want to keep in touch, well, it's no skin off our noses. We can do quite nicely on our own, thank you, without the help of two frosty old biddies like them.'

Miss Boyce clicked her tongue and looked sympathetic. Listening to Clover's accounts she had formed the impression that the Miss Frosts were well-brought-up gentlewomen. As such, they had no right to treat her dear little girl this way, punishing her for something her father did twenty years ago. No right at all. Real caring families stood by each other, steady in adversity.

Over the weeks it became apparent to Bobby Roxburgh that he had something different in Clover. One morning during breaks for the girls to catch their breath after a particularly energetic routine, he went over to the corner where she sat, talking to another of the cast. Without preamble, he said, 'That act you had with your father. Did you sing in it?'

Clover looked surprised. 'Yes, Mr Roxburgh, I did.'

'Old-fashioned love songs?'

'Among others. They were very popular.'

'Well, let's say moonlight and roses ain't exactly up our street. Know anything else, do you? More up to date, like?'

Clover thought of the songs she had sometimes sung while Eddie played the piano, just fooling around when they had the theatre to themselves. A sudden pang of nostalgia struck her and she felt a lump come to her throat. She nodded. 'I used to practise them with my brother.'

He turned and shouted to the piano player, a thin, weedy-looking man with a perpetual cigarette dangling from one corner of his mouth. 'Play something for the little lady, Joe.'

Joe cocked an eyebrow at her and she walked over to stand beside him at the piano. 'Something jazzy,' she said. 'Just start playing, I'll follow.'

She told him the key and a moment later the syncopated rhythm of the latest jazz number had people moving forward to listen.

'Yes, sir, that's my baby. No, sir, don't mean maybe. Yes, sir, that's my baby now . . .' Clover's voice, starting on a quiver, gained strength as some of the cast began to clap in time to the music. She finished with a few dance steps and applause from the rest of the show.

'That was great, Clover,' someone shouted. 'Give us another one.'

She was about to oblige when the stage manager called the cast to resume rehearsals.

The following evening she was tried out at the first house performance. The audience loved it. To the amusement of some of the chorus girls, she received more applause than the striptease artiste who came after her, which was very gratifying. Her name was added to the bills. Miss Blossom. Gave the show a touch of class, thought Bobby Roxburgh.

Chapter Twenty

Spectators roared as the two boxers circled each other inside the roped arena. Wary as jungle cats, their keen eyes watched for a dropped guard, the slightest distraction that meant perhaps they could step in close and land the winning punch on their opponent.

The front seats were occupied by men in evening dress, their ladies in slinky gowns, cut on the cross to show to best effect their lean bodies, more than hinting at the very minimum of underwear. Diamonds glittered in their ears and between the deep cleavage of their gowns. Their voices, however, rose as shrill and excitedly as those sitting at the back of the hall – working men in cheap blue suits or denims, their women in garishly patterned cotton or artificial silk dresses. It was high summer and the hall was stifling even though the side exits had been left open to the night air. Guards had been posted to stop anyone slipping in without paying. The blue haze of cigarette smoke hung over everything, haloing the strong lights above.

Eddie felt the sweat running down his face and into his eyes, temporarily blinding him. His opponent, sensing the brief distraction, lunged to deliver the winning blow; neatly side-stepping, Eddie landed an upper cut on the side of his jaw that had the man sprawling on the canvas. He lay spread-eagled on his back while the referee knelt on one knee beside him counting him out. The crowd yelled, stamping their feet.

The young limey had won most of his fights and was rising fast in the world of boxing. Standing by his side, holding his hand high in the gesture of victory, the referee shouted, 'The winner, folks. Eddie Blossom.'

Maxi Fields climbed into the ring, grinning delightedly. Another triumph for his boy! Things were getting better and better.

Later in the dressing room, he studied Eddie closely as he sat on the high rubbing table, his hands dangling between his knees. Someone had already removed his gloves and Maxi bent to fix a length of plaster to the slight cut on his cheekbone.

He liked Eddie Blossom. Liked the strong, determined jaw line and clear, intelligent eyes. Although the boy was still a little too jumpy, a little raw, he had quite noticeably matured and gained in self-assurance with each fight he won. A potential champion, in the world light heavyweight class.

Tonight, Maxi couldn't contain his excitement. 'Did you see who was sitting in the front row?' he asked.

When Eddie shook his head and said, no, he hadn't, he'd been too busy concentrating on his opponent, Maxi said, 'That movie star. Amorita Kessel. The one they're all talking about.' Then, as though saving the best for last, he added, 'And guess who was with her?'

Again Eddie shook his head. 'Go on, surprise me!' He grinned at Maxi, amused by his interest in movie stars and their friends.

'Nick Farrel, the guy who has just built that studio in Los Angeles. A studio to make movies. People are beginning to call it Hollywood now. She must be his latest flame. Aiming high, is our Nick.'

Eddie pricked his ears up at the name. Nick Farrel. There were probably dozens of Nick Farrels in New York. 'Interested in prize-fighters, is he?' he enquired.

'This Farrel guy?' Teasingly, he added, 'Think he might offer me a job if I'm nice to him?'

Although the words were spoken in jest, Maxi seemed to consider them seriously. Giving Eddie a shrewd look, he said, 'You'd do better being nice to that dame he's with. I hear she's got a hankering for tough young guys who can show her a good time.'

Eddie looked shocked. 'Maxi! I'm a married man. Remember?'

'Oh, she never allows it to get serious. From all accounts, just likes a little fun.' He began to pack away the rolls of bandages and bottles of liniment into a leather bag. 'Joke all you want, but I tell you she could be interested in you.'

Later, when there was a knock on the door, there was no mistaking the message handed to them by a youth who stood waiting in the corridor for an answer. A message from Nick Farrel who said he had enjoyed the fight, that he was glad to see Eddie again and know he was making something of himself, even if it wasn't what he'd planned. 'How about us meeting later, if you're not busy?' he wrote. 'Supper if you can make it. I'll be waiting in Miss Kessel's car at the front entrance if you're interested.'

Eddie passed the note to Maxi, watching the way his eyes widened, the look of incredulity that passed over his face.

'Jesus, you know him?'

Eddie wasn't about to go into details. 'We've met,' he said. 'I tried to get in touch with him once before but he'd . . .' He stopped, thinking back to that day with the rain dripping down under his collar and the acute disappointment of just missing Nick. And the drinks in the bar afterwards that resulted in his getting the job at Maxi's gymnasium. He realised Maxi was watching him.

'You goin'?' Maxi asked, referring to the invitation.

Eddie thought of Imelda waiting at home, waiting for him to arrive so that she could make some excuse to run upstairs to her friends, leaving him alone with Jamie. Normally, unless he was very tired or depressed because he'd lost a fight – not often but it did happen – he enjoyed looking after the little boy, laughing with him as he slapped the bath water with chubby hands or tried to eat the soap bubbles.

Well, just for once, he thought, Imelda could stay at home and see to Jamie herself. How often would he get a chance to meet a famous movie star? And besides, he'd like to see Nick Farrel again.

Dressed neatly in a navy pinstripe suit, his trilby hat set jauntily on his head, he left the building.

Maxi called out after him, 'Tell me what she's like. Take notes if you have to. A real classy dame, that girl. Fortune's smiling on you tonight, kid. Make the most of it.'

The reference to fortune smiling reminded Eddie of Bert and a sudden lump rose in his throat. Then he was crossing the pavement towards the long, black limousine. A uniformed driver stood at attention, holding open the door. Eddie could faintly make out the two figures inside the car and as he bent forward, peering in, he heard a voice: 'How you doin', kid? Good to see you again, and you looking so prosperous.'

Settled beside them on the wide roomy seat, Eddie smiled at the two occupants. Nick sat on one side of Miss Kessel, Eddie on the other. She didn't appear to mind being in the middle of two men. Not in the least. A tiny oval-shaped hat made up entirely of black velvet and veiling dipped over one heavily mascara'd eye. Her mouth gleamed scarlet in the semi-darkness. Her voice when she spoke was low and husky with a decidedly foreign accent. Hungary, he guessed. Or maybe somewhere in deepest Russia.

'I was thrilled by your fight,' she said, edging closer to him. 'You were wonderful.'

Eddie felt himself blushing clear up to the roots of his hair. 'Thank you,' he murmured and felt her shoulder press against his. Her eyelashes, impossibly long and thick, brushed against her cheeks as she assumed a coy expression.

To Nick he said airily, 'Oh, I'm not doing too badly. Keeping the wolf from the door. You saw the fight, then?'

'Yep. And a damned good show you put on. But why boxing? I thought your niche was in vaudeville or whatever you call it in Britain.'

'Beggers and choosers,' said Eddie. 'You know the saying. The man I'm working for had faith in me and with him behind me I've been doing, as I said, not too badly.'

A slim, scarlet-taloned hand rested intimately on his knee, squeezing gently, sending a rush of blood to Eddie's head. He turned away slightly, angling his body towards the window. She allowed her hand to rest there.

Nick asked about Imelda. 'Now, there's a fascinating girl. Unusual looks. With her as your partner, I'd 'ave thought you'd go down well, if not on Broadway then on one of the lesser known theatres on the fringe of town.'

'Imelda was never in my act.' Eddie grinned. 'We have a baby now. A little boy called Jamie. He's almost a year old.'

The fingers on his thigh pressed again. 'I love children and animals,' the movie star said. 'So sweet.'

Nick Farrel laughed. 'Yeah, the way you love beetles and those spiders that climb up the plughole in the bath and scare you half to death.' He looked at Eddie. 'The number of times I've had to rush into the bathroom and rescue some poor little critter from a watery grave out of her bath water.'

Nick's words brought an immediate and very erotic vision of Amorita Kessel huddled at one end of the bath while her rescuer skimmed off the offending insect. As though reading his thoughts, her hand tightened again, this time sliding an inch or two higher. Eddie sat tense and uncomfortable, unsure of how to deal with the situation.

He was saved by the car coming to a halt outside a fancy looking restaurant. Their arrival in the large room caused a flutter of excitement. People stopped eating, and Eddie heard the whispers, 'It's Amorita Kessel!' He was conscious of the curious glances which followed them as the head waiter led them to a secluded table to one side of the room. The place was crowded and few of the diners bothered to disguise their interest. Several men came over to speak to Nick Farrel. Although they addressed him, their eyes lingered on Amorita. Hoping, Eddie guessed, for an introduction. It wasn't forthcoming.

As they waited for their orders, Nick began to question Eddie about his work. Listening intently, after a while he said, 'Have you ever considered the movies? Plenty of scope there for an up-and-coming young guy with your looks and physique.'

Eddie laughed. 'Oh, sure. The motion picture people are falling over each other to secure my services.'

'Don't knock it!' Carefully, Nick considered the good looks, the mop of curly hair, the set of wide shoulders. 'Seriously, kid, if you're interested, I could get you an opening in a movie that's due to start shooting next month. A bit part only, of course, but it would be a beginning and if they liked you, well, who knows where it would take you.'

'What sort of a picture would this be?' Eddie asked casually, thinking of the money he could make, how much Imelda would enjoy the celebrity status, the glamour of the place everyone was now calling Hollywood. Fierce sensations raged through him, pictures flashing though his mind of fame and fortune. How maybe he could afford to pay for Clover to come over on a visit. She'd love Jamie. He realised he'd not been fair to Clover – or Bert, if it came to that. Although his intentions were always good, at first writing regularly, there had come a time, before he joined up with Maxi Fields, when he couldn't even afford the postage of a letter to England. And if he did, Imelda would see the envelope and there would be another scene with her accusing him of spending money they couldn't afford on 'stupid letters'.

'I thought you liked my sister?' he had said. 'You seemed always very fond of her.'

Imelda shrugged. 'I do like her. But she's so far away and we're here and we should concern ourselves with here and now rather than someone thousands of miles away.'

Then he thought of Maxi Fields and the faith Maxi had had in him. He heard Nick Farrel say, 'The picture I had in mind is a cowboy film. Can you ride a horse?'

Eddie grinned. 'I've ridden a donkey across the sands of Blackpool and didn't fall off. I reckon I could learn to ride something bigger without too much trouble.' He hesitated. 'But there's Maxi. He's been good to me . . .'

'Leave Maxi Fields to me. I'll have a word with him.'

Jamie was a perpetual motion machine that crawled, rolled and lurched from one piece of furniture to the next. Ornaments were sent flying, books and newspapers strewn over the carpet. The minute Imelda's back was turned he'd wriggle down from the chair where she'd put him, small hands searching for everything within reach. The whole block heard him when he fell, his bellows seeming to bound from wall to wall.

After ten minutes' exposure to Jamie's phenomenal lungs, Imelda felt she could take no more. Jamie was the cause of everything dreary that was happening to her, she decided. Eddie spent long hours at the gym and on the nights when he had a fight he sometimes wouldn't get home until midnight. She wasn't in the least interested in prize-fights and so attended none of them. All the same, she could think of better things to do with her life than look after a screaming brat. She was, she told herself, literally a prisoner in her own home, and all because of Jamie.

He'd just fallen and bumped his head again and sat screaming on the carpet near the fireplace. Lips firming in anger, Imelda lifted the cushion from the settee and approached the child. It would be so easy. A few minutes with that held over his face and her life would be her own again. She hadn't been put on this earth to be constantly at the beck and call of some man and his brat.

Any more than she had been over the kittens all those years ago or, more recently, Buster Bywater.

As though aware of her thoughts, Jamie stopped screaming and sat looking up at her. The bruises on his forehead, a constant reminder of his frequent falls now that he was pulling himself up against furniture and trying to walk, stood out angrily. His fat little cheeks were scarlet with the exertion of his screaming and he stared at her with large brown eyes.

Imelda laid the cushion back on the settee. The faint sound of whistling caught her attention and going to the window she stood looking down into the street, and the dark young man, as though suddenly aware of her scrutiny, raised his head and gazed back.

All morning he had been working on the car parked at the kerb. The bonnet was still raised. Slowly he lowered it then reached into the car for the oily rag on which to wipe his hands. His eyes never left Imelda's face, outlined through the upstairs window. He grinned, revealing white teeth in the swarthy face.

I'm being picked up, she thought. How about that! By a good-looking young man with a fancy car who lives in the same building. Excitement had her pulse quickening. Well, it's good for what ails you, she thought. Proves that you're not just a housewife and mother after all, but a woman still attractive to other men.

For a moment her animosity towards her son and his father was laid aside for more intriguing thoughts. The good-looking young man was Dot and Julie Amadeo's brother. His name was Johnny and he was staying with his sisters. Imelda gathered he was lying low, as they put it, waiting for the dust of whatever had precipitated his hasty departure from Chicago to settle. Often in the flat when she went upstairs to visit them, making more excuses by the day to do so, it was all too plain that he was attracted to her. She gazed down now at his dark, rather flashy looks and a shiver went through her.

Eddie didn't tell Imelda the good news straightaway. He decided the excitement would grow with the keeping; besides which, he wanted to be quite certain of all the facts before he divulged them to Imelda.

He sat at the kitchen table and thought of all the luxuries he could bestow on her if he proved popular in the film they talked of. Amorita Kessel seemed to have no doubts about it, insisting that Nick Farrel sign him up immediately, before someone else had the notion to. When Nick muttered about a screen test, she waved a negligent hand, saying, 'Screen test? Who needs a screen test? You only have to look at him to know he'll be a sensation on screen.'

In the movie, she was to play the part of a shy, waif-like orphan (a delicious piece of miscasting, Eddie thought with a grin), newly arrived in America from a war-torn European country, one of the thousands of immigrants making for the new lands of the golden West. Eddie was to be a member of the wagon team that was taking them. His English accent wouldn't matter. It was to be a silent picture. The talkies had yet to come into their own.

Sitting at the table, he felt a warm glow of achievement, of deep satisfaction. Behind him at the window, Jamie crawling about at her feet, trying to pull himself up against her skirt, Imelda held back the curtain with one hand, gazing down at the dark young man who was again working on his car, parked in the gutter in the street. She turned her head lazily as Eddie said, 'Have you ever felt you wanted something so badly you could hardly wait to get hold of it?'

Imelda turned back to the window, a smile on her lips. 'You must have been reading my mind,' she said.

A few days later, Eddie climbed the stairs with the bag of groceries Imelda had asked him to get on his way home. That was one of the beauties of New York. The shops were always open. He paused on the landing as Mrs Scholtz, who lived in the apartment next to theirs, opened her door and stood looking at him. Eddie smiled. 'Good evening, Mrs Scholtz. Another fine day.' The old gossip, he thought. Wonder whose reputation she's pulling to pieces this week.

The woman sniffed, as though mortally offended. 'Time you were home, young man,' she said. 'That poor child's been yelling all afternoon. I can't think where its mother is or how she can ignore him like that . . .'

Above her voice, Eddie was suddenly aware of Jamie's crying, pathetic wails that rang through the closed door and had him involuntarily tensing his shoulders. 'Nice of you to be so concerned,' he said. 'Perhaps you'd like to come in with me and see what you can do to help?'

She sniffed again, completely missing the irony. Still she couldn't let the moment slide. 'No use you making fun of me, young man. That wife of yours may think I'm just an old ignoramus who knows nothing about bringing up children, but I wasn't born yesterday and I tell you, if this sort of thing carries on I'm going to do something about it. There are certain authorities who might be concerned.' She gave him a shrewd glance. 'Before it's too late.'

Eddie hefted the bag of groceries from one arm to the other. Listening to this woman's complaints was getting to be an everyday occurrence. He inserted his key into the lock of his apartment door and left her mouthing her fault-finding at the four walls and the other doors on the landing.

There was no sign of Imelda. No sound except the ear-splitting screams of his son. Letting the bag of groceries fall to the table, he ran into the bedroom. 'Jamie! Jamie!'

The little boy clung to the sides of the high wooden cot. He'd obviously pulled himself to his feet and was too frightened to let go. The front of his sleeping suit was soaked in tears and a nappy that had only too plainly not been changed for hours drooped disagreeably about his ankles.

Scooping up the small body in his arms, feeling the uncontrollable sobbing wrack the little frame, Eddie experienced an anger so fierce that for a moment he actually saw red. It wasn't easy to quieten the distressed child. Eventually he succeeded. He bathed Jamie and put fresh sheets and blankets on the cot. He settled

Jamie in it and the little boy, exhausted from all his crying, was soon asleep.

Eddie went into the living room. He sat down heavily and reached for his pack of cigarettes. He carried them out of pure habit, for he seldom smoked these days, taking heed of Maxi Fields' advice that smoking was bad for your wind. The cigarette packet was empty and he crumpled it and threw it on the floor.

Only then did the full significance of what had happened hit him. Imelda had gone off and left the child all by himself God knows how long ago! Mrs Scholtz's words drummed in his ears: 'The poor child's been yelling all afternoon . . .' Where in hell was Imelda? Had she gone out or was she upstairs with those two women, gossiping and drinking the cheap wine they favoured? After the fight, and the shock of finding Jamie alone and in so distressed a state, he didn't really feel like barging in and having words with his wife in front of them. She shouldn't be too long now, surely.

It was another hour before she came in, full of excuses when she saw him sitting there. He cut her short with a gesture. His voice tight with anger, he said, 'If you ever do that again, I swear I'll kill you.'

There was a terrible silence. Children yelled in the street outside. A woman's voice shrilled accusations from the apartment across the hall, backed by loud music from a wireless.

Eddie spoke at last. 'Where did you go?' he asked, his words barely audible.

Without replying, Imelda moved across the room to the mirror above the fireplace. He watched as she titivated before it, running wide-spread fingers through her hair at the back, pulling the ends forward over her cheeks, head sideways, considering the results.

'Where did you go?' he asked again through clenched teeth.

Imelda turned to look at him, immediately shifting her gaze to avoid the quiet rage she saw glimmering in his eyes. Her dark lashes swept down to hide her own thoughts. 'Oh, you wouldn't be interested. Girls' things. I was helping Julie with a skirt she was making. She couldn't understand the paper pattern she'd bought and I was sorting it out for her.'

She spoke so glibly he could almost believe her. But not quite. Not any more. 'If you were only upstairs, why didn't you hear Jamie crying? Mrs Scholtz said he'd been crying for some time.'

'Oh, her!' Imelda shrugged her shoulders, a look of irritation crossing her face. 'Would you rather believe her or me? You know what an old trouble maker she is. Always on the look-out to cause mischief.'

'I know that. But she said Jamie had been crying for ages . . .'

Suddenly she was turning on him, hands on hips, her temper blazing. 'I suppose because she said it that makes it gospel, eh? Do you pay her to spy for you when you go out? You'd think so, the way you're carrying on. There's nothing wrong with Jamie. A good cry at his age is beneficial to the lungs.'

Eddie snorted with disgust. 'Don't be ridiculous!'

'Be sure to ask her all the ghoulish details, won't you. About where I go and for how long. It doesn't matter what I say. You wouldn't believe me anyway.'

'Imelda!' There was a warning in Eddie's voice, but Imelda paid no heed.

'Don't forget she's lived here far longer than we have,' she all but screamed, her face red and ugly, her eyes narrowed into pinpricks of animosity. 'She's probably an expert at spying on her neighbours by now.'

'*Imelda, will you listen?*' Eddie's voice rose on a roar and Jamie in his cot started to cry again. Imelda pointedly ignored him, still fussing with her hair, and Eddie went into the bedroom and soothed him into silence. When he returned, Imelda was standing by the window. He stared at her stubborn back view, willing her to turn round and face him. But she did not move and her shorn black hair, fanning out on her cheeks, for she'd insisted on having it bobbed to be more in the style of the 1920s, revealed the vulnerable nape of her neck and as always his breath caught in his throat at the beauty of her. The artificial silk dress she wore was too short and too tight but it didn't make her any the less tempting. The thought that at one time he would have felt a rush of desire did nothing but infuriate him now. 'You know we can't go on like this,' he said. 'We're going to have to talk.'

Without answering, she went into the kitchen. 'I'll make us some coffee.'

'Not just yet,' he said, following her. 'I want to talk.'

She pouted, placing the kettle on the stove. 'But you'll feel better after a cup of coffee. You always do.'

'Coffee can wait. Let's get all this sorted out first.'

Her face immediately closed up. 'What's to sort out? If you insist on believing that woman's story . . .'

'Of course I don't. Not always, anyway.' He knew Mrs Scholtz for the gossip she was. The whole block knew of her interfering ways, the trouble she'd caused between various husbands and wives. 'But I still can't understand why you didn't hear Jamie crying. God knows he was making enough of a racket.' A thought struck him, something he should have considered long ago when all this first started. 'Why didn't you take him with you? You know he enjoys people.' Jamie was a friendly little chap and it was a joy to see his face light up whenever anyone called, his all too flagrant vying for attention.

Imelda turned towards the stove in an endeavour to

hide the grimace that distorted her face. 'You know I don't like taking him up to their flat. They've got some pretty ornaments and things and the last time I took him he pulled all their books out of the bookcase.' Besides, she thought, still careful to keep her face averted from his sharp gaze, I can't stand the kid constantly trying to pull himself up against my legs. The times he's laddered a new pair of silk stockings I couldn't begin to count.

It seemed they had come to an impasse. He knew she was bored with a life spent looking after him and Jamie. But wives and mothers all over the world did this, considering it their duty, enjoying it.

Belatedly he wondered if this would be a good time to tell her of Nick Farrel's offer. It might well alter matters for the better in their relationship. But some inherent caution stopped him again – what if it all fell through or Miss Kessel changed her mind? She seemed an unpredictable character. How could he face Imelda's scorn afterwards? He'd be better waiting for the right time.

He wondered later what would have happened if he had told her then. Would it have made the slightest difference?

Chapter Twenty-one

Bert continued to play the piano at the Winter Gardens and to Clover's relief he loved it. He'd cut down on his drinking and with money coming in regularly from both of them, life was a lot more relaxed. He insisted on wearing his velvet jacket and it proved to be a great favourite with the ladies. Clover, knowing how fussy he was about his appearance, sponged and pressed it carefully.

On occasion, she guessed, he flirted with the women who took his fancy. Clover didn't blame him. Her mother had been dead for four years and a man like Bert needed a woman's smile to spur him on.

Adam was never far from her thoughts. Even if at times it was difficult to remember how he looked and walked and the way he'd made her laugh over the rainbow and his foolish talk of wishes.

He wrote regularly, accounts of how the new practice was going, of his new partner, how much he missed her bright smile. One evening she returned from the theatre and found a letter from him which said he had a couple of days free and would like to spend them with her. She was overjoyed. Mr Roxburgh was kind enough to let her have two days off.

Even though the weather was cold, the wind blustery, lashing the sea into waves that at high tide crashed against the promenade walls, they spent most of the time strolling the length of the promenade from one end to the other and exploring grass-topped sandhills to the north for unusual shells. They hung over the railings of the harbour, watching the fishing boats bob frantically on the heavy tide and Clover pointed out the small shuttered theatre at the end of the pier.

'That's where we appeared,' she said, proudly. 'The Four Blossoms. We had such a happy childhood, Eddie and me.'

'Do you still hear from him? Your brother?'

'We seem to have lost touch. I haven't had a letter from him for ages, since before Daddy was taken ill.'

'Don't you write?'

'Oh, often. But as I haven't heard back I don't know if he's getting my letters. I imagine he's busy. It must be a very busy place, New York.' She laughed. 'His one aim in life was to set the world on fire.'

Adam grimaced. 'Sounds a distinctly dangerous young man.'

She punched his arm playfully. 'Oh, you know what I mean. Eddie's marshmallow inside, he wouldn't hurt a fly.'

They ventured as far as neighbouring Blackpool, riding in one of the charabancs that ran between the two towns. They made a visit to the Tower with its fascinating interior and marvellous history, wandered around the dark, quiet aquarium with its mysterious array of coloured fish, gazed at lions and other wild animals who endlessly paced their cages, yellow eyes fixed contemplatively on the humans who paused before them.

'Shame!' Clover's sympathetic nature went out to them. 'They shouldn't be caged up like this. It's cruel.'

'I agree. But we're just two voices against thousands who wouldn't.' They moved on to where a cageful of monkeys leaped and chattered, tiny furry hands reaching through the bars for nuts.

'Let's try the ballroom,' suggested Adam. 'It's got elegant golden boxes where the posh people sit and a man plays an organ on a little stage at one end. Years ago, when I was last here, he was playing, "Ta-ra-ra-boomdiay", and people were dancing.'

But to their disappointment today the organ was silent with disconsolate couples strolling aimlessly across a highly polished dance floor.

Adam suggested a cream tea in a café overlooking the sea front and made a great pretence of gazing through the window in search of another rainbow.

'Guess my luck's out today,' he said. 'Nary a sign of one.'

He watched her tucking into the jam and scones, topping the whole with a pat of thick yellow cream from a small dish, thinking she had the appetite of a child. When he heard she had gone back to work, he'd felt anger, although he realised there was no other way.

'The same kind of act you were doing with your father?' he enquired.

Clover avoided his gaze, slowly spooning sugar into her tea. 'Yes, more or less.'

Although it was honest work, somehow she didn't think Adam would approve of the Argyle Theatre. She was thankful that he had only two days, not long enough to see the show. 'It's the first time I've ever accomplished anything by myself,' she told him. 'Before, it's always been with Daddy and the act. It's not even a part, really, but they've given me a couple of songs. They seem to like me and in the theatre one thing can lead to another.'

'You wouldn't rather take a job working in an up-and-coming young doctor's surgery? It could be very rewarding.'

She reached over for another scone. 'Thanks for the kind offer, but I'm quite happy where I am.'

He was introduced to Miss Boyce for the first time and took an immediate liking to the small woman. She invited him and Clover to take tea with her in her room at the top of the boarding house where she lived and it was clear to Clover that she approved wholeheartedly of the young doctor. When Clover left them temporarily to refill the teapot, Miss Boyce leaned forward across the starched white tablecloth and said in a low voice, 'It's not her kind of place at all, you know. This new show she's working in. I'm not at all happy about her appearing there.'

'She seems happy enough. Why do you say that?'

Miss Boyce was stopped from answering by Clover's reappearance carrying the teapot. Adam meditated over her cryptic words.

At the end of his stay she saw him off at the station. Standing on the platform, the train huffing and puffing beside them, doors slamming as people hurried by, he said, 'My practice is doing well. The old man's gone and my partner is a young bloke. Quite fun, really. All the women patients are already madly in love with him.' He gazed directly into her eyes. 'My offer is still open.'

Pretending coyness, she answered, 'What offer is that?'

'That you come back to Moorfield and help us. You could help out in the surgery, be our receptionist.'

'What makes you think I would make a good receptionist?' She grimaced. 'I hate anything to do with doctors or hospitals.' The memory of the long wait that night to hear of her mother's death still haunted her. 'This job I've got is something I have to do, Adam. Besides, I quite like it.'

'It's not even as if your old man needs you now,' he said stubbornly. 'He's fully recovered and is making a life for himself again. He can do it without your help.'

Somehow, she didn't expect this from Adam. 'I've

never left him before. Well, only when I had to, when he was in hospital and at the sanatorium.' She smiled wryly. 'Are receptionists that hard to get in Moorfield? I should have thought any woman with her wits about her could have done the job.'

'Don't prevaricate, Clover. Surely you've guessed what my feelings are for you? When you're old enough I want to make you my wife.'

Clover didn't know what to say. Perhaps it was just as well that the whistle shrilled just at that moment, the guard waved his flag.

Just before the train began to move he drew her into his arms and kissed her soundly and with great pleasure on the lips. 'There, just something for you to think about. Promise me you will?'

Before she could answer he'd climbed into the carriage, pulling the door closed behind him. Releasing the leather strap that lowered the window, he stood watching her as the train juddered, let out an angry exhalation of steam and began to move.

Clover lifted her hand and waved, watching until the train disappeared into the darkness. She had enjoyed seeing him again, she thought. He would be everything a girl asked for in a husband, affable, successful, kind. Then why should the idea of marriage to him fill her with such indecision?

Chapter Twenty-two

The Argyle Theatre was stuffy and heavy with the smell of cigarette and cigar smoke. The musicians were tuning their instruments, the discordant notes drifting to where Harry sat in the auditorium, settling down to see the show. Harry Holt was well pleased with himself. His own new show was proving a great success and tonight he was celebrating with his brother-in-law, John Reid. John had been married to Harry's sister for five years and at present Alice was visiting their mother in London. It was a good opportunity for the two men to enjoy an evening out together. After a good meal in a top-class hotel, Harry had suggested they see what the Argyle had to offer.

Looking about them as they entered, John said, 'One of your old hunting grounds, wasn't it?'

Harry nodded. 'Gave me a leg up on the ladder to better things.' The opportunity to take on the challenge of a new theatre, a new and exciting project, was the best thing that could have happened to him. Although fortune had had a hand in it, hard work and ingenuity had also played an important part. Gone were the days when the music hall with its working-class following held sway over everything. People of all classes were clamouring for the new and glamorous reviews of C. B. Cochran and his contemporaries. The words 'lavish' and 'spectacular' were being used more and more by theatre reviewers in the popular press. The expensive scenery and well-dressed chorus girls of the modern presentations were gaining a wide following.

If his luck continued, thought Harry, he might well find himself on the circuit that led to London and the West End.

Looking about him now as they took their seats in the third row from the front, he remarked lazily, 'The new producer seems to have made the best of a bad job, wouldn't you say?'

The auditorium had been refurbished and a lot of gilt paint added. There were new stage curtains, and Harry had to admit that although the Argyle would never be the amusement centre of the town, if the old adage of 'bums on seats' was anything to go by, the Argyle was enjoying a successful run.

The audience was mostly male; men on their own who smoked and talked a lot. He guessed they would jeer loudly at acts they didn't like and cheer at the others.

The orchestra struck up a rousing tune and as always Harry felt that sense of exhilaration as the curtains swished apart to reveal a make-believe world of high-kicking girls and a family of acrobats who tumbled about the stage as though they were made of rubber. The youngest member of the act, a boy, was sent skimming in the air above his parents' heads; he looked as though he hadn't been walking long never mind flying.

Even so, the skimpily dressed girls began to pall on Harry after a while and he found his mind dwelling on a point in his own production that had been worrying him. When the pure, clear voice of the girl on the stage fell on the suddenly silent audience, it was like a dash of chilled water, alerting his senses. He straightened in his seat, saying to John next to him, 'Who is that girl singing?'

His brother-in-law grinned. 'She's billed as Miss Blossom. You wouldn't know her, old man. She's a lady.'

Harry ignored the sarcasm. 'Working here? What a surprise.' His gaze examined the slim figure under the one spotlight. The pale blue gown, sewn liberally with sequins, sparkled with every move she made, ethereal, light as a summer cloud. The audience were as drawn to her as though she had cast a spell over them.

John Reid looked thoughtful. 'You wouldn't credit it, would you? And don't ask me where old Roxburgh found her, for I wouldn't have a clue. But you must admit she gives the show a bit of much needed class.'

In the interval, John was eager for only one thing, and that was a hasty retreat to the bar. There, to Harry's surprise, he saw the girl again, dressed differently in a short black creation that had the muscles in his jaw clenching with distaste. Busy selling her chocolates and cigarettes, he could see how adroitly she avoided the hands that would try to squeeze her shoulder or steal about her waist.

Watching from the bar, a drink held negligently in his hand, the feeling that he knew her intensified. The name Blossom suddenly fell into place and he wondered how he could possibly have forgotten those wide cheekbones and that perfectly shaped nose which tonight was pink and shining with the heat from the close mass of bodies about the bar. Or the wide, blue eyes that he saw flash with indignation as one of the men pressed too close. Her hair was drawn back from her face as he remembered it, held at the nape of her neck with a tortoiseshell slide, then allowed to fall in a mass of soft waves down her back. A delicious change, he thought, from the almost masculine short bobs of today's fashion.

He turned his head to listen to something John said. When next he glanced back it was to see her struggling with a stout, red-faced man obviously the worse for drink, intent on whispering in her ear. Above the sound of voices and the tinkling of glasses, he heard her voice, raised on the edge of panic. '*No!* Please, sir, don't make a scene.'

Harry heard the man laugh, saw the girl back away, using her tray of cigarettes and chocolates as though it could form an effective barrier between herself and the offensive customer. Placing his glass firmly on the bar top, he decided this would be a good moment to renew his acquaintance with Miss Blossom.

John shook his head as he watched Harry push his way through the crowd.

'My dear Miss Blossom!' Harry said loudly in a genial voice. 'How nice to see you again after all this time.'

Before Clover could speak, he had taken hold of her arm and, smiling over his shoulder, said to the affronted man, 'Miss Blossom and I are old chums.' He transferred his gaze to Clover. 'Aren't we, dearie?'

Clover gulped. Had she swapped one irritation for another? Noting the height of Harry, the width of his shoulders in the dark, well-cut suit, the stout man suddenly lost interest and went to join his friends at the bar.

Harry smiled again. 'I thought you could do with a spot of assistance. I hope you didn't consider it interference.'

Clover lifted her chin. 'I'm quite capable of handling that sort of thing for myself, Mr—'

'You looked anything but capable to me,' he cut in. 'And the name is Holt. Harry Holt.'

'Not a name I could easily have forgotten,' she said icily. 'You were extremely rude and unsympathetic when I came asking for a job a few summers ago. You wouldn't even give me a chance to prove myself.'

'I wouldn't say no to your trying to prove yourself now!'

Her lips twisted. 'I'm doing all right where I am.' A

bell sounded, announcing the end of the interval, and she turned to leave him, pushing her way through the crowd of men slowly returning to the auditorium.

'I'd like to see you after the show,' he called after her. 'I'll come to your dressing room.'

'Please don't bother, Mr Holt.' She turned to look back at him, framed in the doorway. 'You'd have to share me with a dozen other girls. Besides, I can't think of a single thing that you could say that would possibly interest me.'

He continued to regard her, a frown between his thickly marked brows. 'If we don't talk, you'll never know, will you?'

She smiled. 'You don't hesitate about coming to the point, do you?'

'I guess I never did find the bush I'm supposed to beat about. If I ask really nicely to see you later, would you reconsider it?' Before Clover could answer, he went on, 'I bet you think I'm like all the other fellows. Out to get fresh with you.'

'You mean some of you are different?'

His smile widened. 'I hope this doesn't deflate your ego, my dear, but I'm truly not interested in your, um, obvious charms. Just in your talent. You have a lovely voice, a natural grace that is wasted in these surroundings. I'd like very much to put it to good use.'

'Don't worry about me, Mr Holt. I have no intention of wasting myself, as you put it. My talents or anything else. My sights are set on higher things. It just takes a little time and patience, that's all.'

There was a flurry at the entrance of the bar and a voice called, 'Clover? Come on, lass. They're waiting for you.'

Back in his seat, Harry watched as she walked across the stage to the whistles and catcalls of the men in the audience. She placed the board with the name of the

next act embellished in gold letters on its easel, smiled
and walked back into the wings.

John, seated beside him, leaned towards him and
murmured, 'Old Roxburgh certainly expects his pound
of flesh where his girls are concerned.'

Harry felt anger stir in him. His jaw muscles tightened and he wanted to stand up and shout to the noisy
audience to shut up, to be quiet. As though sensing this,
John turned his head to look at him. 'So you knew that
girl after all! Why so uncommunicative all of a sudden?'

'I don't know what you're talking about,' Harry
replied, his voice gruff. 'I'm not remotely interested
in the wench. Except maybe professionally.'

'You could have fooled me,' John responded as the
music struck up and the curtains swung apart.

Seated before the large mirror with its array of picture
postcards stuck into the side of the frame, Clover heard
Harry's name spoken by a couple of the girls seated
near her.

'He can put his shoes under *my* bed any time he
wants to,' joked one. There was a chorus of 'And how'
from other girls sharing the dressing room, followed by
a wave of laughter. 'What a handsome hunk of a man!'
someone remarked, envy plain in her voice. 'Clover
gets all the breaks. Goin' out to supper tonight, are
we, ducks?' A couple of the girls had been in the bar
and seen her talking to Harry.

Used to being teased by the other girls, good-natured
banter that had no sting to it, Clover smiled and made
a noncommittal reply. 'Why don't you wait and see?'
She dabbed at her nose with the huge powder puff and
caught their eyes in the mirror.

'Now, now, Sally. Clover doesn't go in for men. She's
got her daddy's supper to cook. He's got a right, loyal
little helper in Clover, so he has.'

'Wish he'd ask me,' mused her friend wistfully, still on the subject of Harry. 'I know someone who has been to his show. At the Apollo it is, in Blackpool. My friend said it was fabulous. He'd never seen anything like it before.'

'That new boy friend of yours, eh?' Carefully outlining her mouth with scarlet lipstick, Sally leaned closer to the mirror. 'Eyeing up the competition, was he?'

'Come off it! You know Dougie's only interested in me.'

'That's what you think!'

Clover, changed into her outdoor clothes, left them arguing. She could still hear their voices as she walked down the corridor to the stage door.

Emerging onto the street, she stood for a moment allowing her eyes to become accustomed to the darkness. She jumped when a voice at her elbow said, 'Hi!'

With narrowed eyes she peered at the tall figure that had accosted her. Muffled in a greatcoat against the chill air, for winter had arrived with a vengeance, she recognised Harry Holt. His hat was pulled down low over his forehead, his hands thrust deep into his coat pockets.

He'd sent John on his way, apologising for his churlish behaviour, explaining there were one or two matters he'd like to clear up with the girl.

'For someone who's not interested, or only professionally, you seem almighty taken with her,' John had remarked.

Harry grunted. 'Just go on home, there's a good fellow. And thank you for your company tonight. I've enjoyed it. We must do it again sometime.'

'We'll persuade Alice to visit your mother again, fairly soon. Goodnight, old man.'

Harry watched as his brother-in-law disappeared in the direction of the taxi rank, stepping carefully over the icy cobbles.

Was he being a stubborn fool to let the plight of this girl who clearly had no time for him bother him so? And yet it wasn't just that air of vulnerability she carried about her. The lovely singing voice was a gift from the gods. A monstrous pity to waste it on these men who made up the audience at the Argyle. Like casting pearls before swine.

In a cool voice, Clover said, 'Waiting for someone, Mr Holt? I should imagine you'd have a wide choice. Most of the young ladies of the show, in their ignorance, appear to be crazy about you.'

He shrugged, then to her chagrin slipped her hand through his arm as though he'd been doing it for years. 'The story of my life,' he said, with such an air of worldly weariness that she couldn't help but laugh.

The roads were slippery underneath, there was a touch of frost in the air and she could see her own breath in the darkness. Before she realised it, they were crossing the road.

She stopped suddenly and pulled away, looking up at him from under the brim of her hat. It had a small feather of bright yellow stuck into the petersham ribbon at one side and seemed somehow to enliven the dark dreariness of the night. 'Hold on!' she said. 'Where do you think you're going?'

'*We* are going to get a drink and over that drink we are going to have a good long talk about your future.' He looked down into her face. 'You *are* old enough to drink, aren't you?'

Clover lifted her chin. 'Cheek! Not that it's any business of yours. You just can't take no for an answer, can you? If you must know, I go straight home after every performance.'

Harry grinned. 'How restrictive for you! The trouble with you is, you mix with the wrong kind of people. Like that father of yours for a start.'

His rudeness shocked her. 'You've got a cheek!' she said angrily. 'What gives you the right to make critical remarks about my father? You don't even know him.'

He almost said: Everyone in the business knows Bert Blossom, down on his luck and dragging his young daughter along with him. He restrained himself in time, saying instead, 'You can't arrange your life to suit somebody else, you know. No one can do that. And it's true, of course, I have absolutely no right to criticise your father. Let's leave that distasteful subject behind, shall we? What I'm really interested in is why you are appearing in that place. It's not nearly good enough for you.' With one hand he made a gesture towards the lights that still sparkled over the entrance to the theatre. And at that precise moment, like an omen, they went out, leaving everything in deep shadow.

To Clover, superstitious to the core, it was as though an icy finger had touched her. She didn't want to stand on this dark and windy street and talk about her career or anything else. She lifted her chin, looking up at him. 'Why the sudden interest in my career, anyway? You couldn't have cared less what happened to it before.'

Then, before he could think up a reply, she turned away from him, adding, 'Goodnight, Mr Holt. I shouldn't stay out too late if I were you. You might be picked up by one of those chorus girls I was telling you about.'

She knew that he stood and watched her as she walked down the deserted street. Just before turning the corner at the end, she looked back. His outline was visible in the darkness, shoulders hunched against the cold, watching. He reminded her of a hunter, evaluating his prey.

She spied him every night in the audience for the following week. To her secret chagrin, however, he made no further attempt to seek her out. And then on the Saturday night, as she left the theatre by the stage door, she saw him again, standing in the shadows, the smoke from his cigarette pluming in the chill air.

As she stepped forward, he took her arm with the familiarity that irked her. In a bantering tone, he said, 'With your personality and my brains we could go far.'

Clover longed to make one of those spontaneous retorts she'd heard the other girls in the show use. Racking her brains, she couldn't think up a single one. Instead, she murmured, 'We're not going anywhere, Mr Holt. How many times do you need telling?'

'Not even for a little drink? You can't seriously enjoy standing about on a night like this when we could be warm and cosy in some pub with a roaring fire? A few minutes only?' His voice took on a wheedling tone that brought a smile to her face. 'Please!'

Why was she being so childish? she wondered. A young, good-looking man was asking her to have a drink with him, a perfectly innocent invitation, and all she could do was to treat him as though he had the plague.

A letter from Adam had arrived that morning, the first she had received since his return from their weekend. She was usually pleased to get them, but this one had just made her miserable.

'I can't bear to think of you wasting your life exhibiting yourself in front of all those people,' he wrote. 'I meant what I said when we parted at the station. Here with me you would be safe, a happily married woman, helping her husband in his chosen career.' The word pompous sprang to mind but she pushed it aside, continuing to the end of the letter: 'Don't get too attached to that job of yours, for I'm warning you, I have plans for your future which, to me, must take priority above all else . . .'

Even my wishes! she thought testily. What was it about her that made men seem to want to control her, to dominate the way she lived?

If she accepted Harry Holt's invitation and was home later than usual, Bert would worry. The Winter Gardens closed earlier than the regular theatres and so he was always home before she was. She appreciated that. The fire would be built up, a pot of tea waiting. But that was as far as he would go towards preparing their evening meal.

Suddenly her mind was made up. Bert could worry. When had she last caused him any concern? She said, looking up at Harry in the darkness, 'Well, I suppose it would be all right. For a few minutes only, though. I mustn't be too long.'

He placed one hand on his heart, grinning at her. 'Scout's honour. I always knew that one day I'd meet a Cinderella who had to be home before midnight. I didn't think they existed any more.'

She grimaced. 'Well before midnight!' She felt his arm propelling her across the street in the direction of the promenade.

'In any case,' he said, 'it will have to be only a few minutes. They must be on the point of closing.'

They were just in time to order: a whisky for him, and in spite of her objections, a port and lemon for her. The barman hesitated, eyeing Clover. He was on the point of saying something when he caught Harry's look and decided discretion was the better part of valour. Carrying the drinks over to a small table, Harry seated himself opposite. 'See, I even conjured up the fire,' nodding towards the huge old-fashioned hearth where a log fire blazed. He lifted his glass to her in salute. 'To us.'

Clover felt a flush stain her cheeks and lowered her eyes to her own drink, sipping it experimentally. He was so sure of himself! She wished suddenly that she was older and wiser, a woman in her thirties who could exchange badinage with him, could play him at his own game. She remembered his open criticisms of her father and the flush deepened.

When he didn't seem in any hurry to talk, she said, 'Hadn't you better say whatever it is you want to say, Mr Holt? The bartender keeps giving us dirty looks.'

Harry lifted his glass and tossed back the last of his drink. 'Right, I'll do that.' He paused, as though collecting his thoughts. Then he said, 'How would you like to appear at the London Palladium?'

Clover, glass to her lips, spluttered all over the table. When at last she could stop coughing, she said, 'My God, what was in this drink? I could have sworn I heard you mention the London Palladium.'

'You heard right. I asked how you'd like to appear there. Or the Gaiety Theatre? With the plans I have in mind, you could take your choice. You must know, people must have told you before now, that you're a very attractive young woman. With the right encouragement you could improve your situation considerably.'

'My God,' she said again, 'I've heard the girls in the chorus boast of some smart approaches but this takes the biscuit.'

'Do you usually turn down offers of employment as acrimoniously as this?'

Before she could reply, the bartender was at their table, whisking their empty glasses away, saying in a loud voice, 'Come on, folks, time I wasn't here. Haven't you got any homes to go to?'

Harry rose and stood back to allow Clover to precede him through the door. Outside in the dark night, she turned to face him, looking up into his face. 'I don't need anyone to organise my life. I told you before, I can look after myself. Thanks for the drink, however.

Now I really must be getting home.' She put her knitted gloves on, pulling the tight cuffs up to cover her wrists. She heard his sigh.

'From the moment I laid eyes on you I knew you were going to be trouble,' he said. 'Doesn't a thrill go through you at the thought of playing to audiences in the West End? You're not the little trouper I took you for if it doesn't.'

'Everyone in this business dreams of getting into the Palladium and all those other glamorous theatres, Mr Holt. It's just that some of us are more practical than others. Dreams are all very well but they don't pay the rent or put food on the table.' Besides, I've had enough of dreams, she thought, watching his face, hawk-like in the glow cast by a street lamp. I've listened to dreams all my life, listened to my father hold forth on them and my mother smile and pretend she believed all he said. The flame of rebellion that had begun to flicker more strongly with every month that passed blazed into a bright gleam.

It really was as he had said the other night; she was stagnating in the life she presently led. Did she really want to spend the next untold number of years looking after her father, working long hours at the theatre and being leered at by drunken men?

Without asking her permission or even offering her the packet, he lit a cigarette, lifting his head, blowing smoke into the night. As though there had been no break in the conversation, he said, 'I know you keep telling me you can take care of yourself and I'm sure you can. But if by some miracle you should change your mind about my offer, you know where to find me. The Apollo Theatre in Blackpool. King Street.' He summoned up the charm that seldom failed him. 'I'll be expecting you.'

'Don't hold your breath.' Even as she said it, she was thinking: Bert appeared to be over his drinking problem. He was very popular with the regulars at the Winter Gardens. Wouldn't she be a fool not to accept this man's offer?

And Harry, watching that expressive face, thought: she's almost there! A little more verbal prodding and I'll have her.

Bert had been playing all afternoon: slow waltzes, quicksteps, anything the gathering requested. During the afternoon, tea and soft drinks only were served. Several cups and saucers containing the cooling beverage rested on top of the piano. Bert's fingers flew over the keys. He'd have given anything for a drink! That muck they called tea – Earl Grey only, by request of the ladies who seemed to make the Winter Gardens their second home – wasn't Bert's idea of a cup of tea. A good, strong brew like his mother made and which Adele had soon learned to make, so strong you could stand your teaspoon up in it – now *that* was tea!

He sighed and turned his attention to the dancers. Young and elderly alike, they glided past him, their expressions rapt, unheeding of anyone else. Despite the winter chill, the ladies were dressed in knee-length, beltless frocks of light floating material. They didn't seem to feel the cold.

The management kept the temperature comfortable and with the palms and various other fern-like plants growing in large terracotta urns, the illusion was more Mediterranean than north of England.

'Tea for Two' flowed out from under his fingers as Bert continued lazily to watch the passing women and their partners. One woman in particular caught his eye. She was partnered by an elderly gent who looked as though he would far rather be somewhere downing a pint with his mates than trying to concentrate on his partner's nifty footwork.

The woman was slim, with a sweet expression and
faded blonde hair arranged in soft waves about her
face. Difficult to guess her age. He had noticed her
before; exchanged smiles with her. Bert could see
she was a good dancer, with a style and dash that
made all the others on the floor look like clumsy
amateurs.

As he watched, she murmured something to her
partner and with obvious relief he nodded. As soon as
the dance was over, and people stood politely clapping
for an encore, the man gave a quick bow then took her
arm and escorted her back to their table. After a minute
or two the man rose and walked away.

Later, during an interval for more tea and cakes for
those who felt the need, noticing that the woman's
partner hadn't returned, Bert took the opportunity to
venture over to her table.

Placing one hand on the back of an empty chair, he
said, deliberately casual, 'Mind if I join you?'

The woman had fitted a cigarette into a long, ivory
holder. Slowly allowing the smoke to drift from the
corner of her mouth, at first she looked surprised by
Bert's proposal. Then pleased. She smiled, inclining her
head in permission. 'Of course. I've been enjoying your
playing, Mr . . . ?'

'Bert Blossom,' he supplied. On the point of adding,
'But you may call me darling,' a touch of humour that
always brought a gleam to the eye of a female, he
stopped himself in time. There wasn't the least hint
of coquetry in her steady gaze.

'Mr Blossom. You have a wonderfully light touch.'

'Thank you. I saw you dancing.' His gaze wandered
towards the glass entrance. 'Is your friend coming
back?'

'No, I shouldn't think so.'

Bert was intrigued. 'He must be crazy!'

She laughed. 'Inestimably sane. He just doesn't like dancing.'

'Didn't he know he was coming to a *thé dansant*? I mean,' with a gesture that took in the whole room, 'that's what people do at tea dances.'

'I think he was just being polite. He's staying at the same hotel as I am. We struck up an acquaintance.' She gazed around at the fresco of blue sky and clouds that embellished the walls. 'This place has been a Godsend! There's little enough to do here this time of the year.'

'You here on holiday, then?'

'At this time of the year, nearing the anniversary of my husband's death, I'm inclined to get a yearning to revisit Newcombe.' She smiled again. 'You see, we spent our honeymoon here, long before the war, and it seems to help ease the pain. Just a little.' The smile faded.

Bert felt for a cigarette, pulling out the flat silver case from his blazer pocket (today he was having a change from the crimson velvet) and offered it to her. She took one, removing the stub of her old one in the long holder and fitting the new one in its place. She put it between her lips and bent forward for a light. He caught a whisper of her perfume. Light and flowery, reminding him so vividly of Adele that momentarily he closed his eyes, seeming to hear his dead wife's soft laugh.

He heard the woman murmur with a touch of concern, 'Are you all right? You've gone quite pale.'

He feigned amusement. 'Me? Oh, yes, I'm fine.' Drawing deeply on his cigarette he asked, 'Will you be coming here tomorrow?'

She nodded. And then, on an impulse, held out her hand. 'I'm Madge Swanson, by the way. It's so nice meeting you. I'm sure all the other women in the room are positively green with envy, you here, sitting talking to *me*.'

'I'll look out for you,' he said.

'All right.'

'I have some time off tomorrow night. Would you consider coming out for a drink?'

'You don't have to take pity on me, Mr Blossom, just because I told you about my husband.'

'I'm not taking pity on you. I would enjoy it. As you said, there's not much to do in Newcombe this time of the year.'

She relented. Besides, she liked the look of this man. A man who could charm and, she guessed, infuriate. 'Why not?' She began to collect her belongings – a fur coat draped over the back of the third empty chair, gloves, a handbag. 'Goodbye, then.'

'Goodbye, Mrs Swanson. Tomorrow evening. All right?'

'All right.'

'That's a date. Don't forget now!'

'I won't.' She rose from her chair, slipping the coat about her shoulders. Bert watched her go and thought that she was the first woman in whom he'd taken a real interest since Adele's death. Their meeting tomorrow night would be something to look forward to.

Seated at a corner table, a full glass of ale in front of each of them, Bert told her all about his life as a Summer Follies artiste and of all the weird and wonderful people he had worked with. Because he had such a whimsical way with a story he soon had Madge laughing so much she clasped a hand to her side, saying her stays would burst if he didn't stop. The old charm that was never far from the surface emerged and Bert used it to his best advantage.

As the glasses were emptied and then refilled, he enveloped her with his gay, good humour. By the time the landlord had called for last orders, Madge had fallen for him.

In their quieter moments he enquired about her
husband and she told him of the gentle man to whom
she had been married for twenty-five years.

'Owned his own shop,' she said proudly. 'Men's
apparel. Very classy.'

'But you're not from these parts,' remarked Bert. Her
accent told him that.

'No, I was brought up on the south coast, near
Brighton. My husband came from Manchester. That's
where he had his shop. After his death I sold up and
moved back down south. I still have relations there and,
well, it seemed the sensible thing to do.' She stared into
her glass, remembering.

She nodded sympathetically when Bert told her of
Adele, how he'd struggled to take care of his son and
daughter. In hushed tones she said, 'It must have been
very difficult for you. How dreadful for the wee girl,
how she must have missed her mummy.'

Pulling a wry face, Bert agreed. He didn't think it
was necessary to tell her that Clover had been fourteen
at the time . . .

Chapter Twenty-three

Eddie gave a long, satisfied sigh as he finished signing his name to the contract. The sense of relief was overwhelming, just seeing his name there in black and white after all this time of waiting. Handing back the gold-plated fountain pen, he said, 'There, that's done! I only hope for your sake it works out. I'm no actor, you know, even if I did take my first doddering steps on the stage when I was three.'

Nick Farrel grinned. 'You'll do. Amorita is already halfway in love with you and so will half the women in America be by the time that movie's released.'

With a keen eye, he studied the good-looking young man. The tousled hair had been tamed and now lay smooth and glossy with just the hint of a wave on top. Eddie wasn't keen on it but Nick Farrel insisted that it was the look the studio wanted. And Nick Farrel's word was law. Now, to make it legal and above board, Eddie had just signed the contract that was to put Nick even more in control.

'What did Imelda have to say about all this?' he asked with a grin, gently shaking the pages of print to dry the ink. 'Bet she was thrilled.'

'I haven't told her yet.'

Nick looked incredulous. 'You haven't told her! I should have thought you wouldn't have been able to hold it back.' He shook his head. 'She's going to be one almighty surprised young lady when you do get around to it, then. How do you think she'll like living in Hollywood?'

Eddie had put off the telling, waiting until Imelda was in a better frame of mind. Lately, since the day he'd come home and found Jamie crying and alone, things had become increasingly more strained between them. Each little incident was magnified a thousandfold in Imelda's eyes, so that he had begun to dread going home. If it wasn't for Jamie, he often debated whether he would.

Sitting with her in the evenings he had to search frantically for something to say. Anything to break this cold silence of hostility. On the point several times of telling her his good news, a sudden perversity on his part always stopped him and he clamped his lips together and stayed silent. She seemed to exist in a world of her own, seeing to Jamie's needs like an automaton, with barely a word or a smile for the child.

Doggedly he told himself that until she got over this ridiculous phase he would keep quiet. That he was acting as childishly as she was didn't enter his head. He suspected that the Imelda he had yearned for in that seaside summer had never existed, except in his imagination. There had been a time when there wasn't a minute of every hour of every day that he hadn't wanted her. Memories of her were like his heartbeat: always there, a part of him.

Now, after days of frigid silence, Eddie felt he could stand it no longer. Dreading going back to that unwelcoming flat they shared, it was easier in the evening to talk to Maxi Fields in his office, glasses of the Irish whiskey that Maxi still seemed able to buy on the desk before them. Maxi would try to persuade him to go home. 'The little woman'll wonder where you've got to.'

Eddie had given up boxing, at Nick Farrel's insist-
ence, but he still helped Maxi about the busy gymnasium. Once things got rolling, Maxi knew, it would be
different. The kid would have to apply all his thoughts
and energy to his new job. Eddie liked Maxi. The old
man was more like a father to him than Bert had ever
been. He valued his friendship but took little heed of his
admonishments. 'She'll survive,' he'd say when Maxi
spoke like this and Maxi would look at him with concern
written all over his pugnacious features.

Maxi was used to people unloading their troubles on
him. He wondered why the kid was so indisposed to
share his. Of course, being a limey didn't help, stiff
upper lip and all that.

Perplexed, he shook his head. There would be tears
before bedtime, as his old mother used to say. He
watched Eddie light a cigarette, break the match and
then drop it meticulously into the ashtray. 'Tell me
about it, Eddie. What went wrong?'

The little office was suddenly unbearably stuffy.
Eddie got up and went to the window, opening it an
inch to allow the cold winter air to circulate. He said,
'I suppose the fact is that I never really understood her.
What sort of a person she really was.'

Maxi noted the use of the past tense. 'I don't think I
quite get you.'

'Well, meeting her in the beginning, the way things
were.' He'd never told Maxi, or anyone else, details of
his previous life – or, more precisely, Imelda's previous
life – divulging only the bare facts.

He came back to the desk and sat down opposite the
older man. He confided some of the details now to
Maxi. Leaving out Imelda's role in the life of Buster
Bywater, he spoke of the summer they had met, of
the clandestine meetings. 'I think I fell in love with
her the first moment I saw her. She was so lovely, so

– so captivating, I couldn't take my eyes off her. And I knew straightaway that she felt the same.' He coloured a little, gazing down at his clasped hands on the desk top. 'She really was my first love.'

Maxi coughed. 'So what's changed?'

'Everything. She has. For one thing, she can't be bothered with the boy. You can see a mile off that he just annoys her. There's none of the caring mother love that I thought was inherent in every woman.'

Maxi smiled. 'I guess it doesn't come out automatically with the baby. It's probably something you've got to cultivate. Don't worry, kid, your Imelda will come through. You both will.'

'I keep telling myself that. That it's something time will take care of. But every time I go home she's the same. It's either a silence that chills your very bones or the irritability of a wet hen.'

Maxi took a much-needed swig from his glass. 'You said one thing. What's the other?'

'When we do talk it's just rows. We end up shouting at each other.'

'I shout at people all the time. Excellent therapy.'

'Not the way we do it. I hate it. I hate the things she says. I never guessed she knew such things. I keep telling myself that one day I'll come home and it'll all be over, that she'll be back to her old, sweet self. But all the time it's there at the back of my mind, the fear that I did wrong in bringing her all this way, to a strange country, away from the things she knows.'

'Eddie . . .'

He didn't hear the plea in the other man's voice. Now that the words had come pouring out, there seemed no stopping them. 'I can't go on like this, Maxi, hating her and loving her both at the same time. I get to the stage when I don't know what my feelings are. And I'm sure she feels the same.'

'And it's because of all this that you kept mum about Nick Farrel and the movie game?'

Eddie pulled a wry face. 'Crazy, isn't it?'

'I certainly wouldn't argue with you there, kid. You said you keep hoping that one day you'll return home and Imelda will be back to her old sweet and loving self again. Why don't you go home with that in mind, right now, right this minute and put it to the test?'

Eddie stubbed his cigarette out in the ashtray. 'I don't think—'

Ruthlessly interrupting, Maxi went on, 'Staying away like this is just making it a thousand times worse. I would say the merest breath of Hollywood and you'll have her eating out of your hand.'

That wasn't really what Eddie was looking for. He didn't want Imelda 'eating out of his hand', but the Imelda of old, spirited and passionate and fun to be with. He said, 'Do you really think it would work?'

'It's a cinch. Go on, get outta here and tell her how things really are. Whatever the problem is, you're not going to solve it by ignoring it. Life's too short to spend it quarrelling. And keep a hold on that temper of yours.'

Eddie grinned, already on his feet. 'I hear, boss.'

Too restless to wait for a trolley car, Eddie whistled to a passing cab. His thoughts raced ahead, visualising Imelda's delighted face when he broke the good news. News that they would be moving from the tenements she hated to a wonderful place called California where money would be no object and she'd only have to ask for something and it would be hers. Where they could hire a woman to look after Jamie, leaving Imelda free to drive around in that smart yellow car he'd promised all that time ago. Of course she'd have to have driving lessons – so would he if it came to that. Everyone drove cars in California; the Blossoms would be no exception.

Alighting from the cab, he hurried towards his home, grinning and punching the air in that old gesture he used when he was too elated for words. Mrs Scholtz was, as usual, loitering on the upper landing, pretending to rub a duster over the scarred banister rail. She was like a sponge, thought Eddie, soaking up every bit of information she could gather from the different sounds and snatches of conversation filtering through the closed doors.

She looked startled when she saw Eddie, for it was early for him to be home. He gave her a tight grin. 'Good evening, Mrs Scholtz. Busy as usual, I see.'

She jerked her chin up and down in acknowledgement. 'Mr Blossom!'

He felt for his door key and slipped it into the old-fashioned lock. He was as quiet as he could be, not wanting to alert Imelda, wanting to surprise her. And if Jamie had been troublesome and she had just got him to sleep, it would be more than his life's worth to disturb him. He grinned again, picturing her stretched out on their bed, maybe Jamie cuddled up beside her, soft and cherubic, looking as though butter wouldn't melt in his mouth. Imelda would be drowsy, in dishabille, at her most vulnerable. Images played lasciviously in his mind. He saw them making up, begging each other's forgiveness, saying they had both been fools and must never let it happen again. He felt the muscles of his stomach tighten with desire, thinking of the scene that would follow.

The only way to describe Imelda's love-making, when she was in the mood, was tigerish, scratching, leaving marks all down his back.

He stepped lightly across the living room carpet, listening for the slightest sound. Maybe she had gone out and taken Jamie with her. Perhaps she was upstairs visiting those sisters.

At the bedroom door he paused, a slight smile on his lips. Perhaps Jamie wasn't asleep. He could hear . . .

The door opened to his gentle push. Then all thoughts of his wife with Jamie nestled beside her vanished. Stretched out she was all right, shameless in her abandonment, not even a sheet to cover her. Jamie sat in his cot, fat little hands clutching an empty bottle, sucking noisily at the teat. His uncomprehending blue eyes gazed at his mother and the man who lay with her on the bed. Then, as the bedroom door opened, he turned to gaze at Eddie, the bottle dropping to the cot mattress, a beatific smile appearing on his face. 'Dada!' he said, quite clearly and loudly.

Imelda gave a little scream and pushed herself up on the bed with the flat of her hands, her eyes widening in shock. The dark-haired man beside her, who for once hadn't spent the afternoon working on his car, gave a snort of frustration mixed with alarm when he saw Eddie's face, and bounded from the bed.

There followed an undignified scramble for his clothing and an even more undignified departure when Eddie lifted him by the scruff of the neck and all but threw him across the landing and down the stairs.

Mrs Scholtz will really be getting her money's worth today, thought Eddie.

When he went back to the bedroom, Imelda, hurriedly clad in a pair of silk panties and a camisole top, threw her arms about his neck, crying noisily, saying the man had forced his way into the flat and attacked her. 'I tried to hold him off,' she sobbed. 'You saw how much I tried. But he was too strong for me. I couldn't stop him.'

From what Eddie had seen it hadn't looked like she

was trying to hold him off but rather as if she was urging him on. And in full view of Jamie, unintelligible though it might have been to the little boy.

Anger, red and raging, boiled up inside him. He moved swiftly backwards and she felt a stinging blow across her face. 'Don't add to your sins by telling lies, you little bitch,' he growled, and then was shaking her like a maniac, throwing her away from him. She reeled and fell to the ground, the ends of her hair flipping up, covering her eyes.

'Don't, Eddie,' she pleaded. 'I love you so much. You know there's never been anyone but you.' She lay looking up at him, one hand brushing the strands of hair from her face, tucking it behind her ears. She tried the tactics that had so far never failed her, though used infrequently lately. 'Now that you've come home so early, why don't we . . . ?'

Jamie's sudden wail had the fire raging in his eyes again. 'Bitch!' he repeated and bunched his hands into fists. Only the supreme control drummed into him by Maxi Fields stopped him then from killing her.

He sat in the chair in their bedroom, his face in his hands, his head throbbing. He tried to block out the sight that had met him when he opened the bedroom door. But it was no good. Even through closed eyes he could see her, the man with her, their bodies touching . . .

He'd lashed out at her, not caring about the damage he may have caused. For him, for Jamie. And when she'd crouched on the floor, her eyes sharp with hatred, he was suddenly sorry.

'I hate you! I'll hate you for the rest of my life.' Her words echoed in his ears, bringing realisation for the first time. He rose to his feet, unsteady with drink, running a hand over the stubble on his chin and through his tousled hair.

Men always kill the thing they love best. He'd read that somewhere in a book. But what manner of man could want to kill the mother of his child? The scene on the bed came unbidden to his eyes and jealousy possessed him. He knew what manner of man; a man like Eddie Blossom . . .

She stayed hidden away in the apartment for the rest of the week. No word passed between them. Eddie made himself a bed on the hard settee and entered the bedroom only when he needed to take clean linen from the chest of drawers there. Compassion tore into him each time he laid eyes on her, but Imelda remained sullen and withdrawn, for once concentrating only on Jamie. She didn't even emerge to go shopping and Eddie purchased all their needs from the corner shop just down the road. The Greek owner knew Imelda and enquired about her health. Eddie made up a tale of a tummy upset. 'She's taking it easy for a while,' he said, not meeting the shop owner's eyes.

'Ah, yes, these young wifes do not always carry easily. A month or two, my friend, and she will be as right as rain.'

Eddie grimaced. Dear God, that was all he needed! A pregnant Imelda!

He bought flowers, hoping to cheer up the dingy sitting room; little treats of chocolate and fruit. He would have laid the most precious jewels at her feet, plucked the stars from the sky if she'd expressed a craving for them. Anything to have the old Imelda back in his arms.

Mrs Scholtz seemed to have found something else to occupy her time. It was a relief not to have her speculative gaze fixed on him whenever he came in or went out. Johnny Amadeo had vanished as smoothly and as slyly as he had arrived; here one day and gone the next. Going up the stairs one morning, Eddie saw one of the Amadeo sisters coming down but as soon as she saw him she turned and scuttled back to her own apartment.

His visits to the gym were brief, not wanting to leave Jamie too long at a time. One morning, as Eddie slipped on his coat, Jamie looked up from where he was playing with a toy truck on the carpet, pushing it backwards and forwards happily. To Eddie's surprise the little boy rose and on unsteady legs trotted over to him. Clasping his arms about his father's knees, he gazed beseechingly up into his face and said, 'Dada?'

To Eddie, it was a plea he couldn't resist. 'Of course, Jamie, you can come too,' he grinned, scooping the child up into his arms. He found the warm coat he had bought him at the beginning of the winter, and slipped it on the child, buttoning it carefully close to the throat. With Jamie in his arms he went to the bedroom door and tapped gently. When there was no reply he pushed it open and peered in. Imelda lay on the bed, still in her dressing gown, a paperback novel in her hand. She didn't even look up when he said, 'I'm going out for awhile. Taking Jamie with me.'

The little boy loved the trolley ride, jumping up and down on the seat, Eddie's fingers holding him securely from behind, laughing with delight at the sights and sounds of the busy streets.

Maxi and the various men who hung around the gym made a fuss of the little boy and Eddie was gratified that Jamie enjoyed it, too, not clinging to him as he'd seen some children do and crying, but lapping up all the attention happily. 'A fine lad,' proclaimed Maxi. 'What are your plans for him, kid?'

Eddie laughed. 'Too early to say yet. Give the poor little beggar time to grow up.'

Jamie watched, fascinated, as two men in the ring circled each other, gloved hands held before their chests, faces set in a ferocious grimace. Eddie knew they were acting the fool for the benefit of Jamie.

'How's Imelda, then?' Maxi asked. His tone was casual, his hands busy with threading new laces through a glove.

Eddie hadn't told him of the scene that day in the flat. He was too ashamed – of both himself and Imelda – and for all Maxi knew things were all right with them, although he must have wondered just what had transpired that day Eddie had left the gym with such high hopes of reconciliation.

'Oh, she's fine,' he answered. 'She was busy so I thought I'd take the boy out for a bit of fresh air.'

As the afternoon passed it was all too evident that the warm, smoky atmosphere of the gym was making Jamie sleepy. Eddie remembered he usually had a snooze in the afternoon. Carefully he wiped away the remains of the hotdog with which Maxi had taken such delight in feeding him for his lunch. Jamie had loved the soft bun and the spicy sausage and had really made a pig of himself, covering his face with tomato ketchup. Gathering scarves and coats together, Eddie said, 'Better get going, I suppose. He's just about asleep on his feet.'

He returned to an apartment so quiet you could have heard a pin drop. Even the usual cacophony of sounds – shouts from the hordes of children, dogs barking, women screeching to each other across the width of the street – today seemed muffled. Carrying a drowsy little boy in his arms, head resting heavily against his shoulder, Eddie quietly let himself in.

The bedroom was empty, not a sign of Imelda. Carefully, gently, he laid Jamie into his cot, tucking the blankets firmly about him. He made a pot of coffee and rummaged in the pantry for something to cook for supper. When the meal was ready and Imelda still hadn't returned, he dished himself up a plateful, reserving a small amount for the still sleeping boy. Jamie ate what they did now and enjoyed everything that was offered to him. Thank God he wasn't one of those picky children, thought Eddie. Later, he fed Jamie and undressed him for bed, tonight abandoning the usual bath.

Eddie woke in the early morning, stiff and still unrested from the hard settee. He could have used the bed, but the image of Imelda and that man, and what had so obviously just taken place there was still fresh in his mind and he felt he couldn't bear to sleep there.

He saw that Imelda had still not returned home. It was only then that it occurred to him to look through her wardrobe. It was empty. All the pretty, light dresses she'd purchased that summer once the cheques from Maxi Fields were coming in regularly, as well as the thick skirts and blouses and the high-heeled shoes, were gone. Belatedly he scrutinised the bedroom for a farewell note. There wasn't one. Not on the mantelpiece or anywhere else in the flat, either.

At last he had to face it. Imelda had left him. With him and Jamie out of the way, she had seized the opportunity and decamped. Had it been arranged all along with that bloody Casanova, that brother of the Amadeo sisters? he wondered. Should he really be so surprised? Looking back on it, he realised he wasn't. Looking forward to a future without the carping, contrary woman Imelda had become, he was a little shocked to realise he wasn't unduly bothered by that either. With the movie contract safely in his pocket, he felt the future could hold whatever he wished it to hold.

With or without Imelda. He had his little son. He would see that he grew up into a fine young man. And later, when he could afford it, he would return to England, to show them he had made a success of his life. Clover, he knew, would adore Jamie . . .

Chapter Twenty-four

Clover's impression when she met Madge Swanson for the first time was that the woman seemed to be acting a part. Trying to be something other than what she was: an aging widow with peroxided hair, lonely for the company of a man. Overly anxious to please, liking her drink, to Clover she seemed the complete opposite of the type of woman she'd expect Bert to be attracted to. Clover distrusted her from the start. There was no one to tell her that this was a natural reaction to any woman who threatened to take her mother's place.

It was not until the early spring weather was upon them that she began to be seriously concerned. The sun pleasantly warm upon her shoulders, Clover strolled over to the Winter Gardens, intending to give Bert a surprise. Someone else was playing the piano. The man knew Clover and looked up, grinning, saying Bert had stepped out for a moment. 'He shouldn't be long,' he said. 'He's only got a ten-minute break.'

Clover thanked him. It didn't really matter. She'd thought it would be nice to treat herself to a cup of tea at one of the small tables while she listened to Bert playing. They didn't spend nearly enough time together these days. She decided to go out and find him. With the day so nice, the walk would do her good.

Leaving the ornate glass and gilt structure that was the Winter Gardens, she didn't have to walk far before she spied him seated talking to someone

on a wooden bench facing the sea. Behind them in the
spring sunshine early daffodils and primulas gleamed
brightly. Clover hesitated. Then Bert, as though sensing
her presence, looked up from the earnest discussion he
had been engaged in with Madge Swanson, and Clover
felt something inside her cower.

Slowly she approached them. 'Sorry, Dad, I didn't
know you were with someone.'

Madge was unabashed. 'Just come to tell your father
something.' She rose to her feet, smoothing down the
front of her coat with pale hands. She smiled at Bert
who still lounged on the seat, legs crossed, one arm
draped across the seat back. 'I'd better go, Bert. See
you later, eh?'

Bert returned her smile and nodded and Clover said,
hastily, 'Oh, don't go because of me!'

Madge gazed at her with thoughtful eyes. When she'd
first met the girl, she'd hoped the surprise didn't show
in her face. Bert had left her with the impression
that Clover was a little girl. After listening to his
heartrending story of the death of his poor wife, she
could have sworn that was the intention he meant to
give. She didn't quite know what to make of this young
lady who considered her so seriously, and so warily.

She adjusted the fur coat on her shoulders where
she wore it as a cape, clutched the expensive suede
handbag to her breast, and gave a small wave of
farewell.

Clover sat down beside her father, looking at him
intently. He avoided her eyes, gazing out across the
water, pale blue with the sun sparkling on it. A ship
on the horizon trailed long plumes of smoke.

Clover said at last, 'I've got an awful feeling I
disturbed something.'

'I don't know what you mean.' Bert didn't shift his
gaze from the scene before him.

'Don't you?' She laughed. 'You old rogue! Fancy you trying to chat up Mrs Swanson.'

Bert removed his arm from the back of the bench and brushed imaginary dust from the knees of his trousers. 'Madge Swanson's a very worthwhile lady. Very worthwhile. We have a lot in common.'

'Such as?' Clover peered at him intently.

'Well, we're both pretty much the same age. We like the same things. And we're both lonely.'

The same things! thought Clover with a touch of aspersion. Drink and the smoky atmosphere of public houses! Awash with guilt at her unkind thoughts, she leaned forward and laid a hand on the one that rested on his crossed knee. 'Oh, Daddy, I'm sorry. I never guessed you were lonely. You're always so self-contained and sure of yourself.'

'You of all people should know that you don't judge a book by its cover.' His hand moved, turning palm upwards under hers. His fingers clasped hers. 'I loved your mother, Clover. I shall always love her. But that doesn't mean I have to live alone and – and celibate all my life. I'm still a fairly young man and I've been a long time without a woman's arms to comfort me at night.'

Never before had he spoken to her so openly. A warm flush suffused her cheeks, knowing what he meant. And it was true, he was still a young man, well, not yet old, anyway, and who was she to deny him the start of a new life! And yet . . .

She thought of her lovely mother, always so gay, so dainty and ladylike and felt a sudden pang of resentment – there was no other word for it – at the idea of Madge Swanson taking her mother's place.

She drew a deep breath as he said, 'You like her, don't you, lass? Madge is a warm, kind-hearted woman. There's lots of goodness in her.'

'I suppose I can't deny that.'

He realised she hadn't answered his question. 'You *do* like her?'

Knowing he wanted to be reassured, as she had always reassured him when things were going wrong, a sudden perverse desire had her answering in an offhand voice, 'There's nothing to *dis*like.' She almost added: She's too shallow to dislike. A woman who had been around for a long time and was obviously an expert at pulling the wool over a man's eyes. But why must she choose her father?

Bert nodded, his eyes unfocused as he stared across the blue water. 'Your mother was the kindest, sweetest, most beautiful woman who ever drew breath, Clover. No matter what fate tosses my way I shall never forget her.' He turned to her again. 'But Adele was a different life, a different time. Sweet but made distant by the years. You wouldn't deny me the chance of a warm bosom on which to lay my head in the twilight of my years?'

Clover felt the foolish tears spring to her eyes. All she could do was to squeeze his hand and gulp. 'Oh, Daddy!'

His plea for understanding had seemed so heart-rending; it was only later, as she was getting ready for bed, that its familiarity struck her. It was a line from a short sketch her parents had once performed on the stage.

As usual, Miss Boyce was the one to go to with her troubles. The elderly spinster listened to her grievances and tried to reassure her as best she could. She wanted to say, but prudently didn't, that if anything they should be surprised that Bert hadn't been attracted long ago to some woman.

Pouring Clover a cup of tea, handing it to her where she sat in the window, Miss Boyce said, 'I don't know what to think, dear. I suppose your father is old enough to know what he's doing. And I'm sure your dear mother would not have wanted him to be companionless for the rest of his life.' As she had been when the Boer bullet ended the life of her beloved John.

She sighed. She of all people should know how Bert Blossom felt. The loneliness and despair of walking alone . . .

'What should I do if he tells me he wants to marry her?' Clover gazed at her with wide, troubled eyes.

Miss Boyce sighed again. 'A man like your father has to have his head. You won't be able to do anything, my dear, except acquiesce. I know it would be hard and I have my doubts that he would ever take such a headstrong step. The wise thing would be to wait and see and in the meantime consider your own plans.' She gave Clover a shrewd look across the top of her pince-nez. 'What about that young man from Moorfield? Dr Foley? I rather thought . . .'

Clover blushed, turning her gaze away from those astute eyes. She'd thought she loved him. She was sure she did. But lately he'd been getting so possessive, insisting in every letter that she consider his suggestion that she give everything up and go back to Moorfield to him.

'Adam's just a friend. A very dear friend. But nothing else.'

Miss Boyce leaned over the table to pour herself a fresh cup of tea. 'Really? I got the impression he was more than that, dear. Or he would like to be, given the chance.'

Superimposed on her thoughts of Adam came the image of the lean, dark features of Harry Holt. It was as though her thoughts were two-sided, each disputing with the other.

The latest gossip in the Argyle Theatre was that Harry

had plans for touring the provinces with the hope that the show would finish in London.

'As it could well do,' commented Mr Roxburgh, joining a discussion with Clover and a group of chorus girls one morning at rehearsals. 'That doesn't mean any of you lot has permission to go crawling to him seeking a better job. I don't like poachers. Or people who allow themselves to be poached.' And the look he directed towards Clover had her blushing a bright beetroot red. Harry's interest in her hadn't gone unnoticed.

Miss Boyce, too, it seemed had heard the gossip. Giving Clover another shrewd look, she said, 'Getting away from the subject of your father, I've been hearing some things about you, my lady.'

Clover looked startled. 'What things?'

'About a certain producer from a theatre in Blackpool waiting for you at the end of the show and taking you out.'

Clover's lips firmed. It seemed you couldn't do a thing without some busybody at the theatre knowing and spreading the information for all to enjoy.

'Mr Holt produces the show at the Apollo in King Street,' she said. 'I won't deny he's made me an offer.' She recalled his last words to her: 'Won't you at least consider it, Miss Blossom?' and her reply, 'I can't take the chance.' For she knew where she was with Mr Roxburgh. She didn't know where she was with Harry Holt. She'd told him so and he'd grinned and said, 'Don't you ever gamble, Miss Blossom?' She'd assumed an expression that would have done Miss Boyce proud. 'Why, the very idea, Mr Holt!'

Breaking into her thoughts came the insistent tone of Miss Boyce. 'And?'

'And what?'

Miss Boyce gave a longsuffering sigh. 'Are you going to accept the offer? The one the man made?'

Surprising herself, for she thought she'd been quite firm about this, she heard herself answer, 'I don't know. I haven't decided yet.'

'Well, I don't suppose there's any hurry.' Miss Boyce reached for the teapot. 'Have a refill and another piece of shortbread. I made it especially for you, dear, knowing how much you like it.'

When Madge Swanson eventually left to return home, Clover heaved a sigh of relief. She couldn't believe her father could really be interested in the woman, although she supposed you didn't have to be young and foolish to experience a passing fancy for someone. And that's all it had been, surely? A passing fancy?

She got on with her own life, too busy to notice that Bert had become quiet and withdrawn. He was waiting for her each night she returned from the theatre. But where in the past they would chat good-humouredly about the events of the day, now he sat with his supper before him, staring at his plate, totally unaware of the food he was eating.

She had to suppose that Bobby Roxburgh was pleased with her although he never suggested she add another song to her minuscule spot in the show. She still carried the tray of chocolates and cigarettes round in the intervals and was adept at fending off the sly remarks and wandering hands.

Harry Holt seemed to have vanished from the face of the earth. She watched for him each evening, in a perverse way feeling neglected when he didn't turn up. Inevitably some of Bert's melancholy rubbed off on her and the other girls found the good-natured teasing which in the past she hadn't minded now evoked a terse reply.

So one night when Bert broached the subject of

moving on she didn't know whether to feel happy or dismayed.

'I've heard of a job going in Brighton,' he said as she set down supper. 'It might do us good to get away from the north coast for a while and try somewhere new.'

'Brighton? But why go all the way down there?' She stared at him suspiciously as a thought struck her. 'You haven't been sacked, have you?'

'You haven't much faith in your old dad! Of course I haven't been sacked.' He had the feeling that now wasn't the right time to reveal that Madge Swanson lived in Brighton, that she had, in fact, written telling him of the opening in a new stage show, seeing a way of being reunited with Bert. 'It's a step up, lass. The chance I said would come if we believed hard enough. A genuine stage show, a revue they call it. Something that's becoming all the rage. There's bound to be an opening for you in it, too.'

Clover's recent turbulent feelings took over and for the first time in her life she was angry with her father. Surely he could have talked the matter over with her, given her a chance to voice an opinion? She would be eighteen next birthday, no longer a child, and she bitterly resented Bert's overbearing and old-fashioned chauvinistic attitude. In her father's eyes she was still a little girl. In his eyes she would probably never grow up.

She'd gone along with his every wish, stayed with him because he needed her, because she loved him. You didn't desert someone because they neglected to consult you about their future plans. But what alternative did she have if she was ever going to begin to live a life of her own? With a touch more asperity than she meant, she said, 'Well, I'm not going.'

Digesting this, he took a second helping before replying. 'Somehow I thought you'd say that, lass. I suppose I deserve it, dragging you all over the place in search of God knows what, for I certainly didn't. Of course you must stay here if that's what you want. I wouldn't try to persuade you otherwise. Eddie saw his chance of freedom and took it, you must do the same. An old man like me can't expect to cling on to his children for ever.'

Somehow that last sentence didn't quite ring truc. Genial father-types were not Bert Blossom's favourite role.

'And of course there's that young man, that doctor,' he went on. 'That weekend he was here, Clover, I saw a dimple appear in your cheek that I haven't seen since your poor, dear mother died.' He pushed his plate away and, in spite of her frown, reached for the packet of cigarettes lying near him on the table. Through a cloud of smoke, he said, 'I'm a selfish old blockhead, aren't I, expecting you to drop everything and follow to wherever the wind takes me? Without the encumbrance of your old dad I guarantee the next time I see you your name will be up in lights over the best theatre in town. You'll make something of yourself, Clover. You've got all your mother's grace and beauty and to top it all my talent.'

That made her laugh, banishing the initial feelings of anger.

'The only thing I insist on is that you find somewhere else to live. I wouldn't have a moment's peace, thinking of you living in this place.'

She didn't tell him that there was a fair chance she might not be living in Newcombe herself for much longer, that she might be moving on, too. For with a resoluteness she hadn't known she possessed, she had decided she was going to take up Harry Holt's offer.

Finding lodgings not only befitting a young girl on her own but also something she could afford would not be easy. As usual, Miss Boyce came to the rescue. She insisted that Clover apply to her own landlady. 'There's a room recently become available next to mine, Clover. It's a bit poky but the rent is very reasonable.' To Bert, she added, 'Then you won't have to worry. I can keep an eye on the child.'

Clover wasn't slow to accept. Bert could go off to Brighton with an easy conscience, knowing his little girl was in safe hands.

Clover remained dry-eyed on the station platform until Bert's train had vanished from sight, only then allowing herself the luxury of a few tears. On her way to her new home at Miss Boyce's, she thought of the mostly elderly residents, telling herself it would only be temporary, only until she was sure of her job in the show at the Apollo.

For could she really depend on a man as variable as Harry Holt? He could have changed his mind half a dozen times since they last talked, on reflection deciding she was too difficult – 'I knew you were trouble the first moment I saw you . . .'

Not many young struggling artistes would have vacillated as she had done. It had all to do with the way he had treated her at their first meeting, plus the self-satisfied ego of a man who thought he only had to mention a job and she'd fall at his feet in adoration. Plus the fact that all the other girls in the show found him irresistible . . .

Sighing, she entered the rather grim, grey house with the white-painted sign over the door: Guest House for Ladies and Gentlemen. She had the feeling that a door was closing on yet another compartment of her life. Like the one that had closed on her blissful childhood with Eddie and Adele; and on that summer day with Bethany and Hazel. Now she really would be alone.

But independent, she reminded herself with great satisfaction. At liberty to do whatever she wanted from now on. Climbing the rather musty smelling staircase to her room at the top of the house, smiling a greeting to an old man who clutched at the banister rail as she passed, his hand trembling with age, she decided that tomorrow she would take a charabanc over to Blackpool and visit Mr Holt.

King Street was a part of Blackpool she wasn't familiar with. When she alighted from the coach she asked the first kindly looking woman who passed and was directed to a wide street at the back of the Tower. At this time of day, early afternoon, the theatre looked closed and shuttered. But as she hesitated outside, a woman in a blue pinny came out and began an assiduous polishing of the brass handles of the doors.

Clover approached her. 'Can you please tell me if the producer is in the theatre?'

The woman paused in her work, saturated the rubbing cloth with strong-smelling Brasso and turned to look at her. 'Don't know, love. The door's open. Go in and if he's around he'll be in his office.'

Clover thanked her and pushed open the swing door, careful to avoid touching the gleaming brass. This was the time of the day when the theatre would be at its quietest, after the morning's rehearsals were finished and the first house began. There was no one about to ask but Clover knew enough about theatres to guess where the office might be.

Harry Holt looked up from the paperwork littering

his desk. He raised his brows in surprise as Clover peered round the edge of the door.

'Hello!' She smiled, then a feeling of irritation overcame her at the smug look he gave her. He was in his shirtsleeves, the knot of his tie pulled down. And, surprising her, a hat perched on the back of his head.

Without answering her greeting he continued to look at her. Then, lazily, he said, 'I expected you long before this. What kept you?'

Firmly she told herself she would not rise to his baiting. 'I don't rush into things, Mr Holt,' she said primly. 'But once I'd made up my mind I came straight over.'

He leaned back in his chair, that disconcerting look making her feel uneasy. 'What made you so sure I'd be waiting here to welcome you with open arms?'

She flushed. 'I wasn't sure. It was . . . I thought I'd try, that's all.' She turned, one hand reaching for the door handle. 'But if I've wasted my time, I'll be getting back.'

'Oh, for God's sake come in and shut the door! And sit down. I can't talk to you while you're dithering about like that.'

Lips firmed into a tight line, she did as she was told. No one had ever spoken to her as he did. She was sure that if they had she would have given them a right ticking off. It had been the same that other time when she had faced him across a desk, asking for a job. She wondered about the background that could have produced a man like Harry Holt. What kind of a childhood had he had to make him so unremittingly arrogant and abrasive?

She remembered the time he had come to her aid in the bar of the Argyle Theatre when the man had been pawing her. For a moment she had glimpsed a concern for her welfare that was touching – and totally inconsistent with the look he was giving her now. Head up, she returned his look. 'All right, I'm sitting.'

His lips twitched. 'So you've decided to swallow your pride and come and work for me, have you? You won't regret it.'

She inclined her head. 'I've still got to give notice to Mr Roxburgh, though.'

'You haven't told him yet?'

'Of course not. I told you before, I'm not a gambler. I can't afford to be, especially not now when . . .' She hesitated, unsure whether to bring Bert into it or not.

His eyes softened. 'Why especially now?' he asked.

'My father's gone off to Brighton, to appear in a new production down there, if he's lucky.' She lifted her head, catching his look. 'Oh, I don't mind. It was for the best, believe me. The job he was doing, playing the piano at the Winter Gardens, was only temporary and not really for a gifted performer like my father.'

'Leaving you high and dry after all the loyalty you've shown him!'

Clover's chin came up, her eyes a sudden furious blaze of blue. 'It had to happen sometime. I've got to start leading a life of my own sometime.'

'As I well remember telling you one dark and bitterly cold night outside the theatre.'

'It was for the best.' Foolishly, she heard herself repeating the words and she wondered if she would ever get over the habit of defending her father all the time.

'It seems we agree on some things, then.' Thick, spiky lashes came down to hood his look. 'When do you think you can start?'

'I'll have to let you know. I'll come over—'

'Telephone.' He indicated the black upright on its stand on his desk. 'I'm usually here. If I'm not, someone will take a message.'

Clover looked alarmed. 'I've never used one of those things before,' she said and bit her bottom lip. 'I'd really much rather come over.'

'Rubbish! That is the very reason they are inventing these new gadgets all the time, to save people time.' The hint of a smile touched that straight mouth. 'It won't bite you.' He stood up and came round the desk, one hand going under her elbow to pull her to her feet. 'And don't let old Roxburgh bully you into staying. You didn't sign a contract or anything like that, did you?'

'No.'

'Well,' he grinned, 'is it agreed, then?'

'Agreed,' she replied and took his hand in hers and to his vast amusement shook it.

The door had barely closed behind her when the telephone on his desk started ringing. It was his brother-in-law, asking if he was free for a late supper after the show that evening. Harry said he was and they talked awhile until John said, quite out of the blue, 'Did you get your little songbird?'

It seemed such a coincidence, when Clover had hardly left his sight, that for once in his life Harry was nonplussed. Then he said, 'Not yet. But I'm working at it.'

'Can't for the life of me see why you're so interested in her, old man. She's only a kid and girl singers are two a penny.'

'That may well be true. It just happens that I want this one.'

He heard John laugh. 'Alice always did say you were a big softie at heart. Just because you feel sorry for her.'

Harry frowned, and said easily, 'I don't think it's pity I feel. Not pity.'

John laughed again. 'Anyway, whatever it is, don't let it go to your head. And don't be late for supper. You know how Alice hates having her dinner spoiled!'

Bobby Roxburgh didn't take too kindly to his protégée giving notice to leave. After all he'd done for her, too! Sourly he reminded her of his warning about poaching and poachers. When Clover didn't argue but just stood there, chin up, that inflexible expression on her face, his manner softened and he ended up by offering her a larger part in the show. Her little musical number had gone down well, and he'd received numerous compliments about the singer in her blue gown. His voice entreating, he said, 'A larger part would mean more money, Clover. And what about acting as understudy to our leading lady? Now there's a chance you'd be very foolish to refuse.'

Clover shook her head. Her mind was made up. 'Thank you, Mr Roxburgh. You have been very kind. I appreciate it, believe me. But I must reach out for other things.'

He nearly blurted out that he wasn't being kind. The thought of the gap this girl would leave in his production had nothing to do with kindness.

He shrugged and turned away. 'Well, if you've made up your mind, I suppose that's it. And I wish you every luck with Harry Holt. He's rude, unpredictable and impossible to get along with, but he's also a damn good producer. As long as you remember that he eats little girls like you for breakfast.'

Miss Boyce didn't allow the dismay she felt when Clover told her of her new plans to show. Or her alarm that her promise to Bert about keeping a watchful eye on his daughter would now be broken. Like Bobby

Roxburgh she gazed into those implacable blue eyes and knew nothing she could say would make the slightest difference. She almost felt she no longer knew this girl who faced her so defiantly.

Clover guessed the thoughts that ran through the little woman's mind. She hugged her tightly, her voice reassuring. 'Don't worry, Boycie. I'll be fine. You can come over in the charabanc and see me in the show. I'll send you some tickets.' She laughed. 'Bring Mr Grantham with you,' mentioning an elderly man whom she'd caught winking at Miss Boyce across the lounge.

Miss Boyce sniffed. 'That's not funny, Clover.'

'Anyway, I promise I won't talk to strangers or behave in any way you and Mum would find unbecoming in a lady.'

'They will *all* be strangers. You won't know any of them.'

'I'll know Mr Holt. He's a bit of a dragon and I'm sure he's very strict with his employees.' It was a good description, she thought; there had been moments during their brief meetings when she could easily have visualised him breathing fire. She grinned at the image it conjured up.

But Miss Boyce didn't know the half of it. Didn't know about the terrible, degrading conditions they had endured on their last stay in Moorfield, before Bert was taken ill, before Adam came into her life, working so earnestly to contact her aunts, to put a roof over her head . . .

She experienced a sudden pang of guilt, thinking of Adam. He wrote such affectionate letters, the last of which lay unanswered on the dressing table. Each one insisting she leave the life she was leading and seriously consider joining him in Moorfield. Irritated, she had tucked it back into its envelope. She should, she knew, acquaint him of this latest move. Deliberately she'd kept back the information that Bert had left, knowing that if it was at all possible he'd be over in a flash, worrying just as Miss Boyce was worrying now, making plans for her.

Chapter Twenty-five

The chorus girls at the Apollo eyed her with suspicion. Harry Holt introduced her and then, beckoning to a pretty but tired-looking girl with blonde hair, he said to Clover, 'This is Rosie Thomas. She'll show you around, where the dressing rooms are, the cheapest place to buy supper, and so on. I hope you won't mind, but I took the liberty of renting a room for you in the boarding house where Rosie and most of the girls stay. It's clean and moderately priced. I think you'll find it comfortable.'

Clover blinked. Talk about organising her life! But there had not been time to find anywhere to stay and so this really was a break. And she'd be with the girls she worked with. She smiled at Rosie, not realising that the answering smile hid a seething mass of resentment. Rosie didn't like newcomers. Especially not newcomers in whom Mr Holt took such an interest. Finding her a room, indeed! she thought. Bothering his head about whether she would find it comfortable or not! Who did she think she was, anyway? The bloody Empress of China!

Harry looked from one to the other, eyebrows raised. 'All right, then? Any questions, Miss Blossom?'

'No questions.'

Aware of the gossip prevalent in all such companies and not wanting to display too much interest in her, Harry ignored her for the next few days. Rosie showed her the steps of a dance to go with her music, surprised that Clover picked it up so quickly.

'I've been singing and dancing since I was a little girl,' Clover explained with a smile. 'You only have to play a song a couple of times and I know it off by heart.'

Rosie gave an unladylike snort, anger at the cool confidence of this girl boiling up inside her. When Clover sang as she always had, hands still, head up, facing the audience, Rosie tut-tutted peevishly and said, 'No, not like that! That isn't what Mr Holt wants at all. Put some life in it. Haven't you heard of his motto: Gals, Guys, Glamour and Giggles! Put a bit of *that* into it. Here, let me show you.' Hands on hips, scarlet mouth pouting, eyes narrowed to what she imagined was a sexy squint, Rosie strutted across the stage, her whole demeanour conveying meanings to the words of the simple song Clover was quite sure were not there.

Oh, well, thought Clover and did as she was told. The following day, practising to an empty theatre, Harry came upon her and Rosie. Unobserved, he stood for long moments, watching from the wings. Halfway though Clover's song, he strode onto the stage, frowning, looking fierce. 'No! *No!* If I'd wanted that sort of thing I wouldn't have hired *you*. Don't tell me somebody actually *taught* you to sing like that?'

Clover didn't answer, aware of Rosie's twitching ears.

'I need something quite different,' he went on. 'A complete contrast to the act that comes before. Try it again, only this time keep it simple and sweet, the way the songwriter intended it to be. You *can* do that, can't you?'

Clover nodded and the pianist started up again. It was easy to revert to the style of her childhood, the way she and Adele had sung together.

'That's better,' said Harry, privately delighted. 'Now

try and keep to that and don't get carried away by trying out other arrangements, okay?' Instinct told him that Clover's demure appearance and manner would evoke nostalgia for the Golden Age of Music Hall which audiences adored. She had both wit and style uncluttered by the false coyness of other artistes.

He nodded and said again, 'Yes, that's better.' And walked away.

Clover stared after him, and Rosie said in a complacent tone, 'Don't take too much notice of Harry. He's up one minute and down the next. I 'spect that wife of his is playing him up again.'

'I didn't know Mr Holt was married!'

'He keeps it quiet. But it somehow leaked out. Not much you can keep secret in our job.'

'But why?'

Rosie shrugged. 'Doesn't want people to know, does he!'

'What people? And if that's the case, how come you know?'

Rosie shrugged again, a favourite gesture with her, it seemed. 'All us girls know.'

Intrigued, Clover's fancies flew every which way, imagining all sorts of things: a dizzy flapper with bare knees, flashy and liking a good time; someone Harry had married when they were very young and was now ashamed of; a girl from the country who hated the bright lights and so stayed at home with the children . . . And where did he keep her? In a nunnery or something? Where was she when he was out waiting at stage doors for girls?

Harry Holt went down a peg or two in her estimation.

Clad in a floating dress of palest grey chiffon that danced with every step she took, Clover gazed at herself in the long mirror in the dressing room. The dress just skimmed her knees, revealing a length of pale, shiny silken beige hose. It was like being dressed in moonlight, she thought. She left her hair the way she preferred it, long and flowing, its newly washed softness spilling down her back. A long chiffon scarf of the same filmy material held it back from her face.

They had prepared a twenty-minute act of singing, followed by a short dance before going into the final chorus. But an enthusiastic audience refused to let her go. After a signal from Harry, standing in the wings, she improvised for a further ten minutes, urging the crowded rows of upturned faces to join her in a selection of the old sentimental numbers her parents had sung. She possessed, thought Harry, the kind of nostalgia that could make the trite little songs worthy of tears. He watched, unable to take his eyes off her.

At last, bowing to an unmistakable success, she left the stage, to be greeted by delighted members of the cast flocking all about her, their words of congratulations ringing in her ears. All but Rosie, who stood on the outskirts of the group, the expression on her face unreadable.

The auditorium was abuzz with people commenting on and discussing the show. The buzz had an excited approval about it that was music to Harry's ears. The girl had clearly gone down well. It was time to celebrate.

'Very sexy, in a pure, sweet kind of way,' he overheard one young man say to his partner. 'I'd pay well over the top to see and hear her any old day.'

The observation surprised Harry. Annoyed him, too, in an odd sort of way. Funny, he'd never thought of the Blossom girl as sexy.

He paid a visit to the bar and then made his way to

the large dressing room shared by the chorus. 'Very good, girls, very good,' he said, pushing open the door to the sound of laughter and many voices. He carried two bottles of champagne. The girls squealed with excitement as a popped cork bounced off the ceiling. The second one flew towards Clover, narrowly missing her. Another member of the cast came in a moment later, carrying a trayful of glasses and for the first time in her life Clover tasted champagne.

She decided she liked it. There was an elegance about it that appealed to her, exactly matching the way she felt right at this moment.

Harry appeared at her side, pouring more of the golden liquid into her glass, topping it up every time she took a drink. 'You did all right tonight, Clover, but then I knew you would.' She smiled, the drink already making her feel tipsy. She lifted her glass and took too great a gulp, making her splutter.

'Careful!' She heard the laughter in his voice and felt her face redden with embarrassment. 'That's good champagne. You're supposed to sip it.' And then he was gone, moving down the row of dressing tables, congratulating each girl in turn.

Clover cleansed her face of the stage make-up then changed out of her costume into her street clothes. After a moment's hesitation, she added a little lipstick, touching her lips lightly with a pale pink.

'You meetin' your fella?' asked the girl next to her, busy doing the same.

Clover smiled. 'My "fella" doesn't live here. I don't see him all that often.'

The girl laughed. 'Don't worry, ducks, we can soon alter that. I guarantee a string of 'em lining up at the stage door eager to take you out.'

Again Clover shook her head. 'I don't think so.'

The girl gave her a look of disbelief, catching her eye

in the mirror. 'Where you bin hiding yourself all these years? That's the way it always goes.'

'I know that. If that's what you're looking for, that's fine. It's just that I'm not interested in anyone else.'

'Who is he? Someone connected with the theatre? Is he famous?' The girl looked ready to settle into a spicy bit of gossiping.

'No, not in the theatre. Far removed from it, in fact.' She thought of Adam Foley and again the pang of guilt struck her, reminding her that she still hadn't written to tell him the news. Miss Boyce had promised she would redirect any letters that came for her, as well as keeping in constant touch herself.

A week went by and still she hadn't written. Each time she entered Harry's office she contemplated the telephone on its upright stand, pleased that she had got over her initial fears and used one at last when she phoned Harry to tell him when she would be joining him.

Overcoming her nervousness had been a kind of watershed, not nearly as frightening as she first thought. Watching her one morning, Harry said, 'Is there someone you want to phone, Clover? You keep looking at that thing as if it was the Holy Grail.' He leaned back in his chair. She noticed he hadn't put his jacket on or tightened his undone tie. A soft felt hat was perched on the back of his head.

Here was her chance, she thought. Without bothering to write, she could let Adam know of the new job and hear his reaction in his voice.

'Well, yes,' she admitted. 'There is someone who was kind to me when my father fell ill. When we were living that winter at Moorfield. I haven't written to tell him about my change of job. Or about Daddy going down south.'

A wave of the hand indicated the telephone. 'Be my

guest. Go ahead, I won't charge you. Do you know the number?'

She didn't, of course. How stupid of her! You had to know the telephone number to get anywhere on this modern invention.

'All right,' he said and leaned forward to pick up the receiver. 'Tell me who it is and where he lives and I'll get it for you.'

'Dr Adam Foley.' She gave the address of the surgery and watched him dial the operator. Moments later he handed the instrument to her, once more sitting back, obviously intending to remain in the room.

Adam was surprised to hear her voice. The first thing he said was: 'Are you all right? What's happened?'

Quickly, Clover quelled his fears. There was a long silence when she broke the news about Bert and then told him of her new job in the Apollo Theatre.

'A new job?' he said. 'Didn't you get my letter?'

'Yes, I got it.' And all it did was make me cross.

'Then you read what I wrote?' His voice had sharpened to a tone she'd never heard him use before.

'Adam, please try and understand. I like my work. It's all I know. Settling down in one place is a lovely idea, but not yet. Not for a long time yet.'

'Does that mean you will – someday? I'd be perfectly content if you told me that now.' There was an undercurrent of anger in his voice.

She thought of his kindness, his generosity in helping her father, of seeing her safely to her aunts' house. 'Oh, Adam, don't let's quarrel. Wish me luck and say you'll be back to see me soon. You'll like the show, I promise. I'll get you some tickets and you can judge for yourself.'

His answer was a grudging, 'We'll have to see about that. We're very busy just now, I'm thankful to say. I don't know when I can make it but I'll try for a couple of days soon. And, Clover . . .' His voice softened, as though making amends. She waited, feeling Harry's gaze resting on her face. 'Of course I wish you luck. You've always had that, as well as all my love.'

As she hung up, Harry said cryptically, 'He's your lover, eh?'

His eyes surveyed her thoughtfully and there was something in their depths that made her flush, made her heart begin a swift pitter-patter. Taking a deep breath, trying to sound nonchalant, she said, 'Not at all.' And some little devil inside her made her add, watching him, 'Not yet, anyway.'

The intense look in his eyes deepened. 'You're much too young to become involved in anything like that,' he said, all expression gone from his face. 'Anyway, you'll barely have time for love affairs, innocent or otherwise. There'll be too much to do.'

'I've been in this game a long time, remember. I know how things are done.'

He rose and came round the desk towards her. 'Just be sure you keep your mind on your work and don't let anything interfere with it, okay?'

She met his eyes squarely and nodded. 'Thanks for letting me use the phone,' she said and escaped quickly through the open door.

Miss Boyce wrote to ask if it was all right to come over and see her, adding that she had a letter from Bert and might as well bring it herself instead of readdressing it. Besides, she said, she wanted to see how Clover was getting on.

Bert wrote that he was happy in his new life, had got the position he wanted in the new revue and that his digs were comfortable, although he still missed his little girl's agreeable presence.

Clover folded the letter and tucked it back into its

envelope. She had insisted on treating Miss Boyce to tea, taking her to the café where she had been with Adam on that weekend. 'They do a nice cream tea,' she explained. 'I know how much you appreciate home baking and the cakes and scones they serve are the best in Blackpool.'

Miss Boyce was pale, and seemed rather quiet, not her usual chirpy self. When Clover asked her if she was unwell, she insisted she was all right. In fact, she'd been feeling very tired lately, though she couldn't think why she should.

She took a sip of the reviving tea and gazed out at the busy promenade where holidaymakers enjoyed their freedom, children running, making a bee-line for the ice cream cart that parked at the far end. The sun was shining, the water sparkling. She thought back to her childhood, to the words of a prayer her mother had often quoted, 'God's in His heaven and all's right with the world.' She drew a deep breath and turned to smile at the concerned face across the table from her. 'Dear Clover,' she said brightly, 'you mustn't worry about me. I'm feeling my age a bit, that's all. I've so looked forward to seeing you again, to seeing the show.' She had decided that she would go to the first house performance. That way she wouldn't be too late getting home, for she still had to face the long drive in the coach afterwards. She didn't care to be out alone in the dark. 'Your father must be very proud of you,' she went on. 'And your dear mother, if she only knew. But I'm sure she must know, for deep in my heart I have no doubt she keeps an eye on you.'

'And on Eddie,' said Clover, suddenly wistful. 'I wish I knew how he was.' She looked at Miss Boyce. 'You do think Ma Ruggles is forwarding the letters on to you?'

'I'm sure she would, dear. She was always very fond

of you and your brother – ' When Clover had left her aunts, she'd written to Ma Ruggles and asked if she would mind forwarding any letters that should arrive to Miss Boyce '– So you can be sure you will get them,' said Miss Boyce.

Chapter Twenty-six

The reporters, gathered outside the Los Angeles theatre, watched the parade of celebrities in evening dress alight from their limousines and enter the ornate doors on their way to the preview of Amorita Kessel's new picture.

Cameras flashed and reporters called out, 'Miss Kessel, would you look this way, please?' and 'Over here, Miss Kessel. Can we have one more picture? A big smile, now.'

There were movie stars and their partners of the moment, producers and directors, all there to celebrate Amorita Kessel's latest venture. And to judge the new man in her life. The crowds were held back by a roped-off area where the long, sleek cars slid to a stop. The occupants stepped out to a barrage of flash bulbs and cameras clicked frantically. Overhead, bright beams of searchlights slid across the night sky, creating a dream world of motion and light.

The crowd 'ohhhed' and 'ahhed' and craned their heads to watch. Then turned their attention back to the scene unfolding before them. Most of the female stars were draped from head to toe in fur, chinchilla, sable, mink, their faces heavily made-up, eyes dark with mascara, lips impossibly red.

In contrast, Amorita had on a gown that could have been spun from a spider's web. Fragile black lace clung to the slim, svelte figure. Her arms and shoulders were bare, startlingly white against the raven black of the gown. She was a knock-out and she knew it. At her side, Eddie Blossom knew it, too. Although he wasn't Eddie Blossom any more. Not right for the American taste, they had told him. It was Eddy Hart now.

The aura of excitement that constantly surrounded her had become second nature to Eddie. Used to audience reaction since he was a little boy, this adulation that greeted Amorita wherever she went was different. These crowds were so extravagant in their emotions, so excessive. Amorita lapped it up like a cat lapping cream. Eddie wondered what she would do if it ever stopped.

Being new to the world of the silver screen, fame had still to find him. Hardly anybody recognised him, for the lurid posters outside the theatre were mainly of Amorita, with just the hazy figure of a man in the background.

The making of the film had been hard work but Eddie had enjoyed it. He rented a house on a quiet, dusty road, bought a small car and drove to the studio each day. Behind the house, near enough to smell the blossom in summer time, a lone orange grove was a sad reminder of times not so long ago, when the land hereabouts had been covered in citrus groves.

A woman had been engaged to look after Jamie and Eddie had amused Amorita by insisting on interviewing the applicants himself.

'Jamie is the most precious thing in my life,' he told her stubbornly. 'I have to be very sure of the kind of person I have taking care of him. These are his most formative years. I couldn't leave him with just anyone.'

Amorita had clicked her tongue and pressed a scarlet mouth against his cheek. 'The oh so good dadee! Jamie is a lucky little boy. And you, my darlink, are lucky to have such a fine son.'

Thinking of it now, as Amorita posed for the attention of the cameras, Eddie remembered the first women interviewed. Dragons, every one of them, so formidable he wondered how they could ever have got work looking after children. Maybe some people wanted that for their children. Not him. Then a young woman came forward who looked so fresh and – gentle, there was no other word for it – that he knew straight away she was the one. She introduced herself as Miss Kate Barrie. Dressed in a simple white frock, not too short, with a Peter Pan collar and neat cuban-heeled strap shoes, she looked perfect. Her hair was the palest shade of blonde, arranged in a neat chignon at the back of her neck. Soft curls clustered over her forehead. Her smile was luminous, making him think of spring sunshine.

He waited while deep blue eyes examined him politely, as though it was she who was conducting the interviewing and not he. She had, she told him, held various nannying positions which had all ended when the families moved back to New York.

'Why didn't you go with them?' he asked.

'My mother is a widow. I would prefer to be near her.'

'What would you say to going to live in England?'

She didn't even blink. 'Yes, I noticed the accent. I'll be honest. I couldn't do that, so maybe I'd better leave and let you interview someone who will be more suited to your needs.'

He held up a restraining hand. 'Don't go.' He smiled into those friendly blue eyes. 'I don't plan on going home yet awhile. So if you think you would like to work for me, I'd be delighted to have you.'

'Eddieee!' Amorita Kessel's faintly petulant voice made him suddenly aware of the occasion and how his mind had been wandering. It seemed the cameras were finally finished with her, focusing on the next glamorous star to step into the limelight.

He turned, smiling, and took Amorita's arm to lead her through the crowd into the auditorium and their seats. The lights were dimmed and a hush fell over the audience. Amorita sat up, ever eager to admire herself on the silver screen. Eddie, however, felt like sinking so low into his seat that nobody present would know it was him up there making such a fool of himself.

The titles flashed black against a white screen: *The Lone Prairie*. He'd managed to learn how to ride a horse without much difficulty; after the first few mishaps it had come naturally to him. As the story advanced, he sat up straighter, relaxing as he heard the murmurs of appreciation echo about the theatre, felt Amorita's fingers pressing into his forearm through his dark evening jacket, heard her low, throaty whisper, 'They like you, *mon ami*.'

There was a stage-coach chase; a waggon train attack by hundreds of Indians, a cavalry charge. No movie had been so impressive. Eddie recalled the real-life scout and buffalo hunter who had acted as adviser on the film and who had insisted he appear in some of the scenes.

As the film ended and the lights went on, people turned in their seats, grinning at each other. Eddie was thumped on the shoulder as he escorted Amorita to the crowded lobby and her waiting car.

'Great, kid. You were great.' From somewhere Nick Farrel appeared, grinning from ear to ear. 'Didn't I tell you?' he enthused as he caught up with them. 'Didn't I tell you? Excellent, me boy. Excellent.' Even though Eddie's part had been small, it was clearly evident he had a natural talent.

More used to compliments being showered on her, Amorita waited, foot in its narrow pointed black shoe tapping impatiently, scarlet lips pouting. It was a look portrayed in hundreds of publicity pictures, sold in movie magazines all over the country. Tonight it didn't seem to be having the effect on Nick Farrel that it usually did; he kept on talking to Eddie, almost as if he was ignoring her.

To everyone's surprise, she declined the invitation to the party celebrating the premiere. Eddie, too, declined, saying he would see her home. On the drive back to her mansion in the Beverly foothills of Hollywood, she was quiet. Unusually quiet for Amorita. When he kissed her lightly on the lips at her front door, her uniformed chauffeur waiting discreetly in the car to drive Eddie home, she smiled invitingly through her thick lashes.

'Aren't you coming in?'

He hadn't intended to, though he knew there was no reason for him to hurry back to the white Spanish-style house on the outskirts of the small town. Jamie would be sound asleep by now and Kate would be there.

That gave him a feeling of great satisfaction. Kate Barrie had proved invaluable, taking charge of Jamie like a seasoned veteran, quietly spoken and genteel. Jamie had taken to her at once, all big, solemn eyes as he listened to her read aloud from his favourite book of nursery rhymes.

To Amorita's question, Eddie replied, 'You must be tired, sweetheart. Far better to get some beauty sleep than to think of entertaining me at this late hour.' He smiled down at her in the warm darkness. 'We can congratulate ourselves on the film tomorrow.'

She gave another of those famous pouts, making him think of a spoiled child. But a very lovely spoiled child. 'I wasn't thinking of talking, *chéri*! Do you English think of nothing but that?' She lifted one hand and trailed a long finger across his lips. 'So dull! So dreary! I'm sure if I asked nicely you would change your mind, no?'

'I thought you and Nick . . .' he began, intrigued

by her proposal. She gave a low, tinkling laugh at his
naivety. 'Nick's just a friend. A very *good* friend, I'll
admit. While you, dear, darlink Eddieee, could be so
much more.'

And Eddie was tempted, feeling the white-scented
arms steal up about his neck, pulling his head down to
hers. For a brief heartrending moment there was the
echo of the tinny jangle of a merry-go-round, the hot
smell of oil lamps mingling with candyfloss. And a girl
with midnight dark eyes who had betrayed him . . .

Life, he decided, was too fleeting to grieve over
the past. With a sigh he lowered his mouth to cover
hers, feeling her move closer in her spider-web gown
of black lace.

The studios encouraged it, this new romance between
their brightest star and their new discovery. They were
seen together at all the right parties, a white hand
clutched possessively on his sleeve, those inscrutable
eyes gazing loftily into the cameras. They were frequent visitors to Playfair, that lovely house built by
Mary Pickford and her husband, Douglas Fairbanks.
Rudolph Valentino danced his famous version of the
tango with Amorita and was showered in red roses by
admiring onlookers.

Two movies in quick succession followed *The Lone
Prairie*. Both Westerns, both with Amorita Kessel. In
both Eddie was given a larger part. He had the rigid
discipline of Maxi Fields to thank for his fine, strong
physique and the muscles that enabled him to lift a
girl from the ground onto a horse in one breathtaking,
swooping movement as effortlessly as if he was flicking
a lace cuff. His acting held an ironic enjoyment that
never failed to communicate itself to the audience. They
found his sense of fun delightful. It was as though
he knew he was irresistible and wickedly gloried in

it, relishing every turn of the fast-moving, farfetched stories.

Eddie drove each morning to the studio, a rather grandiose title for the corrugated iron structure that was more like a large warehouse than anything else. Parking his car, calling greetings to everyone who passed, for he was a great favourite with the people who worked there, he strode through the large, echoing lots. On one they would be shooting a comedy, full of slapstick and custard pies. Stopping briefly to watch, he'd laugh at the antics of the small, brilliant man who played the tramp, all long shoes and little black moustache.

Cheek by jowl, a tear-jerking melodrama of tribulation and eventual triumph would be acted out by the Gish sisters. Eddie preferred the gangster movies, with shiny, rain-washed pavements and tommy-guns shattering the night. Here he would linger, until a boy sent by the director of his own movie found him and reminded him they were waiting.

He loved the work but he wasn't really taking it seriously. It was all still a game to Eddie: the near-hysterics of the Hungarian director who sat in a canvas chair on the set and screamed abuse at everyone, the nervous twittering of the bevy of girls who hung onto his every word. Eddie refused to be intimidated by him or anyone else in the studio and did what was required of him with unaffected ingenuousness.

Only for the most dangerous shots would Eddie allow a stunt man to take over from him. The films were instant box office successes, encouraging the producers to seek out more and more scripts. In Eddie they had found a new, wholly convincing Western actor, virile, natural and likeable.

When Amorita complained of the dust and the constant smell of horse flesh, Eddie was the one sent to chivvy her out of it.

But for all his enjoyment in his sudden fame, his constant worry was that he might be neglecting Jamie. The boy had just turned two, into everything, running everywhere, mischief his second name. Eddie fully realised that Kate had her work cut out just to keep up with the lively child. However, she never complained, seeming to take it all in her stride. Her love for the little boy was indisputable, his affection for her plain for everyone to see.

On the rare days when Eddie got home and it was still daylight, the afternoon still warm and sunny, he would find her sitting on the shady white verandah, reading a novel, or a piece of delicate sewing in her lap, keeping an eye on Jamie as he played on the square of lawn at the front.

Eddie thought the verandah, with its gracefully rounded arches built in the Spanish style, a blaze of fiery bougainvillea twined through the white trellis work, a perfect place for her cool prettiness. Once he'd asked her why no one had yet snapped her up for the movies and she'd laughed and shaken her head. All he knew of her was that her father had died a few years ago and lately her mother had moved in with her married brother and his wife. He knew Kate visited them whenever she could, lately asking permission to take Jamie with her. 'They have a young family,' she explained. 'I'm sure Jamie would love it.'

Everything was going so well. Too well. He should have known that fate kept a blow up its sleeve for when you were least expecting it.

He received a telephone call at the studio from Kate one day. She said that someone had come to the house demanding to see him. 'Normally I would never bother you at the studio,' she said, 'you know that, but she – this woman – is so insistent it's made me nervous. She picked Jamie up and cuddled him and the poor little fellow didn't like that at all. As I said, she's made me very nervous . . .'

Warning bells rang in Eddie's brain. 'Where is Jamie now?' he barked. 'You haven't left him alone with her, have you?'

'No, Mr Blossom, he's all right. He's with me.' She hesitated. 'She – the woman – said she was Jamie's mother . . .'

'Stay there,' he shouted into the phone before banging it down and racing out to his car.

Making herself completely at home, Imelda sat back in the big chair in the lounge and looked about her. Hmmm, nice! Very nice! By the look of this place, Eddie was certainly doing all right for himself. Certainly better than she had done. Perhaps if she hadn't been so hasty . . .

Fat use telling herself that now. At the time of her break-up with Eddie, she hadn't been able to see further than the end of her nose, hadn't been able to think of anything but the handsome features of Johnny Amadeo, hear his voice murmuring sweet nothings in her ear. He was the most exciting man she had ever met. That day when Eddie had found them hadn't been the first time, either. With each day that passed she grew more impatient for his caresses.

Eddie hitting her had been the last straw. Why should she hang around and take such treatment? Not just from Eddie but from any man? With Johnny she could start a new life. Johnny was a soft touch. She'd have no problems handling him.

So had gone her thoughts on that last day in New York. After Eddie had left the apartment, she had packed her belongings and slipped away, keeping a wary eye out for Mrs Scholtz.

The bright picture of her life with Johnny had turned out to be another fiasco. A small-time hood, belonging to a gang in Chicago, Johnny's job was to collect the takings from the various establishments the gang ran and deliver them to the boss. Pronto. Only Johnny didn't quite see it that way and once before had tried to hold on to some of the cash for his own benefit. Hence his hasty departure to the safety of his sisters in New York. Now, back in Chicago, he offered his services to a rival gang. Things had gone all right for a time. Then, old habits being hard to break, Johnny once more found himself in hot water with his bosses.

It had meant another move. And then another. And so it had gone on for the next eighteen months. While Eddie had been sitting pretty, making enough money to buy this beautiful house and employ a woman to look after their kid!

When Eddie entered the room, she smiled at him, the smile that had always sent his senses reeling.

Eddie felt his stomach muscles tightening, the palms of his hands breaking out in a cold sweat. One look at his face as he'd climbed from the car had sent Kate into the garden, taking Jamie with her. He could hear them now, Jamie's laughter shrill and joyful as Kate pushed him on the swing. Eddie had fixed it himself to the branches of an ancient orange tree where in spite of its age, creamy, sweet-smelling blossoms still burst forth in the spring.

'Hi!' Imelda's voice broke the silence, her tone soft, conciliatory. She looked tired, even though she'd tarted herself up with bright lipstick and rouge, lots of mascara on her eyes. Her dress was daringly short, completing the picture of licentiousness. But she was still lovely enough to capture any man's heart. He wondered what had happened to that Amadeo bastard and if she was still with him.

'Why the hell are you here, Imelda?' The air around

them seemed to seethe with the contained violence of his demand.

Her eyes hardened. Meekness was not in her nature and she wasn't about to show any of it to him now. 'You know why I came. To see Jamie.'

'You have no right to be here,' he told her brutally. 'You gave that right up when you walked out on us.'

'That doesn't stop him being my baby.'

'Jamie is *my* son.' There was no mistaking the emphasis of possession. 'You didn't want him. You didn't even want to know how he was getting on or if he was happy. You just didn't care.'

Imelda stiffened at his deliberately cruel reminder. 'Why do you think I went to all the trouble to find you both if I didn't care?' she retaliated. 'I couldn't stand being apart from him. I tried to forget. I tried to tell myself he was better off without me. But I couldn't. I wanted my baby.'

'Do you really expect me to believe that?' Eddie jeered. 'You never displayed the slightest curiosity before. How can you expect me to believe you now?'

'How do you know?' she flared. She was losing her temper, not even trying to control it, just letting go of all the emotions that boiled up inside her. She felt a childish urge to assault him physically. She rose from her chair and took a few short steps towards him, fists curling at her sides. 'You don't know anything of what I've been thinking or feeling these past two years – wondering if my baby is happy and healthy.'

'Well, you can stop wondering,' Eddie interjected in a harsh voice. 'Jamie's fine, as if you really cared.'

'I do care, I do.' She thrust her face forward, eyes snapping. 'I love my baby. That's a stinking thing to say, Eddie Blossom. You know it isn't true.'

'I'm not particularly interested in what you think, Imelda. I haven't been for a long time.'

Nothing she said seemed to move him and she wondered at the change in the vulnerable youth who had loved her so ardently to this hard-faced man whose unyielding, masculine features displayed nothing to indicate if her anguished pleas would ever touch him.

'All I know is that you relinquished all claim to our son when I came home and found you with that man.'

'I know. I know I'm a rotten mother. But I'm still that, his mother.'

'You *were* his mother.' He stressed the past tense. 'Not any more.'

'But I am! Whatever you say is never going to change that. Any more than saying you are not his father.'

'I'm glad you recognise that I am his father,' he said grimly. 'At least you admit that.'

Imelda felt like screaming. This wasn't going the way she'd planned. 'Oh, Eddie,' she cried. 'Why are we quarrelling? You used to love me, used to say you'd do anything for me.'

'I'd have torn the moon out of the sky and given it to you on a plate if you'd asked me. But that was then. Now I can't stand to be anywhere near you. Do you honestly believe I'd allow you to have him, after all you did?'

'You've had him all to yourself for the past two years, watched him start to walk, heard him say his first words. Surely it isn't too much to ask you to let me share him with you again.'

His hands reached out and clasped her shoulders, pulling her forward, bringing her face to face with him. Looking down into her eyes, his grip tightened, biting into the flesh, making her whimper. Then he pushed her away as though he was revolted by the merest physical contact with her. 'No!' he said, his voice harsh.

He turned and began to make for the door. Imelda ran after him, catching at his arm. Abruptly he shook her off. She pushed in front of him to block his way, pressing her back against the door. 'Why won't you listen to me?' she shouted, almost hysterical. 'Why are you treating me like this?'

'I listened to you long enough,' he returned evenly. 'You should have thought about that when you left Jamie alone that time, not knowing or caring how long it might be before I returned. Before you took another man to your bed, with Jamie looking on. Now you want him back. I suppose you expect me to feel sorry for you. Well, I don't.'

'And what about Jamie? Don't you think he needs a mother's love?'

'He has my love and protection, plus the love of a woman who cares for him more than you ever did. As far as I'm concerned, our life is perfect just now and I have no desire for it to be any different.'

'I—'

'Can you imagine what it was like after you'd gone?' Eddie cut in. 'Can you? How confused he was? How confused *I* was?' He shook his head. 'No, Imelda, I never want to go through that again.' He turned to the desk set before the wide window affording a view of the garden. 'I'll give you a cheque. At least I can do that much.' Sitting writing at the desk, he could hear the sound of Jamie's shrill laughter through the open window.

He looked over to where Imelda waited, eyes fixed greedily on the chequebook spread out on the desk top. He tore the slip out and handed it to her. 'You live your life and I'll live mine – but with Jamie. Don't try to see him again.'

There was a warning in his voice that made her shudder. His complete lack of feeling towards her was a shattering discovery. She had always been so sure of her hold on him, on any man she set her sights on. Tight-lipped she went to the window and stood staring out. When she turned, her face was set in a defiant sneer. 'Don't think just because you've given me money that this is the end of it, because it isn't. I'll go to court if I have to. I'll—'

He laughed, cutting her off. 'You wouldn't stand a snowball in hell's chance.'

'Wouldn't I?' Her eyes narrowed with hatred. 'Do you think that once I've described the set-up here, that woman you've got living with you, that Kessel bitch you spend so many nights with – oh, yes, don't look surprised, your tender love affair is well documented in the popular movie magazines – do you really think a court would give you custody of Jamie? *Do* you?' she insisted when he didn't answer.

'And you're living such a blameless life, I suppose, that they'd hand him over to you like that?' He turned to her, trembling with cold fury. 'Where *are* you living, anyway? What gullible fool has been taken in by your pitiful stories this time and is giving you bed and board?' He didn't believe for one moment any of the pleas about missing her baby she had trotted out. He imagined those kind of emotions were completely foreign to her. 'How did you find me, anyway?' he asked.

'It wasn't hard. You're a big name now, Eddie. Pity I wasn't able to gaze into the future, like my old grandma. Seeing all this,' with a gesture of her hand about the luxurious room, 'I might not have left you.'

His jaw tightened. 'You've got your money. Now go. I don't want to set eyes on you again, understand?'

'Well, that's something you'll have to wonder about, isn't it? You'll never know where I am or when I'll turn up to haunt you. Whether the court gives Jamie to me or not, I'll still have him.' She smiled, so cold it made his flesh creep. 'With you away all day and half the night, who's going to stop me? Certainly not that silly milksop of a girl you've got looking after him.'

'I told you to go,' he said, his words coming out tight and angry.

At the door she paused, looking back at him. 'You never did get me that yellow car you promised, did you?'

Memories came rushing back, making his heart turn over. 'Oh, Imelda!'

And in spite of everything, she could see the hurt beneath the tough exterior, betrayed by the misery in his eyes and the bitter twist of his mouth.

Waving the cheque in her hand, she said airily, 'Oh well, maybe a few more of these and I'll be able to treat myself to one.'

Passing through the garden she waggled her fingers at Kate and her little son in a farewell gesture. The smile on Jamie's face faded, his excited words to Kate died on his lips and he sat quite still on the wooden seat of the swing, solemnly staring as she passed along the short driveway to the road. Johnny had parked their dilapidated car further along the road, on a dusty side turning. He much preferred to stay out of Imelda's little deals, though he was not averse to sharing whatever proceeds might result.

Closing the gate behind her, Imelda turned to look back one last time. She watched the blonde girl hurrying to Jamie's side, enfolding the boy in her arms in a protective gesture and she wondered at the sudden feeling of chill emptiness that enveloped her.

Chapter Twenty-seven

Clover received the surprise of her life one evening when Harry tapped on her dressing room door and poking his head in said, 'Hey, Clover, you've got a visitor.'

She turned on her stool before the dressing table mirror, already dressed for her part in the 'Beside the Seaside' number: long pantaloons, a long-sleeved bodice with a frill about the neck, a large gawdy bow perched on the back of her hair. She saw the face peering behind Harry's shoulder and her own face broke into a delighted grin. 'Daddy!' She rose from the stool, throwing her arms about him, hugging him tightly. 'Oh, Daddy, it's so good to see you. Why on earth didn't you write you were coming? I could have sent you some tickets.'

'It was a spur of the moment thing,' said Bert, his grin equalling hers in delight. He looked fit and relaxed, dressed neatly in a navy blue suit with a crisply starched white shirt. Someone was obviously looking after him well. He turned to beckon to the woman who hovered in the corridor outside.

'And guess who has come with me.'

Clover tried not to look surprised when she saw Madge.

'You'd never guess, would you,' Bert went on, 'but Madge lives in Brighton.'

Clover made an effort and smiled, holding out her hand to the woman. 'Is that so? Nice to see you again, Mrs Swanson.' Aware that Harry was dawdling

just inside the door, she said, 'Dad, I want you to
meet—'

'No, don't tell me. You're Harry Holt.'

Despite the aversion he felt, remembering Bert's past
behaviour, the way he'd treated his daughter, Harry
shook hands. 'I'm pleased to meet you. But how did
you know it was me?'

'Clover writes so much about you it couldn't be
anyone else.'

Clover blushed, saying quickly, 'Mr Holt has been
very good to me, Daddy. Encouraged me no end. I've
got a couple of spots singing and leading the chorus in
a dance number.'

A fact that hadn't gone down too well with various
members of the cast, Rosie Thomas for one. That and
getting her own dressing room.

'I'm not at all surprised,' said Bert complacently.
'I've said it before, only a blind man could miss that
talent. And,' to Harry, 'I don't think Mr Holt is a
blind man.'

A knock came on the door. 'Five minutes, Miss
Blossom.'

'I've got to go,' smiled Clover, turning for one last
glance in the mirror. 'I'll see you after the show. You
go on and take your seats. I hope you got good ones!'

'Yep, right near the front.'

'Well, then . . .' She reached out to plonk a kiss on
his cheek. 'Give us a kiss for luck.'

Both hands raised, Harry pushed her out of the dressing room. 'Off you go. We'll see you after the show.'

The stage curtains swished aside, revealing a setting of
sands and a curving bay with sailing boats; white sails
against blue water. The Union Jack fluttered on top of
a striped canvas tent. The chorus girls were dressed
in 1880s style bathing suits, all with bows of varying

colours in their hair. The male dancers wore similar costumes of red and white striped cotton, each with a straw boater hat. They strutted between the girls who twirled parasols over one shoulder, flirting outrageously. The tent flaps parted and Clover emerged and they joined together in a song, Clover twirling from one dancer to the next, smiling, her footwork neat and sprightly, moving to the music.

The snide looks that had been exchanged between the girls when Harry had given her her own number, the muttered asides – 'You can see who's bin giving him a bit of how's yer father, can't you?' – were completely lost on Clover. 'I don't think it was like that,' another of the girls remarked. 'Clover's a nice girl. I'm sure she wouldn't resort to getting what she wants in that way.'

Rosie Thomas's lips had curled. 'You reckon?'

Harry had stood in the wings and watched her perform for a whole week before he took the bull by the horns and decided to give her the lead in a couple of numbers. The 'Beside the Seaside' number with the boys and girls dressed in swimming costumes was an inspired choice. She threw herself into the part with a spirit that had the audience clamouring for more. Her performance in this was the direct opposite to her solo appearance singing the more leisurely sentimental songs, the one, blue spotlight highlighting her slim figure in its grey chiffon. She suited the title of the show perfectly: *Stardust*.

After the performance Bert and Madge came back to the dressing room and Harry suggested they all go out for a late supper. 'My treat,' he smiled, catching Clover's eye. 'I know a place that's not too noisy, where the music's soft and smoochy and the food excellent.'

'What more could a man ask for?' grinned Bert. 'I like your friend, Clover. He knows a good thing when he sees it.'

Harry's look was cool, quizzical. 'Meaning?'

'Meaning that my lass has made a wise choice in you.'

This time Clover blushed a fiery red and glared at her father so fiercely that Madge coughed and quickly took charge of the conversation. It was quite obvious that the two young people were attracted to each other and that Clover wasn't prepared to acknowledge it yet. Silly girl! thought Madge. The man was a knock-out. Had she been a few years younger she might have given Clover a run for her money. Although she suspected Clover didn't really approve of her, she was glad the girl had accepted her presence here with equanimity. As it was, she and Bert were doing very nicely, thank you. At her age she supposed she should be thankful for small mercies. She knew Bert had every intention of making an 'honest women' out of her – some day. But he still had to coax approval from young Clover. One of the reasons for their visit here.

Smiling at the girl, she said, 'You looked really captivating. Brought tears to my eyes with that second number of yours.'

'The ability to make people cry is an endearing quality,' said Harry. 'Clover has it down to a fine art.'

'Just like her dear mother,' said Bert. 'She could have a whole audience in floods of tears with one of her old songs.' He grinned at Clover. 'Do you remember – "To comfort and cheer you, just to be near you, to teach you the right from the wrong. She'd sigh for you, cry for you, yes, even die for you, that's what God made mothers for . . ." '

'Yes, very nice,' said Harry. 'The old sentimental numbers always were popular. Now, if we're going out we'll have to give Clover time to change. Come and have a drink with me, and Clover can join us in the bar when she's ready.'

At that time of night the restaurant to which he took them was fairly quiet, most people having eaten and gone on to other things. The small orchestra in its alcove of palms and potted ferns played discreetly, perking up when Harry rose and asked Madge if she'd care to dance.

Leaning back in his chair, Bert lazily watched them circle the floor then, in a reflective tone, said, 'He's the sort of man who will always be able to catch the barman's eye in a packed bar, obtain a table in a crowded restaurant and get a taxi in the rain.'

'Daddy!' Clover turned in her chair to look at him. He knew well that tone in her voice and gave a little laugh.

'Oh! Oh! What have I done wrong now?'

'I just don't want you to talk about me and Mr Holt like you did. He's my boss, nothing else. It's – it's embarrassing, Daddy. Besides, he's married.'

'I didn't know. I just thought I detected a certain inflection in your voice when you were introducing him.'

'Well, you thought wrong. I haven't got time for that sort of thing anyway. Neither has he. Did you know he's negotiating with a theatre in the West End of London for *Stardust*?' Her face lit up as she spoke. 'They've staged reviews there by people like C. B. Cochran, very up-market, Harry says. He thinks *Stardust* has a good chance of transferring well.'

Bert gazed at her thoughtfully. 'Whatever happened to that nice Dr Foley? I had hoped you and he . . .'

Again the bright colour flooded her cheeks. She picked up one of the heavy silver forks that lay on the table and began to make patterns with it, pressing it into the white damask tablecloth. That way she didn't have to meet Bert's eyes. 'I haven't got time for that now, Daddy. All sorts of things are happening, too quickly for me to really understand them.' She didn't explain that with Adam she would have to give them all up, become a housewife. Adam would insist upon it. 'He's been awfully busy in his new practice. He tells me it's doing well. He's been very lucky, his new partner seems a real asset.'

'I'm glad for his sake. Not many in my lifetime have been as kind or considerate as that young man. I don't know what we would have done without him. And the way he helped you!' He shook his head. 'With me in hospital, and you alone in that awful house. What would you have done, girl? It doesn't bear thinking about. Better not to think about it, I suppose.'

He reached for his glass, taking a long sip before going on to the thing that had been worrying him most. 'Do you remember me asking you once what you thought of Madge? And you replied there was nothing to *dis*like about her? Do you still feel that way?'

Clover's tablecloth drawing ceased. She put the fork down and lifted her head, meeting his eyes. 'You're going to marry her.' It came out flatly, without a trace of emotion.

'Would you mind very much if I did? She's a nice woman, Clover, and very good for me.'

'So you really came to ask me that? Not just to see my act or the show?'

'We came for a number of reasons, not the least of which was to see your show.' He reached across the table and took her hand. 'But would you mind all that much, lass? We *would* like your blessing.'

'She's not a patch on my mother. She's completely different, Dad. What do you *really* see in her?'

'I see pleasant company and friendship and someone to take care of in our later years. Isn't that what everyone wants, lass, when you get down to the nitty-gritty? What I wanted with your mother but was cruelly denied?'

Clover had to laugh. He could make the most simple statement sound so dramatic at times. And he'd always got his way, always. Gazing at the woman as Harry whirled her round to the music, her face upturned to his, excited, gay, Clover thought: I don't care! I'm blowed if I'm going to fall in with his wishes, just like that. Look at her, blatantly flirting with Harry. 'You would never have caught my mother carrying on like that. Funny that she lives in Brighton, isn't it? Was that the real reason you went down there?'

'And I couldn't have made a wiser move. Anyway,' Bert pressed her hand, 'we've got a few days to think about it. We're not going back till Monday.'

'Where are you staying?'

'We've booked into a little place behind the Tower. Not too far from the Apollo. We thought tomorrow we'd take a trip over to Newcombe, see if any of my old mates are still about.'

It really had nothing to do with her so why should she experience this sudden sinking of the heart at the picture conjured up by his words? She heard him say as the dancers returned to the table, 'Maybe look in on old Buster Bywater. I hear he's still with the Follies.' He looked up at Madge, flushed and smiling at something Harry had said. 'I'm sure Madge would enjoy meeting him.'

Noting the glowing cheeks, the coquettish looks she was directing at Harry, Clover said tartly, 'Oh, I'm sure she would love it.'

She wondered if she should conjure up some excuse when two days later Madge telephoned, using the theatre number, and asked Clover if she could meet her for lunch. Her voice coolly casual, Clover agreed. 'Is it about my father?'

'It's about both of us.'

Madge was late. Sitting at the table in the busy

restaurant, sipping from a glass of fortifying Tio Pepe, Clover went through all the things she wanted to say. When she finally arrived, Madge seemed as nervous as she was. They ordered a light lunch, then for a while they talked casually of the weather, what a fine summer it was promising to be. Madge spoke of her love of gardening and said she had a garden front and back of her house. Madge was on her best behaviour and Clover could see how a man might be won over by her charms. 'Yesterday, when we were in Newcombe,' she said, sipping her drink, 'Your father took me to see an old friend of your family. Miss Boyce.' She smiled. 'Doesn't anyone ever call her anything else? Very formal, surely!'

'That's exactly what she is, very formal. My mother gave her the nick-name Boycie and sometimes called her Joyce. But people usually refer to her as Miss Boyce. Or little Miss Boyce.'

'She's a nice old dear. Your father wanted her to come over to Blackpool and we could have made up a little dinner party before we go back, but she said she hadn't been well. I could see your dad was quite concerned.'

'He would be. Miss Boyce is part of our life. I'll really have to make an effort to get over and see her. The trouble is, these days I seem to have so little time to myself.' Clover sighed. 'And when on earth I'll find enough time to travel all the way down to Brighton to see my father, I don't know.'

'Well,' said Madge, complacently, 'we're counting on you to find time. We'd both like to see you.' She looked at Clover, a frown between her thinly arched brows. 'Did your dad tell you what our plans are?'

'You mean about getting married?'

Madge nodded. 'What are your views on the subject?'

Clover sighed. 'I had this speech all worked out, but

it's gone. The idea of my father marrying again isn't something I could take lightly. I don't know why I should feel so strongly about it, but . . .' She drew a deep breath, wondering if she would ever find the words to make sense of what she was feeling. 'No, that's silly. I *do* know why. I was jealous. It's been Dad and me for so long I think I'd be jealous no matter who it was. This doesn't make sense, I know, but I hoped that when – if – my father ever decided to marry again, she'd be just like my mother. I suppose I dreamed of having her around again. I'm sorry, Madge. This *doesn't* make sense . . .'

Madge leaned across the table, taking her hand. 'Of course it does. It makes perfect sense to me. I'm sorry I'm not like her but I can always try. And I'd take care of your father just as well as she would.'

Clover sighed. 'She's been gone for so long I suppose I've kept a pretty idealised picture of her in my mind. It's not fair to expect anybody to live up to that. I've been childish. I just hope we can be friends.'

'Oh, we can, lovey. We've got so much in common, after all.'

Clover looked up and Madge laughed, high, uninhibited laughter that had diners at nearby tables turning to gaze at them in amusement. 'We both love Bert.'

'Yes, that's true.' Clover felt suddenly as though a heavy load had been lifted from her shoulders.

'Look,' said Madge, 'I'll make a deal with you. I don't have to pretend to be anybody else and you don't have to call me Mum!'

And Clover couldn't help but join her laughter with Madge's.

She held out her hand.

'Deal.'

Harry insisted on going with her to see her father and Madge off at the station. Bert embraced her warmly while Madge stood in the carriage, leaning from the open window, looking on with a fond smile.

'Goodbye, my little love,' Bert said softly and Clover could have sworn there were tears in his eyes. 'Come down soon to see us, promise.'

'I will, Daddy. Just as soon as I can.'

'And, Clover . . .' Madge called from the carriage window, 'I wouldn't say no to you bringing that handsome specimen with you, either.'

'Oi! Oi!' laughed Bert. 'I'll have less of that kind of talk, if you don't mind! You're making Harry blush.'

As she bent from the carriage window to hug Clover, Madge whispered, 'Whoever it is you've got your eye on, dear, he must be some bloke. Your dad told me all about him. He sounds a real gentleman. Even so, you'd be a fool to let this one get away.'

Clover felt her cheeks flush, catching Harry's eye, wondering if he'd overheard. 'Oh, Adam is,' she said quietly. 'A very special bloke.'

Madge sighed gustily. 'And special blokes are hard to come by.' Her gazed lingered on Bert, shaking Harry firmly by the hand. 'I've found mine.'

Harry and Clover walked back from the station, silently introspective, busy with their own thoughts. Madge's words were still fresh in Clover's mind and suddenly her thoughts were filled with Harry's maleness and potency. She had been conscious of it on previous occasions, but nothing like as strongly as she was now. She had to agree with Madge that he was an attractive man. Very attractive. A shiver went through her. At once Harry was turning, looking at her enquiringly.

'Are you cold?'

'Just a goose walking over my grave, that's all.'

Although when they had emerged from the station it had seemed dark, she saw it was not really dark at all. The sky was bright with stars, the night blown through with the buffeting wind that smelt of the sea. Breaking the silence, Harry said, 'Do I take it there's soon to be wedding bells for your father and his delightful friend?'

Clover nodded. 'I think so. She's all right. Isn't she?'

She sounded so badly in need of reassurance that Harry grinned, gently taking her arm to lead her across the wide street fronting the promenade. When they reached the other side, he still held it, his fingers warm pressing against her forearm. 'You don't sound too sure. Don't you approve of the lady?'

'I suppose I should be happy my father's found someone who loves him. Although I wasn't at all sure at first. I thought she was a bit – flashy. But they seem genuinely fond of each other so I suppose it'll be all right.' Her lips twisted ruefully. 'My father really does need a woman to take care of him, you know. He's not much good on his own.'

For a moment Harry's fingers on her arm tightened. 'Well, you of all people should know.' She remembered the way he'd spoken about Bert on previous occasions and made to pull her arm away. Again his grip tightened, holding it securely as he went on smoothly, 'You really must stop worrying about him, you know. Madge will make sure he toes the line from now on if I'm any judge of character.'

Clover sighed. 'It will be nice for him to settle into a proper house instead of living in an assortment of boarding houses. Madge has her own house, she tells me, with a garden front and back.'

'Somehow, I can't see your father digging the garden at weekends, planting cabbages and potatoes, worrying over greenfly on his roses.' Harry sounded amused.

'I'd love it.'

'Worrying over greenfly or planting cabbages and potatoes?'

'Just being able to live in a house. All I've ever known is boarding houses and the backstage of theatres. Did you ever look out of a train window at night and see all those little towns? Cottages, gardens, lights in windows?'

Something in his voice changed as he said, 'Yes, all the time.'

'They all seem so quiet and peaceful and – and *real*. Nothing in the theatre is real. It's what I dreamed about as a little girl, a house with a garden.'

'Correct me if I'm wrong, but if the indulgent doctor disapproves of your continuing with your life on the wicked stage, you won't mind giving it up, then?'

When Clover was slow to answer, he went on, his voice terse, 'Just don't go organising a wedding when my plans for the West End opening are almost completed.'

Matching his tone, she said, 'You'll be given fair warning, don't worry.'

There was a tense silence, then he said, 'Do you really intend to marry your doctor?'

Torn between her love for the stage and her affectionate gratitude to Adam, she said, 'He'd be bitterly hurt if I didn't, some day.'

'You can't be expected to marry a man just because he'd be bitterly hurt if you didn't. Are you sure you're not just trying to talk yourself into something, Clover?'

'No, I'm just counting my blessings. He's a fine man and I owe him so much.'

'A lot of people confuse duty with love. It's a dangerous emotion.'

She remembered Rosie's gossip about his wife. The mystery surrounding her.

Unable to stop herself, she said softly, 'Is that what happened to you?' He didn't seem surprised that she knew.

'No. Not at all. We were both very young. She came from a strict background, parents who treated her more like a little girl than a grown woman.' He fell silent, staring out over the dark sea. They had stopped walking and were standing on the promenade, leaning against the railings. A few couples strolled in the distance.

Staring at his profile in the darkness, she said, 'Don't talk about it if it bothers you. I shouldn't have asked.' She hesitated. 'It's just that – well, I'd heard about you being married and it surprised me. I've never heard you mention your wife before now.'

He gave a harsh laugh then turned to look at her. 'They say confession is good for the soul, don't they? I want to talk about her. I haven't done for so long it seems like our marriage was a dream. A very exquisite dream while it lasted, but not real. And, of course, like a good many dreams, this turned into a nightmare . . .'

Her eyes filled with compassion. She placed a hand on his arm, pity filling her. What terrible thing could have happened to make him look like this? she wondered.

'She was such a pretty little thing. She had a little-girl-lost look about her that was so appealing no one could resist her. We ran away to get married in the face of her parents' opposition. It was nineteen fifteen, the war had been raging for a year, and I was expecting to be called up at any minute. We had two months together and then, before I knew what had hit me, my papers came and I was in France. Up to my ears in mud, trying to kill another human being because he wore a different colour uniform to me. I was twenty-one. After a particularly horrific charge with fixed bayonets, I was badly wounded and left in the field for dead.'

Clover remained silent, her hand tightening on his sleeve.

'Lucy had written to tell me she was pregnant and when word came informing her I was missing, presumed killed in action, she lost the baby and went into a kind of shock. The doctors could never give me a satisfactory explanation. I don't think they knew.' He gave a long, shuddering sigh that she felt go right through his body. 'She never came out of it. When I came home she didn't even know me. Just sat smiling in a chair, her arms folded as though she held a baby in them.'

Softly, Clover breathed, 'Where is she now?'

He took so long to answer that she worried that she'd hurt him deeply. 'She's dead. Lucy's dead. She died last year after being in that place for six years. And in all that time, whenever I went to see her, she didn't know me. I blamed myself for making her pregnant in the first place. I'll never forgive myself, never.'

'I'm glad you told me.' It made understanding him so much easier. Understanding all those impossible moods of his, the way he worked himself so hard and expected others to do the same. Almost as though he was afraid to let up in case the memories came flooding back.

He drew a deep breath, feeling for a cigarette in the crumpled packet he took from his pocket. Lighting up, gazing down at the glowing tip, he said, 'Never mind. Life can't always be full of happy endings.'

Chapter Twenty-eight

On Monday a letter arrived that sent her thoughts all in a turmoil. She felt alarm as she read the neatly written page, telling her of Miss Boyce's stroke. Brief, businesslike, it explained that Miss Boyce had been brought into the Ashby Home for the Elderly after having spent a week in the General Hospital. 'The reason I am writing this is because her right arm is paralysed and is quite useless. She gave me your name and asked me to write to you. She is a patient in a wing in the Home where residents are kept until they are able to join the rest of our people.'

It was signed Mabel Norris, Superintendent.

Clover felt sick. A stroke! Miss Boyce! She could hardly believe it. That spirited little woman confined to her bed in an old people's home! Unable to write her own letter! Clover shook her head in disbelief.

Tucking the letter back into its envelope, she went to find Harry. Funny, these days whenever she needed help or advice, Harry was the one she turned to. She found him in his office, seated at his desk – as usual in his shirt sleeves, as usual wearing his hat on the back of his head, as though he had just come in from the street and had been too preoccupied to remove it.

He beckoned with one hand for her to sit down, then continued with the long column of figures in the big leatherbound ledger. Clover contained her impatience as best she could.

While she waited she studied the dark, good-looking face bent over the ledger, the skin stretched tautly over the high cheekbones, the virile thickness of his black hair partly covered by the felt hat.

He was the only man she knew who could wear a hat indoors and at that rakish angle, perched always on the back of his head. Totally free of inhibitions. And yet, somehow, the things he'd revealed to her about his late wife made him more vulnerable than he would ever admit.

Finally he put down his pen and closed the ledger. Looking up at her, he said, 'Well, what is it? You look as though you've seen a ghost.'

Pulling the letter from her pocket, she said, 'Read that.'

His eyes studied the lines of writing. Handing the letter back, he said, 'Didn't you know anything about it?'

He knew about Miss Boyce, had met her the one time she'd come over to see Clover in the show.

She shook her head. 'No, I didn't. I want to go over and see her, Harry. Can you let me have time off? A whole day?'

'Of course. One of the other girls can take your place for the matinée. Tomorrow?'

'That would be great. I'll get the train, it'll be quicker than the charabanc. I should be back before nightfall.'

'Don't worry about it.' She read the compassion in his eyes and her pulses leaped. 'If there is anything I can do, just let me know.'

'Thank you, Harry. I appreciate it.'

The Ashby Home for the Elderly was on the outskirts of Newcombe. Clover hired one of the taxi cabs that were parked in the forecourt of the station and asked the driver to take her there. It would be her luck, she thought, to get a man whose hobby was an abundant knowledge of the many privations suffered by the unfortunate inhabitants of the Home. By the time she arrived at the dour-looking building she was depressed and worried.

Inside the front hall, a vast, inhospitable place where her footsteps echoed in the silence, she found a woman who directed her down a long corridor at the end of which she found the wing where the bedridden patients lived.

Double swing doors opened up onto a small ward. She walked quietly along the row of beds, her eyes searching for the much-loved face.

Frail as a child beneath the covers, Miss Boyce lay in a narrow hospital bed at the very end of the row. Her face was so peaceful that for a moment Clover thought she was too late. Then she opened her eyes and smiled faintly at the girl.

Dismayed by the change in her, Clover pulled up a chair and sat, taking hold of one thin hand and clasping it tightly. It was icy cold, heavy, the bones beneath the yellowed skin as brittle as a bird's.

'You came, child.' Her voice was thin and threadlike. Clover's mouth was dry as she leaned closer. 'I knew you would. I asked that woman to write, although I didn't really like worrying you.'

Clover clicked her tongue in exasperation. 'Didn't like to worry me, indeed! Whatever next? I'm cross that you didn't let me know sooner.' She gazed about her at the white painted walls, the sterile aspect of the place. She wondered how anyone, especially the half-dozen women who lay in beds on each side of the ward, could be expected to get well in such a forbidding atmosphere.

'Tell me what happened, Boycie.'

The story she told, of feeling suddenly unwell,

slumping from her chair to the floor, had Clover's heart turning over. 'Luckily I was in my room when it happened. I dread to think how embarrassing it would have been if it had been anywhere else. In public, say.' Clover's lips twisted. Even now, the little spinster had a horror of being shown up in public.

'It was so unexpected, all I could do was lie there until my landlady came up to tell me something. They took me to the hospital and then I was brought here.'

Clover patted the thin hand reassuringly, saying, 'Well, you're safe now. We'll soon have you home, as good as new. Why did they send you here? Why didn't they keep you in the General?'

'They said there was nothing else they could do for me. Besides, they needed the bed. And, Clover . . .'

She tried to lift herself from the pillows, her eyes shining like beads. It was too much for her. She fell back and Clover said, 'Just rest, dear,' and her voice was unsteady although she managed to check the tears.

'I wondered if you'd bring that bit of knitting in? The new jumper I was knitting for you. You know where I keep it, beside the chair by the fireplace.'

Clover nodded obediently. 'Of course I will. The next time I come.'

She stayed as long as they would let her, her chair pulled close to the bed, Miss Boyce's hand in hers. When it was time for her to leave, she spoke quietly to the nurse, asking to be informed if there was any change in her condition.

The nurse shook her head. 'I doubt there will be. She'll never walk again, you know. And, Miss Blossom, you needn't bother to bring that knitting in. She won't be able to finish it.'

Undaunted, Clover said, 'I'll bring it anyway. You can phone me at this number,' scribbling the telephone number of the Apollo on a scrap of paper. The nurse assured her she would.

She felt too upset to discuss it with Harry when she got back and, respecting her feelings, he didn't probe. He insisted she go again at the weekend and Clover was again forced to listen to the same taxi driver and the same dire warnings on the drive from the station.

She had brought grapes and a small bottle of Miss Boyce's favourite lavender water, as well as the knitting she had requested. But it was obvious nothing would get done, for Miss Boyce's right arm seemed completely useless. Clover placed the needles and wool on top of the locker, next to her spectacles case. If ever she was able to take it up again it would be near to her hand.

Clover bent and kissed her cheek. 'How are you, Boycie?' Again she sat holding the yellow, bird-like hands, alarmed at the way the veins stood out on the backs. There were bruises that had not been there the first time she visited. She traced one finger over the marks. 'What have you been doing to yourself?'

Miss Boyce glanced fearfully about her, checking that no one was listening, before she spoke. The other elderly women in the ward stared listlessly into space or turned the pages of dog-eared magazines. She whispered, as though revealing a well-kept secret, 'I fell off the toilet seat. Wasn't that silly of me? Bruised my arms.'

Clover frowned. 'You must be more careful.' She looked at the woman's seemingly useless right arm. 'Wasn't anyone, a nurse or a helper, there to give you a hand? You shouldn't be going anywhere on your own.' Hadn't that nurse said Miss Boyce would never walk again?

'They take you into the bathroom and leave you. I sat there for ages . . .' She coloured slightly, then added in a lowered voice, 'My bottom was getting numb and when I called and called and no one seemed to hear, I tried to push myself up. I fell to the floor and thought I'd crawl along the corridor to my bed. But my right leg wouldn't move and I got so cold, lying there on the tiled floor with only my nightie on. Finally someone came and took me back to bed and scolded me for not waiting.'

'Boycie!' Clover expressed all the horror she felt in that one word, so angry she was sure steam was going to explode through her ears at any moment. 'You mean they just ignored your cries for help? That's scandalous!' She looked about her, her cheeks flushed. 'I'm going to have a word with someone over this, you see if I'm not.'

'No, please, dear, don't make any trouble.' Miss Boyce looked so disturbed Clover forced herself to relax, and tried to smile.

'Maybe they truly didn't hear you,' she said gently. 'A place this size, with so many people to take care of, they must be run off their feet.'

'I expect that's it, dear.'

Adroitly, although she was still simmering, Clover changed the subject, talking animatedly about things in the theatre. 'Has anyone been to see you besides me?'

'A couple of girls from the chorus came yesterday, and I had a nice letter from Mr Ryder, telling me to get well soon.'

Clover smiled, relieved to hear she wasn't the only one to visit. 'I've still got that velvet dress you helped me make out of those curtains. And Dad has his jacket still. Madge calls it his smoking jacket, very posh, and says she likes him to wear it on chilly evenings.'

She went on to tell her about the wedding plans. Miss Boyce seemed to be having trouble taking it in. She frowned. 'Is that the woman he brought to see me the last time he came to Newcombe? I really didn't know what to make of her, Clover.'

'I wasn't too sure at first either. But I think she'll

be good for him. And he can't go on for ever on his own.'

'And what about you?'

Clover laughed. 'Oh, I'm much too busy at the moment to bother my head about anything else but the show.'

The day had been lovely; long, hot and sun-soaked. As the bus from Blackpool station drew near the dropping off point at the sea front, Clover could see that the tide was out, revealing a wide, clean stretch of sand. Everything would have been perfect if it hadn't been for the picture of Miss Boyce in the forefront of her mind. It was a situation in which she felt completely helpless.

She bit her lip, gazing at the beach littered with bright spots of colour: bathing towels, huge inflatable rubber balls, children kneeling in the sand, engrossed in making turrets in a smoothly rounded sandcastle.

As she alighted from the bus, she could hear the shrieks of gulls, soaring and swooping overhead, their screams matched by the cries of children piercing the still, hot afternoon air.

With an ache she remembered the summers when on her long solitary walks by the sea Miss Boyce would join her, and how they would chatter. Miss Boyce had never treated her as a child but always on the same level, not afraid to discuss any subject.

Clover walked back to the boarding house that was now her home, pushing open the front door, suddenly eager to kick off her high-heeled shoes, to relax in her own room. The landlady heard her come in and appeared from the direction of the kitchen. She wiped her hands on a blue print pinny, leaving white flour marks. 'Oh, Miss Blossom, you've got a caller. I hope you don't mind but I let the young man wait in your room. The poor dear looked so tired I thought it wouldn't do no harm.' She simpered. 'Such a nice young man, so well spoken. He said he was your fiancé, otherwise I would never have taken such liberties . . .'

Clover was already halfway up the stairs. 'That's all right, Mrs Wiseman. How long has he been waiting?'

'Oh, about an hour.'

Clover leaped the last few steps and hurried along the landing to a door at the far end. At this time of the day the place was quiet, the other girls who had digs here out enjoying themselves. With a matinée-free afternoon, their probable destination would be the beach, taking advantage of the weather, catching a tan.

Adam lay sprawled in her one easy chair, legs extended before him, eyes closed. Quietly shutting the door behind her, she walked over to stand looking down at him. His hair fell untidily over his forehead and she bent, brushing it back with gentle fingers. He mumbled drowsily and turned his head. Clover lowered herself onto the broad arm of the chair as his eyes opened and he said, 'Hmmm, I fell asleep. Must be the air in here.'

She gave a little laugh. 'What are you doing here?'

'I'm surprising you.'

'Well, you certainly did that. But why on earth didn't you write and tell me you were coming?'

'I got a sudden, irresistible urge to see you.' He sat up straight, stretching his arms, easing the muscles in his neck. 'God, I'm tired! Moorfield has just been through a diphtheria epidemic and I've done nothing but peer down sore throats and comfort parents for weeks. They all expect never to see their children again once they've been sent off to an isolation hospital.'

'I'm sorry. I didn't know.' That explained the long lapse between his visits, she thought. Diphtheria! How awful!

As though reading her thoughts, he said, 'That's why I couldn't come before. We've been rushed off our feet. I feel as though I haven't had a proper night's sleep for ages.' He grinned and made a grab at her, pulling her across his knees. 'But enough of that. Come here, you little wretch, and tell me where you've been all afternoon. Your landlady said you'd been away all morning, too.'

'I've been over to Newcombe.' Acutely aware of his arms holding her close to his chest, she began to explain about Miss Boyce. 'I've been trying to see her whenever I get the chance. It's such a shame, Adam. She's in an old people's home and you should see the insensitive way they treat the residents there. I hate walking away after my visits, knowing she's got to stay behind.'

'She shouldn't have to. Doesn't she have any money of her own? Enough to pay for a private nursing home? I know of several hereabouts that have a very good reputation.'

Clover knew Miss Boyce had some money put by to keep her when she was no longer able to work, but she doubted very much if the little woman had the means to pay for private nursing. 'I shouldn't think so for one minute,' she replied. She lifted her head to look at him. 'They say she won't ever recover. Can that be true? Surely, in time . . .'

He frowned, gazing down into those worried blue eyes. 'Do you really want me to answer that, Clover?'

It was there in his eyes, the answer she couldn't bear to hear. Abruptly she pushed herself away from him. Struggling to her feet, she went over to the small table in front of the window and helped herself to an apple from the bowl of fruit there. Polishing the rosy skin on one hip, she took a bite and stood chewing, her eyes fixed unseeingly beyond the window. There wasn't much to see, anyway. Roofs of houses, gardens parched with the unusually dry spell of hot weather, treetops shivering in a light breeze. And, glimpsed through the buildings, the criss-cross pattern of steel soaring into the blue sky, denoting the Tower.

Behind her she heard his voice saying lightly, 'Don't you know what they say about apples? That they keep the doctor away? Or are you trying to tell me something?'

She discarded the half-eaten apple in the wastepaper basket, then settled back at his feet, one arm clasped across his knees, her head resting against it.

'Why did you tell Mrs Wiseman I was your fiancée?'

'Because that's the way I always think of you.' He laid one hand on her head, long fingers entangled in the soft hair, caressing the scalp beneath. 'Don't you, Clover?'

She mustn't reveal how much the touch of his hand was affecting her, making her tingle all over. She forced a laugh. 'She wouldn't have let you in for any other reason.'

'Well, that's as it should be, isn't it?' His voice mocked gently. 'I wouldn't like to think of you entertaining other men in your room. Oh, Clover . . .' He attempted to pull her onto his lap again and she leaned back, resisting him amiably. He frowned, letting his hands fall to the arms of the chair. 'Why are you so afraid of showing your emotions?'

'Because emotions just muddy the subject. You can't think straight when you let your emotions take over.'

'You *are* a funny little thing! I've always enjoyed the company of women. But somehow I've never found one I can trust completely. Until you.'

This time she didn't reply, not knowing what to say.

'Did I ever tell you you're the most sensible girl I've ever met? Most girls think of nothing but their looks, clothes and make-up and how much money they can wheedle a man into spending on a night out. You're not like that, darling Clover. You could never be like that.'

'We've not exactly had the chance to spend much time together, have we? You don't really know how I could be.' She lifted her head, looking from the corners of her eyes, teasingly. 'I could be a real gold-digger for all you know.'

'Don't be daft! You're the type who will make a perfect wife, a discerning receptionist for our practice and a trustworthy assistant. Someone I can relax with.'

Clover was touched. At times, the thought of being in his arms, safe from the world and men like Harry Holt with their aggressive and domineering ways, was very enticing.

Still she couldn't help saying, provokingly, 'Is that all you want me for, as a receptionist and assistant?'

'Don't forget I mentioned a wife, too.'

And suddenly, instead of feeling joy at his declaration, she found herself shying away from it. A moment later he was feeling inside his waistcoat pocket and producing a small blue velvet-covered box. Opening it, he withdrew a ring, a sapphire and diamond cluster set in gold. Taking her left hand he slipped the ring gently over the third finger.

'Adam!' She couldn't find words to describe her feelings. She hadn't been expecting this. And yet – why hadn't she been expecting it? He'd made no secret of his feelings towards her. 'It's beautiful!' she breathed, holding her hand out to the light coming from the window. 'It must have cost a fortune.'

Then, determinedly, she began to slip it from her finger. 'But I can't accept it, Adam.'

'Why not? Give me one good reason why you can't accept it.'

'It must have cost a fortune,' she said again. 'Really, Adam, it's too much.'

'No, it's not. Wearing this, I'll know you belong to me. Only to me.' Seeing her frown, her lips forming objections, he smiled and went on, 'Don't tell me you didn't mean what you said that time you phoned? About settling down in one place?'

'I did mean it. But as I explained, not just yet.'

'I'm a fairly patient man, Clover, but I can't wait for ever.' As though bored of sitting, he rose to his feet, fumbling for a cigarette from the packet in his pocket.

'I'm not asking you to wait for ever. Only until . . .' She paused and he cut in, quickly.

'Until what? Until you've had your season in the West End, got all that nonsense out of your system? Is that how long?' He turned away, drawing the smoke deep into his lungs, clearly exasperated. 'That *could* take for ever. If you ever do get it out of your system.'

She felt her hackles rising at his tone. 'I can't change how I feel.' She reflected on Harry's words: You can't marry a man just because he'd feel bitterly hurt if you didn't. And was immediately ashamed. She looked down at the ring on her finger, denoting his love. 'You really shouldn't have spent so much money on me.'

'We're not talking about money here. We're talking about love and – duty.' He reached for her left hand and took the ring between his forefinger and thumb and turned it a little, to and fro, as though he was screwing it on.

'Duty?'

'Yes. Don't you think you owe me something?' He dropped her hand and stood, gazing down into her face. 'I thought we had got pretty close during that time of trouble. You seemed to like my company. And your aunts liked me.'

'They did, yes. Although they didn't say it in so many words, I guessed they thought you were an admirable catch.' She laughed.

'That's good, because I wrote and told them I was going to marry you.'

'You told them *what?*' Clover was shocked.

'Oh, darling, do listen. I told them I was going to marry you—'

'Wasn't that rather pre-empting matters? It could be years yet before I—. In any case, you would need my father's permission, not theirs.'

'Before you tire of the stage and settle down to a proper respectable life? I got the impression, that afternoon in the café, with you worrying your silly little head about the rainbow, that you did love me. I'm seldom wrong about anything, Clover. Don't tell me I was this time?'

She turned away from his searching gaze. 'I – don't know. I really don't know, Adam. You'll think I've been leading you on and I suppose I have, in a way. But I swear I didn't mean to. I was just so grateful for everything you did.'

'Well, I must say you were pretty convincing in your play-acting. You really had me fooled. But then I suppose you've had excellent training.'

'Play-acting?'

'Well, wasn't it?'

She shook her head. 'Not entirely.'

'You don't sound very sure.'

'I'm not. I'm not sure about anything at the moment. I'm worried about Miss Boyce and whether I'll be able to cope with a big part in a London production. And my father's future happiness . . .'

'If you were married to me you wouldn't have to worry about a thing. I promise. Not a thing for the rest of your life.'

She sighed. How could anyone promise that? 'You make it sound so tempting . . .'

'I'm doing my best.'

Bending his head, he leaned forward until his mouth touched hers. She kept her own lips closed, feeling nothing, telling herself it was because of all her worries that she felt like this. When at last he lifted his head he continued to stare at her, his eyes fixed intently on hers. 'There,' he said, 'sealed with a kiss.' As though her attempts at explanation had meant nothing to him.

Clover felt as though a snare had been set into which she had unwittingly strayed. Turning away from him, making her voice light, she said, 'How long are you staying this time?'

'Just until tomorrow evening, I'm afraid. I feel like a thief, even then, taking time off when we're so rushed.'

'And you're pleased with your new partner?' She felt she had to say something, anything to get away from the subject she'd rather not face. To her relief Adam began to tell her of his practice in Moorfield. She knew it was a subject dear to his heart and so listened quietly. As he talked she could see, in her mind's eye, those mean, rubbish-littered streets, the small groups of round-shouldered, unemployed men on the street corners, eyes ever alert for the end of a cigarette dropped in the gutter. The carefully retrieved tobacco from half a dozen of those would make a roll-up. She could hear the shrill voices of the women gossiping over back fences, their conversation liberally sprinkled with obscenities as they moaned about their housing conditions and their out-of-work husbands.

She felt again the soul-shattering destitution of living in that squalid house, the disgusting crawling creatures that rustled away into the darkness whenever the oil lamp was lit.

Even though, if she married Adam, she wouldn't be living in those same conditions, she would be seeing them every day. They would be all about her. No escaping from them. Just the thought of the front door of the house where Adam had his surgery, where she had waited on that dark, terrifying night while his housekeeper went to fetch him, chilled her very bones. If she married Adam she would have to go through that door every day of her life, the memory of that terrified girl, shivering in the thin coat that covered her nightdress, always with her.

She tried to repress the shudder that went through her. During a pause in Adam's monologue, she asked, 'Have you booked into a hotel for the night?'

'I didn't have time. I came straight here from the train – only to find you gadding off to Newcombe . . .'

Seeing the way her expression changed, he added quickly, 'I'm sorry, that wasn't fair. I understand your distress for the old girl but she really isn't your concern, Clover. Doesn't she have any family of her own?'

'No, she hasn't – apart from a sister she hasn't heard from for over twenty years.'

'I see. Still, no doubt the place she's in will come up with something. And I shouldn't worry too much about the way you say they are treating her. Often to the outsider it looks like neglect, but you must remember the nursing staff are very busy people and don't have time to pander to each particular need, much as they would like to.'

Without answering, Clover turned and picked up another apple from the bowl, taking a vicious bite out of it. She heard him laugh. 'Ouch! I felt that!'

When Mrs Wiseman knew he had nowhere to stay for the night, she insisted he used the tiny spare room at the top of the house, a room kept for the height of summer when people would put up with anything just to get a bed to lie on. 'I'm afraid it isn't much, Dr Foley,' she apologised, 'but as it is only for one night, I'm sure you'll find it comfortable enough.'

'It will do me fine, Mrs Wiseman,' Adam assured her. 'As you say, it's only for one night.'

She went out and closed the door behind her, but not before giving Clover a warning look. It said: And I'll have my ears pricked for any creeping up the stairs during the night, young lady. So just think on . . .

Clover went to sit on the side of the bed. She ran her hand over the prim and cold-looking white spread. One side of the room's ceiling sloped halfway down to the floor and Adam had to bend his head as he moved about. He came to sit beside her. One hand brushed the silky hair from her cheeks. 'This will do all right for me,' he said softly, 'until the day when I can stop living like a monk and be with my own little Clover.' He took her into his arms, holding her fiercely against him. His body was hard against hers and she could feel his desire for her, unexpected and frightening. It made her tremble.

'Really, doctor,' she said though her senses were swimming, 'would you have my landlady walk in and find us misbehaving? She's more than likely to return, you know. She doesn't trust any of us girls from the stage one little bit.'

'Don't tempt me,' he said, his eyes sparkling. 'Besides, you forget, we're engaged. Doesn't that give me some rights?'

She pushed him away and stood up. 'Not the sort of rights you have in mind,' she said and went to the door.

He followed her and at the door he took her hands and kissed her fingertips so gently that she again felt that unexpected trembling start up all over again.

'Goodnight,' he said. 'Sweet dreams.'

The door closed on her and for a moment he stood listening to her footsteps as she descended the stairs.

* * *

During breakfast the following morning the other girls at the table eyed Adam with profound interest and there was much speculation about his sudden presence there.

Elbows nudged and Clover heard muffled whispers: 'Who is he? I must say that Clover's a sly one!' 'Do you think he stayed the night . . . ?' 'Of course. Why else would he be having breakfast with her?' 'Do you think – in *her* room . . . ?'

This provoked stifled giggles and Adam looked up from his bacon and eggs, brows raised enquiringly. He caught Clover's eye and grinned, as though he enjoyed being the topic of conversation, for she supposed he must have overheard some of the comments.

'I really put the cat among the pigeons,' he remarked after breakfast as he walked with her to the theatre. Rehearsals that morning would give her the opportunity to introduce him to Harry. She was looking forward to the two men meeting. She wondered what Harry would make of Adam. And vice versa!

She didn't want to have to explain about the sapphire and diamond ring and so slipped it from her finger and into her handbag. 'It's not a good idea to wear jewellery at rehearsals,' she told Adam. 'It will be safer in my bag.'

Harry as usual was in his office. This time when Clover knocked and entered he removed his hat, his gaze resting on the man who followed her into the room. Expertly he skimmed the felt trilby across the room, aiming for the tall hatstand in the corner behind the door. It landed neatly on the top peg.

As she introduced the two men, Clover was struck by the difference between them. Harry, so energetic, so full of life; Adam, reflective, quiet, taking in everything but saying little.

'Clover has told me all about you,' said Adam as they

shook hands. 'I hope you're taking good care of her. She's inclined to be too trusting for her own good.'

Harry's eyes flickered, resting on Clover's face. 'But of course! The very best of care. Eh, sweetheart?' Clover blushed, meeting his eyes. He'd never used such an endearment before to her.

He came round from behind his desk, standing beside her, smiling at Adam. Before she could edge away he'd slipped one arm about her waist, drawing her to him, saying, 'As I said, the very best of care. You know, Dr Foley, I've ruffled a few feathers and stepped on a few toes in my time, but I want to assure you that's all over now. Since Clover appeared I've abandoned my evil ways.'

Blushing furiously, wondering if he'd been drinking before they arrived, Clover stepped back from his arm, mumbling something about rehearsals. She wouldn't have been in the least surprised if Harry had patted her on the shoulder – or bottom! – and said in that patronising way, 'Off you go, then, little woman.' Instead, to her relief, he returned to his desk and buried himself in his mass of paperwork.

Neither she nor Adam mentioned the incident. He didn't hang about to watch rehearsals but said he'd come to the afternoon matinée. 'Then I'm afraid it will be off to catch my train.'

It was the first time Adam had seen her perform on the stage. He didn't know what he'd been expecting but it certainly wasn't the tastefully costumed dancers, both girls and boys, who faced the audience when the curtains parted. They formed a half-circle, the men kneeling on one knee while the girls perched on their laps. They wore long, Edwardian-style gowns, sumptuously decorated with diamanté and frills, a fan of ostrich feathers at the back of their hair. The men wore full evening dress with shiny top hats.

As Clover appeared from a rose-covered archway at the back of the stage, they stood and began to sing the chorus of a popular song. Dressed identically in a long gown of rose-coloured satin, she danced lightly between them, twisting and turning gracefully, her long satin train draped over one extended arm. Joining her voice with theirs, she began to sing. The rest of the dancers fell silent, forming a half-circle about her, listening while she sang alone.

Adam could hardly believe it. That was his Clover up there, holding an entire theatre full of people captivated with a voice as pure as a crystal stream. *His* Clover!

From his seat in the front stalls he gazed about him, taking note of the spellbound faces, hearing the deafening applause at the end of the number. The audience shouted for more, young men in shirtsleeves, hair slicked back with an abundant application of Brylcreme, girls in summer dresses, their bare arms pink from too much sun. It certainly gave a man food for thought.

At the railway station when he kissed her goodbye, he held her away from him and gazed deep into her eyes. 'You were wonderful, Clover. I never once realised how talented you were.'

Clover felt a warm glow at his words of praise. 'Adam . . .'

Silencing whatever it was she was going to say, he kissed her again, moving his mouth on hers in a long, mind-drugging kiss. The engine blew a shrill whistle of steam, making them start, the guard at the door of the last carriage waved his green flag. Just before Adam released her, he said softly, 'Yes, wonderful. But just remember, one way or another, Clover Blossom, you are going to marry me.'

* * *

Clover walked back from the station, past the decorative iron scroll benches which dotted the promenade, past the gardens which in spring were quilted in primroses. The sea was quiet, dark as ink, the tide out, leaving the wet sands gleaming like satin.

After the show that night, she hung around until all the rest of the cast had gone. She walked on silent feet along the uncarpeted corridor, seeking Harry. He looked up as she entered the room, busy packing away some papers in a file. 'Do you mind?' she asked, uncertainly. 'Am I disturbing you?'

His lips twisted. 'No more than usual.'

'If I am—'

'There's no one in the whole, wide world I'd rather see walk in that door right now than you.'

Clover blinked at him, then hurried on, 'I saw your light. I thought, perhaps, if you weren't busy for a little while . . .'

'No, no, just tidying up.' He added another sheaf of papers to the thick file and closed it. He laid it with a pile of others on his desk. Then he rose from his chair and came round to push the door firmly closed. 'Feeling depressed with the good doctor going away, are we?'

She didn't reply.

'Look,' he said, 'you've not eaten yet, have you?'

She shook her head.

'Well, instead of eating alone, why not come out and have it with me? Somewhere where there's music and gaiety.'

'I think I'd like that,' she replied quietly.

He took her to the restaurant where they had been before with Bert and Madge. This time the place was busy, the laughter and voices mingling with the tinkle of glasses and the music from the small ensemble. A number of people were dancing.

Seeing the crowd, Clover drew back. 'It's very busy. We'll never get a table . . .'

As she spoke, the head waiter came hurrying over, smiling at Harry, addressing him by name. 'It's nice to see you again, Mr Holt. Just the two of you, is it? Please, come this way,' and Clover was reminded of her father's remarks about Harry, of how he was the type of man who could always command a table even in the busiest restaurant.

They ordered a light meal then sat and watched the dancers, until Harry caught her eye. 'Care to?' She nodded.

The feel of his hand in the small of her back, guiding her into his steps, his other hand clasped in hers, sent tingling sensations she would rather not have felt all the way through her. Was it a fearful sort of apprehension she felt or just nerves because he was holding her more closely than normal good manners decreed? She wanted to push him away, then suddenly hated the thought of when the music stopped and he would have to release her.

How could she feel this attraction towards Harry and at the same time long for the comforting assurance of Adam's presence? Really, falling in love was all very perplexing. Then suddenly, the spell was broken. He was asking in a casually deceptive tone, 'So what did the good doctor think of our little show? Did he approve?'

'Yes. He said it was very well done. And please don't keep on calling him the good doctor.'

'Why, isn't he a good doctor, then?'

She knew he was teasing and a flicker of annoyance made her cheeks flush. 'Of course he is. An excellent doctor. Only, the way you say it, it sounds so cynical.'

'I'm sorry. I'm sure I had no intention of being cynical about the good – sorry, about Dr Foley.' He gave her an expert twirl, twisting her out from his body with one arm, then pulling her back and holding her tightly against him. '*Are* you going to marry him, Clover?'

The question came so unexpectedly that her step faltered. Losing the beat of the rhythm, she fell against him, an excuse for him to hold her even more tightly.

'I think I'd like to sit down,' she said. Without a word he followed her back to their table. After a moment, she said, 'Adam's given me a ring.'

He raised enquiring brows. 'And?'

'An engagement ring.'

His eyes rested on her bare left hand. 'Then why aren't you wearing it?' He grinned. 'Don't tell me it was so cheap you couldn't bring yourself to show it off to the rest of the girls?' He'd seen newly engaged girls, flashing their rings under everyone's noses, smiling and chattering endlessly about their fiancé.

'I know he's the most wonderful person in the world, but . . .' She bit her lip, unable to find the words that would express her feelings.

'But being the most wonderful person in the world isn't enough, is it? Not when you don't love him.'

She met his eyes angrily. 'I didn't say I didn't love him. You don't know anything about my feelings.'

He looked amused. 'And you do? Clover, you're so mixed up you don't know whether you're coming or going. What you need is someone who can show you what love really is.'

She glared at him. 'And who would you suggest that person is?' You, I suppose, she thought, trying not to reveal it in her eyes.

'I'm open to all offers.'

She reached for her handbag. 'Really, you are the most opinionated, self-centred man I've ever met. You . . .' Conscious of the amused glances from nearby tables, she stood up and began to walk out of the restaurant. Harry followed meekly behind. The head waiter came hurrying after them, looking pained, enquiring if there was anything wrong. Harry turned to assure him everything was all right, thank you. Madam had a slight headache. Nothing to worry about.

In the darkness of the evening they walked back to where she lived. Before she entered her front door she stopped, turning to look at him. Harry stood close, gazing up at the distant stars. 'Just because he's given you a ring doesn't make it Gospel,' he said. There might never have been a break in their conversation at the restaurant. 'And it doesn't mean that I have to stop caring for you, Clover. Because I could never do that.'

Before she could guess his intentions, he bent his head and kissed her. A light kiss such as one would bestow on a child. 'There, that wasn't so bad, was it?'

Trying not to show how much it had affected her, Clover stepped back, a tight smile on her lips. 'Remember what you said about keeping my mind on work? Not letting anything interfere?'

'Yes, well . . .' He pulled her close and kissed her again. 'That's just to show you how adaptable rules can be.'

She didn't have to ask him what he meant. It was there on his face and in the thickly lashed eyes studying her so intently.

The moon came out from behind the clouds, silvering the road and casting ghostly grey shadows over the tiny front garden of the boarding house. Clover took a deep breath and, leaving him standing there, went into the house. She talked to the other girls who were in as though there was not a cloud on her horizon to worry her, but deep inside she was trembling and uncertain, wondering how she was ever going to sort out the different men in her life.

Chapter Twenty-nine

She made another visit to the dreaded place that was now Miss Boyce's only home. Something must be done, she thought. I can't bear to leave her here indefinitely like this, visiting whenever I can. What about when we leave for London – touching the wooden panelling that lined the long corridor for good luck – what about then?

The nurse stood waiting impatiently for her to catch up. 'Come on, dear, Miss Boyce is looking forward to seeing you.'

Quickening her pace, she followed to where the little woman lay in her high bed. Nothing had changed, except maybe the number of bruises standing out so alarmingly on the poor, thin arms.

To Clover's exclamation of distress, the nurse said, 'Yes, not a pretty sight, is it? But Joyce is an independent old soul and will insist on trying to do everything on her own. She just doesn't realise she's not capable of it.' She looked down into the pale face, her own expression showing not the slightest trace of compassion. 'Do you, Joycie?'

Clover knew Miss Boyce would have an old-fashioned antipathy to being called by her Christian name by anyone except friends. Everyone in the theatre usually used first names, but even they addressed her by her proper title.

An alarming purple bruise, quite fresh, covered almost the whole of one cheek. Clover felt her anger boiling but she waited until they were alone before saying, trying not to sound too shocked, 'Hello, Boycie. How are you?'

The greying head turned restlessly on the pillow. So grey now, when there hadn't been a trace of it before. 'As you can see, Clover, not too good.'

'Perhaps you should ask the nursing staff for help instead of trying to do things on your own.' Clover tried to make her suggestion smooth, uncritical. 'That's what they're there for, to help.'

'In theory, maybe. Not in practice. No, dear, it's not that easy. Last night I was determined to get back by myself from the bathroom and this time managed to pull myself up by the washbasin, then fell, catching my cheek on the edge of the basin. It was very painful, Clover. I could hardly sleep afterwards. The nurse was very angry. She told me in future I must call for a bedpan and then wait for them to bring it.' She grimaced, looking up at the shocked girl with apologetic eyes. 'I'm sorry, dear, it's not a very pleasant subject to discuss in front of a girl like you. But I *hate* the thing, so immodest, so coarse. They don't even bother to bring a screen for a bit of privacy.' A sudden flush heightened the pale cheeks as she added, heatedly, 'And do you know what the worst thing is, Clover? They won't let me smoke!'

Clover hid a smile at that. 'This is all too ridiculous,' she said. She rose from her chair. 'Who's in charge here? I'm going to have a word about this.'

The little woman looked alarmed. 'Oh, no, dear, don't do that! They don't like criticism. And it would only make it worse for me after you've gone.'

Clover felt like weeping. 'How can I ignore it? I must do something.'

Miss Boyce's good hand reached out and pressed hers. Her grasp was weak. The other hand didn't move but lay limp on the bedclothes, like the hand of some waxen

418

statue. Clover held the hand tightly in both of hers, trying to convey all the love she felt for the little woman in that clasp.

The faded eyes turned away to gaze at where some of the women were being coaxed to leave their beds for their tea. Shepherded by a woman in a blue striped apron, they made their way with various degrees of agility to a long table set in the middle of the ward with chairs all round it, Miss Boyce murmured, 'It's tea time, dear. There's chocolate biscuits today. I don't want to miss them . . .'

'Let me help.' Clover reached for the dressing gown that lay across the foot of the bed, holding it out for the woman to slip round her shoulders. The nurse looked over at them and clicked her tongue impatiently, as she would to a reluctant child. 'Come *on*, Joycie. We haven't got all day. You want a biscuit, don't you?' And Clover cringed inwardly at the look of consternation that flooded her old friend's face.

As though missing a chocolate biscuit might be the end of her world . . .

'Just look at you,' said Harry. 'Standing there like a little bantam hen, your feathers all ruffled up and your cheeks as red as rowan berries. And all for a woman who isn't even a relative.'

'That is beside the point.' Clover in her anger almost spat the words at him. 'Miss Boyce is my dearest friend. She has no one else to help her and I can't just turn my back on her.' She looked at him from under her eyelashes. 'Could you, were you in my shoes?'

She heard his sigh, faintly exasperated, seeming to say: women! 'I suppose not. All right, what do you want me to do?' Then he frowned. '*Me?* What have *I* got to do with it? You look at me with those big blue eyes and you've got me saying things I never intended to say. Let me amend that by saying, what are *you* going to do about it?'

She wrinkled her nose. 'Always trying so hard to sound the big, impermeable businessman, aren't you? Just as well I know you better than to believe that.'

'Don't try and change the subject.' They stood facing each other across the width of the room. They were in Harry's office where she had gone immediately on arriving back from her visit to Miss Boyce. 'Well?' he said, sounding impatient.

'I thought if I could get her into a nice place, a private place, I wouldn't worry nearly so much. And she'd be so much happier.'

He nodded, thinking of his late wife and her long sojourn in the private nursing home. He heard Clover say, hopefully, 'I'm sure there are places, Harry. Adam spoke of them when he was here.'

He made up his mind. 'Of course there are. We'll think of something, love. Don't worry.'

With the air of quiet determination that possessed him whenever he had a special project in mind, Harry made enquiries about private nursing homes. The few he selected were visited by him and Clover and they finally found one they liked: a red brick building built just before the war, standing in its own grounds surrounded by spacious lawns and pretty gardens. The nursing staff seemed genuinely pleasant and caring. Clover liked it straightaway. The feeling was right, she decided. And if she liked it, she knew Miss Boyce would like it, too. The one thing that worried her was the high fees they charged. Mouth turned down at the corners, she said to Harry, 'They're not cheap!'

'Nothing worthwhile is cheap, Clover. Oh, I know the song tells us that the best things in life are free, but that isn't always so. Isn't your little Miss Boyce worth it?'

Clover flushed. 'Of course she is.'

Harry was waiting for her when she arrived for rehearsals a week later. He handed her the letter that had arrived by that morning's post, informing them of Miss Boyce's acceptance into the new nursing home. It went on to say that the home's private ambulance would be at their disposal whenever it was convenient. 'There,' he said, grinning. 'Everything's fixed.'

He followed her into her dressing room, closing the door behind them, whistling softly under his breath. He seemed almighty pleased about something. It couldn't just be Miss Boyce in her new abode. As though reading her thoughts, he said, 'My sister and her husband are celebrating their sixth wedding anniversary tonight, Clover. They asked me to bring you to their dinner party as a guest.'

'Why me? I don't even know them.'

'Because you are soon to be my new leading lady. Because what they have seen of you, they like. And because I twisted my sister's arm, declaring that if they didn't invite you, I wouldn't come either.'

From those sentences, all Clover really heard was the bit about his new leading lady. She turned from the dressing table, eyes wide, sparkling, 'Does that mean . . . ?'

'It does. It means that you can start thinking about London and the West End, about new costumes and new songs and dances to be learned. You, my little-star-in-the-making, are going to be so busy you won't have time to draw breath.'

Clover gave a cry of delight and flew at him, flinging her arms about his neck, planting a kiss on his cheek. 'Oh, Harry, that's wonderful! When are we going?'

He laughed, holding her at arm's length. 'Hold on a minute! Time for all that sort of thing later. Negotiations are still in progress, that's all I can say, but it shouldn't be long now.' Releasing her, he turned towards the door. 'Better get on with those rehearsals, hadn't we? We'll go straight to Alice and John's place from here after the last show. And dress up. It's going to be a prestigious affair.'

She hugged herself, smiling at her reflection in the mirror.

That night when he came to the dressing room to get her, his eyes swept over her appearance, not missing a single detail. She wore a gown of her favourite blue, a gauzy chiffon, just skimming her knees. A short floating cape of the same material, falling in graceful folds to her elbows, was sewn with a fine sprinkling of sequins that sparkled whenever she moved. 'You'll dazzle them,' he said. Resplendent in black, he wore the formal attire with ease. Instead of making him look more civilised, though, he looked more dangerous.

'You're not so bad yourself,' she answered with equanimity.

To her surprise, he carried a short white fox cape, also elbow-length, which he placed gently about her shoulders. 'It's nippy out,' he explained. 'And there doesn't look much warmth in that dress you're wearing, charming as it is.'

She ran her hand over the soft fur, admiring it. 'It's lovely! How do you come to have such a beautiful thing?'

'I keep it for emergencies such as this,' he replied tersely. 'Now, come on or we shall be in Alice's bad books. She hates to be kept waiting.'

The dinner party was a great success. Clover took an immediate liking to Alice, and John made her laugh, relating all kinds of outrageous jokes. 'Careful!' she heard Harry murmur at one time. 'Not for young ears.'

John's glance rested on Clover, her flushed cheeks, bright eyes. His voice lowered, he said, 'Yes, I forgot you took a certain interest in her, although fatherly or not I wouldn't like to say.' He gave his brother-in-law a keen look. 'How is she taking the idea of moving to London?'

'She's thrilled, of course. What else could she be?'

Clover hadn't once mentioned Adam Foley since he'd told her the news in the dressing room that morning. And he certainly wasn't going to worry his head about that side of her life until she chose to bring it up herself.

He drove her back later to her boarding house. Before getting out of the car, she turned to him and said softly, 'You made a real effort to be nice tonight. I should take it as a compliment, I suppose.'

'For you, my lady, anything. We aim to please.'

She laughed. 'Thank you for a wonderful evening. I really enjoyed meeting your sister and her husband.'

'John's seen you before, that evening in the bar when that man was pestering you.'

'Yes, I remember.'

There was a brief silence, then Harry said, 'We'll have to do it more often.'

She gazed at his profile in the car, feeling her heart start to race, her pulses flutter. She was too young and too inexperienced to recognise the violent swings of attraction and then rejection she suffered in this man's presence. Long ago she'd shied away from getting too close to him. Now twin devils fought within her, knowing she had a duty to Adam and yet with all the perversity of her nature longing to be with Harry. When she remained silent for so long, he asked, 'What are you thinking about? You look a million miles away.'

She shook her head. 'Nothing. Nothing important, anyway.'

'You could have fooled me. Sweet dreams, those were. I may not be the most sensitive of men but I could hazard a guess as to what they were.'

My God, I hope not! she thought. 'I don't think—'

'You're wondering about Adam, about how it will affect your relationship if you go to London with the show. But how will it affect you, Clover, if you turn it down? If you follow what you misguidedly think is your duty and retire to a life of being Mrs Adam Foley?'

Suddenly she was angry. She didn't want him putting into words all the things she already knew. She would deal with them in her own good time. She didn't need his interference. In the close confines of the car she turned to face him. 'Look, I don't remember asking for your opinion, so I'll thank you to keep it to yourself. I've said I'll come with you and the show to London. I'll do the wretched show. I'd be a fool to quit now, just when things are going so well for me.' Her voice softened, lowered. 'I'm grateful to you for giving me the chance, Harry, but that doesn't give you the right to meddle in my affairs.' She took a deep breath. 'And what I decide to do after the show is entirely my own business.'

He gave a low laugh, pulling her close before she could object, kissing the tip of her nose. 'You are the perfect woman, Clover Blossom. Stubborn, tortuous and obstinate.'

Clover made the by now familiar journey to visit Miss Boyce. Unable to hold back the wonderful news of the new show, she blurted out the reason for her visit. The little woman's face glowed with pleasure. 'I knew some day someone would recognise the real talent in you, Clover. You deserve the best and London will offer you just that.'

'And besides that we've found a wonderful new place

for you,' enthused Clover. 'It's in an ideal setting, with pretty gardens and walks and when we were there – Harry came with me – we saw people sitting out on the lawns in the sunshine. The staff seemed very attentive. I'm sure you'll love it, Boycie.'

'Mr Holt went with you?'

'Harry's gone to a lot of trouble finding somewhere where we hoped you would be happy.'

'That's very good of him.' Gazing up, suddenly earnest, Miss Boyce added, 'Is it expensive, Clover? It sounds as though it might be.'

Thinking of Harry's words – 'Isn't your little Miss Boyce worth it?' – Clover said, 'I'm sure, between us, we'll manage. You mustn't worry about that.'

'I've still got a bit tucked away. It's not a fortune but I'm sure it will last out any time I have left.'

Clover bent to kiss her cheek. 'Don't let's get morbid, now. Even though I'll be away I'll write and try to get up to see you whenever I can. And I'm sure someone from the Follies will always be here.'

Madge had found that a new man in her life didn't bring her the companionship she'd hoped for. She still spent a lot of her time at the pictures, on her own. Of course, she couldn't blame Bert. His work in the theatre kept him busy and she knew what she'd taken on when she discovered what he was. In any case, she was used to going to the pictures on her own. As long as it was a good film, full of emotional scenes, she was satisfied. She didn't particularly want someone trying to talk when she was enjoying a good weep over the plight of some little orphan girl.

Cowboy pictures weren't really her cup of tea. But she'd read so much about the new epic currently showing in town that she felt she had to see it. *The Lone*

Prairie. And her favourite actress, that lovely Amorita Kessel, was in it.

She came out into the sunlight blinking, the image of the supporting actor fresh in her mind. Eddy Hart his name was. It didn't ring a bell. Even so, she was sure she'd seen him before. The strong, good-looking features were very familiar. When she got home, the silver-framed picture of the Four Blossoms that took pride of place on the mantelpiece caught her attention, and she realised why the face was so familiar. Her stepson-to-be a film star! She couldn't wait for Bert to get home to tell him . . .

Chapter Thirty

After handing over the first cheque, Eddie had known there would be further demands, the amount probably increasing each time.

He hadn't been wrong. Over the last year half a dozen cheques had followed the first one, all to different addresses from which Imelda had written the begging letters. He was just thankful that she stuck to letters and, in spite of her threatening words, didn't try to see Jamie again.

Kate would never forget the viciously brooding look directed at her by Imelda as she passed through the garden that day.

Kate had her own thoughts about this. Sending regular cheques was only leading Imelda on, in her opinion. 'Why do you do it, Eddie?'

Eddie sighed. 'Because I've got it to give, Kate. If I hadn't, well, it would be a different kettle of fish.'

His relationship with Kate had changed over the time she'd worked for him. He encouraged her to speak openly about her opinions. His gaze fell on the little boy who played happily on the lawn in front of them. They were sitting on the wide, shaded verandah, sharing a last cup of coffee before Eddie left for the studio. He wasn't needed until later today and so relished the time it gave him to spend with his son and Kate. 'Besides,' he added quietly, 'I've got Jamie and all the money in the world couldn't make up for that.'

Many times since Imelda's desertion, Eddie had debated on whether to begin divorce proceedings or not. It sounded so irreversible, so final. Imelda was lost to him for ever, he understood that and wouldn't have had her back at any price, but putting the whole messy business into the hands of a lawyer was something he was loath to do. The studio wouldn't be too pleased. A messy divorce case involving their hero of the moment would not be at all to their liking.

Then, like a light being switched on in a dark room, the idea came to him. Turning to Kate, he grasped both her hands in his and said, 'Do you still have the feeling that you can't leave your mother?'

She hesitated. 'Well, Mom seems to have settled in quite nicely with my brother and his family. She adores the grandchildren.' She lifted her head to gaze at him with that directness that he loved. 'Why do you ask?'

His grasp on her hands tightened. 'Look, the studio bosses are giving me some time off before I start my next movie. They're still searching for a suitable script; it seems we can make them quicker than they can write them, so it may be some months before they need me again. For a long time I've wanted to go back to England and see how my father and my sister are doing.'

His mouth twisted as though in pain. 'It was a rotten thing to do, to go off and desert them like that. Especially to Clover, my little sister.' Not so little now, he reminded himself. Clover would be nineteen this year. 'I haven't written for so long I wonder how they are and what they're doing. So while the opportunity presents itself, Kate, I'm taking it to go home.'

'Men are the very worst letter writers. Does your sister even know about Jamie and your new career?'

He grimaced. 'I'm ashamed to admit it, but no. So many things have happened that I just haven't been able to keep up with time. But won't we have a lot to tell her

when we do see her? And won't she just love Jamie.'
He looked at her. 'And I'm taking you with me.'

'But what about Imelda and the divorce—?'

Eddie released her hands and made a small, airy
gesture. 'Before we go, I'll put it into the hands of
my lawyers. They can take care of it. Anything they
need to know they can write and ask. But I'm going
home.' The exclamation came out with such an air of
triumph that she had to smile.

'And I suppose you think they'll be hanging around
waiting for you to show up? Surely they will have moved
on by now?'

To her consternation, he leaned forward and kissed
her lightly on the lips. 'Well, if they have, there are
people who'll know where they will be. Ma Ruggles
for one. And Miss Boyce. Or *her* landlady. Someone
will know where they are.'

Kate frowned. 'I still think you've been awfully lax
in not writing.' She bit her lip. It really wasn't anything
to do with her.

'I know that, and that's the very reason I want to
make it up to her now.'

Kate gave him a look. 'And your father?'

Eddie nodded. 'My father too.'

Although delighted at the thought of the show leaving
the provinces and opening in London, much of Clover's
happiness was dimmed by the inability to make up her
mind what to tell Adam. His last words, spoken before
the train pulled out – 'One way or another, you are
going to marry me' – returned again and again to
haunt her.

Noticing her restlessness, the abstracted manner in
which she attended rehearsals these days, Harry tackled
her about it. Calling her into his office one day between
shows, he demanded, 'Well, what's wrong? Something

is, I can tell. Not having second thoughts about coming to London, are you?'

'Of course not. It's just that . . . well, I just wish I knew what to do about Adam. I don't know how he's going to react.' Or rather, she did know and dreaded the argument she knew would follow when she told him she was leaving Blackpool for the West End.

Harry's gaze fell upon her left hand, still bare of jewellery. Not once had she worn her engagement ring, for he'd have been the first to notice if she had. It took a moment for him to reply. Then, as he had once before: 'Telephone him,' he said brusquely.

'That seems very cold-blooded. Besides, I haven't made up my mind what to say yet.'

'Tell him the truth, that you're going with *Stardust* to the West End. You can' – it took courage to say it, but he managed it – 'still get on with your life afterwards. It won't be for ever.'

Clover glanced at the upright black telephone as though it might suddenly leap up and bite her. There was a long pause while he gazed at her, amusement twisting his mouth. 'Go on, pick it up and tell him. He can't do anything drastic over the phone.' He glanced up at the wall clock over the door. 'He'll be home now, won't he? Nine o'clock?'

'Unless he's been called out on a case.' She bit her lip indecisively, praying that he had. 'All right.'

'Do you want me to get the number for you?'

She shook her head and he pushed the telephone towards her.

It seemed to ring for ages before it was answered. 'Clover! How nice to hear your voice. Everything all right?'

'Hello, Adam. Everything's fine. I just wanted to tell you something.'

'You've decided to pack it all in and marry me?'

Although he teased there was an undercurrent of hope in his voice, plain to hear.

'No, not that.'

Harry wondered if he should leave the office, allowing her to speak in private. Sheer stubbornness made him stay. All right, he thought, so I'm a snide, egotistical pain in the neck but I love the girl and she's too good a little trouper to allow some village doctor to carry her off under my nose. Anything worth having was worth fighting for. And he didn't care what anyone else thought, either. He wasn't in love with anyone else.

He heard her say, 'Please try to understand, Adam . . .'

Harry bent and pulled out the bottom drawer of his desk. Inside was a half-bottle of whisky. Two glasses stood on the broad windowsill. He fetched them, poured himself a liberal measure and stood sipping the amber liquid. His gaze remained fixed firmly on her back. She'd turned one shoulder so that he couldn't see her face, but he could hear the anguish in her voice and he felt his temper rise.

By the time she'd finished speaking, talking in snatches with many interruptions from Adam, he'd finished the first drink and was pouring a second.

She hung up the receiver on its stand, then turned and looked at him, her eyes bright with unshed tears.

'I take it the doctor wasn't amused,' Harry said. He stood leaning against the desk, glass in his hand, his gaze fixed intently on her face.

'He said he's coming over as soon as he can get a train. Tomorrow morning that will be.' She gave a wry smile, her lips quivering. 'I think I'm in for a battle, Harry.'

He banged his glass down on the desk so forcibly that he spilled some of the contents. She heard him say her name and in two strides he had covered the space between them. When he took her in his arms she did not protest, but went willingly, nestling against him like a child coming home on a dark night. His lips were soft, nuzzling against hers, breathing fire into her mouth. His hands were against her back, pressing her ever closer to his responsive body. 'Clover! Clover!' he breathed. There really was nothing else to say and they clung together for what seemed to the bewildered girl an eternity. Then suddenly he moved away and she was left sagging, clutching at the back of a chair for support.

Harry was breathing harshly and contrarily she felt a burst of fierce gratification to see him shaken out of his arrogant self-control.

But his mask of assurance was firmly back in place when he said, 'I think a drink is called for, don't you?' He lifted the bottle and poured a tiny measure into the second glass, offering it to her, gazing at her flushed cheeks. 'Drink this. It will do you good.'

Raising his glass in a toast, he said, 'To our health, Clover, and to you making the right decision where your future is concerned.'

He lifted his glass to his lips, tossing the whisky back in one gulp while Clover held hers, watching him. What he had done had been unexpected. She should be furious. Yet she had enjoyed it, every nerve and cell in her body hungering for more. The knowledge made her regard herself with bitter self-contempt. She was in danger of losing her head. And over the wrong man! Was she really so naive that she imagined she could resist the primitive, purely physical reaction she had experienced in this man's embrace?

'Perhaps I've already decided,' she answered, more calmly than she felt. 'Thanks for letting me use the phone.' She put her glass, still untasted, down on his desk. 'I won't have the drink. I've got a headache.' She realised it was true. She really did have a splitting headache. All this emotion was not good for her . . .

He stood and watched her, the empty glass still in

his hand. About to pour himself another one, he shook his head, his mouth tightening in contempt at his own weakness and thrust the bottle away, out of sight and temptation as he heard the door close behind her.

One of the delights of the seaside was that even at the end of a warm and particularly stuffy day, there was always a breeze along the promenade towards evening. Thunder hung in the air and since early morning the temperature had risen steadily. Dark clouds had gathered on the horizon and people said maybe a good downpour would cool things down a little.

The shops were hot and crowded, the parks dusty and the trampled grass turning brown. But here, as she and Adam sat in the glass shelter facing the sea, gusts of cool, salt-laden air swept in from the sea.

Adam had arrived about midday, spoiling for a fight. She'd tried to explain but he wouldn't listen. 'I don't know how you expect me to take it,' he said tightly. 'You know my thoughts on the subject, and yet you let it get this far without telling me. London! *London!* How can a child like you go gadding off to London with someone like that Holt fellow? I wouldn't give tuppence for your chances of staying . . .' He nearly said undefiled but changed it quickly to, 'innocent, down there.'

'That's not very charitable.'

'I didn't mean it to be charitable. You don't merit charity. You're obsessed by all the glamour, the chance of parading before a crowd of lecherous men who have nothing better to do with their time and money—'

'Adam!'

'There will be fancy cars and flats in London and wild parties every night. And money, money and more money. You'll never be satisfied, Clover. Whatever you get will never be enough.'

Clover couldn't believe he was describing her. Surely he didn't see her like that?

'A doctor's wife has a certain responsibility to the community he serves. She must be above reproach,' he went on heatedly.

'And being on the stage gives grounds for reproach, does it?' Clover was so angry her voice trembled. She never dreamed he could be so stuffy and narrow-minded. A woman beyond reproach! How biblical!

At first they had sat in her room while she had made tea and offered him a plate of biscuits. He'd refused anything heavier. Later, when the small room became unbearably hot and stuffy, they walked along the sea front, their conversation punctuated by long, morose silences. Now dusk was beginning to set in; the promenade lights came on.

'Once you get involved in that kind of life you won't want to come back. You'll become so deeply involved that eventually you'll . . .' He took a deep breath. 'Well, use your imagination.'

Clover's lips twitched. 'You're being very melo-dramatic.'

'It's simply a matter of getting your priorities right,' he forged on, 'and knowing that people, people who *love* you, matter more than possessions.'

'People who love me? My father has no objection to my going to London. If he can trust me then why can't you?' She laughed aloud. 'As if I'd do, or even be interested in, any of the things you mention. I'd hate fast cars and loud parties, although I wouldn't mind a nice flat in London. And the money, money, money part of it sounds a bit of orl right.' Deliberately she put on a Cockney accent.

'That isn't all,' he said, ignoring her attempt to lighten the conversation. 'I want to speak to you about that man.'

'Man? What man?' she asked, sure he meant her father.

'That manager or whatever he calls himself. Harry Holt.'

Clover's pulses leaped in warning. 'What about him?'

'I somehow got a strong feeling when I saw you together that he has taken a liking to you.'

'You mean, apart from admiring my voice?'

'He's too brash, too much of a Borstal boy for a girl like you to be associated with.'

'Nonsense. He comes from a very good family.' She thought of his sister and her husband and the lovely home they had on the outskirts of town. The obvious wealth that surrounded them all. 'He's not in the least like a Borstal boy, whatever that may mean.'

'When we're married I shall insist—'

Clover allowed him to go no further. 'I'm sorry, Adam, but I have to tell you, I really can't marry you.'

The little shelter suddenly seemed unbearably stuffy. She stood up and walked to the iron railing that lined the promenade. She heard him come up behind her but didn't turn around. 'We wouldn't be happy, Adam. I'd make you miserable and you'd end up hating me.'

'Not in a million years.'

She felt his arms go round her, trying to turn her, but stubbornly she kept her face averted, gazing out to sea. 'Yes, you would. I know it.'

'Then you know more than I do.' When she still wouldn't turn, he said, 'Are you telling me that you've just been playing with my affections? That I'm expendable now that something better has come along? I've served my purpose and am not needed any longer?'

Clover felt wretched. 'You make it sound terrible. It's not like that, Adam. Really it's not.' She turned to face him at last. 'I'm sorry, Adam. I really did love you – for a time. Puppy love, I suppose. After all, I was only sixteen. How can one know about love at that age?' To her horror she heard her voice start to shake. She went back into the shelter and sat on the bench, her arms huddled about her, her body trembling. She longed to be away from here, back in the theatre with Harry's hawk-like face grinning at her, the chorus girls running past on their way to the stage.

He came and sat down beside her. She heard him sigh. 'It wasn't puppy love that I felt for you, Clover.' And suddenly, despite her efforts, she started to cry. Without a word he handed her his handkerchief, still neatly folded and crisp from the iron, and she shook it out and wiped her eyes and then her nose.

'I'm sorry, Adam,' she said again.

'You'll feel different in the morning. Look, I'll go home, there's a train in about an hour's time. I'll catch that. Then I'll telephone you tomorrow. When is the best time? When will you be at the theatre?' He smiled, so sure of himself, repeating, 'You'll feel different in the morning.'

'No, Adam, I won't. I'll feel exactly the same. It wouldn't be fair to you, marrying me. I admire you, Adam. More than I can say. And I'll never be able to repay you for all your help when my father was ill. But it isn't enough. I've been raised in the theatre, it's really all I know. I wouldn't be happy anywhere else.'

'Not even helping me look after people less fortunate than ourselves who make up the bulk of my practice? It's a worthwhile job, Clover. It would bring you more satisfaction than what you plan.'

She shook her head. 'I don't think so, Adam. But I wish you luck in everything you undertake.' She'd almost forgotten. She opened her handbag and pulled the ring out, handing it to him. He moved back as though she had made to assault him.

'You're making a big mistake, Clover. A terrible mistake.'

She shook her head. 'I know if I went ahead, *that* would be a mistake. Please, wish me luck . . .'

He took the ring, almost snatching it from her, and dropped it into his coat pocket. 'Wish you luck?' He shook his head. 'I don't think I can bring myself to wish you luck in the life you intend to lead. Now, I'd better go.'

'I'm so sorry . . .' The tears started again.

'Don't be. I'll survive. I'll be too busy with my practice to brood.' He gave her one last look. 'Goodbye, Clover.'

Through a blur of tears she watched him stride away, as though anxious to be gone from her sight. She stood for a long time, gazing out at sea while the purple shadows gathered about her. The curve of the big bay seemed strung with a necklace of coloured lights, reflected in the shimmering water. Suddenly exhaustion consumed her. Never had a day seemed so long. She collapsed back onto the wooden seat. A young family passed the shelter where she sat, the father carrying a toddler, the mother dragging an older child by the hand. 'I don't want to go home, I want to stay here, I don't care if it *is* dark . . .'

Clover caught the young mother's eye, sympathising with her. She thought of herself as a child, sitting with a group of other children on the sand, watching the Punch and Judy show. Of Eddie coming to find her and her heartfelt pleas: 'Just a few minutes more, Eddie, I want to see the end . . .' A warm breeze, like the breath of someone sitting beside her, caressed her cheek and she felt Adele's presence, strong and compelling, heard the soft whisper, 'Buck up, love. Everything will be all right, you'll see.'

She saw the lights of an electric tram moving towards

her along the prom, whizzing past the small shelter. Further along to the right, one of the piers jutted out into the sea, alive with noisy holidaymakers.

She could understand why the old magic reasserted itself, time after time, year after year, luring people back. Even though at times she might secretly long for one of the houses and gardens she had described to Harry, the smell of greasepaint, of oil paint, the musty smell of old velvet, it was all in her blood.

She drew a breath of the fresh salty air deep into her lungs, wiped her eyes with the backs of her hands, for Adam had claimed his handkerchief before leaving her, and turned her face towards her future.

Towards Harry.

JOSEPHINE COX

In the grand tradition of Catherine Cookson

OUTCAST

'A classic is born'
LANCASHIRE EVENING TELEGRAPH

On a fateful night in 1860, Thadius Grady realises, too late,
that he has made a grave mistake. In blind faith he has put
himself and his daughter Emma at the mercy of his sister and
her conniving husband, Caleb Crowther – for he has
entrusted to them his entire fortune and the daughter he
adores. With his dying breath he pleads to see his daughter
one last time – but Caleb's heart is made of stone.

A feared Lancashire Justice, Caleb Crowther is a womaniser
and a gambler, and now the inheritance due to Emma is as
much in his hands as is the beautiful Emma Grady herself.
But Caleb lives in fear of the past, for how did Emma's
mother mysteriously die? And what made Thadius and Caleb
hate the river people so intensely? History seems likely to
repeat itself when Emma falls helplessly in love with Marlow
Tanner, a young bargee. For Marlow and Emma, it is an
impossible love – a love made in Heaven, but which could
carry them both to Hell...

FICTION/SAGA   0 7472 4075 2

More Compelling Fiction from Headline:

DEE WILLIAMS

CARRIE OF CULVER ROAD

A warm-hearted Cockney saga

As a little girl, brought up in an orphanage, Caroline
Parker had always been told that Dept Ford was the place
her disgraced mother had come from. So when years later
her husband dies, leaving her penniless and with three
young children to support, Caroline's first thought is to
head for the place she has envisaged as home: Dept Ford.
But to her horror, she arrives at her local station to find
that Dept Ford is not the country village she'd imagined,
but in the middle of London, a huge, teeming city the
likes of which she's never seen.

Luckily a kindly passer-by takes pity on her and her weary
children and puts them on the tram to a place where she
might find lodgings which, as it turns out, is in
Rotherhithe, not Deptford. And so it is Culver Road that
becomes her true home, where Carrie – as her neighbours
christen her – and her family, helped out by the
irrepressible Flo and her soft-hearted docker husband Alf,
find themselves battling through times both good and
bad: through strikes and street parties, weddings and
funerals, through the first war, with Kaiser Bill, and the
tense build-up to the next. And it is in Culver Road that
Carrie meets Jim, the enigmatic sailor who is to change
her life...

"A book that will give pleasure to many"
Betty Burton, author of *Jude*

FICTION/SAGA   0 7472 3607 0

HARRY BOWLING

The new Cockney saga from the bestselling author of GASLIGHT IN PAGE STREET

The Girl from Cotton Lane

Cotton Lane in dockland Bermondsey is one of the many small cobbled streets which serve the wharves. And on the corner is Bradley's Dining Rooms, the favourite eating place of the rivermen, trade union officials and horse and motor drivers. Since her marriage to Fred Bradley, Carrie has been building up the business, and trade has picked up considerably since the end of the Great War. Yet everything is not well between Carrie and Fred. And though they have a little daughter they both adore, neither of them is truly happy.

Carrie's parents, Nellie and William Tanner, live in Bacon Buildings, the tenement they were forced to move into when George Galloway sacked William after thirty-seven years. But their hearts lie in Page Street, their old home, and with their friends there: redoubtable Florrie 'Hairpin' Axford and her gossiping companions; scruffy old Broomhead Smith; the fighting Sullivans, and young Billy, who, unable to box after a wound sustained in the trenches, is determined to set up a gymnasium to help the local youngsters keep off the streets; and new arrivals, Joe Maitland, who's doing well with his warehouse in Dockhead, though his dealings are not always strictly above board, and Red Ellie, the stalwart Communist who brings the street together to fight their slum landlord, George Galloway.

Don't miss Harry Bowling's previous Cockney sagas, GASLIGHT IN PAGE STREET, PARAGON PLACE, IRONMONGER'S DAUGHTER, TUPPENCE TO TOOLEY STREET and CONNER STREET'S WAR, also available from Headline.

FICTION/GENERAL   0 7472 3869 3

A selection of bestsellers from Headline

LONDON'S CHILD	Philip Boast	£5.99 □
THE GIRL FROM COTTON LANE	Harry Bowling	£5.99 □
THE HERRON HERITAGE	Janice Young Brooks	£4.99 □
DANGEROUS LADY	Martina Cole	£4.99 □
VAGABONDS	Josephine Cox	£4.99 □
STAR QUALITY	Pamela Evans	£4.99 □
MARY MADDISON	Sheila Jansen	£4.99 □
CANNONBERRY CHASE	Roberta Latow	£5.99 □
THERE IS A SEASON	Elizabeth Murphy	£4.99 □
THE PALACE AFFAIR	Una-Mary Parker	£4.99 □
BLESSINGS AND SORROWS	Christine Thomas	£4.99 □
WYCHWOOD	E V Thompson	£4.99 □
HALLMARK	Elizabeth Walker	£5.99 □
AN IMPOSSIBLE DREAM	Elizabeth Warne	£5.99 □
POLLY OF PENN'S PLACE	Dee Williams	£4.99 □

All Headline books are available at your local bookshop or newsagent, or can be ordered direct from the publisher. Just tick the titles you want and fill in the form below. Prices and availability subject to change without notice.

Headline Book Publishing PLC, Cash Sales Department, Bookpoint, 39 Milton Park, Abingdon, OXON, OX14 4TD, UK. If you have a credit card you may order by telephone — 0235 831700.

Please enclose a cheque or postal order made payable to Bookpoint Ltd to the value of the cover price and allow the following for postage and packing:
UK & BFPO: £1.00 for the first book, 50p for the second book and 30p for each additional book ordered up to a maximum charge of £3.00.
OVERSEAS & EIRE: £2.00 for the first book, £1.00 for the second book and 50p for each additional book.

Name ....

Address ....

....

....

If you would prefer to pay by credit card, please complete:
Please debit my Visa/Access/Diner's Card/American Express (delete as applicable) card no:

Signature ....Expiry Date ....